Melymbrosia

Melymbrosia

by

VIRGINIA WOOLF

EDITED WITH AN INTRODUCTION

by

LOUISE DESALVO

CLEIS
PRESS

Melymbrosia was edited from Virginia Woolf's early manuscripts and typescripts now in the New York Public Library's Henry W. and Albert A. Berg Collection of English and American Literature.

Published in the United States by Cleis Press Inc.,
P.O. Box 14684, San Francisco, California 94114.
Printed in the United States.
Cover design: Scott Idleman
Cover photograph: Courtesy of the Mary Evans Picture Library, London
Book design: Karen Quigg
Cleis Press logo art: Juana Alicia

**First Edition
First Printing**

Library of Congress Cataloging-in-Publication Data

Woolf, Virginia, 1882-1941.
    Melymbrosia / by Virginia Woolf ; edited with an introduction by Louise DeSalvo.
        p. cm.
    ISBN 1-57344-148-1 (cloth)
        1. Young women—Fiction. 2. Triangles (Interpersonal relations)—Fiction.
    3. British—South America—Fiction. 4. Man-woman relationships—Fiction.
    5. Ocean travel—Fiction. I. DeSalvo, Louise A., 1942- II. Title.
    PR6045.O72 M45 2002
    823'.912—dc21
                                    2002024484

To
Ernest J. DeSalvo

Acknowledgments

I would like to thank Frédérique Delacoste at Cleis Press for her enthusiasm for publishing this edition of *Melymbrosia*. I am grateful to Felice Newman for her careful reading of the introduction to this edition. Thanks, too, to Don Weise for the energy that he has brought to this, and other projects.

I owe an enormous debt of gratitude to Edvige Giunta, who provides the kind of support that permits a writer to keep working. I thank Hunter College President, Jennifer J. Raab for her unwavering support of my work and for revitalizing Hunter College with the challenges of a new century in mind. I thank, too, Acting Provost, Ann Cohen, Acting Associate Provost, Vita Rabinowitz, Dean Robert Marino, Professor Richard Barickman, Chair of the Department of English at Hunter College and Professor Harriet Luria, Deputy Chair.

Ernest J. DeSalvo first persuaded me that editing *Melymbrosia* would be worthwhile; I thank him for all the help he has provided during the production of this volume. Frederick B. Adams, Jr., David V. Erdman, Alice Fox, James W. Haule, Elizabeth Heine, W. Speed Hill, Mitchell A. Leaska, Jane Lilienfeld, Jane Marcus, the Modern Language Association's Committee on Scholarly Editions, David J. Nordloh, Susan M. Squier, Lola L. Szladits, and G. Thomas Tanselle, were all enormously helpful with work on the original volume.

I would like to thank Isaac Gerwitz, Curator of the Henry W. and Albert A. Berg Collection. And finally, I would like to express my gratitude to the Author's Literary Estate for permission to produce this volume, and to Elizabeth Haylett for her help and her enthusiasm for the publication of this edition.

Contents

"A Wound in My Heart":

Virginia Stephen and
the Writing of *Melymbrosia*

In June 1910, Virginia Stephen entered a nursing-home at Twickenham for a rest cure. She had not been well since March, when she was finishing the draft of her first novel, *Melymbrosia*, presented in this volume. The completion of major projects would always be a dangerous time for her throughout her writing life. Near the end of her work on *The Years*, for example, she succumbed to suicidal despair, blaming her disintegration on the book. She had been working at a frenetic pace and was feeling overwhelmed and stressed. This time, the tumult of a flirtatious relationship with Clive Bell, her sister Vanessa's husband, and Virginia's guilty feelings about the affair, complicated the final stage of her work on *Melymbrosia*.

There has been much speculation about the causes of Virginia Woolf's depressions and mental breakdowns throughout her life. That she was sexually abused in 1888 at age six by her half-brother Gerald Duckworth and, later, when she was a teenager through 1904 when she was in her twenties, both by him and her other half-brother George, is surely supremely important.

In a memoir, "22 Hyde Park Gate," read aloud to friends in the 1920s, Virginia Woolf publicly described how, as a very young woman, she would undress for bed, and, almost asleep, she would hear the creaking of her door. George Duckworth would enter her room and implore her not to turn on the light. "Beloved," he would say, as he "flung himself" onto her bed and took her in his arms. But, Woolf said, no one in her family's privileged circle in London knew that George was not only brother, but also "lover" of both her and her sister Vanessa. Virginia Woolf, one of the twentieth century's greatest novelists, was an incest survivor.

Her breakdowns, then, can be understood as evidence that she suffered from post-traumatic stress disorder. Woolf had many of its symptoms—periods of overwhelming sorrow; mental anguish; negative feelings about her body; feelings of emotional coldness, emptiness, and detachment; sleep disturbances; inexplicable headaches; food disorders; fear, anxiety, and mistrust. And her heroine, Rachel Vinrace, in *Melymbrosia*, also manifests several of these symptoms.

Virginia Stephen was born on January 25, 1882, into a household in which incest, sexual abuse, physical violence, and verbal abuse towards girls and young women were common. In contemporary parlance, the Stephen family was extremely dysfunctional. Like many writers who achieve fame, her initial impulse to create was fueled by loss, grief, and sexual abuse. These experiences form the emotional bedrock of her first novel.

Virginia Stephen envisioned the kind of novel that she would write one day almost immediately after the death of her father in February 1904. The inspiration for *Melymbrosia* can be traced to this time, although there is no evidence that she began working on the novel this early. She was writing reviews and essays, but she now started thinking about a project sufficiently lengthy and compelling to take her mind away from her father's death.

The loss of Virginia's brother Thoby Stephen in 1906 also contributed to the novel. After his death, Virginia wandered the streets of London in grief chanting lines from Alfred Lord Tennyson's *In Memoriam*. For years, Thoby had been her intellectual companion, the sibling with whom she had discussed Shakespeare and the Greeks, who showed respect for the quickness of her mind. With him, she first engaged in equally matched, heated intellectual debates. In losing Thoby, she lost the person who provided her with access to the world beyond her Victorian household, the home to which she had been largely confined (much like her heroine Rachel) by both social custom and frequent illness.

Thoby had contracted typhoid on a holiday the family took in Greece. Virginia became responsible for his care because Vanessa and a family friend, Violet Dickinson, were also ill. Virginia, though she believed her brother's doctor was incompetent (as Terence Hewet believes that Rachel's doctor is in *Melymbrosia*), was persuaded by him not to consult another. But the doctor misdiagnosed Thoby's typhoid as pneumonia and there was a botched operation as well.

Virginia blamed herself for his death, and she wished she had died instead. In one sense, because her heroine shares so many of her character traits, Rachel's death in *Melymbrosia* can be read as a symbolic substitute of her own death for that of Thoby's. And Virginia surely drew upon this event in writing Rachel's deathbed scenes late in the novel.

Virginia's sister Vanessa agreed to marry Clive Bell only two days after Thoby's death. After their marriage, the couple moved into the house that Vanessa, Virginia, Thoby, and her younger brother Adrian had shared, displacing Virginia, and forcing her to share accommodations with Adrian, with whom she did not get along.

Virginia was furious that Clive had taken her sister away from her by marrying. She expressed her rage at Vanessa by trying to steal her husband's affections. After the birth of Vanessa and Clive's first child, she and Clive carried on what was perhaps the most passionate heterosexual relationship of Woolf's life. It was dangerous and self-destructive, however, for it alienated her from her sister Vanessa's attentions which she counted on for emotional sustenance.

There were kisses between Virginia and Clive, we know, and perhaps more. On one joint holiday, Clive and Virginia abandoned Vanessa to care for the squalling baby (which made Clive nervous). They took long walks together, looked at the sea, talked about her novel in progress, discussed the differences between women and men, and professed their love (as Rachel and Terence do in *Melymbrosia*). Clive and Virginia continued to steal moments away from Vanessa for passionate embraces and to protest their love for each other, throughout the composition of *Melymbrosia.*

Virginia drew upon her affair with Clive to describe many of the emotional entanglements in her novel, including its many triangular relationships, especially those of Evelyn Murgatroyd; of Ridley Ambrose, Helen Ambrose, and St John Hirst; of Helen, Rachel, and Terence. But she recreates her romance with Clive most dramatically in the scene in which Rachel, an unmarried young woman, and Richard Dalloway, a married man, kiss.

Though Rachel has in some sense welcomed his attention, there is something deeply troubling about Rachel's encounter with Dalloway. In this scene's troubling aftermath, Virginia is describing the deleterious effect of her experience with taboo sexual relations. In loving her sister's husband, Virginia was reenacting the hypersexualized, incestuous hot-house atmosphere of her past. This emotional reality, she described in *Melymbrosia.*

As *Melymbrosia* opens, Helen and Ridley Ambrose are on their way to the *Euphrosyne*, the ship which will transport them from London to Santa Rosa in South America so that Ridley can work on an edition of Pindar. Helen cries, thinking about her two children, who have been left at home, cared for by a nurse. Ridley doesn't share her grief; he seems not to be attached to his children at all. The choice to leave them apparently hasn't been Helen's. Still, being separated from one's children (leaving them, sending them off to boarding school, having others raise them) is part of a cultural pattern for people of their class. Willoughby, for example, has left Rachel in the care of two aunts indifferent to her well-being so he could traverse the ocean to build a mercantile empire. The most significant feature of childrearing among the privileged classes in England, Virginia Stephen shows the reader, is that children are often neglected and contact between parents and children is minimized. When it occurs, it is often unpleasant.

Because the boys of Helen's class must be educated for the sake of empire, the impact she has upon her son must be squelched or minimized. The powerful, developing bond between a mother and her children must be severed to minimize her influence. If Helen had her choice, she would be close to her son. But he is not her son; he is England's.

Clarissa Dalloway, wife of Richard Dalloway, former Member of Parliament, clarifies this—she and Richard board the vessel when it stops at the mouth of the Tagus River. Clarissa knows that imperialism depends upon "sending out boys from little country villages" to rule, something that would be unlikely if strong family bonds were forged. More than anything, Clarissa wants a son, not because he would be an important addition to their family, but because he could be useful to the empire.

Woolf's satire of British mores and of colonialism and imperialism is often ferocious. "I can't stop thinking of

England," Mrs. Dalloway says, "what it really means to be English. One thinks of all we've done, and our navies, and the people in India and Africa, and how we've gone on century after century." What Mrs. Dalloway means is that to be English is to rule others, to dominate, subjugate, and colonize.

Ridley does not need to leave London to do his work. But away from London, he can dominate his wife's attentions without their children's competition. He demands a kind of maternal care from Helen that might not be forthcoming if their children were present. He is infantile, self-absorbed, and narcissistic.

Commanding attention from women is a male pattern of behavior in *Melymbrosia*. Richard Dalloway's household revolves around his needs and desires: Clarissa, his wife, does his bidding; she flatters and cajoles him, assures him that he is her superior; he believes that a woman's responsibility is to provide emotional support so her husband can actualize his desire, and Clarissa fulfills this role. Although both Hewet and Hirst have received the finest education their culture provides, both are immature, inept, and needful of a woman's attentions. Hirst wants Helen to take care of him as soon as he meets her; while her children do without her in London, she mothers a virtual stranger while abroad. Hewet is unsuited for a mature emotional relationship. In a conversation with Rachel, Hewet admits that he despises women, and that he has flitted from one woman to another because he resists emotional demands made upon him. It seems, too, that he and Hirst are intimate.

During a storm at sea, in one of the novel's most important scenes, the married Richard Dalloway embraces Rachel and kisses her; he says that she tempts him. That night, she awakens and experiences the extreme aftermath of this event.

The Dalloways soon disembark and Helen and Rachel discuss the effect of Richard's kiss. Helen, by this time, has established herself as Rachel's confidant and friend, although she is not altogether favorably disposed toward this young woman, thinking her childish and naïve. Rachel is her niece, her sister's daughter, but Helen sees nothing of the mother's pluck in this young woman. Despite their blood tie, and Rachel's mother's death, Helen has taken no interest in Rachel before this voyage. Though Helen is ostensibly interested in Rachel's well-being, she ridicules and berates Rachel, calling her "the dupe of the second-rate". She also competes with her, admitting that she wishes Dalloway had kissed *her* instead of kissing Rachel.

Rachel has never had maternal protection because her mother has died and because her caregivers have been disconnected from her and unconcerned about her welfare. So Rachel has never learned how to protect herself; she is an extremely vulnerable young woman and the novel suggests that Helen is not necessarily desirous of Rachel's success in the world, though she appears to be.

Helen believes that Rachel thinks and acts like a child, that she is unable to care for herself, to make astute judgements about the people she meets. It is true that Rachel has been provided with no real knowledge of the world. She believes that it is an unpredictable place, that "the world might change in a minute and any thing appear." She has spent most of her life alone. When she has asked questions of her aunts, who were ostensibly responsible for her care, though they ignored her, she was treated as if her curiosity was a pathology. She has been taught, too, that the expression of feelings is equally pathological.

Sometimes, though, Rachel's self-understanding is keen. She knows that she lives with "the burden of lies" that have been told to her and that she hasn't received the nurturing necessary for growth. Even her passion—music—she realizes she has been kept from cultivating by her father who strictly prescribes the amount of time she is permitted to devote to it.

Helen soon persuades Willoughby to allow Rachel to accompany her and Ridley to Santa Rosa instead of taking her on his journey up the Amazon River. Helen's motives are not altogether clear. She seems to want to assist in the young woman's education; she seems to feel a newfound responsibility for her. But it seems, too, that Rachel's future becomes something that Helen wants to manipulate.

After the *Euphrosyne* leaves them at Santa Rosa and the Ambroses and Rachel take up residence in a villa there, Rachel meets Terence Hewet, a young Englishman staying at a hotel nearby. Helen and Rachel begin to spend time with the hotel guests, and Terence's friend, St. John Hirst, becomes interested in Helen. Hewet and Hirst set about trying to teach Rachel about books and about life under Helen's watchful eye.

In describing encounters between women and men throughout *Melymbrosia*, especially those in which men try to instruct women, discourse upon their areas of expertise or engage in study, Virginia Stephen's satire is biting and savage. She ridicules the very best that male society and male education has produced. Mr Pepper's disquisitions upon the art of road paving and upon the comparative longevity of elephants and tortoises parody engagement with worldly concerns and the traditions of significant academic discourse. Richard Dalloway tries to teach Rachel about politics but interrupts his discourses by kissing her, leaving her with the memory of her visceral response to his embrace rather than with a knowledge of the difference between liberals and conservatives. Ridley Ambrose is incapable of finding a chair for himself to work in; he treats drafts from cracks in windows as if they were catastrophes and impediments to learning. He needs the organizational skills of his far more capable wife to begin his work on the Greeks, one that Helen knows will be read by no more than twenty-four people. Terence Hewet pontificates to Rachel about the weakness of her sex, about women's lack of logic and reason, while he himself writes muddles instead of masterpieces; his creative work is so hopelessly maudlin that even he can't take himself seriously. Though Terence is enormously self-assured, he admits to having written an idiotic tragedy that has derailed because he has introduced a cow into the dramatic events for no apparent reason.

Meantime, Rachel is not permitted time to perfect her piano playing. Mrs Dalloway, though she is clearly interested in politics, leaves this work to her husband. Helen's only aesthetic outlet is embroidery. Susan Warrington's time is completely devoted to self-sacrifice. Evelyn Murgatroyd has boundless ambition but no outlet for it. Only two major characters in the novel are working women: Mrs Flushing, who seems to have a keen entrepreneurial spirit; and Miss Allen, who works diligently on her book.

Rachel Vinrace joins Hewet and other hotel guests on a donkey trip up a nearby mountain. On the expedition, two of the hotel guests, Susan Warrington and Arthur Venning, become engaged. Their lovemaking, witnessed by Terence and Rachel, is extraordinarily upsetting to her. After a party celebrating their engagement, Rachel and Terence wonder if they too are in love.

Soon after the party, Mrs Flushing, an Englishwoman who is staying at the hotel, invites Rachel to her room to view her paintings, and Rachel agrees to take a steamboat ride up a nearby river on an excursion including Helen, Terence and St John. Ostensibly, the reason for the trip is to see life as the indigenous people live it. Really, though, Mrs Flushing and her husband plan to purchase native goods. It seems as if they trick their companions into sharing expenses for a journey that they will profit from when they sell these native goods in England at inflated prices.

When the steamboat stops so the travelers can explore the countryside, Terence and Rachel take a walk alone together. They discuss their childhoods, the difficulties of loving, and Terence's past sexual encounters. They embrace passionately, about which Rachel has conflicting emotions— that what they have done is terrible but that it also brings her happiness.

Terence and Rachel seem unsuited to form a relationship, though they enter one because it is expected of them. Rachel deplores the physical expression of love; she is terrified of men. Earlier, when she and Terence had watched Susan Warrington and Arthur Venning embracing, she tells Terence, "how I hate it—how I hate it!" Terence, recognizing that she has been harmed in some way, asks, "What has the world done to you?" She tells Terence she has some deep wound in her psyche, a "wound in my heart."

On yet another walk, Helen, perhaps realizing that Rachel is drifting from her, pursues her, tumbles her to the ground, and professes *her* love in an early and explicit rendering of lesbian love. During an embrace, Helen tries to force Rachel to admit that she loves her better than she loves Terence. Perhaps Rachel's ambivalence about heterosexuality is rooted in unacknowledged lesbian desire.

After their return from this trip upstream, Rachel suddenly falls ill, and soon dies of a disease described by several of the hotel guests as a fever.

In *Melymbrosia*, Virginia Stephen has used the ancient symbol of the sea journey for the soul's journey. But she has subverted its age-old meaning, for Rachel is utterly unfit emotionally and intellectually to make her way through life because of her childhood. And, symbolically, this is one reason why she dies.

Melymbrosia bristles with social commentary and impresses the reader with Virginia Stephen's engagement with the most significant political issues of her time. In these pages, she comments upon the trade union movement and labor unrest; the suffrage movement (which she herself joined) and its increasing militancy; the parliamentary debates which threatened to alter the very structure of British government; the issue of whether artists, writers, and musicians or politicians did more good for society; the effect of political leaders like Balfour and Lloyd George; the Lords' rejection of the budget; the problem of reconciling humanism with empire building; the effect of the declining birth rate upon empire. She discusses whether women owed it to their country to produce many children; the changes occurring in religion; the effect of new developments in psychology; the contradictions within liberalism; the Irish nationalist movement; the protectionist movement; legislation affecting the welfare of the poor, the aged, and women; the limited means society provided women who needed to earn their livings; the impossibility of crossing class lines to marry. She describes the effect of illegitimacy upon personality; legislation affecting the education of women; the need to secure foodstuffs to feed a population whose agricultural productivity has declined; the allure of less circumscribed ways of social and sexual behavior; the excitement of airplanes; the problem of road repair; the impending specter of war with Germany; the Moroccan crisis; the effect of the revolution in Portugal; the problem of developing naval power; the issue of the Dreadnoughts; colonialism and its origins.

Rachel Vinrace's life is portrayed against these issues. It is impossible to read *Melymbrosia* and think of Virginia Stephen as an effete dreamer spinning out her private fantasies in the solitude of her study between bouts of madness. Here is a writer engaged with the most important issues of her day even as she struggled with mental illness; here is a woman who understands that every encounter between women and men occurs within the context of shifting and conflicting social and political forces.

Virginia Stephen was cognizant of the objections critics would make to her work because of her critique of culture. In 1909 she wrote Lytton Strachey, "A painstaking woman who wishes to treat of life as she finds it and to give voice to some of the perplexities of her sex, in plain English, has no chance at all."

At the earliest stages of its composition, she had showed *Melymbrosia* to Clive Bell, who supported Virginia's decision to become a novelist. He commented on her work-in-progress, offering advice about style and substance. And although he was generally supportive, he once severely criticized what he believed to be the serious imbalance in her portraits of women and men. Why, he asked, were the women rendered with such empathy while the men were drawn with such rancor? Why were the men depicted as ignorant despite their education, and rude or vulgar, self-involved, vain, even tyrannical? She replied that she would keep his objections in mind, and she did, for in *Melymbrosia,* the portraits of Evelyn Murgatroyd, Susan Warrington, Mrs Dalloway, and Mrs Flushing, for example, are as sharply satirical as those of the men. But she told Clive Bell she believed that, as a man, he was not a very good judge of how, in private, women regarded men. And she said that she wanted to write her own views on the subject of the relationship between the sexes, not his, and that although her boldness sometimes terrified her, she would persist in trying to pen her own account of the subject.

After Clive Bell criticized her portraits of men early in 1909, and though she worked on it through 1912, Virginia never showed him—or anyone—this completed draft of

Melymbrosia. And until I edited the manuscripts for the work's first publication, it was unknown and unavailable to the general reading public.

Although *Melymbrosia* is a substantial, highly polished, immensely political, often savagely satirical piece of work, Virginia Stephen chose not to publish it. Among Virginia Stephen's most important achievements in *Melymbrosia* are an insightful portrayal of the effects of abuse upon the psyche of a young woman; a fierce critique of imperialist and sexual politics; a discussion of the interrelationship among childrearing practices, empire-building, and oppression as insightful and profound as that of her later *Three Guineas*; an innovative use of the form of the female *bildingsroman*; descriptions of the natural world that rival those she penned later in her career; and hilariously savage character portrayals.

She surely could have released it to the world had she chosen, for the novel is as significant and well-written as, say, E. M. Forster's *A Room with a View*, published in 1908 (and given a mixed review by her). Indeed, both *Melymbrosia* and *A Room with a View* treat the theme of a young woman's passage from innocence to knowledge. Virginia's work, though, is far more experimental and subversive than Forster's.

But no matter how accomplished and risk-taking this first novel was, Virginia Stephen continually expressed fears about publishing it, about having it seen, exposed, and criticized. To her sister Vanessa Bell, she wrote that she hid her manuscript whenever anyone entered a room and she wondered if she would ever dare print it. Woolf, though, was often immensely hard on her work throughout her lifetime, often considering it unworthy.

But her feelings about *Melymbrosia* were not consistently negative. She also believed that she would write innovative, controversial work. Though Virginia Stephen sometimes had doubts about this work, she nonetheless believed that she was in the process of re-forming the novel with the boldness of her vision which sometimes terrified her. She was telling the heretofore untold story about the relationships between women and men. She was describing sexual politics in an imperialist culture. She was examining the emotional aftershocks of incestuous abuse although, because of the times during which she was writing, she would have to disguise her meanings if her work was to see print. (Ironically, the firm owned by Gerald Duckworth, one of the half-brothers who had molested her, published *The Voyage Out,* a later version of *Melymbrosia.*)

Why Virginia Stephen chose not to publish *Melymbrosia,* she never disclosed. Perhaps she was not entirely pleased with her efforts and thought she could do better. Perhaps it was because the novel was too close to her own experience. Perhaps she feared making it public because of the nature of her material. Perhaps, too, it was because Clive Bell's critique of her male portraits forewarned her that the ironic portraits of the educated men of her class presented in the novel would cause male critics of the work (who would come from the very class she satirized) to spurn it and she did not feel able to endure public ridicule.

Instead of publishing *Melymbrosia,* Virginia Stephen began rewriting the novel some time after she recovered from the illness that attended the completion of the version presented here. She penned two more complete drafts, finishing the one she chose to publish in 1912, after her marriage to Leonard Woof. She called it *The Voyage Out.*

But *Melymbrosia* is, in many ways, a bolder rendering of that later work. Overall, Virginia's tendency, as the years progressed, was to blunt the clarity and savagery of *Melymbrosia,* to make her meanings more ambiguous, to make Rachel more naïve and dreamy, less fury-filled. In *Melymbrosia,* the issues of the aftermath of sexual abuse, same-sex love (treated overtly in Rachel's and Helen's relationship), and the critique of imperialism, are more overt and piercing than in the later version. In *The Voyage Out*, the meanings are muted; it is a more mythic, and a less socio-political work of art.

Virginia Stephen disassembled *Melymbrosia* when she began to work anew, cannibalizing her first novel for later drafts. It remained undiscovered and unread until, in the 1980s, I organized it from the many extant pages of all the novel's versions deposited in The Berg Collection of English and American Literature of The New York Public Library after her death. They were in a remarkable state of disarray, and it took seven years for me to reassemble *Melymbrosia* and edit it into the readable volume printed here.

After working for several years with the manuscripts of Virginia Woolf's *The Voyage Out* at the Berg Collection of English and American Literature of The New York Public Library, I had realized that there might be a complete early text of the novel submerged within the manuscripts as they are presently arranged. It seemed as if Woolf had used some specific pages of an early version of the novel as the basis for another, later, version. It appeared that she had taken that former version, dismantled it, cut its pages into pieces, rearranged them, cancelling words, phrases, lines or paragraphs on some pages or overwriting passages on some pages as she worked. If, in fact, she had done this, I believed that pages of a very early version of *The Voyage Out*, which Woolf called *Melymbrosia* in its earliest incarnations, might be scattered throughout the extant manuscripts, and that I might recover it.

The Berg Collection of The New York Public Library had acquired manuscripts of *The Voyage Out* from Leonard Woolf. When they came to the Berg, they were in no apparent order. In 1962, he discovered another holograph volume of the novel and presented it to the Berg Collection. In addition to the pages which are extant, Leonard Woolf states that his wife had once burned many pages of earlier versions of the novel. Although Woolf customarily destroyed the typescripts of her novels, saving only her handwritten or holograph drafts, she did not destroy the typescript of *Melymbrosia*. It seems as if she wanted her first completed full-length fiction to survive.

The Berg Collection grouped the manuscripts of *The Voyage Out* into six major categories: Holograph, volumes I and II; Holograph and Typewritten Fragments; Earlier Typescript; Later Typescript; Final Typescript; Fragment. These categories were established by Lola Szladits, the Berg's Curator at the time, and the extant drafts were sorted by her, but each entity, the catalog warned, was composed of various drafts so that the "Earlier," "Later," and "Final" typescripts, for example, were not necessarily entities in and of themselves and were not necessarily written in the order suggested by the labels. The study of the early development of Woolf's craft was, in fact, greatly impeded by this arbitrary system of organization and classification.

The major problem, then, in establishing the text of *Melymbrosia* was that the manuscripts in the archive had not been sorted into earlier and later drafts of the novel as Virginia Woolf herself had written them. It was therefore necessary for me to reconstruct the drafts *as they once existed* before the earliest extant draft could be identified.

I sorted the extant manuscripts into tentative drafts on the basis of internal evidence and physical characteristics (for example, paper type, paper size, watermark, ink color, typewriter ribbon color, pin holes in the manuscript—Woolf sometimes used dressmaker pins to assemble the pages of her chapters). But the sorting, sequencing and dating of these drafts could not be accomplished with any degree of certainty without external evidence from letters, diaries, memoirs, biographies, and autobiographies describing the novel. Particularly important were letters stating that Woof was about to begin a new draft, that she was not working, or working hard, or working only occasionally. Particularly important, too, were dated letters or datable manuscripts written on paper with the same watermark as sheets of the novel.

What propelled my work was my conviction that if I could locate those pages, date them, put them in their original order, determine when Woolf made the changes that appeared on each page, then a very early version of *The Voyage Out*, which no one but Virginia Woolf herself had seen, might be discovered. The recovery and subsequent publication of the earliest attempt at fiction of one of the 20th century's greatest literary stylists, I believed, would be of enormous interest to readers.

For over seven years, I studied the extant manuscripts, determined the number of drafts represented, established approximate dates of composition for each draft by reading the then unpublished letters and diaries which referred to the work in progress. As it turned out, two submerged nearly complete texts and fragments of several other drafts emerged from this textual work. In all, I found evidence of about nine drafts or fragments of drafts. But the most important one, consisting of about 390 typescript pages of what had originally been a 414-page draft—the earliest draft—is presented here. It is significant because it is Virginia Woolf's first completed novel.

Virginia Woolf's title for the work was *Melymbrosia*. The meaning of the title remains a mystery, but it might have been intended as an ironic combination of the Greek words for *honey* and *ambrosia*: Woolf refers to the ambrosial fields of Greece in a diary she kept on a journey there.

A complete description of the method I used to establish the text of *Melymbrosia* and to determine that it is the earliest example of a novel written by Virginia Woolf is fully described in *Melymbrosia by Virginia Woolf: An Early Version of* The Voyage Out (New York: The New York Public Library, 1982).

The original manuscript is owned by the Berg Collection of English and American Literature, the New York Public Library in New York City. The Gale Group has microfilmed the work. To order a copy, go to www.galegroup.com/psm or to find a library that possesses a copy of the microfilm, do an advanced search at www.google.com, using the phrase "Virginia Woolf Manuscripts."

In reading *Melymbrosia*, Virginia Woolf's first novel, one is privileged to witness the early flowering of one of the 20th century's creative geniuses. It stands in relationship to *The Voyage Out* as *Stephen Hero* does to James Joyce's *A Portrait of the Artist as a Young Man*. But *Melymbrosia* is also a significant work of art in its own right. It demonstrates how remarkably talented Virginia Stephen was in this, her first voyage into the art of fiction.

The young Virginia Stephen who wrote *Melymbrosia* was heroic. She was an incest survivor who wrestled throughout her life with its aftermath in a society that did not offer her a paradigm for understanding what had happened to her. This, instead, she did herself. For she was an enormously courageous woman and a prescient one, who determined that there was a relationship between her abuse and her depression. She used her writing to try to understand her life, and the world about her, and to repair the rift in her own psyche, and to express these insights to others. Although she killed off her heroine in this, her very first completed novel, and although its creation was attended by bouts of mental illness and despair, in the long run, the writing of *Melymbrosia* helped her to stay alive, to become that writer,

Virginia Woolf, who changed the course of literary history, who penned *To the Lighthouse*, *Mrs Dalloway*, and *The Waves*—among the most important works of the twentieth century. Hers was a long and distinguished career, one that began with the work presented in this volume, with *Melymbrosia*.

Louise DeSalvo
Sag Harbor, New York
December 1, 2001

Note to the Reader

Melymbrosia is missing several pages, unfortunately, some at the very beginning of the novel. To provide the reader with a coherent text, the missing material has been supplied, within square brackets, from later versions of the manuscript. That of Chapters One, Two, Thirteen, Fourteen, and Nineteen is supplied from the first edition of *The Voyage Out*. That of Chapters Five, Six, Nine, and Eleven, is from later typescript versions. That of Chapter Twenty Two, is from a handwritten draft. Editorial transitions appear in double square brackets.

Virginia Woolf's idiosyncratic use of punctuation and paragraphing has been retained; although sometimes quirky, it seems she was experimenting with these elements and that she had made deliberate choices about them.

CHAPTER ONE

[As the streets that lead from the Strand to the Embankment are very narrow, it is better not to walk down them arm-in-arm. If you persist, lawyers' clerks will have to make flying leaps into the mud; young lady typists will have to fidget behind you. In the streets of London where beauty goes unregarded, eccentricity must pay the penalty, and it is better not to be very tall, to wear a long blue cloak, or to beat the air with your left hand.

One afternoon in the beginning of October when the traffic was becoming brisk a tall man strode along the edge of the pavement with a lady on his arm. Angry glances struck upon their backs. The small, agitated figures—for in comparison with this couple most people looked small—decorated with fountain pens, and burdened with despatch-boxes, had appointments to keep, and drew a weekly salary, so that there was some reason for the unfriendly stare which was bestowed upon Mr. Ambrose's height and upon Mrs. Ambrose's cloak. But some enchantment had put both man and woman beyond the reach of malice and unpopularity. In his case one might guess from the moving lips that it was thought; and in hers from the eyes fixed stonily straight in front of her at a level above the eyes of most that it was sorrow. It was only by scorning all she met that she kept herself from tears, and the friction of people brushing past her was evidently painful. After watching the traffic on the Embankment for a minute or two with a stoical gaze she twitched her husband's sleeve, and they crossed between the swift discharge of motor cars. When they were safe on the further side, she gently withdrew her arm from his, allowing her mouth at the same time to relax, to tremble; then tears rolled down, and, leaning her elbows on the balustrade, she shielded her face from the curious. Mr. Ambrose attempted consolation; he patted her shoulder; but she showed no signs of admitting him, and feeling it awkward to stand beside a grief that was greater than his, he crossed his arms behind him, and took a turn along the pavement.

The embankment juts out in angles here and there, like pulpits; instead of preachers, however, small boys occupy them, dangling string, dropping pebbles, or launching wads of paper for a cruise. With their sharp eye for eccentricity, they were inclined to think Mr. Ambrose awful; but the quickest witted cried "Bluebeard!" as he passed. In case they should proceed to tease his wife, Mr. Ambrose flourished his stick at them, upon which they decided that he was grotesque merely, and four instead of one cried "Bluebeard!" in chorus.

Although Mrs. Ambrose stood quite still, much longer than is natural, the little boys let her be. Some one is always looking into the river near Waterloo Bridge; a couple will stand there talking for half an hour on a fine afternoon; most people, walking for pleasure, contemplate for three minutes; when, having compared the occasion with other occasions, or made some sentence, they pass on. Sometimes the flats and churches and hotels of Westminster are like the outlines of Constantinople in a mist; sometimes the river is an opulent purple, sometimes mud-coloured, sometimes sparkling blue like the sea. It is always worth while to look down and see what is happening. But this lady looked neither up nor down; the only thing she had seen, since she stood there, was a circular] iridescent patch slowly floating past, with a straw in it; this sometimes swam behind a great tremulous tear. Tears dropped when the consciousness came over her, like a gust of pain, that her arms no longer closed upon the bodies of two small children. Then the physical desire would be replaced by the memory of the words. "We saw a dog with a bandage on its leg, mummy." Those were the words, which her son had suddenly spoken after good bye had been said, as she left the room. She being gone, the nurse would answer him. He expected her to come back. He might feel lonely. To leave them for four months was intolerable pain. The wild animal in her determined to go back. Nevertheless though feeling a rush all through her, she stood still weighted down as if her feet were cast in lead, by the knowledge that to go back was impossible. She did not remember why, but she knew that it was. There was no reason, life being a compromise.

"Lars Porsena of Clusium

By the Nine Gods he swore

—The first two lines sounded loud in her ear—

"That the great house of Tarquin

Should suffer wrong no more."

The last two were fainter, and showed that her husband had passed her in his walk. Yes, she would go back to all that; but at present she must weep. Screening her face she sobbed more steadily than she had yet done; her shoulders rose and fell quite evenly. It was this figure that her husband saw, when having reached the polished Sphinx, he turned; the stanza stopped. He came up to her, laid his hand on her shoulder, and said, "Dearest." His meaning [was "We must live." His voice was supplicating. But she shut her face away from him, as much as to say, "You can't possibly understand."

As he did not leave her, however, she had to wipe her eyes, and to raise them to the level of the factory chimneys on the other bank. She saw also the arches of Waterloo Bridge and the carts moving across them like the line of animals in a shooting gallery. They were seen blankly, but to see anything was of course to end her weeping and begin to walk.

"I would rather walk," she said, her husband having hailed a cab already occupied by two city men.

The fixity of her mood was broken by the action of walking. The shooting motor cars, more like spiders in the moon than terrestrial objects, the thundering drays, the jingling hansoms, and little black broughams, made her think of the world she lived in. Somewhere up there above the pinnacles where the smoke rose in a pointed hill, her children were now asking for her, and getting a soothing reply. As for the mass of streets, squares, and public buildings which parted them, she only felt at this moment how little London had done to make her love it, although thirty of her forty years had been spent in a street. She knew how to read the people who were passing her; there were the rich who were running to and from each others' houses at this hour; there were the bigoted workers driving in a straight line to their offices; there were the poor who were unhappy and rightly malignant. Already, though there was sunlight in the haze, tattered old men and women were nodding off to sleep upon the seats. When one gave up seeing the beauty that clothed things, this was the skeleton beneath.

A fine rain now made her still more dismal; vans with the odd names of those engaged in odd industries—Sprules, Manufacturer of Sawdust; Grabb, to whom no piece of waste paper comes amiss—fell flat as a bad joke; bold lovers, sheltered behind one cloak, seemed to her sordid, past their passion; the flower women, a contented company, whose talk is always worth hearing, were sodden hags; the red, yellow, and blue flowers, whose heads were pressed together, would not blaze. Moreover, her husband walking with a quick rhythmic stride, jerking his free hand occasionally, was either a Viking or a stricken Nelson; the sea-gulls had changed his note.

"Ridley, shall we drive? Shall we drive, Ridley?"

Mrs. Ambrose had to speak sharply; by this time he was far away.

The cab, by trotting steadily along the same road soon withdrew them from the West End, and plunged them into London. It appeared that this was a great manufacturing place, where the people were engaged in making things, as though the West End, with its electric lamps, its vast plate-glass windows all shining yellow, its carefully-finished houses, and tiny live figures trotting on the pavement, or bowled along on wheels in the road, was the finished work. It appeared to her a very small bit of work for such an enormous factory to have made. For some reason it appeared to her as a small golden tassel on the edge of a vast black cloak.]

Observing that they passed no other hansom cab, but only vans and waggons, and that not one of the thousand men and women she saw was either a gentleman or a lady, Mrs Ambrose understood that after all, it is the ordinary thing to be poor. This was the city of the poor. Philosophy, which she liked to read, is only read by a drawing room full of people; their ears are charmed by music; they see pictures; innumerable fires and carcases keeping them warm, their brains work. But the rest have never heard a sound of the music, or a word of the disputations that have been going on in the drawing room since the beginning of time. Startled by this discovery, and seeing herself tracing a circle all the days of her life round Piccadilly, she was greatly relieved to pass a building, put up by the London County Council for Night Schools.

"Lord, how gloomy it is!" said her husband. "Poor creatures!" But as one only saw these things when one was unhappy, they might be traced to the mood; on the other hand the mood might be the right one. People in numbers, she tried to console herself, always depress one. What with misery for her children, the poor, and the rain, her mind was like a wound exposed to dry in the air.

At this point, the cab stopped; it was in danger of being cracked like an eggshell. The wide embankment which had had room for cannon balls and squadrons, had now shrunk to a cobbled lane, steaming with smells of malt and oil, and blocked by waggons. They stood beneath the warehouses and were being fed by sacks. Rippling on the other side of the warehouses was the river, with floating ships. From them the sacks were picked that went into the waggons.

Half an hour later Mr and Mrs Ambrose sat in a small rowing boat, and looked down the two banks, along the edges of which a gigantic child had placed bricks—some square, some oblong, some immensely tall and narrow. All were washed the same smoke grey. The river, which had a certain amount of troubled yellow light in it, ran with great force; bulky barges floated down swiftly, escorted by tugs; police boats shot past everything; the wind went with the current. The open rowing boat in which the Ambroses sat, bobbed and curtseyed across the line of traffic. A frail and ancient waterman, who had been found on a flight of steps, rowed them. Once he said, he had taken many passengers across; he seemed to recall an age when his boat, moored among rushes, carried delicate feet across to lawns at Rotherhithe. "They want bridges now," he said, indicating the monstrous outline of the Tower Bridge. Mournfully Helen regarded him, who was putting water between her and her children. Mournfully she gazed at the ship they were approaching; anchored in the middle of the stream, they could dimly read her name; "Euphrosyne."

"Ships all the world over" the waterman said "fly that flag the day they sail." It was a moment for presentiments.

CHAPTER TWO

[D]own in the saloon of her father's ship, Miss Rachel Vinrace, aged twenty-four, stood waiting her uncle and aunt nervously. To begin with, though nearly related, she scarcely remembered them; to go on with, they were elderly people, and finally, as her father's daughter she must be in some sort prepared to entertain them. She looked forward to seeing them as civilised people generally look forward to the first sight of civilised people, as though they were of the nature of an approaching physical discomfort,—a tight shoe or a draughty window. She was already unnaturally braced to receive them. As she occupied herself in laying forks severely straight by the side of knives, she heard a man's voice saying gloomily:

"On a dark night one would fall down these stairs head foremost," to which a woman's voice added, "And be killed."

As she spoke the last words the woman stood in the doorway. Tall, large-eyed, draped in purple shawls, Mrs. Ambrose was romantic and beautiful; not perhaps sympa-thetic, for her eyes looked straight and considered what they saw. Her face was much warmer than a Greek face; on the other hand it was much bolder than the face of the usual pretty Englishwoman.

"Oh, Rachel, how d'you do," she said, shaking hands.

"How are you, dear," said Mr. Ambrose, inclining his forehead to be kissed. His niece instinctively liked his thin angular body, and the big head with its sweeping features, and the acute, innocent eyes.

"Tell Mr. Pepper," Rachel bade the servant. Husband and wife then sat down on one side of the table, with their niece opposite to them.

"My father told me to begin," she explained. "He is very busy with the men.... You know Mr. Pepper?"

A little man who was bent as some trees are by a gale on one side of them had slipped in. Nodding to Mr. Ambrose, he shook hands with Helen.

"Draughts," he said, erecting the collar of his coat.

"You are still rheumatic?" asked Helen. Her voice was low and seductive, though she spoke absently enough, the sight of town and river being still present to her mind.

"Once rheumatic, always rheumatic, I fear," he replied. "To some extent it depends on the weather, though not so much as people are apt to think."

"One does not die of it, at any rate," said Helen.

"As a general rule—no," said Mr. Pepper.

"Soup, Uncle Ridley?" asked Rachel.

"Thank you, dear," he said, and, as he held his plate out, sighed audibly, "Ah! she's not like her mother." Helen was just too late in thumping her tumbler on the table to prevent Rachel from hearing, and from blushing scarlet with embarrassment.

"The way servants treat flowers!" she said hastily. She drew a green vase with a crinkled lip towards her, and began pulling out the tight little chrysanthemums, which she laid on the table-cloth, arranging them fastidiously side by side.

There was a pause.

"You knew Jenkinson, didn't you, Ambrose?" asked Mr. Pepper across the table.

"Jenkinson of Peterhouse?"

"He's dead," said Mr. Pepper.

"Ah, dear!—I knew him—ages ago," said Ridley. "He was the hero of the punt accident, you remember? A queer card. Married a young woman out of a tobacconist's, and lived in the Fens—never heard what became of him."

"Drink—drugs," said Mr. Pepper with sinister conciseness. "He left a commentary. Hopeless muddle, I'm told."

"The man had really great abilities," said Ridley.

"His introduction to Jellaby holds its own still," went on Mr. Pepper, "which is surprising, seeing how text-books change."

"There was a theory about the planets, wasn't there?" asked Ridley.

"A screw loose somewhere, no doubt of it," said Mr. Pepper, shaking his head.

Now a tremor ran through the table, and a light outside swerved. At the same time an electric bell rang sharply again and again.

"We're off," said Ridley.

A slight but perceptible wave seemed to roll beneath the floor; then it sank; then another came, more perceptible. Lights slid right across the uncurtained window. The ship gave a loud melancholy moan.

"We're off!" said Mr. Pepper. Other ships, as sad as she, answered her outside on the river. The chuckling and hissing of water could be plainly heard, and the ship heaved so that the steward bringing plates had to balance himself as he drew the curtain. There was a pause.

"Jenkinson of Cats—d'you still keep up with him?" asked Ambrose.

"As much as one ever does," said Mr. Pepper. "We meet annually. This year he has had the misfortune to lose his wife, which made it painful, of course."

"Very painful," Ridley agreed.

"There's an unmarried daughter who keeps house for him, I believe, but it's never the same, not at his age."

Both gentlemen nodded sagely as they carved their apples.

"There was a book, wasn't there?" Ridley enquired.

"There *was* a book, but there never *will* be a book," said Mr. Pepper with such fierceness that both ladies looked up at him.

"There never will be a book, because some one else has written it for him," said Mr. Pepper with considerable acidity. "That's what comes of putting things off, and collecting fossils, and sticking Norman arches on one's pigsties."

"I confess I sympathise," said Ridley with a melancholy sigh. "I have a weakness for people who can't begin."

"...The accumulations of a lifetime wasted," continued Mr. Pepper. "He had accumulations enough to fill a barn."

"It's a vice that some of us escape," said Ridley. "Our friend Miles has another work out to-day."

Mr. Pepper gave an acid little laugh. "According to my calculations," he said, "he has produced two volumes and a half annually, which, allowing for time spent in the cradle and so forth, shows a commendable industry."

"Yes, the old Master's saying of him has been pretty well realised," said Ridley.

"A way they had," said Mr. Pepper. "You know the Bruce collection?—not for publication, of course."

"I should suppose not," said Ridley significantly. "For a Divine he was—remarkably free."

"The Pump in Neville's Row, for example?" enquired Mr. Pepper.

"Precisely," said Ambrose.

Each of the ladies, being after the fashion of their sex, highly trained in promoting men's tale without listening to it, could think—about the education of children, about the use of fog sirens in an opera—without betraying herself. Only it struck Helen that Rachel was perhaps too still for a hostess, and that she might have done something with her hands.

"Perhaps—?" she said at length, upon which they rose and left, vaguely to the surprise of the gentlemen, who had either thought them attentive or had forgotten their presence.

"Ah, one could tell strange stories of the old days," they heard Ridley say, as he sank into his chair again. Glancing back, at the doorway, they saw Mr. Pepper as though he had suddenly loosened his clothes, and had become a vivacious and malicious old ape.

Winding veils round their heads, the women walked on deck. They were now moving steadily down the river, passing the dark shapes of ships at anchor, and London was a swarm of lights with a pale yellow canopy drooping above it.]

The unfortunate city of London was not the place they had left, but the place they would come back to. For the first time since she had seen her blush, she took a look at Rachel. Straggling haired, with whipped cheeks, amused, in high spirits, Rachel under a lamp, she thought, was a nice strange creature; as for beauty, how seldom even beautiful people, look beautiful? She looked wild. Even under favourable conditions however, Helen could not get over her repugnance to a raw girl. As she believed that it took them many years to feel anything, and the chances were that when they felt they felt crookedly, her manner to her own sex was just, but not merciful. Rachel showed no signs of politeness. Slowly the intoxication of the movement died down, and the wind became rough and chilly. Long cigars were being smoked in the dining room; they looked through a chink and saw Mr Ambrose throw himself violently against the back of his chair, while Mr Pepper crinkled his cheeks as though they had been cut in wood; the ghost of a roar of laughter came out to them and was drowned at once in the wind. In the dry yellow-lighted room, Mr Pepper and Mr Ambrose were oblivious of all tumult; they were in Cambridge; it was the year 1875.

"They're old friends" said Helen, smiling at the sight. "Is there a room for us to sit in?"

Rachel opened a door. "It's more like a landing than a room" she said. Indeed it had nothing of the shut stationary character of a room on shore. A table was rooted in the middle; seats were stuck to the sides. Happily the tropical suns had bleached [the tapestries to a faded blue-green colour, and the mirror with its frame of shells, the work of the steward's love, when the time hung heavy in the southern seas, was quaint rather than ugly. Twisted shells with red lips like unicorn's horns ornamented the mantelpiece, which was draped by a pall of purple plush from which depended a certain number of balls. Two windows opened on to the deck, and the light beating through them when the ship was roasted on the Amazons had turned the prints on the opposite wall to a faint yellow colour, so that "The Coliseum" was scarcely to be distinguished from Queen Alexandra playing with her Spaniels. A pair of wicker armchairs by the fireside invited one to warm one's hands at a grate full of gilt shavings; a great lamp swung above the table—the kind of lamp which makes the light of civilisation across dark fields to one walking in the country.

"It's odd that every one should be an old friend of Mr. Pepper's," Rachel started nervously, for the situation was difficult, the room cold, and Helen curiously silent.

"I suppose you take him for granted?" said her aunt.

"He's like this," said Rachel, lighting on a fossilised fish in a basin, and displaying it.

"I expect you're too severe," Helen remarked.

Rachel immediately tried to qualify what she had said against her belief.

"I don't really know him," she said, and took refuge in facts, believing that elderly people really like them better than feelings. She produced what she knew of William Pepper. She told Helen that he always called on Sundays when they were at home; he knew about a great many things—about mathematics, history, Greek, zoology, economics, and the Icelandic Sagas. He had turned Persian poetry into English prose, and English prose into Greek iambics; he was an authority upon coins, and—one other thing—oh yes, she thought it was vehicular traffic.

He was here either to get things out of the sea, or to write upon the probable course of Odysseus, for Greek after all was his hobby.

"I've got all his pamphlets," she said. "Little pamphlets. Little yellow books." It did not appear that she had read them.

"Has he ever been in love?" asked Helen, who had chosen a seat.

This was unexpectedly to the point.

"His heart's a piece of old shoe leather," Rachel declared, dropping the fish. But when questioned she had to own that she had never asked him.

"I shall ask him," said Helen.

"The last time I saw you, you were buying a piano," she continued. "Do you remember—the piano, the room in the attic, and the great plants with the prickles?"

"Yes, and my aunts said the piano would come through the floor, but at their age one wouldn't mind being killed in the night?" she enquired.

"I heard from Aunt Bessie not long ago," Helen stated. "She is afraid that you will spoil your arms if you insist upon so much practising."

"The muscles of the forearm—and then one won't marry?"

"She didn't put it quite like that," replied Mrs. Ambrose.

"Oh, no—of course she wouldn't," said Rachel with a sigh.

Helen looked at her. Her face was weak rather than decided, saved from insipidity by the large enquiring eyes; denied beauty, now that she was sheltered indoors, by the lack of colour and definite outline. Moreover, a hesitation in speaking, or rather a tendency to use the wrong words, made her seem more than normally incompetent for her years. Mrs. Ambrose, who had been speaking much at random, now reflected that she certainly did not look forward to the intimacy of three or four weeks on board ship which was threatened. Women of her own age usually boring her, she supposed that girls would be worse. She glanced at Rachel again. Yes! how clear it was that she would be vacillating, emotional, and when you said something to her it would make no more lasting impression than the stroke of a stick upon water. There was nothing to take hold of in girls—nothing hard, permanent, satisfactory. Did Willoughby say three weeks, or did he say four? She tried to remember.]

A tall, burly man entered the room; this was Willoughby Vinrace; Rachel's father. He shook Helen's hand with an emotional kind of heartiness.

"It's a great pleasure that you have come," he said. "For both of us."

"M-m-m-" said Rachel, in obedience to her father's glance.

"We'll do our best to make you comfortable. And Ridley? We think it a great honour to have him. Pepper will have some one clever enough to talk to. This child has grown, hasn't she?" Still holding Helen's hand, he drew his arm round Rachel's shoulder, and made them come uncomfortably close.

Helen forebore to look.

"D'you think she does us credit?" he continued.

"I'm sure she does" said Helen.

"We expect great things of her, don't we?" he said, squeezing his daughter's arm and releasing her.

"I like your ship, Willoughby" Helen broke off.

"You haven't tested her yet" he said. "But we can give her a good character, can't we Rachel?"

"Some people can't" said Rachel.

"But about you now"—they sat down—"Did you leave the children well? They'll be ready for school, I suppose? Do they take after you or Ambrose? They've got good heads on their shoulders I've no doubt?"

Helen brightened, and explained that her son was six and her daughter ten. Everybody said that her boy was like her, and her girl like Ridley. As for brains, they were quick brats, she thought[, and modestly she ventured on a little story about her son,—how left alone for a minute he had taken the pat of butter in his fingers, run across the room with it, and put it on the fire—merely for the fun of the thing, a feeling which she could understand.

"And you had to show the young rascal that these tricks wouldn't do, eh?"

"A child of six? I don't think they matter."

"I'm an old-fashioned father."

"Nonsense, Willoughby; Rachel knows better."

Much as Willoughby would doubtless have liked his daughter to praise him she did not; her eyes were unreflecting as water, her fingers still toying with the fossilised fish, her mind absent. The elder people went on to speak of arrangements that could be made for Ridley's comfort—a table placed where he couldn't help looking at the sea, far from boilers, at the same time sheltered from the view of people passing. Unless he made this a holiday, when his books were all packed, he would have no holiday whatever; for out at Santa Marina Helen knew, by experience, that he would work all day; his boxes, she said, were packed with books.

"Leave it to me—leave it to me!" said Willoughby, obviously intending to do much more than she asked of him. But Ridley and Mr. Pepper were heard fumbling at the door.

"How are you, Vinrace?" said Ridley, extending a limp hand as he came in, as though the meeting were melancholy to both, but on the whole more so to him.

Willoughby preserved his heartiness, tempered by respect. For the moment nothing was said.

"We looked in and saw you laughing," Helen remarked. "Mr. Pepper had just told a very good story."

"Pish. None of the stories were good," said her husband peevishly.

"Still a severe judge, Ridley?" enquired Mr. Vinrace.

"We bored you so that you left," said Ridley, speaking directly to his wife.

As this was quite true Helen did not attempt to deny it, and her next remark, "But didn't they improve after we'd gone?" was unfortunate, for her husband answered with a droop of his shoulders, "If possible they got worse."

The situation was now one of considerable discomfort for every one concerned, as was proved by a long interval of constraint and silence. Mr. Pepper, indeed, created a diversion of a kind by leaping on to his seat, both feet tucked under him, with the action of a spinster who detects a mouse, as the draught struck at his ankles. Drawn up there, sucking at his cigar, with his arms encircling his knees, he looked like the image of Buddha, and from this elevation began a discourse, addressed to nobody, for nobody had called for it, upon the unplumbed depths of ocean. He professed himself surprised to learn that although Mr. Vinrace possessed ten ships, regularly plying between London and Buenos Aires, not one of them was bidden to investigate the great white monsters of the lower waters.

"No, no," laughed Willoughby, "the monsters of the earth are too many for me!"

"If it weren't for the goats there'd be no music, my dear; music depends upon goats," said her father rather sharply, and Mr. Pepper went on to describe the white, hairless, blind monsters lying curled on the ridges of sand at the bottom of the sea, which would explode if you brought them to the surface, their sides bursting asunder and scattering entrails to the winds when released from pressure, with considerable detail and with such show of knowledge, that Ridley was disgusted, and begged him to stop.

From all this Helen drew her own conclusions, which were gloomy enough. Pepper was a bore; Rachel was an unlicked girl, no doubt prolific of confidences, the very first of which would be: "You see, I don't get on with my father." Willoughby, as usual, loved his business and built his Empire, and between them all she would be considerably bored. Being a woman of action, however, she rose, and said that for her part she was going to bed. At the door she glanced back instinctively at Rachel, expecting that as two of the same sex they would leave the room together. Rachel rose, looked vaguely into Helen's face and remarked with her slight stammer, "I'm going out to t-t-triumph in the wind."]

Suddenly Helen felt, "Of course one loves Theresa's child." Yes, but that did not mean that one could show it. "Good night" she said, without even shaking hands. An hour later all the passengers lay horizontal upon their ledges, hearing noises that told them that the voyage was begun, and resigned, for nothing they could do would make any difference. The eye of Heaven could see the Euphroysne moving slowly up a gash in the land, through the rippling silver spaces and the black shadows, until she came out into a wide breadth of the sea, and her reds and yellows began to shine in the dawn.

CHAPTER THREE

It is true that they all came in to breakfast on the following morning. Mr Pepper was punctual, having passed an almost sleepless night. Helen came next; and ordered the coffee. Then Vinrace appeared; then Ridley; then Rachel.

"The first day of a voyage is an excellent time for making good resolutions, Rachel" her father said. "Your Aunt has had to give us our coffee."

But his tone was kindly. "The first day of a voyage"—that was the feeling that made them all kindly. The voyage had begun; friendship perhaps had begun too. The sense of untapped resources was comforting; and it depended upon a great number of years and events which were present in the mind, and gave the breakfast a kind of beauty. When Ridley said, "She's not like her mother," when Helen sighed, "Of course one loves Theresa's child" when Rachel groaned "How I hate old friends!" when Willoughby mused, "How strange that Theresa isn't here" when Mr Pepper wondered, "There are advantages in a fortunate marriage, I daresay" they were all making the first breakfast memorable. In after years, very probably, the entire voyage would be represented by this one hour; and the hooting of the sirens perhaps the night before. Nothing is stranger than the position of the dead among the living, and the whole scene was the work of one woman who had been in her grave for eight years.

Thus Helen, as she mixed milk and coffee, and spoke kindly about the weather, the rheumatics, and the habits of sailors, was thinking on from the text, "I wonder why Theresa married you." Theresa might have married any one; a Professor, or a painter of pictures, that is to say; she had married a business man. Nor was he merely a rock of a man, to whom a brilliant woman might cling for support; on the contrary he was a sentimental man who imported goats for the sake of the empire, and ruled his daughter because he knew that life without a sense of duty is bound to be tragic. Again, he was sentimental in his reverence for book learning, and sentimental in his hatred for arts which display the person, acting, singing, piano playing and fiddling. He was certainly sentimental about his wife and daughter. On anniversaries he shut himself up, and grieved; in ordinary life, he never spoke of the dead naturally, and veiled his affections beneath sternness and humour. Having taken life very seriously from the start, he was now in a position to do his country good. One little wine merchant's office in Hull had grown, had burst its walls, been carried off in a cart, re-risen in great blocks, which showed like mountains at night; while ships went out at his command and lured thousands upon thousands of tawny little goats from the uplands of South America into their holds. To have established one's family, so that they need only draw dividends as long as the world lasts, and to be able to do something for one's country by the time one is forty is a great achievement; it was probable that Willoughby Vinrace would be one of the exceptional people who make an accurate image of themselves in some kind of substance before they die, and render it back to the world.

Undoubtedly, Helen was prompted to go on saying 'sentimental' by the fact that she was comparing her husband with Theresa's husband. Between friends who marry at the same time, there must always be these profound comparisons. That is the staple of their talk—What has life done for me?—for you? For me, (I believe in my secret heart) it has done rather better than for you. "Still, I don't know what Willoughby feels," Helen was bound to own; nor did the word 'sentimental' cover every thing. No one could call Ridley sentimental. But, he was poor and they did not see a great deal of life. One may take it for granted that scholarship is better than business; but at times it seemed as though Theresa had chosen the more adventurous career. They were building a new factory when Ridley was bringing out the third volume of Pindar. Then Theresa died, and the comparisons were at an end, which was one form of sorrow. There was no other woman one could tell things to. Rachel—? What an absent minded, dreamy looking creature she was, pouring milk from a height, as though to see what kind of drops it made! "At twenty four we weren't as chill as that," Helen mused. "It will be ten years before she feels a thing. Theresa was always after something. She was darker, bolder, softer, more animated. This girl might be a boy." One could be hard upon the child because one had loved the mother. The points in Rachel's' favour were her lack of chatter, and her charming face, which would have been attractive if, &c &c; but Helen meant to know her.

"Pepper knows, but Pepper won't say" said Willoughby.

"I do not know; and therefore I cannot say" said Mr Pepper.

This was the only help he gave to what civilised people think necessary—talk at meals. Mr Pepper was in advance of civilisation. He said, when it was worth while to say it, that one should only speak when one has something to say; and it was many years since he had had anything to say at breakfast, his circulation, being, he supposed defective. Then one must be sure about one's meaning; half the ideas that came to him died when examined. Consequently he issued facts more frequently than ideas; and was never in a muddle about his feelings. While he sipped his tea, and cut his toast into long bars, he was cracking many a doubtful idea up in his workshop. How far should one let oneself be influenced by her beauty in judging Helen's niceness? Some kinds of beauty probably set up an emotional fiction which it is the right to submit to. Yes that was undoubtedly present, to some extent, in this case. Blandly he passed her the jam. She was talking nonsense, but not worse nonsense than people usually do talk at breakfast. It is never right to yield because a woman is a woman. Therefore, he stuck to his "I do not know." Then he rambled. About marriage, for instance. It is advisable in certain circumstances; for when childbirth is over, there remains companionship, which has obvious advantages over solitude. There must be many small things one can say to a woman when one is undressing; but after a certain age the formation of habits is an insuperable bar. Are habits bad? He reviewed his habits. He committed not only poetry but prose to heart a good deal; he was fond of dividing numbers; he read Petronius in May, and so on. But the human affections are the best things we have. His circumstances had not been altogether favourable. Condemned to toil for twelve years in a railway station in Bombay, he had seen few women that commanded his respect. He had applied his mind to the service. He had perfected a system. There was nothing to regret in his life, except fundamental defects, and no wise man regrets them. There is always the present. He looked round the table, and smiled.

"What's that old thing smiling for?" Rachel mused. "I suppose he's chewed something forty seven times."

"Chewing" summed up much—too much; indeed the poor man was nothing but a summary of middle age to her. One person stood for age, another for business, another for society. It was a convenient short cut. More often than not they gained in the process, becoming featureless but dignified. The figures of elderly women, and beautiful young women in particular, gained a beauty like that of people on the stage, which they would not have had, if Rachel had dispensed with symbols. The cruelty of the process was now shown; she met Mr Pepper's smile with an intelligent stare, and possibly clouded his conviction that their understanding was deep and lasting, though not a thing one talked about. So kindly was the morning, showing blue through the windows, that she pitied him— a man who had no future, a man who knew all about himself.

"Are your legs bad to day, Mr. Pepper?" she asked, with the smooth and charming voice of youth, which conveys balm if not sympathy.

"It was not my legs but my arms" he corrected her. "They don't change."

"Not even on a beautiful autumn morning like this?"

"Beauty has no effect upon uric acid that I am aware of" he said.

"What are you going to do today?" Rachel pursued.

"I shall begin the works of an author you have never heard of." The name sounded like Maccabaeus.

"He's a fascinating man. He tells one about the making of roads. He was a kind of Mac Adam; only the system was different. Naturally it had to be, because of the soil. Do you realise what an important thing a road is Rachel?"

"Begun by rabbits, they were continued by men" said Rachel idly.

Mr Pepper went on,

"The best roadmakers were the Romans by a long way. We lost the art, to recover it, and lose it again. I have the habit of cycling through Richmond Park every morning before breakfast. I have observed the futility of modern methods. I have been at the trouble of explaining. 'With the first heavy rainfall,' I have told them, 'your road will be a swamp.' Again and again my words have proved true. I have advised them to read Maccabaeus. Yet the old method goes on. What they do is this"—He crumbled his bread to represent a heap of small pebbles; Rachel understood him to say that they were too small; then in her mind's eye she soused them in coffee to represent the state of the roads of Richmond after a heavy fall of rain. Then Mr Pepper advanced upon his bicycle and red tinged water went squirting on either side. He dismounted, picked up a pebble, and begged a man with a pick axe to examine it. Meanwhile she had lost every word of the explanation, which interested Helen, because she liked to know how things were done.

"And so our rates rise" she sighed.

"Precisely" said Mr Pepper. "And so they will continue to rise, so long as present methods endure." He laughed lightly at the stupidity of mankind.

"So long as we let things be done for us" said Helen. "Why aren't you on a Council Mr Pepper?"

"I was" said Mr Pepper. "But I had to resign. It took up too much time."

"They were too stupid I suppose" said Helen. "How one resents stupidity! I'm almost sure that the nurse has taught Margaret the Lord's Prayer by this time!"

"She'll soon forget it" Ridley growled. "You attribute too much power to Christianity, my dear. I'll sweep her little head clear in half an hour. Besides, the child is sensible."

"It's the waste I hate" said Helen.

"Oh a little religion hurts nobody" said Mr Vinrace, awkwardly trying to turn the conversation with a laugh.

"Don't you think so?" said Helen, fixing him with her large severe eyes.

"I would rather my daughter told lies than believed in God; only they come to the same thing."

"If you think that," shrugged Willoughby, "we can't argue; and we don't want to quarrel, do we Helen?"

Theresa, the dead woman, again made herself felt.

"There is no reason for quarrelling because one disagrees" said Helen. "But when I think of a child of mine sitting up on its haunches and babbling nonsense to a God because an ignorant woman cajoles it, my blood boils!"

Ridley laughed out loud. "Oh Helen, what a goose you are!"

She neatly flicked a piece of toast across the table, so that it lodged in his beard. The conversation ended.

"Let's take the air" said Helen. She stood with her feet on the ladder and her head in the open.

"Oh look!" she cried. "We're out at sea!"

Standing upon the deck, they saw that all the smoke had disappeared, and the houses; and that the ship was out in a wide space of sea, very fresh and clear, though colourless. They had left London, sitting on its mud. A very thin line of shadow tapered on one side, scarcely thick enough to stand the burden of Paris, which nevertheless rested upon it. A strange exhilaration came over them, when they felt that they were free of roads, and were taking their way, alone, across the sea. The ship went very quickly over small waves that slapped her and then fizzled, almost like effervescing water. Above was the colourless October sky, thinly clouded as if by the trail of wood-fire smoke. Ridley snorted like a horse; William Pepper grasped the rail and chuckled, without pain or derision; and Mrs Ambrose turning her long sloping cheek up to her husband, drew his arm within her cloak. The pair moved away; it could be seen that they kissed each other; and then Ridley had something private to communicate. Rachel guessed that it had to do with her father. An emotion stirred within her. How beautiful the sight of a couple arm in arm is! She now looked upon Helen as a type of maternity, to whom reverence was due. The interfering old friend was gone. Mrs Ambrose was a melodious figure. Looking into the bubbles in the water below, Rachel longed for music.

"I give you till ten-thirty tomorrow Rachel" said her father, "Enjoy your meditations now; and let's have done with them! Why, you'll turn into a stone woman one of these days, and what use will she be to me, eh? If anyone wants me, I'm busy till one—And Rachel, I expect you to be punctual." He pressed her shoulder, and made off. In his cabin there waited him a stout leather case; locked; and stuffed with documents. It was his delight to feed upon such matter until it was consumed. The present stock would last him exactly the length of the voyage. When working he felt that his ship— the great ship of his destiny—was forging ahead. An immense satisfaction was given off by his person (one could almost hear him thump and throb) as he leant across the table and dealt with papers. His small grey eyes glowed in the chase. Above him was pinned a photograph of his wife. She had a thin humorous face, and her eyes, though vague as Rachel's eyes, would light up sooner than Rachel's, and laugh. "My dear," one could fancy her saying, "Why work so hard? What does it all matter? Be happy!" Occasionally he looked up at her and groaned. More doggedly then did he drive his pen; more powerfully score his sheet. No one knew how he was tempted and wounded and driven to despair as he forged ahead; nor did any one know what vanities and visions came to solace him as he voyaged alone. He took it for granted that all men who master the world are as lonely as he was. He could not help hoping that it might not be necessary for Rachel to master the world.

The hours which he had granted his daughter for meditation were brutally cut short. She was still standing, still watching the bubbles race, when she heard a cough. Mrs Chailey, who coughed, walked the deck like a web-footed fowl. She was short and fat, as respectable as a woman can be, and her toes had lumps on them, smoothly outlined in felt. An expression of straightforward indignation was upon her honest face.

"Might I speak to you Miss?" She looked round stealthily to see that no gentry were near.

"I don't know how ever we shall get through this voyage, Miss Rachel" she began. "I never saw the things in such a state. Why there's only sheets enough for yourselves, and the master's has a rotten place in it, you could put your finger through." As Rachel showed no signs of agitation, she continued, "Did you notice the counterpanes last night? I thought to myself a poor person would have been ashamed of them. The one I gave Mr Pepper you could see your face through. I'll show you miss."

Together they descended and inspected a large pile of linen, heaped upon a table. Mrs Chailey ran through the sheets with experienced fingers. Some had yellow stains; others had places where the threads made long ladders. But otherwise they seemed as sound, Rachel thought, as sheets usually are.

"Couldn't they be mended?" she asked.

"No Miss Rachel," said Mrs Chailey vehemently, "they could *not* be mended; they're only fit for dust sheets they are. Why, if one sewed one's fingers to the bone over sheets like those one would have one's work undone next time they went to the laundry."

Her voice in its indignation wavered, as if tears were near.

"We can't buy any now" said Rachel, for she had to lean a hand against the wall to steady herself. The sea was beneath them.

"And then Miss Rachel you could hardly ask a living creature to sit where I sit. I'll show you Miss."

Mrs Chailey was expected to sit in a cabin which was large enough, but too near the boilers.

"I can hear my heart go when I've been in here five minutes" she declared. "Your mother would never have asked it of me."

"But of course, if it's bad, you must change" said Rachel desperately. "Where could you sit, Mrs Chailey?"

"I've thought Miss that as you weren't using Number sixteen at present—I could turn out directly you wanted it."

"You shall have Number sixteen... But about the sheets?"

"I'll tell you Miss Rachel what I think best to be done; I could take the master's sheet and join it down the middle and if Mr Pepper had the one with the spots, we could manage at present, so long as no one looks too close."

"No one ever notices—at least I shouldn't think they did."

"Ah Miss Rachel you *should* notice and not leave things to servants the way you do. Your mother would have known every sheet in her house."

Her mother no doubt would have forced Mrs Chailey to tell the truth. Or would she not have succumbed to shyness, when she saw this competent woman of fifty as much upset in her temper as a child and forced to evasions, because she wanted to sit where she had not leave to sit?

Luckily for Rachel's peace of mind, generally as placid as a deep pool, little phrases were apt to come between her and the facts.

"It's the burden of lies" she thought to herself, as she withdrew; "We carry the burden of lies."

Meditating on the burden deposited hundreds of years ago upon the shoulders of all of us, she did not consider the particular case.

Mrs Chailey folded her sheets, but though indignation was gone, her expressions testified to flatness within. Miss Rachel didn't care—that was it.

"Chailey, you old wretch, what d'you come bothering me for?" that was how Rachel's mother would have spoken.

"New sheets? You ought to be ashamed of yourself! Let me look at them. Nonsense! They're as good as new. It's your temper that wants mending. Tell me what's at the bottom of it...... Oh—you want another room do you? Well, I don't see how I'm to manage it." There was no getting round Mrs Vinrace; many was the brush that Chailey had had with her; yet at the end one always felt better; one knew where one was. Thus pondering, Mrs Chailey took up her abode in the room which she had won so easily. Before she considered a room her own, she had to stand several tiny ornaments on the dressing table; she had to dot a number of little photographs on the wall. One might have read the story of her life in these absurd china pugs, and faded cartes de visite. Presented, generally with tears, at some crisis, a wedding or funeral, bought one day when "we'd gone for a treat, that summer you had a house in Sussex," given by widowed publicans in memory of their wives, treasured from the death bed of her mistress, Chailey had here the tokens of a life. Supreme among them all—a sun round which the stars were arranged—hung a large picture of Theresa Vinrace. Those privileged to look behind the frame read that it was given to a faithful servant in gratitude by Willoughby Vinrace. When a woman has spent thirty of her fifty years among the pots and sheets of one house, the tokens of her life do not take up much space; but the little figures and hair pin boxes (made of queer stone and stamped with city arms) are not rubbish; any more than a hole in a sheet is a trifle. Owning such possessions, Mrs Chailey never took kindly to a ship. Unknown to any one, she had cried yesterday when the lamps were lit; she would cry this evening; she would cry tomorrow. It was not home. At this moment tears were not distant; but that was because—because she got things too easily now. No one ruled her; no one really knew what things she was lazy about, what things she did quite beautifully. Miss Rachel not caring, well, one couldn't help being lazy. But life wasn't as good as it used to be.

Pinning up photographs, she moralised; and, as she drove a nail in for her mistress to hang from, concluded, "So long as I'm with you, and can do something for your family, I've no cause to complain." Indeed, she was right; the family was everything, and if Rachel one day put her child in Mrs Chailey's arms, she would feel as the keen novel reader feels when the story reaches its gorgeous climax, and ends happily, and one drops off to sleep, content.

"Mrs Chailey?" some one was calling outside the door. "Oh Mrs Chailey, do you think you would help me?" It was Mrs Ambrose who asked for help, and Chailey was once more a competent woman.

"I can't find Miss Rachel, and I'm trying to arrange my husband's room. Mr Vinrace has given him a room to read in. But there's no chair."

In saying this she was not strictly speaking the truth; there was a chair, an arm chair, but it was too high a chair to read Greek in. Again, for reading Greek one does not want a big heavy table but a little movable table. And then a piercing rod of draught coming right down one's neck chills the Greeks. These defects accumulating had resulted in a roar of anguish, which came to Helen's ears as she devastated the saloon of all that Mr Grice held lady like. Ridley pointed with a lean forefinger.

"It's as though they'd taken pains to torment me!" he cried. The fictitious comfort of chair and table for the moment deceived Helen; but she was too wise to show her perplexity. "How can one read with one's feet in the air? I can no more move that table than a Rhinoceros. This breeze blows down my spine. Really, one might have credited Vinrace with more sense!" He went on to damn the foolhardy rashness which had led him—"people told one such lies—I ought to have known better" to trust his corpse to a ship.

"Take three turns, and you shall find it all ready" said Helen. "A low chair—we'll find another table."

"But, my dear, the draught—? I shall have to sit in my great coat."

"There's such a thing as flannel."

"I don't understand you, Helen."

"No; but you will."

Ridley shrugged his shoulders with foreboding, like a child whose canary bird has flown, and cannot believe that all the gold in his mother's purse will really buy a new one. Still, mothers sometimes work miracles.

It was at this crisis that Mrs Chailey was called in. To her considerable though mute amazement, it was explained to her that no gentleman could read Greek in a high chair.

"Why it's the master's own chair!" she exclaimed, as though Emperors might be proud to dictate despatches in it. "I daresay Mr Ambrose isn't very strong" she added. In that case, she would do anything, and Helen gladly accepted this diagnosis of what ailed her husband.

In a low chair, flanked by a light table, behind a door frilled with flannel, Ridley could soon communicate with the Greeks. Having placed him, and received his thanks, "the thanks of an ineffectual creature who could not exist without you" Helen watched him start. First, he looked comfortable, and stroked his thighs; then he looked intent; gradually innumerable fine lines came in his face. His eyes saw something noble close to him, which could only be seen looking very steadily. Communication was now established; and an intense stillness was in the room where the Greeks were. How random and flurried the world seemed, when Helen shut the door, and came out on the gusty deck where sailors were scrubbing, with gulls above their heads!

Yet she never left him without wondering. Illiterate herself (it could be proved that she had read Hamlet, but as to the lesser plays of Shakespeare there was reason for doubt) she respected readers; but sometimes wondered about Greek. Hide it though she might, she knew quite well that there were only twenty four people who enjoyed Ridley's books; this innermost circle was enclosed by wider rings, containing those who read because they had to; and those who knew that such books were important without reading them. Very soon the force of his fame was spent; and the world surged in complete indifference to it. That was ungrateful of the world, considering how Ridley forsook its pleasures to give his brain to Greek. The joys of lighted halls, midnight wanderings, laziness in the sun, all reckless expenditure of energy, were cut from his life, leaving it is true, a noble and delightful man, whose standard was very high, whose mind was very pure, whose digestion was very delicate, whose head often ached, who was (here she frowned a little) an egoist certainly, with very little sympathy for fat women and stupid men.

How abominable for instance was his treatment of poor Willoughby! Groans at the sight of him, yawns when he spoke, and worse than either a kind of half veiled insolence towards him, as to a well-meaning, perspiring, industrious, agricultural labourer. She could excuse his prejudice against the man his sister had married; she could not excuse his contempt for clumsiness. Willoughby read encyclopaedias instead of books; but Helen, who called him sentimental, believed that there was no dismissing human force, and that to patronise the form it takes is to proclaim oneself a dandy. On the whole, that was her grudge against Greek; or, more justly, her grudge against the Ambroses. Indeed when one cast one's mind back to the grandparents, and uncles and aunts, to the first editions, and good etchings and nice chairs, to the traditions of scholarships and deaneries and posts, how could one blame Ridley or Rachel either? if as Helen suspected, she shared the family taint. They had been born beneath green shades. Dwelling with unusual satisfaction upon the thought of her uncle the brewer, and her brother the stockbroker, she completed her work, and turned the saloon into a bare but pleasing sitting room, with charming yellow curtains.

CHAPTER FOUR

Great tracts of the earth lay now beneath the October sun. The whole of England from the bald moors to the Cornish rocks, was lit up from dawn to sunset, and showed in stretches of yellow, green and purple. Even the roofs of the great towns glittered. In millions of small gardens, millions of dark red flowers were blooming, until millions of old ladies came down the paths, snipped through their juicy stalks, and laid them upon cold stone ledges in the village church. Thousands of picknickers coming home at sunset, cried, "Was there ever such a day as this?" "It's you" the young men whispered; "Oh, it's you" the young women replied. All old people and many sick people were drawn, were it only a foot or two, into the open air, and prognosticated pleasant things about the course of the world. As for the confidences and expressions of love that were heard not only in cornfields but in lamplit rooms, where the windows opened on the garden, and men with cigars kissed women with grey hairs—they were not to be counted. Some said that the sky was an emblem of the life they had had; others that it was a promise of the life that would be theirs. Long-tailed birds clattered and screamed, and crossed from wood to wood, with golden eyes in their plumage.

But very few people thought about the sea. They took it for granted that the sea was calm; and there was no need, as there is in many houses when the creeper taps on the bedroom windows, for the couples to murmur before they kiss,

"Think of the ships tonight" or "Thank Heaven, I'm not the man in the light house!" For all they imagined, the ships when they vanished on the skyline, dissolved, like snow in water. The grown up view was not much clearer than the view of the little creatures in bathing drawers who were trotting in to the foam all along the coasts of England, and scooping up buckets full of water. They saw white sails or tufts of smoke pass across the horizon, and if you had said that these were waterspouts, and petals of white sea flowers, they would have agreed.

The people in ships however took an equally singular view of England. Not only did it appear to them to be an island, a very small island, but it was a shrinking island in which people were imprisoned. One figured them first swarming about, like aimless ants, and almost pressing each other over the edge; and then, as the ship withdrew, one figured them making a vain clamour, which, being unheard, either ceased, or rose into a brawl. Finally, when the ship was out of sight of land, it became plain that the people of England were completely mute. The disease attacked other parts of the earth; Europe shrank, Asia shrank; Africa and America shrank. It seemed doubtful whether the ship would ever run against any of those wrinkled little rocks again. But, on the other hand, an immense dignity had descended upon her; she was an inhabitant of the great world, which has so few inhabitants. She travelled all day across an empty universe, with veils drawn before her and behind. She was more lonely than the caravan crossing the desert; she was infinitely more mysterious, moving by her own power and sustained by her own resources. The sea might give her death, or some unexampled joy, and none would know of it. But when the sun shone, and the long still days were blue, her state was far more wondrous than the state of England. She was a bride going forth to her husband unattended.

"Loe! where she comes along with portly pace,
Like Phoebe, from her Chamber of the East."

After three perfect days it was natural to feel for the Euphrosyne as for some vast, consoling woman. One of the miracles wrought by the sea is that it smooths away differences and makes people appear much alike—heroic, bored, hungry or indolent; it does with them as it does with broken bottles and proves that we are all glass. On board the Euphrosyne, the passengers were serene and indolent; but with regard to the crew, such a statement would be rash; for no one could possibly know what those lean housemaids were feeling. No one ever seemed to speak to them; but Captain Cobbett who appeared at odd hours and was ready to conduct tours into refrigerators, and engines, had communicated several facts about ports and life at sea to Helen; with William Pepper listening.

These conditions were much to Rachel's liking. She liked the warmth, the monotonous blue, the serenity and indolence. To enjoy them at her ease, she retired soon after breakfast to her room, her music room, she called it, for her little piano was placed there. When the ship was full, this apartment bore some magnificent title; and was the resort of elderly sea sick ladies, who left the deck to their youngers. By dint of up setting a cube sugar box full of books on to the floor, and appropriating a large pale arm chair, Rachel had stamped the room for her own. Her father believed that when she slammed the door, she addressed herself to the German language, which he said, is the foundation of all knowledge. She believed that she divided the time equally between practising the piano, and reading—the things one wanted to read. But a spectator would have wondered. There lay the German work which her father, with a pathetic wish to conciliate her, had procured—"Tristan," with an English translation.

There lay her music books, with a late Beethoven sonata spread upon the little piano. There lay several odd volumes, selected very much at random from the literature of England; Wuthering Heights; Cowper's Letters, the life of Colonel Hutchinson by his widow, and the History of Sailing Ships. Old envelopes jutting out at different thicknesses showed that while she was well started in them all, she had finished none. Then there was a looking glass, which perhaps, was in use too. It was obviously the room of a person without a system. Coming up here on the fourth of the blue days, Rachel thrust the windows open as far as they would go. No; there was nothing to be seen but blue waves; not a spout of smoke even on the horizon. Lying back in the arm chair she could just see the blue, but she tried, for a moment to obscure it. She held Tristan before her eyes, and read that engaging passage which, running thus in the German

> *Der zagend vor dem Streiche sich flüchtet*
> *wo er kann weil eine Braut er als*
> *Leiche für seinen Herrn gewann!*
> *Dünkt es dich dunkel mein Gedicht?*

goes like this in English.

> *In shrinking trepidation his shame*
> *he seeks to hide*
> *While to the king his relation*
> *He brings the corpse like Bride.*
> *Seems it so senseless what I say?*

It must be admitted that a grudging student of the German tongue had some reason to lift the eyes with delight. But in Rachel's case, lifting the eyes meant getting them filled with sun warmed blue. There was that far horizon, wavering in a soft haze, to plunge into. A resolute mind would have escaped; but an irresolute mind which allows the eyes to expand to their full width is lost. Rachel's book slipped and sprawled and she ceased to smile; an immense vagueness filled her. Then it appeared to her that this sitting indoors with niggling little books was insufferable, and she lifted a chair out into the sun. Yet one can't sit and look at things; one must have a book convenient. Cowper's Letters was convenient; the kind of book that offers a sentence and then, so to speak retires modestly while you see what you can do with it. She read about his desk which came along the road so slowly, and the little boys who threw mud at his windows on the fifth of November, and how he took refuge in his greenhouse from a storm, and about the sheets of the Task. She got an idea of him, slim and pale with delicate hands, dwelling in a red brick village with excessively muddy roads. She had never read a word of his poetry save what is printed in the Golden Treasury. In short this slim phantom was all that remained of William Cowper, as far as she was concerned. Dipping here and there, she gave him qualities; what an egoist he was; how vain of his poetry, how lonely, owing to the state of the roads and people's view of madness. That he would go mad again was evident; the deeps of melancholy were all about him. One peopled the low dark room with demure women. Here was Mary Unwin—here Lady Hesketh. They awaited the poet's return, and were politely tart with each other. "They are real, these dead people," was her conclusion. She put her hand up, and fancied she felt the faint shock of the things he had thought over a century ago, tingling, like wireless messages upon her palm. Thinking was going on then as now; and thinking after all, is the flesh and blood of life; action seemed to her all out of proportion, as though people came and waved flags in your face. (This was an allusion to Mrs Chailey, who had been bothering her about the tea and bacon.) "Come, Spirits" she murmured; and was instantly fortified by a sense of the presence of the things that aren't there. There were the beautiful drowned statues, there were the glens and hills of an undiscovered country; there were divine musical notes, which, struck high up in the air, made one's heart beat with delight at the assurance that the world of things that aren't there was splendidly vigorous and far more real than the other. She felt that one never spoke of the things that mattered, but carried them about, until a note of music, or a sentence or a sight, joined hands with them. That was why she read Cowper's Letters. The world that was sunk a little way beneath time seemed to her of the nature of a spirit. Her quarrel with the living was that they did not realise the existence of drowned statues, undiscovered places, the birth of the world, the final darkness, and death. To the one man who had yet asked her to marry him, she had said that it seemed to her ridiculous. Why, she half expected to come up next year as a bed of white flowers. Since she had been conscious at all, she had been conscious of what with her love of vague phrases, she called, "The Great War." It was a war waged on behalf of things like stones, jars, wreckage at the bottom of the sea, trees stars and music, against the people who believe in what they see. It was not easy to explain, supposing Rachel knew what she meant.

But when Miss Clara Vinrace gave at dinner a minute account of her afternoon's visit to Kensington, and how, suddenly remembering that it was Mrs Phillipses day at home, she had left the sale at Barkers, although she was not really dressed for calls, 'I had on my old Tweed jacket' 'But I always think your fur looks so nice'—and had been so glad afterwards, because Marion Phillips was home from Aberystwyth, and she always thought that one could leave blankets to the last day of a sale, not like blouses which got snapped up—

Rachel struck a very crude blow at her Aunt's world by asking what she supposed Kensington High Street was like in the days of William the Conqueror? "Didn't they dig up a mammoth under Pontings the other day?" She felt that if only one could begin things at the beginning, one might see more clearly upon what foundations they now rest.

"Did they? Oh, I didn't hear of it—but a shilling on a blanket isn't more than Gosling allows, only one is certain about the quality......"

The wounds that Rachel received hurt considerably.

"Oh Rachel never dreams of helping one" her Aunt would gasp, while she struggled to disentangle her prince nez from the curl on the nape of her neck. Or, "Rachel, think of others" came at her out of the blue; or "Don't be morbid dear" which meant that she had said that the smell of broom reminded her of funerals. "I always think it such a cheerful plant" said Miss Bessie, and threw her niece into a passion.

But they were kindly ladies, and would have done much to feel what in private they mourned that they never did feel, that Rachel would 'come' to them, as they called it.

They encouraged her when she tried to give expression to her theories. There was a theory about what things were real, which grew out of a casual remark of Miss Clara's to the effect that at ten thirty every morning she expected to find the housemaid brushing the stairs. It seemed odd, when Rachel thought of it, that one ever should ever expect to find a housemaid brushing the stairs.

"Couldn't we get behind the system and see what it's all about?" she suggested. Somehow they slipped from the organisation of labour to real feelings. As became Christian ladies, the Misses Vinrace maintained that no human being if she is doing her duty is either ugly or inferior.

"What is mud on your boots Rachel," Miss Clara explained, "is good earth in the street." Therefore it followed that one's feeling to a housemaid was as good a feeling as one could get.

"I shudder when I pass them" Rachel confessed. "I'd rather have at tooth out than speak."

They explained that of course one couldn't share the feelings of another class; and it was a great mistake to try. But a good servant never went beyond her place. Then followed a long inquisition. Granted that one could not feel anything much for servants, (but the Misses Vinrace did not grant it) what did one really feel for—for "you and me" in short? "Should you say that you had a strong feeling for Aunt Clara, now?"

The Aunts did not like this, but a longing that their niece should 'come' to them made them gentle.

"Certainly. What questions you do ask!"

"How does it show itself?"

"I can't say I've ever thought 'how'" said Miss Vinrace. "If one cares, one doesn't think 'how' Rachel."

"And do you care for me?"

"You dear thing, you know I do!" said Miss Vinrace, suddenly venturing over the line which separates ordinary conversation from special conversation. "Because you're your mother's daughter if for no other reason. And there are plenty of other reasons. But I sometimes wonder how much you care for us?"

At once Rachel perceived that the talk had left the rail she had planned, and had spilt them all into a scene. She had wanted to find out what they thought. She had wanted to say that there must be some kind of structure in the background which kept them all living together, just as there was a reason for that housemaid on the stairs; though—she meant to wind up—"we seem to be dropped about like tables or umbrellas." While she paused to think this, she cut Miss Vinrace to the quick; she made her blush. For, on a sudden impulse, she had lifted a veil which, she thought, had better not be lifted; and Rachel had taken advantage of it to hurt her. On the whole, Rachel gave as sore wounds as she received.

"Shall we go for a turn?" Miss Vinrace resumed, in her brave chilly voice. "It's going to be fine, I believe, in spite of Shaw."

The veil was dropped; it became a curtain.

That was the result of wishing to share one's feelings; and the conclusions must be that to feel anything strongly is to create an abyss between oneself and others, who too, feel strongly, but differently. One had recourse to symbols. Let all people be images; worship spirits; wage the great war. Therefore, her Aunts were images; Helen was an image; Mr Pepper was an image. Music was real; books were real; all things that one saw were real; and all that one thought. These were the spirits. The war was waged chiefly at meals, when one had to keep on knowing that the things that were said were all misfits for ideas, or did not try to fit anything. Mr Pepper's remark about the comparative longevity of elephants and tortoises for instance was a husk; Helen dealt largely in misfits, because she tried to keep talk going. Ridley however seemed to be on the side of the spirits, because he was so vain, and could hide nothing. Yet—yet—affection seemed to come in. Her little compartments did not fit all that she had to put in them. Her dreams began to include a new dream, about saying what one thought, and getting it answered. She dealt tentatively in misfits herself, and thrilled to feel Helen's eye upon her, dark with sympathy. Although these were symptoms of a war to come far subtler than any she had yet engaged in, she did not rise and go to meet it consciously. Uneducated, in the sense that no one had ever required her to know anything accurately, she was ill-fitted to keep her eye upon facts; correspondingly tempted to think of the bottom of the sea. "Why should I go bothering about my feelings, and other people's feelings," her meditations ran, "while the gulls are squawking above, the sea is running round the world, and the plants are opening on earth? I live; I die; the sea comes over me; it's the blue that lasts." Conveyed between sea and sky on a little platform which trembled with the waves, it was tempting to expand as though the entire being were one eye; blue haze was poured into that until it brimmed over; meanwhile the waters swished and sighed. There was no other sight or sound. Now fortified by the presence of all the spirits, she floated; her soul was like thistledown kissing the sea, and rising again, and so passing out of sight. It passed, indeed, to sleep. The midday sun grew hot.

"Yes," said Helen, finding that she had read the same passage twice, and was preparing to begin a third ascent, "It's really too hot to think."

"Your book requires thinking?" enquired the slightly sarcastic voice of William Pepper, who had drawn his deck chair close to hers.

"Philosophy" said Helen shortly. "Why do they bind books in black?" She displayed the volume. "How ugly university arms are! Lord, how glad I am that Ridley was never a Professor! Think of Cambridge on a day like this!"

"It might be pleasant, underneath the trees" mused Mr Pepper. I wonder if the foliage has done well this autumn. It is time for the cactus to be in blossom. I always make a point of seeing that."

"Oh yes, under the trees, if one's an undergraduate" said Helen. "I was thinking of intelligent conversation. Dons. Weekends—a—h—h—h!" She yawned.

"Yes," said Mr Pepper, "it's quite hard to remember that anything matters—much, on a day like this. I really think I've been asleep." He yawned.

"Why don't you try to sleep again" said Helen, "after your bad night?"

He took a bottle of white tabloids from his pocket and swallowed two. "That's done" he said, replacing it. "If you've finished with your philosopher, perhaps—" But Helen's great eyelids were closed, and her fingers unclasped. Pepper looked at her. "She's asleep" he said to himself. Helen heard him vaguely strike a match. Was it the flame of that, or of the sun, that was so warm upon her cheek? Warmth embraced her. Down down she went into the depths of sleep ...... up up she came into the daylight. There was Mr Pepper opposite, with his head drooped upon his shoulder, and his cheek a little flushed. After losing him several times and seeing him several times, and each time getting him clearer, she looked at her watch. Three quarters of an hour had been spent among those wavering sea weeds. It was near lunch time. She would walk to clear her head from the fumes of sleep. She wondered what Rachel had done with herself. Behold—her chair! Rachel was curled up asleep, with her cheek upon her palm, and her head bare in the sun. She looked like a victim dropped from the claws of some winged beast of prey. Helen thought her beautiful and unprotected. Sleep seemed to rob her of her weapons, and to expose what was covered when the eyes and lips were lively. Symmetry was restored. But why did she feel pity, looking upon the unlined face of youth, inscrutable in sleep?

"Because you have suffered something in secret, and will have to suffer more" she concluded. But knowing how awkward it would be if Rachel woke and saw her, Helen looked, thought, and moved on noiselessly.

CHAPTER FIVE

"He's a politician, and she's a lady of distinguished family—I can't remember which. That's what Dabson told me, and that's all I can tell you, ladies, I'm afraid."

But William Pepper could supply unimpeachable facts.

"He was member for South Cowley in the last Parliament; a Tariff Reformer; his wife is the daughter of the man who owns the estate there."

"A good member?" asked Helen desiring really to know the colour of his eyes and the nature of his temper.

"Neither good or bad, particularly," said Mr Pepper. "He lost his seat in the last election, but he will probably regain it next time. He was on the County Council."

This jogged Willoughby's memory.

"Oh! that fellow" he said. "A good man. I'm glad. I thought it was the other one, you know. Now Rachel you must attend for a minute. They will want things nice. Come along with me, and show me where you're putting them. We can't be luxurious, but we can be comfortable and I look to you to see to it my dear."

This unilluminating conversation took place on the 6th day of the voyage, in the mouth of the Tagus, where the Euphrosyne was anchored; and had reference to Richard Dalloway, once member of Parliament, and his wife, Clarissa. Being unable for a season at least to serve his country in Parliament, Mr Dalloway was serving it indirectly by broadening his mind. For that purpose the Latin countries did very well, though the East would have done better. He had been through France; he had stopped at manufacturing centres, where, producing letters of introduction, he had been shown over works, and noted facts in a pocket book; in Spain, he and Mrs Dalloway had mounted mules, for they wished to understand how the peasants live. Are they ripe for rebellion, for example? Mrs Dalloway insisted upon a day at Madrid, with the pictures. They arrived at Lisbon, just before the revolution, and spent five days which, in a journal privately issued afterwards, they described as "of unique interest." Richard had audiences with ministers; and foretold a crisis at no distant date "the foundations of government being incurably corrupt. Yet how blame &c &c &c" which as the world knows, were soon justified. Clarissa inspected the royal stables, and took several snap shots, showing men now exiled, and windows now broken, of equal interest. She photographed Fielding's grave, and let loose a small bird, which some ruffian had trapped, "because one hated to think of any thing in a cage, where English people lie buried."

The point of the tour was that it was unconventional. Their plans were decided as much by the foreign correspondents of the Times as by any other force. Mr Dalloway also wished to look at certain guns. All along those coasts, things were desperately unsettled. They wanted a slow inquisitive kind of ship, not a tramp exactly, but certainly not a liner, which would stop for a day or two at this port and that, taking in coal, while the Dalloways saw things for themselves. This had justified Richard's romantic statement on the steps of the Reform Club. "Expect to hear of me next in Petersburg or Teheran." But a disease had broken out in the East, there was cholera in Russia; and he was heard of in Lisbon.

The Euphrosyne was precisely the kind of boat that they wanted. She was of a fair size; a cargo boat, with accommodations for passengers, who, by pulling a certain wire, would be conveyed, as a favour. There was scarcely a situation in Europe which could not be alleviated by the mention of the name of some one Richard knew. Old women in omnibuses (if Richard ever travelled in them) were almost impelled to offer up their corner seats by the mere look of him.

On this occasion a card, with a pencilled line, dropped at Mr Dabson's door, and followed by a call, and a cup of tea, got them a cabin, although it was not Mr Vinrace's intention to take any passengers on this trip; indeed the Vinrace line only took passengers incidentally, the purpose being, after all, to forge one of those mystical tunnels which carry love and gold and energy from one fragment of the earth to another.

A boat took them out to the ship in the dusk. Pale lamps were beginning to shine, and the hills above the town were misty. "Like Whistler" said Mrs Dalloway. The new passengers appeared to Rachel, summoned by her father to receive them, as a tall slight woman, wrapped in a fur cloak, and a sturdy man, dressed like a sportsman on an autumnal moor. Many solid leather bags of a rich brown hue, surrounded them; in addition to which, Mr Dalloway carried a despatch box, ornamented with his card, and Mrs Dalloway a case, in which Rachel suspected a diamond necklace, and bottles with silver tops. Of their faces she got no clear impression, because the light was bad and she was shy. She was more than shy; she was humiliated. The evident distinction of the pair came at her like a sound or a stroke.

"There's my world shattered again" she said to herself, as she showed them to their rooms. The penalty of having a world was surely great. Three solid boxes, two live figures, with distinguished ways of turning and looking (they had scarcely spoken) a despatch box, and a jewel case, shrivelled up the smooth blue dome in which Rachel had enclosed the entire world for four days. Luggage and gestures, yes but there was something else. She could not think of Cowper with out blushing; mermaids, caves, the unseen things, suddenly deserted her; she was disrobed, an incompetent, insignificant, unattractive girl. Women too, she remembered, are more common than men; and Darwin says they are nearer the cow.

"One must act" she goaded herself. But Helen had arranged the flowers. Helen was making the smoking room more habitable. "If one can give men a room to themselves, where they will sit" she said sagely to Rachel, over her shoulder, "it's all to the good." She had sacrificed her own arm chair.

"Arm chairs are *the* important things" she said, wheeling it to an angle.

"Now Rachel, what are you going to wear?"

Rachel felt her ignominy. To accept such compromises, for Helen was giving way, now to men, now to the fact that these people were guests, seemed base; but cowardice and vanity forbade protest; and she was overwhelmed by the stream of an incomprehensible world; she was overwhelmed by the rush of Helen's vitality. Helen did not niggle. Whatever Helen thought best she would wear—her silk in short.

An hour later, Mrs Dalloway realised, with an enormous sense of relief that Mrs Ambrose had at least a way of shaking hands much like her own. The slight sketch given her before dinner by Mr Vinrace had made her a trifle uneasy.

"There's my brother-in-law, Ambrose, the scholar— I daresay you know his name, and his wife, and my old friend Pepper, a very quiet fellow, but knows everything, and that's all."

She had never heard of Ambrose—was it a surname?— but she knew that scholars married, practically any one; girls they met in farms, on reading parties; or little suburban women, who said, "Of course I know it's my husband you want, not *me*." Helen's appearance reassured her; it was eccentric, indeed, but not untidy; and her voice had restraint in it, the sign of a lady. That balanced the unfavourable effect of Mr Pepper, who had not changed his neat ugly suit.

"A quiet queer little thing" she thought him.

"But, after all," she said to herself, "*Every*one's interesting, really." Theoretically, her husband shared her belief; but in practise, he gave precedence to men educated at public schools, and to women who did their hair. Ambrose and Pepper he decided, sliding his eye round the table discreetly between mouthfuls of soup, scarcely passed the test; Willoughby was probably all right; Helen, from the soft loops of her hair, was obviously considered beautiful in artistic circles; and Rachel,—he could not suppress a smile— Rachel was conscious of her virginity. He put her age at twenty one (it was twenty four); and limited her experience to the walls of a middle class drawing room, and the dormitories of a provincial high school.

Under these circumstances, Richard and Clarissa signified across the table that they grasped the situation, and would stand by each other loyally.

"What I find so tiresome about the sea," Mrs Dalloway began immediately, like the first flourish of a fiddler, "is that there are no flowers in it. Imagine fields of hollyhocks and violets in mid ocean! How divine!"

"But dangerous to navigation" boomed Richard. "Why, weeds are bad enough aren't they, Vinrace? I remember crossing in the Mauretania once, and saying to the captain 'Now tell me what perils you really dread most for your ship, Captain Richards?' expecting him to say ice bergs, or derelicts, or fog, or something to that effect. Not a bit of it. 'Sedgii Acquaticus' he said, 'A kind of duck weed.'"

"Strange" said Mr Pepper.

"They have an awful time of it those Captains" said Willoughby. "Three thousand souls on board!"

"Yes indeed," said Clarissa; "I'm convinced people are wrong when they say it's work that wears one; it's responsibility. That's why one pays one's cook more than one's housemaid, I suppose."

"According to that, one ought to pay one's nurse double; but one doesn't" said Helen.

"No—but think what a joy to have to do with babies instead of saucepans!" said Mrs Dalloway, looking with greater interest at Helen, a probable mother.

"Still, that doesn't do away with the responsibility" said Helen.

"Mothers always exaggerate" said Ridley. "A well bred child is no responsibility. I've travelled all over Europe with mine. You just wrap 'em up warm and put em in the rack."

"How like a father!" cried Clarissa. "My husband's just the same. And then one talks of the equality of the sexes!"

"Does one?" said Mr Pepper

"Oh some do!" cried Clarissa. "My husband had to pass an irate lady every afternoon last session, who said nothing else I imagine."

"She sat outside the house; it was very awkward" said Dalloway. "At last I plucked up courage and said to her, 'My good creature, you're only in the way where you are. You're hindering me, and you're doing no good to yourself.'"

"And then she caught you by the coat, and would have scratched your eyes out."

"Pooh—that's been exaggerated" said Richard. "No; I pity them, I confess. The discomfort of sitting on those steps must be awful."

"Serve them right" said Willoughby curtly.

"Oh, I'm entirely with you there" said Dalloway. "Nobody can condemn the utter folly and futility of such behaviour more than I do; and as for the whole agitation, well! may I be in my grave before a woman has the right to vote in England! That's all I say."

The solemnity of her husband's assertion made Clarissa grave. "It's unthinkable" she said. "Don't tell me you're a suffragist?" she turned to Ridley.

"I don't care a fig one way or t'other" said Ambrose. "If any creature is so deluded as to think that a vote does him or her any good, let him have it. He'll soon learn better."

"You're not a politician I see" she smiled.

"Goodness no" said Ridley.

"I'm afraid he won't approve of me" said Dalloway aside, to Mrs Ambrose.

"Don't you ever find it rather dull?" said Helen.

"If you ask me whether I ever find it rather dull," said Richard, considering the nature of the question, "I am bound to say yes; on the other hand, if you ask me what career do you consider on the whole, taking the good with the bad, the most enjoyable and enviable, not to speak of its more serious side, of all careers, for a man, I am bound to say, 'The politicians.'"

"The Bar or politics I agree" said Willoughby. "You get more run for your money."

"All one's faculties have their play" said Richard. "I may be treading on dangerous ground; but what I feel about poets and artists in general is this; on your own lines, you can't be beaten; granted; but off your own lines—puff—One has to make allowances. Now I shouldn't like to think that any one had to make allowances for me."

"I don't quite agree Richard" said Mrs Dalloway. "Think of Shelley. I feel that there's almost everything one wants in Adonais."

"Read Adonais by all means," Richard conceded. "But whenever I hear of Shelley I repeat to myself the words of Matthew Arnold 'What a set! What a set!'"

"Matthew Arnold was a detestable prig" snapped Ridley.

"A prig; granted; said Richard; "but a man of the world. That's [where my point comes in." We politicians doubtless seem to you (he grasped somehow that Helen was representative of the arts) a gross commonplace set of people; but we see both sides; we may be clumsy but we do our best to get a grasp of things. Now your artists find things in a mess. Shrug their shoulders, turn aside to their visions—which I grant may be very beautiful and leave things in a mess. Now that seems to me evading one's responsibilities. Besides we aren't all born with the artistic faculty."

"It's dreadful" said Mrs Dalloway who, while her husband spoke had been thinking.

"When I'm with artists I feel so intensely the delights of shutting oneself up in a little world of one's own, with pictures and music and everything beautiful, and then I go out into the streets and the first child I meet with its poor hungry dirty little face makes me turn round and say "No I can't shut myself up—I won't live in a world of my own. I should like to stop all the painting and writing and music until this kind of thing exists no longer—Don't you feel," she wound up, addressing Helen, "that life's a perpetual conflict?"

Helen considered for a moment. "No" she said. "I don't think I do."]

Mrs Dalloway laughed.

"I didn't expect you to say that" she said.

"Aren't I a living example of it?" he asked.

"That's not the general opinion anyhow" she said. "By the way, I was so fearfully interested by the Agamemnon at Cambridge the other day. I wish you'd tell me all about it."

Ridley graciously inclined his ear.

"Don't you think it's quite the most modern thing you ever saw? It seemed to me I'd known twenty Clytemnestras. But of course, I know nothing about it."

"If you enjoyed it you're as good a judge as any one," said Ridley.

"I don't understand a word of Greek, but I could listen to it for ever. I suppose it's the sound."

Την δ' ἀπαμειβόμενος προσέφη νεφεληγερέτα Ζεύς
Τέκνον ἐμόν, ποῖόν σε ἔπος φύγεν ἕρκος ὀδόντων.
Πῶς ἂν ἔπειτ' Ὀδυσῆος ἐγὼ θείοιο λαθοίμην,
ὃς περὶ μὲν νόον ἐστὶ βροτῶν, περὶ δ' ἱρὰ θεοῖσιν

struck up William Pepper.

"Pepper can go on like that for hours" said Ridley.

"Isn't it very difficult?" asked Mrs Dalloway. "I never could learn any thing by heart—"

"Not if you make a habit of it" said Mr Pepper. "I learnt ten lines as I shave in the morning; and ten as I wash my teeth at night."

"The dreadful little creature only washes his teeth once a day" Clarissa calculated.

"I'd give ten years of my life to know Greek" she said.

"I could teach you the alphabet in half an hour" said Ridley, "and you'd read Homer in a month. I should think it an honour to instruct you."

Helen, engaged with Mr Dalloway and the habit, now fallen into decline, of quoting Greek in the House of Commons, noted, in the great commonplace book that lies open as we talk, the fact that all men really like women to be fashionable. Clarissa exclaimed that she could think of nothing more delightful. For an instant she saw herself in her drawing room in South Street with a Plato open on her knees. She could not help believing that a real scholar, if specially interested, could slip Greek into her head with scarcely any trouble.

Ridley engaged her to come tomorrow.

"If only your ship is going to treat us kindly!" she exclaimed, drawing Willoughby into play. For the sake of guests, and these were distinguished, Willoughby was ready to vouch for the good behaviour, even of the waves.

"I'm dreadfully bad; and my husband's not very good" sighed Clarissa.

"I am never sick" Richard explained. "At least, I have only been actually sick once. That was crossing the channel. But a choppy sea, I confess, or still worse, a swell, makes me distinctly uncomfortable. The great thing is never to miss a meal. You look at the food, and you say, 'I can't'; you take a mouthful, and Lord knows how you're going to swallow it; but, persevere, and you often settle for good ...... My wife's a coward."

They were pushing back their chairs. The ladies were hesitating at the doorway.

"I'd better show the way" said Helen, advancing.

"We sit in here." She opened the door of the saloon.

"Wonderful human beings"—rose, like a sigh, to Rachel's lips, as she followed them. Would that too become a phrase? Wonderful was Mrs Dalloway; still more wonderful was Mr Dalloway. While the rest had talked, she had sat, in her humiliation, trying to grasp the world. What was it that Mrs Dalloway revealed? She was a tall slight woman, of thirty five perhaps. She wore a white muslin dress, in the bosom of which a flower shone; a pearl necklace drooped round her throat. Half way through dinner she had sent out for her fur cloak. A scent floated from her; a chain tinkled. Sitting lightly upright, she seemed to be dealing with the world as she chose. A touch here, a touch there, and the enormous solid globe spun round this way and that beneath her fingers. She gave none of those awkward blows which people like her father and Helen even, indulged in. She went lightly, but directly, to the point; it seemed that she could speak of any thing.

"To live in a world of one's own"—that of course was what they all did; and Mrs Dalloway's world was the real one. But Richard rolling that deep deliberate voice was even more impressive. He grasped things so loosely; he made others appear (She thought of her Aunts) like old maids' cheapening remnants. It seemed to her that he came from the humming oily centre of the machine, where the polished rods are sliding and the pistons thumping, to see how the tiny wheels on the outskirts were doing their work.

"You play?" said Mrs Dalloway to Mrs Ambrose, opening the score of Tristan which lay on the table in the saloon.

"My niece does" said Helen, laying her hand on Rachel's shoulder.

"Oh! How I envy you!" Clarissa addressed Rachel for the first time.

"D'you remember this? Isn't it divine?" She played a bar or two with ringed fingers upon the page.

"And then Tristan goes like this and Isolda—Oh—it's almost too thrilling! Have you been to Bayreuth?"

"No I haven't" said Rachel.

"Then that's still to come. I shall never forget my first Parsifal—a grilling August day, and all those fat old German women, come in their stuffy high frocks, and then the dark theatre, and the music beginning, and one couldn't help sobbing. A kind man went and fetched me water I remember; and I could only cry on his shoulder! It caught me here" (she touched her throat) "It's like nothing else in the world! But where's your piano?"

"It's in another room" Rachel explained.

"But you will play to us?" Clarissa entreated. "I can't imagine anything nicer than to sit out in the moonlight and listen to music—only that sounds too like a school girl! You know," she said turning to Helen, "I don't think music is altogether good for people—I'm afraid not."

"Too much strain?" asked Helen.

"Too emotional somehow" said Clarissa. "One notices it at once when a boy or girl takes up music as a profession. Sir William Broadley told me just the same thing. Don't you hate the kind of attitudes people go into over Wagner—like this." She cast her eyes to the ceiling and assumed a look of intensity. "It really doesn't mean that they appreciate him; in fact I always think it's the other way round. The people who really care about an art are always the least affected. D'you know Henry Phillips, the painter?" she asked.

"I've seen him" said Helen.

"To look at one might think he was a successful stockbroker, and not one of the greatest painters of the age. That's what I like."

"There are a great many successful stockbrokers, if you like looking at them," said Helen.

Rachel wished vehemently that her Aunt would not be so perverse.

"It's the combination," said Clarissa. "When you see a musician with long hair, don't you know instinctively that he's bad?" she asked Rachel.

"Yes" said Rachel, valiantly advancing.

"One's only to think of Joachim and Watts."

"—And how much nicer they'd have looked with curls!" said Helen. "The question is, are you going to aim at beauty or not?"

"Cleanliness!" said Clarissa. "I do want a man to look clean!"

"By cleanliness you really mean well cut clothes" said Helen.

"There's something one knows a gentleman by" said Clarissa. "But one can't say what it is."

"Take my husband now, does he look like a gentleman?"

The question seemed to Clarissa in extraordinarily bad taste,—"one of the things one can't say" she would have put it. She could find no answer, but a laugh.

"Well, anyhow," she said turning to Rachel, "I hope you'll escape." There was that in her manner that made Rachel love her.

Mrs Dalloway hid a tiny yawn, a mere dilatation of the nostrils, "D'you know," she said, "I'm extraordinarily sleepy. It's the sea air. I think I shall escape."

A man's voice which she took to be that of Mr Pepper, strident in discussion, and advancing upon the saloon, gave her the alarm.

"Good night—good night" she said. "Oh I know my way—Do pray for calm! Good night!"

Her yawn must have been the image of a yawn. Instead of letting her mouth droop, dropping all her clothes in a bunch as though they depended on one string, and stretching her limbs to the utmost end of her berth, she merely changed her dress for a dressing gown, with innumerable frills, and, wrapping her feet in a rug, sat down with a writing pad on her knee. Already this cramped little cabin was the dressing room of a lady of quality. There were bottles containing liquids; there were trays, boxes, brushes, pins. Evidently, not an inch of her person lacked its proper instrument. The scent which, in Rachel's mind clung to her words, pervaded the air. Thus established, Mrs Dalloway began to write. A pen in her hands became a thing one caressed paper with. She might have been stroking and tickling a kitten as she wrote—"Picture us, my dear, afloat in the very oddest ship you can imagine. It's not the ship, so much as the people. One does come across queer sorts as one travels. I must say I find it hugely entertaining. There's the Manager of the line—called Vinrace—a nice big Englishman, doesn't say much—you know the sort. As for the rest—they might have come trailing out of an old number of Punch. They're like people playing croquet in the sixties. How long they'd all been shut up in this ship, I don't know; but one feels as though one had boarded a little separate world; and they'd never been on shore, or done ordinary things in their lives. It's what I've always said (don't laugh!) about literary people—they're far the hardest of any to get on with. The worst of it is these people—a man and his wife and a niece—might have been one feels, just like everybody else, if they hadn't got swallowed up by Oxford or Cambridge or some such place, and made cranks of. The man's really delightful (if he'd cut his nails!) and the woman has quite a fine face, only she dresses of course in a potato sack, and wears her hair like a Liberty shop girl's. They talk about art, and think us such poops for dressing in the evening. However, I can't help that; I'd rather die than come into dinner without changing—wouldn't you? It matters ever so much more than soup. It's odd how things like that *do* matter so much more than what's generally supposed to matter. Then there's a nice shy girl—poor thing—I wish one could rake her out before it's too late. She has quite nice eyes and hair, only of course she'll get funny too. We ought to start a society for broadening the minds of the young—much more useful than Missionaries, Hester! This child might marry a decent man. Oh, I'd forgotten—there's a dreadful little thing called Pepper. He's just like his name. He's indescribably insignificant, and rather queer in his temper, poor dear. It's like sitting down to dinner with an ill-conditioned fox terrier, only one can't comb him out, and sprinkle him with powder as one would one's dog. It's a pity sometimes one can't treat people like dogs! When he sneezes the black berry juice runs out of his nostrils. Disgusting! But you'd die laughing. It's all so queer. The great comfort is that we're away from newspapers, so that Richard will have a real holiday this time. Spain wasn't a holiday—"

"You coward!" said Richard, almost filling the room with his sturdy figure.

"I did my duty at dinner!" cried Clarissa.

"You've let yourself in for the Greek alphabet anyhow."

"Oh my dear! Who *is* Ambrose?"

"I gather that he was a Cambridge don; lives in London now; and edits classics."

"Did you ever see such a set of cranks? The woman asked me if I thought her husband looked like a gentleman!"

"It was hard to keep the ball rolling at dinner certainly" said Richard. "Why is it that the women, in that class, are so much queerer than the men?"

"They're not half bad-looking really—Only—they're so odd!"

They both laughed, thinking of the same things.

"I see I shall have quite a lot to say to Vinrace" said Richard. "He knows Sutton and all that set. He can tell me a good deal about the conditions of ship building in the North."

"Oh I'm glad. The men always *are* so much better than the women," said Clarissa.

"One always has something to say to a man certainly" said Richard. "But I've no doubt you'll chatter away fast enough about the babies, Clarice."

"Has she got children? She doesn't look like it somehow."

"Two. Boy and girl."

A pang of envy went through Mrs Dalloway's heart.

"We *must* have a son Dick" she said.

"Good Lord, what opportunities there are now for young men!" said Dalloway, for his talk had set him thinking. "I don't suppose there's been so good an opening since the days of Pitt."

"And it's yours!" said Clarissa.

"To be a leader of men" Richard soliloquised. "It's a fine career. My God—what a career!"

The chest slowly curved beneath his waistcoat.

"I can't stop thinking of England" said his wife, leaning her head against his waistcoat. "Being on this ship seems to make it so much more vivid—what it really means to be English. One thinks of all we've done, and our navies, and the people in India and Africa, and how we've gone on century after century, sending out boys from little country villages—and of men like you Dick, and it makes one feel as if one couldn't bear *not* to be English! Think of the light burning over the House Dick! When I stood on deck just now I seemed to see it. It's what one means by London."

"It's the continuity" said Richard. A vision of English history, King following King, Prime Minister Prime Minister, and Law Law, had come over him while his wife spoke. At the summit of this great pyramid of Prime Ministers was Richard himself. He ran his mind along the line of conservative policy, which went steadily from Lord Salisbury to Alfred, and gradually enclosed, as though it were a lasso that opened and caught things, enormous chunks of the habitable globe.

"It's taken a long time but we've pretty nearly done it" he said. "It remains to consolidate."

"And these people don't see it!" Clarissa exclaimed.

"It takes all sorts to make a world" said her husband. "There would never be a government, if there weren't an opposition."

"Dick, you're better than I am" said Clarissa. "You see round, where I only see *there*" she pressed a point on the back of his hand.

"That's my business, as I tried to explain at dinner."

"What I like about you, Dick, is that you're always the same, and I'm a creature of moods."

"You're a pretty creature anyhow" he said, gazing at her with deeper eyes.

"You think so, do you? Then kiss me."

He kissed her passionately, so that her half written letter slid to the ground. Picking it up, he read it without asking leave.

"Where's your pen?" he said; and added in his little masculine hand, ["R. D. loquitur; Clarice has omitted to tell you that she looked exceedingly pretty at dinner and made a conquest by which she has bound herself to learn the Greek Alphabet. I will take this occasion of adding that we are both enjoying ourselves in these outlandish parts and only wish for the presence of our friends—(yourself and John to wit) to make the trip perfectly enjoyable as it promises to be instructive ...." Voices were heard at the end of the corridor. Mrs Ambrose was speaking low; William Pepper was remarking] in his distinct and rather acid voice, "There's nothing to be said for her that I can see."

But neither Richard or Clarissa profited by the verdict, for, directly it seemed likely that they would over hear, Richard crackled a sheet of paper.

"I often wonder," Clarissa mused in bed, over the little white volume of Pascal which went with her everywhere, "whether it is really good for a woman to live with a man who is morally her superior, as Richard is mine. It makes one so dependent. I suppose I feel for him what my mother and women of her generation felt for Christ. It just shows that one can't do without *some*thing."

CHAPTER SIX

Clarissa was early afoot next morning, much like in appearance, one of the slender white gulls, with tapering bodies. Twice she circled the ship observing with swift turns of her head the labours of kneeling sailors here and there. She bridged the gulf which Rachel thought unbridgeable.

"Isn't that very hard work?" she said, stopping by a young man who was polishing brass. Encouraged by her voice he told her how other kinds of work were much harder; and about the winter seas. Next, she fell in with Mr Grice, and begged him to explain the use of an instrument. Mr Grice had long marvelled at the placid ignorance of landsmen about the sea. Considering that the earth is a very small part of the universe, it seemed to him that their attitude was arrogant. It made him sad. Once or twice he had contributed articles about marine wonders to learned journals; but his style was of the mechanical kind—information issued in strips. Still, his confidence was firm that if only someone could be found to popularise the sea as Kipling and other authors had done the land, it would take its place as the great wonder and blessing of the world. The benignant nature of the sea moved his eloquence; vexed, it is true by a few evil passions, scarcely comparable with the volcanoes and catastrophes of land, it offered unparalleled benefits to mankind. The ignorant rapacity of fishermen, continuing for centuries, had scarcely lessened its bounty; fish still swarmed;

and the deep seas could sustain Europe unaided supposing every earthly animal died of the plague tomorrow. He bade Clarissa think of those streets in London, where men and women stood in regiments hour after hour waiting for a mug of greasy soup. "Many a time I've watched them, and many a time I've thought of the good flesh down here waiting and asking to be caught. It makes one wish for the days of Popery to come back. Why? Because of the fasts."

Meanwhile he showed her the few treasures which the great ocean had bestowed upon him—pale fish in greenish liquids, blobs of jelly with streaming tresses, fish with lights in their heads, they lived so deep.

"They have swum about among bones," Clarissa sighed.

"You're thinking of Shakespeare" Mr Grice said, and taking down a copy read aloud, his finger pointing the words, in an emphatic nasal voice,

Full fathom five thy father lies; ......

"A grand fellow Shakespeare" he said replacing the volume.

Clarissa said she was so glad to hear him say so; which was his favourite play?

"I wonder if it's the same as mine?"

"Henry the Fifth" said Mr Grice.

"Joy!" cried Clarissa. "It is!"

Hamlet was too what-you-might-call introspective for Mr Grice; the sonnets too passionate; Henry the Fifth was to him the model of an English gentleman. Among other benefits bestowed by the sea was that it gave one time for serious reading, whereas on shore there was always the music hall or some tomfoolery to waste one's time. Huxley and Herbert Spencer—"although they're not precisely ladies' books"— were among his favourites, also Emerson and Thomas Hardy.

Clarissa was intensely interested. What it is to be a sailor was shown so vividly, that she could hardly tear herself away to breakfast. She promised to come back, and be shown things.

"I've had the most interesting talk of my life!" she exclaimed taking her seat beside Willoughby.

"A very interesting fellow—that's what I always say" said Willoughby, distinguishing Mr Grice. "But Rachel there finds him a bore."

"When he gets on to currents" said Rachel, anxious for an excuse.

"I've never met a bore yet!" said Clarissa.

To that Helen answered that the world in her opinion was full of them.

"I agree it's the worst one can possibly say of any one" said Clarissa. "How much rather one would be a murderer than a bore! One can fancy liking a murderer. It's the same with dogs. Some dogs are awful bores, poor dears."

"We had a dog who was a bore and knew it" said Richard to Rachel. She noticed that he wore clean linen, with blue rings round the cuffs; and had a signet ring upon brown hands. His tone was cool and easy.

"He was a Skye terrier, one of those long chaps, with little feet poking out from their hair like—like caterpillars. Well, we had another dog at the same time, a black brisk animal—a Shipperke I think you call them. You can't imagine a greater contrast. The Skye so slow and deliberate, looking up at you like some old gentleman in the club, as much as to say 'You don't really mean it do you?' and the Shipperke as quick as a knife—I liked the Skye best I must confess. There was something pathetic about him."

The story seemed to have no climax.

"What happened to him?" Rachel asked.

"That's a very sad story" said Richard, lowering his voice, and peeling an apple. "He followed my wife in the car one day, and got run over by a brute of a cyclist."

"Was he killed?" asked Rachel.

But Clarissa had heard.

"Don't talk of it" she cried. "It's a thing I can't bear to think of to this day."

Surely those were tears in her eyes?

"That's the painful thing about pets" said Mr Dalloway; "they die. The first sorrow I can remember was for the death of a dormouse. I regret to say that I sat upon it. Still, that didn't make one any the less sorry. Here lies the duck that Samuel Johnson sat on, eh? I was big for my age."

"One might give children ravens or tortoises for pets" said Rachel.

"It's a fallacy that ravens live longer than other birds" said Mr Pepper.

"If I were honest, I think I should call *you* a bore" Clarissa thought to herself.

"Then we had canaries, a pair of ring doves, a Lemur, and at one time a Martin" continued Richard.

"Did you live in the country?" asked Rachel.

"We lived in the country for six months of the year" he explained. "When I say 'we,' I mean four sisters, a brother and myself. There's nothing like coming of a large family. Sisters are particularly delightful."

"He as thoroughly spoilt" Clarissa explained.

"Appreciated" said Richard.

Wonders were moving like shapes in a mist, before the eyes of Rachel. Why, people would talk about their lives, their pets, their sisters, the things they had seen, if one asked them. Even distinguished men, like Mr Dalloway, would share things. Bubbles swam, met and clustered in her tea cup. Such was life. But before the bubbles burst, her chance was gone, and her image falsified. Mr Dalloway was gravely considering his wife's version of Mr Grice's politics; and politics though spoken of by human lips, had little to do so Rachel thought with the human soul. Popery and fish—the percentage of Catholics in England—what had happened or would happen in France; it was easier to imagine a square white house in a wood, where the Dalloways lived, than to follow them from fact to fact. From the image of bubbles, one fell into the image of abysses, ink-blue spaces, between high rocks, dividing soul from soul. The sounds of laughter, deep genuine laughter from Helen, a derisive twitter from Mr Pepper, came to her across the deeps; but, having loosed her grasp completely, she could not say why popery should make them laugh.

Appealed to by Mr Dalloway—"I'm sure Miss Vinrace has secret leanings towards Catholicism"—she made a lame chill answer, missing the spirit of the remark; and provoked Helen once more to irritation.

"Rachel *ought* to attend."

Still, it was not Helen's blame that she dreaded, but the low opinion of the Dalloways. The move from table to deck however, took away her chance of retrieving herself.

"I always think religion's like collecting beetles" Clarissa said to Helen as they walked together. "One person has a passion for black beetles; another hasn't; it's no good arguing about it. What's your black beetle now?"

"I suppose it's my children" said Helen.

"Ah, that's different" Clarissa breathed. "Do tell me. You have a boy haven't you? Isn't it detestable, leaving them?"

It was as though a blue shadow had fallen across a pool; their eyes were deeper, their voices more cordial. The tears suddenly rushed to Rachel's eyes.

"They might know I've no mother" she said; and left them abruptly for her music.

She played well. Of half the young ladies in Kensington that might be said without adding as one added in Rachel's case, that they were born to play. They were born for a thousand other reasons; to marry, to nurse, to ride, to fill the world; music, with painting and a knowledge of English history, was like a tiny tin sword which was clasped into heir hands, to fight the world with, if other weapons failed. To change the figure, it was like a little bridge on to the back of a great plain, one might escape by it, supposing the house one lived in was burnt to the ground. The house one lived in flourishing, one stood sometimes at the windows and took a look at the view. They could play the slow movements in Beethoven sonatas, when the dusk fell, and some one said, "It's an age since I heard you play." Then a certain discontent would come over them. "One does have to sacrifice a lot for children doesn't one?" they would complain. But how triumphantly the sum balanced on the right side! There were lights in all the windows; one heard children crying in the nursery, as one opened the front door.

Rachel spread her Bach before her, and sat down to it.

"You're my black beetle" she said, and her faculties began to work. It was the expression on her face, sensual and absorbed, that proved she was born to play; and the supple and workmanlike movements of her fingers. Although her notes were sometimes wrong, and her phrases fragmentary, she inspired a listener with confidence; she seemed to have a shape in her mind; she would carry the listener, not drop him; which is the virtue too of some imperfect books. The notes were attempts to form the design. As for the design, words, in describing it, would pin down what should fly free. But Mrs Dalloway when she talked of black beetles, was hinting at something common to arts, religions and maternity. One wants to do something without an audience, Rachel was far away from all looking glasses.

If, when the person was thus without personality, and conscious only of love, a superhuman form had risen at the end of the avenue, a religion might have come into being.

For Rachel there was not a superhuman form; but the love—of what?—of unseen things. The door opened impulsively. A looking glass flashed bright in Rachel's eyes. Mrs Dalloway had come to find her. Why? The shape of the Bach fugue crashed to the ground.

"Don't let me interrupt" Clarissa implored. "I heard you playing, and I couldn't resist. I adore Bach!"

Rachel flushed and fumbled her fingers in her lap.

"It's too difficult" she said.

"But you were playing quite splendidly! I ought to have stayed outside."

"No" said Rachel.

She slid Cowper's letters, and Wuthering Heights out of the arm chair, so that Clarissa was invited to sit there.

"What a dear little room!" she said. "Oh Cowper's Letters! I've never read them. Are they nice?"

"Rather dull" said Rachel.

"He wrote awfully well didn't he?" said Clarissa, "—if one likes that kind of thing—finished his sentences and all that. Wuthering Heights! Ah—that's more in my line. I really couldn't exist without the Brontës! Don't you love them? Still, on the whole, I'd rather live without them than with out Jane Austen."

"I don't like Jane Austen" said Rachel.

"You monster!" Clarissa exclaimed. "I can only just forgive you. Tell me why?"

"She's so—so—well like a tight plait" said Rachel floundering.

"Ah—I see what you mean. But I don't agree. And you won't when you're older. At your age I only liked Shelley. I can remember sobbing over him in the garden. 'He has outsoared the shadow of our night—Envy and calumny and hate and pain' you remember?—'can touch him not and torture not again—From the contagion of the world's slow stain'—

how divine!—and yet what nonsense! I always think it's *living* not dying that counts. I really respect some snuffy old stockbroker who's gone on adding up column after column all his days, and trotting back to his villa at Brixton with some old pug dog he worships, and a dreary little wife, sitting at the end of the table, and going off to Margate for a fortnight,—I assure you I know heaps like that—well, they seem to me *really* nobler than poets whom every one worships, just because they're geniuses, and die young. But I don't expect *you* to agree with me!"

She pressed Rachel's knee.

Rachel tried, but could not lay hands upon the argument.

—"'Unrest which men miscall delight'—when you're my age you'll see that the world is *crammed* with delightful things. I think young people make such a mistake about that—not letting themselves be happy. I sometimes think that happiness is the only thing that counts. I don't know you well enough to say, but I should guess you might be a little inclined to—when one's young and attractive—I'm *going* to say it!—everything's at one's feet." She glanced round as much as to say "not only a few stuffy books, and Bach."

"I long to ask questions" she said. "You interest me so much. If I'm impertinent, you must just box my ears."

"As if talk weren't the only thing in the world!" said Rachel at which Mrs Dalloway looked amused but checked her smile.

"D'you mind if we walk?" she said. "The air's so delicious."

She snuffed it like a race horse as she stood on deck.

"Isn't it good to be alive?" she said, and drew Rachel's arm within hers.

"Look! Look! How exquisite!"

The land was beginning to lose its substance; but was still the land though at a great distance. Little towns were sprinkled in the folds of the hills; they were very peaceful. Mountains rose behind them.

"Honestly though" said Clarissa having looked, "I don't like views. They're too inhuman." They walked on.

"How odd it is!" said Clarissa impulsively. "This time yesterday we'd never met. I was packing in a stuffy little room in the Hotel. We know absolutely nothing about each other—and yet I feel as if I *did* know you!"

"You have children—your husband was in Parliament."

"You've never been to school, and you live—?"

"With Aunts at Richmond."

"Richmond?"

"You see, my Aunts like the Park."

"And you don't! I understand!" Clarissa laughed.

"I like walking there alone; but not with the dogs."

"Some people *are* dogs, aren't they?" said Clarissa. "But not everyone—oh no, not everyone."

"Not everyone" said Rachel and stopped.

"I can quite imagine you walking alone" said Clarissa; "and thinking—in a little world of your own. But how you will enjoy it—some day!"

"You mean, I shall enjoy walking with a man" said Rachel.

"I wasn't thinking particularly of a man" said Clarissa. "But you will."

"I shall never marry" said Rachel.

"I shouldn't be so sure of that" said Clarissa. Her side long glance told Rachel that she found her attractive.

"One man did ask me" said Rachel. "But—"

"What?"

"It seemed—well, why marry?"

"That's what you're going to find out" said Clarissa. Her face kindled in joy over the secret she knew.

Rachel followed her eyes and found that they rested, for a second, on the robust figure of Richard Dalloway, who was engaged in striking a match on the sole of his boot; while Willoughby expounded something.

"There's nothing like it" she said. "Do tell me about the Ambroses. Or am I asking too many questions?"

"I find you easy to talk to" said Rachel.

The short sketch of the Ambroses was however a little perfunctory. "He's my uncle."

"Your mother's brother?"

When a name dropped out of use, the lightest touch upon it tells. Mrs Dalloway went on,

"You are like your mother?"

"No; she was different; she was very amusing" said Rachel. She determined to tell this stranger what she had never told Aunts or friends; that she wanted her mother, and had loved her. Clarissa's eyes filled with tears.

"How strange!" she said. "That's what I felt directly I saw you." She too, had no mother; and no one understood, until she met Richard who gave her all she wanted; but Richard was quite unlike other men—"Don't think I say that because I'm his wife; I see his faults more clearly than I see anyone else's"—He was man and woman too. He kept one at one's best—which was what one wanted of a husband.

"I often wonder what I've done to be so happy" she went on, allowing one tear to slide.

"How good life is!"

Helen passed them at this point, and was slightly irritated to see that they walked arm in arm. Often as she had said that expression was what Rachel wanted, she did not mean this particular expression; it was too emotional.

They were joined by Richard; Vinrace had dived down to his documents, more exhilarated than he had been for a long time by his talk with an influential man.

"Observe my Panama" said Richard.

"Are you aware Miss Vinrace how much can be done to induce fine weather by appropriate head dress? I have determined that it is a hot summer day; nothing you say will shake me. Therefore I am going to sit down. I advise you to follow my example." Three chairs invited them.

Richard surveyed the view.

"That's a very pretty blue" he said. "But there's a little too much of it. Variety is essential to a view. Thus, if you have hills you ought to have a river; if a river, hills. The best view in the world in my opinion, is that from Boars Hill on a fine day—it must be a fine day, mark you—A rug?—oh thank you my dear …… In that case you have also the advantage of associations—the Past."

"D'you want to talk Dick, or shall I read aloud?"

Clarissa had fetched a book with the rugs.

"Persuasion" announced Richard, examining the volume.

"That's for Miss Vinrace" said Clarissa. "She can't bear our beloved Jane."

"That—if I may say so—is because you have not read her" said Richard. "She is incomparably the greatest female writer we possess."

"The Brontës?" Rachel hinted.

"She is the greatest" said Richard, "for this reason, if for no other; she does not attempt to write like a man. Every other woman does; on that account, I don't read 'em."

"Produce your instances, Miss Vinrace," he went on; joining his fingertips. "I'm ready to be converted."

He waited, while Rachel scrambled over the names of great women, and discovered that she had not read their books.

"I'm afraid he's right" said Clarissa. "He generally is— the wretch!"

Rachel bowed to the oracle; after all, he had done things.

"I brought Persuasion" said Clarissa "because I thought it was a little less threadbare than the others—though, Dick, it's no good your pretending that you know Jane by heart, considering that she always sends you to sleep!"

"After the labours of legislation, I deserve sleep" said Richard.

"You're not to think about those guns" said Clarissa, seeing that his eye rested upon the land meditatively "not about navies, or Empires or anything."

"'Sir Walter Elliot, of Kellynch Hall, in Somersetshire, was a man who, for his own amusement, never took up any book but the Baronetage'—don't you know Sir Walter? 'There he found occupation for an idle hour, and consolation in a distressed one' she does write well, doesn't she? 'there—'" she read on, in a light humourous voice. She was determined that Sir Walter should take her husband's mind off the guns of Britain, and divert him in an exquisite, quaint, sprightly and slightly ridiculous world. Then it appeared that the sun was sinking in that world; and the points becoming softer. Rachel looked up to see what caused the change; Richard's eyelids were closing and opening; opening and closing. A nasal breath announced that he no longer considered appearances. He slept.

"Triumph!" Clarissa whispered at the end of a sentence.

Suddenly she raised her hand in protest. A sailor hesitated; she gave the book to Rachel, and stepped lightly to take the message—"Mr Grice wished to know if it was convenient" &c. She followed him. Ridley who had prowled unheeded, started forward, stopped, and, with a gesture of disgust, strode off to his study. The sleeping politician was left in Rachel's charge. She read a sentence; and took a look at him.

In sleep he looked like a coat hanging at the end of a bed. There were all the wrinkles and the sleeves and trousers kept their shape though no longer filled out with legs and arms. You can then best judge the age and state of the coat. She looked him all over until it seemed to her that he must protest.

"A lemur, a dormouse, and some canaries" she ruminated. "A house in a wood—no, that was my invention; sisters who spoilt you; I wish foreheads had keys, and one could open them." She could fancy a strong machine inside Mr Dalloway's brow; a great many bars, wheels, and one wide spring expanding regularly, in a clear yellow light. Poor Jane Austen! She was impotent beside this body. She talked of unreal things.

A strange sense of her own weakness shook Rachel queerly. She looked at her right hand; then at Richard's hand. She realised the unimportance of her life. "I should have to give you what you asked" she reflected "because—because—" The reason was not found, for Richard woke.

He grunted and looked odd, as short sighted people look when you snatch away their spectacles. It took him a moment to recover from the impropriety of having snored and grunted before a young lady.

"I suppose I have been dozing" he said. "What's happened to every one? Clarissa?"

"Mrs Dalloway has gone to look at Mr Grice's fish" said Rachel "over there."

"I might have guessed" said Richard. "It's a common occurrence. And how have you improved the shining hour? Have you become a convert?"

"I don't think I've read a line" said Rachel.

"That's what I always find. There are too many things to look at. I find nature very stimulating myself. My best ideas have come to me out of doors."

"When you were walking?"

"Walking—riding—yatching—I suppose the most momentous conversations of my life took place while perambulating the great court of Trinity. I was at both Universities. It was a fad of my father's. He thought it broadening to the mind. I think I agree with him. I can remember—what an age ago it seems!—settling the basis of a future state with the present secretary for India. We thought ourselves very wise. I'm not sure we weren't. We were happy, Miss Vinrace, and we were young—gifts which make for wisdom."

"Have you done what you said you'd do?" asked Rachel.

"A searching question! I answer—Yes and No. If on the one hand I have not accomplished what I set out to accomplish—which of us does?—on the other I can fairly say this; I have not lowered my ideal."

He looked resolutely at a sea gull, as though his ideal flew there.

"I'm stupid" said Rachel, "But what *is* your ideal?"

"There you ask too much Miss Vinrace!" said Richard playfully.

"But I do want to know" Rachel pressed.

"Well, how shall I reply? In one word—Unity. Unity of aim, of dominion, of progress. The dispersion of the best ideas over the greatest area."

"The English, you mean?"

"I grant that the English seem on the whole, whiter than most men; their record's cleaner. But Good Lord, don't run away with the idea that I don't see the drawbacks—horrors—unmentionable things done in our very midst! I'm under no illusions. Few people I suppose have fewer illusions than I have. Have you ever been in a factory Miss Vinrace?—no, I suppose not—I may say I hope not."

Rachel had only walked through poor streets, dreaming.

"I was going to say that if you'd ever seen the kind of thing that's going on round you, you'd understand what it is that makes me and men like me politicians. You asked me a moment ago whether I'd done what I set out to do. Well, when I consider my life, there is one fact I admit, that I'm proud of; owing to me some thousands of girls in Lancashire and many thousands to come after them—can spend an hour every day in the open air which their mothers had to spend over their looms. I'm prouder of that, I own, than I should be of writing Keats and Shelley into the bargain."

It became painful to Rachel to be one of those who write Keats and Shelley. She liked Richard Dalloway and warmed as he warmed.

"I know nothing!" she exclaimed.

"It's far better that you should know nothing" he said paternally. "And you wrong yourself, I'm sure. You play very nicely, I'm told and I've no doubt you've read heaps of learned books."

Elderly banter would no longer check her.

"You talk of unity" she said. "You ought to make me understand."

"I never allow my wife to talk politics" he said severely. "For this reason. It is impossible for human beings, constituted as they are, both to fight and to have ideals. If I have preserved mine as I am thankful to say that in great measure I have, it is due to the fact that I have been able to come home to my wife in the evening and to find that she has spent her day in calling, music, play with the children, domestic duties—what you will; her illusions have not been destroyed. She gives me courage to go on. The strain of public life is very great" he added.

This made him appear a battered martyr, parting every day with some of the finest gold, in the service of mankind.

"I can't think," Rachel exclaimed, "how any one can endure it!"

"Explain, Miss Vinrace" said Richard. "This is a matter I want to clear up."

He gave her a chance, and she determined to take it, although to talk made her heart beat.

"It seems to me like this" she began. She would really expose her shivering private visions.

"There's an old widow in her room, somewhere let us suppose in the suburbs of Leeds."

Richard bent his head to show that he accepted the widow.

"In London you're spending your life, talking, writing things, getting bills through, missing what seems natural. The result of it all is that she goes to her cupboard and finds a little more tea, a few lumps of sugar, or a little less tea and a newspaper. Widows all over the country I admit do this. Still, there's the mind of the widow—the affections; those you leave untouched. But you waste your own."

"If the widow goes to her cupboard and finds it bare," Richard answered, "her spiritual outlook we may admit will be affected. If I may pick holes in your philosophy, Miss Vinrace, which has its merits, I would point out that a human being is not a set of compartments, but an organism. Imagination, Miss Vinrace; use your imagination; that is where you young liberals fail. Conceive the world as a whole. Now for your second point; when you assert that in trying to set the house in order for the benefit of the young generation I am wasting my higher capabilities, I totally disagree with you. I can conceive no more exalted aim; to be the citizen of the Empire. Look at it in this way, Miss Vinrace; conceive the state as a complicated machine; we citizens are parts of that machine; some fulfill more important duties; others (perhaps I am one of them) serve only to connect some obscure parts of the mechanism, concealed from the public eye. Yet if the meanest screw fails in its task, the proper working of the whole is imperilled."

It was impossible to combine the image of a lean black widow, gazing out of her window, and longing for someone to explain about the soul, with the image of a vast machine, such as one sees at South Kensington, thumping, thumping, thumping.

"We don't seem to understand each other" she said.

"Shall I say something that will make you very angry?" he said.

"It won't" said Rachel.

"Well then; no woman has what I may call the political instinct. You have very great virtues; I am the first, I hope, to admit that; but I have never met a woman who even saw what is meant by statesmanship. I am going to make you still more angry. I hope that I never shall meet such a woman. Now, Miss Vinrace, are we enemies for life?"

Vanity, irritation, and a thrusting desire to be understood, urged Rachel to another attempt.

"Under the streets, in the sewers, in the wires, in the telephones, there is something alive; is that what you mean? In things like dust carts, and men mending roads? You feel that all the time when you walk about in London, and when you turn on a tap and the water comes?"

"Certainly" said Richard. "I understand you to mean that the whole of modern society is based upon co-operative effort. If only more people would realise that, Miss Vinrace, there would be fewer of your old widows in solitary lodgings!"

"Then are you a Liberal or a Conservative?"

"I call myself a Conservative for convenience sake" said Richard smiling. "But there is more in common between the two parties than people generally allow."

[There was a pause. It did not come on Rachel's side from any lack of things to say; as usual she could not say them, and the time for talking probably ran short. And she was haunted by absurd ideas—how if one went back far enough, everything perhaps was intelligible; for the mammoths who pastured in the fields of Kensington High Street had turned into paving stones and boxes full of ribbon, and her aunts.

"Did you say you lived in the country when you were a child?" she asked.

The minds of raw girls seemed to Richard odd; but he was flattered. Her interest was so genuine.

"I did" he smiled.

"And what happened?" she asked—"or do I ask too many questions?"]

"Are you sure you haven't got a novel up your sleeve Miss Vinrace?"

"I ask too many questions, I suppose?"

"I'm flattered, I assure you. But—let me see—what happened? Well, riding, lessons, sisters. There was an enchanted rubbish heap I remember, where all kinds of queer things happened. Odd, what things impress children! I can remember the look of the place to this day. It's a fallacy to think that children are happy. They're not; they're unhappy. I've never suffered so much as I did when I was a child."

"Why?" asked Rachel.

"I didn't get on well with my father" said Richard shortly. "He was a very able man; but hard. Well—it makes one determined not to sin in that way oneself. Children never forget injustice. They forgive heaps of things grown up people mind; but that sin is the unpardonable sin. Mind you—I daresay I was a difficult child to manage; but when I think what I was ready to give! No I was more sinned against than sinning. And then I went to school, where I did fairly well, and then as I say my father sent me to both universities ...... D'you know, Miss Vinrace, you've made me think? How little, after all, one can tell any any body about one's life! Here I sit; there you sit; both I doubt not, chock full of the most interesting experiences, ideas, emotions; yet how communicate? I've told you what every second person you meet might tell you."

"I don't think so" said Rachel. "After all, it's the way of saying things, isn't it, not the things?"

"True" said Richard, "Perfectly true. When I look back over my life—I'm forty two—what are the great facts that stand out? What were the revelations, if I may call them so? The misery of the poor and—(he hesitated and pitched over) love!" Upon that word he lowered his voice; it was a word that seemed to unveil the skies for Rachel.

"It's an odd thing to say to a young lady" he continued. "But have you any idea what—what I mean by that? No; of course not. I don't use the word in a conventional sense. I use it as young men use it. Girls are kept very ignorant, aren't they? Perhaps it's wise—perhaps—You *don't* know?"

He spoke as if he had lost consciousness of what he was saying. He called upon the same furtive spirit in Rachel.

"No; I don't" she said.

"Warships Dick! Over there! Look!"

Clarissa skimmed towards them gesticulating.

She had sighted two sinister grey vessels, low in the water, and bald as bone. Consciousness returned to Richard instantly.

"By George!" he said, and stood shielding his eyes.

"Ours, Dick?" said Clarissa.

"The Mediterranean Fleet" he answered.

The Euphrosyne was slowly dipping her flag. Richard raised his hat. Convulsively Clarissa squeezed Rachel's hand.

"Aren't you glad to be English!" she said.

The warships drew past, casting a curious effect of discipline and sadness upon the waters. At lunch the talk was all of valour and death, and the magnificent qualities of British admirals. Clarissa quoted, Willoughby quoted. Life on a man of war was splendid; death, doing one's duty was heroic.

No one liked it when Helen remarked that it seemed to her as wrong to keep sailors as to keep a Zoo, and that as for dying on a battle field, surely it was time we ceased to praise courage—"or to write bad poetry about it" snarled Pepper.

But Helen was really wondering why Rachel looked queer and flushed.

CHAPTER SEVEN

That salute to the navy of England was almost the last act showing a happy confidence in the world on the part of the Dalloways before they were laid low. Instead of padding over the waves like some broad-backed dray horse, upon whose hind quarters pierrots might waltz, the Euphrosyne took to cantering and swerving like a colt in a field. Her pulse no longer beat so steady day and night that you might time your own heart by it. At dinner the company heard her groan and strain as though a lash were descending. The plates slanted, and Mrs Dalloway's face blanched for a second as she helped herself and saw the potatoes roll.

"Not yet" she said bravely, in answer to the inevitable humour of her husband—"Feeling queer Clarissa?"

"It's going to be nothing, I assure you" Willoughby encouraged her. He called upon Pepper to testify to the extraordinary qualities of the ship. She had all the virtues of character, and none of the vices of intellect. Willoughby always endowed his own property with the qualities he admired. He would talk in much the same way of dear crusty old Chailey. But no consideration of this kind would prevent William Pepper from silence to begin with, and, when pressed, from a concise statement that in his opinion they were now in for a period of bad weather not necessarily prolonged.

"I should ask Captain Cobbett" he concluded. But no one felt any wish to confirm his prophecy. The dinner was gloomy.

"I think I'll go to bed" said Clarissa when, being alone with two women there was not much reason to pretend. Though pale, she was able to smile as she left them at the absurdity or being sea sick. Helen considered, but decided that there was nothing to offer.

Next morning it was impossible to overlook the fact. The storm, call it breeze if you would, was on them; and manners would not stand the strain. Clarissa did not appear. Richard came to breakfast, to lunch, to tea, at all three meals he swallowed firmly; but at dinner certain glazed asparagus, swimming in oil, showed him the kind of thing he would have to face, if he persisted. He shook his head, smiled grimly, and ejaculating, "That beats me" went.

"We are alone once more" said William Pepper; and looking round the table smiled benignly, as though they must all take his point. But they were thinking of different things.

On the following day they met; but as flying leaves meet in the air. Sick they were not; but the wind propelled them hastily into rooms, violently down stairs. They passed each other gasping on deck; they shouted across tables. They wore fur coats; and Helen was never seen with out a bandanna on her head. For comfort they retreated to their cabins, where with tightly wedged feet they let the ship bounce and tumble. Their sensations were the sensations of potatoes in a sack on a galloping horse. The world outside was merely a violent grey tumult. For two days they had a perfect rest from their old emotions. Rachel had just enough consciousness to suppose that a donkey on the summit of a moor in a hailstorm, with its coat blown into furrows, felt as she felt; then she became a wizened tree, perpetually driven back by the salt Atlantic gale.

Helen on the other hand, staggered to Mrs Dalloway's door, knocked, could not be heard for the slamming of doors, and the battering of wind, and entered.

There were basins of course. Mrs Dalloway lay half raised on a pillow, and did not open her eyes. Then she murmured, "Oh Dick is that you?"

Helen shouted—for she was thrown against the wash stand—"How are you?"

Clarissa opened one eye. It gave her an incredibly dissipated appearance.

"Awful" she gasped. Her lips were white inside.

Planting her feet wide, Helen contrived to pour champagne into a tumbler with a tooth brush in it.

"Champagne" she said.

"There's a tooth brush in it" said Clarissa, and smiled; it might have been the contortion of one weeping. She drank.

"Disgusting" she murmured, indicating the basins. Relics of humour still played over her face, like moon shine.

"Want more?" Helen shouted. Speech was again beyond Clarissa's reach. The wind laid the ship shivering on her side. Pale agonies crossed Mrs Dalloway in waves. When the curtains flapped, grey lights puffed across her. Between the spasms of the storm, Helen made the curtain fast; shook the pillows, stretched the bed clothes, and smoothed the hot nostrils and forehead with cold scent.

"You *are* good!" Clarissa gasped. "Horrid mess."

She was trying to apologise for white underclothes, scattered on the floor. For one second she opened a single eye, and saw that the room was tidy. "That's nice" she gasped.

Helen left her; far far away she knew that she felt a kind of liking for Mrs Dalloway. Her petticoats however rose above her knees.

Quite suddenly the storm relaxed its grasp. It happened at tea. The expected paroxysm of the blast gave out just as it reached its climax and dwindled away; the ship instead of taking the usual plunge went steadily. The monotonous

order of plunging and rising, roaring and relaxing was interfered with, and every one at table looked up and felt
something loosen within them. The strain was slackened and
human feelings began to peep again, as they do when daylight shows at the end of a tunnel.

"Try a turn with me" Ridley called across to Rachel.

"Foolish" cried Helen, but they went stumbling up the
ladder eagerly. Choked by the wind their spirits rose with a
rush, for on the skirts of all the grey tumult was a misty spot
of gold. Instantly the world dropped into shape; they were no
longer atoms flying in the void; but people riding a triumphant ship on the back of the sea. Wind and space were
banished; the world floated like an apple in a tub.

Having scrambled twice round the ship and received
many sound cuffs from the wind, they saw a sailor's face positively shine. They looked, and beheld a complete yellow
circle of sun; next minute it was traversed by sailing strands
of cloud, and then completely hidden.

By breakfast time next morning, however, the sky was
swept clean; the waves were steep, but blue; and after their
view of the strange underworld, people began to live among
tea pots and loaves of bread with greater zest than ever.

Richard and Clarissa however still remained on the
border land. She did not attempt to sit up; her husband stood
on his feet, and contemplated his waist coat and trousers.
The gulf between him and all that his clothing stood for was
still not to be bridged. He lay down, and resigned himself
once more to vagueness.

At four o'clock however, waking from sleep, he lay for
some minutes admiring the redness of a plush cover. Slowly,
the warm delightful world slid into his mind through that
channel. His waistcoat and trousers were still foreign to him;
but when he stood in the passage, dressed, he too was ready
to begin again.

"How nice you look, Dick" said Mrs Dalloway when he stood beside her. She meant that he smelt of soap, and that his shirt as he bent crackled. She too had been in dreadful places where one ceased to believe in such things.

"Go and get a breath of air. You look quite washed out" she said.

"I don't like leaving you, poor little woman" he said.

"Oh, I'm much better. It's only my head spins rather. But that kind woman was so good to me. Be nice to her, Dick."

Being nice to Helen was not altogether easy, nor always pleasant. Sometimes she did not answer; sometimes she said "Um-m" and took time to consider what the speech amounted to. Richard was slightly disconcerted by a manner which dispensed with politeness. Man of the world as he was, he could take his cue from an onion seller with a barrow; but for educated people to go tampering with the conventions appeared to him an irritating waste of time. It landed one too in dreadful arguments.

Helen had pity on his white cheeks.

"You look very ill" she said. "You'd better have some tea."

He was impressed by her beauty. She had a certain charm. The hands that moved about the cups were beautiful.

"You've been very good to my wife" he said. "She's had a very bad time. You came in and fed her with champagne I hear. It was awfully good of you. Were you among the saved yourself?"

"I haven't been sick for twenty years—sea sick I mean" said Helen. "But you—are you better?"

"There are three stages of convalescence I always say," broke in the hearty voice of Willoughby. "The milk stage—the bread and butter stage—and the roast beef stage. I should say you were at the bread and butter stage." He handed him the plate. "That's good. Now, I should advise a hearty tea; then a brisk walk on deck well wrapped up, and by dinner you'll be clamouring for beef, eh?" He went off laughing.

"What a splendid fellow he is!" said Richard. "Always keen on something!"

"I shouldn't have said that" said Helen and stopped.

"This is a great undertaking of his" Richard continued.

"I suppose I'm wrong but I never can see that business needs brains" said Helen.

"It's the responsibility" said Richard. "To be a mere man of business I grant you, is no proof of ability; but to have a constructive mind—to see the links and combinations as Vinrace does—we always get on this subject" he smiled.

"It's interesting" said Helen. "But I expect your head's aching."

"It is muzzy still" Richard owned. "It's humiliating to find what a slave one is to one's body in this world. D'you know I can never work without a kettle on the hob? As often as not I don't drink tea, but I must feel that I can if I want to."

"That's very bad for you" said Helen.

"It shortens one's life; but I'm afraid, Mrs Ambrose, we politicians must make up our minds to that at the outset. We've got to burn the candle at both ends, or—"

"You've cooked your goose!" said Helen brightly.

"It's very difficult to make you take us seriously!" Richard protested.

"But I'm so grateful to you" said Helen. "You do all the dirty work."

"And get precious little thanks" said Richard.

"I've got to go home to all the horrors of a contested election while you—read philosophy in the sun."

He had seen her book.

"Shows my sense" said Helen.

"I believe you're right" he said, ruefully turning the leaves of the black volume. "'Good then, is indefinable'" he read. "How jolly to think that's all going on still! 'and yet so far as I know there is only one ethical writer, Prof. Henry Sidgwick, who has clearly recognised and stated this fact.' I suppose that's the kind of thing you think important?"

"Yes" said Helen.

"So did I when I was an undergraduate," said Richard. "Why, I can remember arguing for six hours with the present secretary of state for India upon the reality of matter. What's the view now? Is it real or not?"

"That depends—"

"No—no—don't ask me to define what I mean by reality. Be merciful to a sea sick politician." He dropped the book, and handed his cup for more tea.

"Seriously, I respect no one more than a philosopher or a scholar like your husband. They pass the torch—they keep the light burning by which we live. By the way, what does your husband think of the new appointment?"

"I really don't know" said Helen.

"I had some reason to be interested in it" said Richard. They did me the honour to consult me. I was on the Commission at the time. I thought it a thoroughly sound appointment myself, though some, I gather, were disappointed."

But Mrs Ambrose yielded no information; either she had none, or did not wish to share it.

"What the devil *is* she interested in then?" Richard thought to himself.

"I hope your husband is getting on with his great book?" he said aloud.

"I don't think they'll ever make *him* a Professor" Helen smiled.

"Aha" thought Richard. "There's jealousy at the bottom of it."

"To men of his worth, such distinction can make little difference" he observed with cumbrous diplomacy.

"The difficulty would be his clothes" said Helen. "He's not a good lecturer either. I sometimes think," she mused, "that he'd have done better as a judge. Greek is such—niggling work. But if you can't write yourself, perhaps it's the next best thing. Now—what about fresh air? I'm going to take your wife some tea."

Richard was dismissed. "A hard woman" he concluded; as he twisted his muffler.

Willoughby's advice had been good. The body which had grown white and tender in a shaded room tingled all over in the fresh air. Richard exulted in the thought that he was a man undoubtedly at the prime of life. Pride glowed in his eye as he let the wind buffet him and stood firm. With his head slightly lowered he sheered round corners and met the blast. There was a collision. For a second he could not see what the body was he had run into. "Sorry. Sorry." It was Rachel who apologised. They both laughed, too much blown about to speak. She drove open the door of her room, and stepped into its calm. In order to speak to her, it was necessary that Richard should follow. They stood in a whirlpool of wind. Papers began flying round in circles. The door crashed to, and they tumbled laughing into chairs. Richard sat upon Bach.

"My word! What a tempest!" he exclaimed.

"Fine, isn't it?" said Rachel. Certainly the struggle and wind had given her a decision she lacked. Her hair was down.

"Oh what fun!" he cried. "What am I sitting on? Is this your room? How jolly!"

"There—sit there" she commanded. Cowper slid once more.

"How jolly to meet again" said Richard. "It seems an age. Cowper's Letters…Bach—Wuthering Heights—Is this where you sit and meditate on the world, and then come out and pose poor politicians with questions? In the intervals of sea sickness, I've thought a lot of our talk. I assure you, you made me think."

"I made you think? But why?"

"What solitary ice bergs we are Miss Vinrace! How little we can communicate! There are lots of things I should like to tell you about—to hear your opinion of…. Have you ever read Burke?"

Rachel had not.

"No? Well then I shall make a point of sending you a copy. The Speech on the French Revolution—the American Rebellion? Which shall it be, I wonder?" He noted something in his pocket book. "And then you must write and tell me what you think of it. This reticence—this isolation—that's what's the matter with modern life! Now, tell me about yourself. What are your interests and occupations? I should imagine that you were a person with very strong interests. Of course you are! Good God! When I think of the age we live in, with its opportunities and possibilities, the mass of things to be done and enjoyed—Why haven't we ten lives instead of one? But about yourself?"

"You see, I'm a woman" said Rachel.

"I know—I know" said Richard—throwing his head back, and drawing his fingers across his eyes.

"How strange to be a woman! A young and beautiful woman" he continued sententiously, "has the whole world at her feet. That's true, Miss Vinrace. You have an inestimable power—for good or for evil. What couldn't you do—" he broke off.

"What?" asked Rachel.

"You have beauty" he said. The ship lurched. Rachel fell slightly forward. Richard took her in his arms and kissed her. He held her tight, and kissed her passionately. She felt the hardness of his body and the roughness of his cheek. She fell back in her chair, with a tremendous beating of the heart. It sent black waves across her eyes. He clasped his forehead in his hands.

"You tempt me" he said. It was his voice that was terrifying. He seemed choked in fight. They were both trembling. Rachel stood up and went. Her head was cold; and her knees shaking. The physical pain of the emotion was so great that she could only keep herself moving above the great leaps of her heart. She leant upon the rail of the ship, and gradually ceased to feel, for a chill crept over her. The heart slackened. Far out between the waves little black and white sea birds were riding.

"You're peaceful" she said. She became peaceful too.

A kind of exaltation dwelt with her.

But moving washing dressing disturbed this, and by dinner time she was hardly able to face the awkwardness of seeing Richard.

Richard was talking emphatically when she came in; he slid his eyes over her, and they were uneasy. It was obvious, as soon as she listened, that his talk was empty; but ringing platitudes always woke a response in Willoughby, who reverenced formal heartiness.

"Beef for Mr Dalloway!" he shouted cheerfully. "Come now—after that walk you're at the beef stage!"

The old voyage in the Mauretania did service again. How did big ships differ from small ships in storms? Ingenious games. Then Richard asked about wages, and promotions. He asked questions too quick to pay much attention to the answers; but old hoards of information came to his rescue. He kept talk going, which did not include the ladies.

Helen, to all appearances was taken up with the management of her husband. Ridley's intimacy with the Greeks made him terribly hard upon the living. He knew when they spoke the truth; he knew when they were stupid. Only physical beauty concealed these faults from him; and men are seldom beautiful.

"Barnacles again" he pished; when Richard began, "Crossing in the Mauretania six years ago"—

"Barnacles?" Pepper inquired.

"My dear Pepper you've missed the point" Ridley informed him.

Pepper took reproofs with a smile.

"I can't conceive why I haven't been teaching you Greek, Rachel" was his next remark. "Much better for you than those eternal scales."

Rachel, as Helen suspected, had touches of her uncle's temper, oddly embedded in an indolent disposition.

"Greek must be worse than German" she answered. "Why should one learn anything? What makes you learn? You are learned aren't you—more learned than any body; but I don't see why." She spoke rashly.

"Don't talk nonsense, my dear" said Ridley. "You ought to thank your stars you have the chance of learning. When you're old and people bore you" he glanced significantly at the talkers. "But I'm not the one to preach the advantages of learning."

The remark was made with a profound groan, which Helen interpreted to mean that there was no brown sugar for his pudding.

"They'll bring it" she nodded.

"—a worn out old creature like me" he concluded and helped himself copiously.

"Considering your letters" said Helen, "you deserve beating." He had three letters, she explained; stuffed with praise. One, from a lady, praised not only his books, but his beauty. She had compared him with her idea of Shelley, if Shelley had been spared to middle age, and had, presumably, grown a beard.

Rachel laughed.

"How cruel of you!" Ridley shot at her.

"Then there was another, equally fulsome, praising his modesty" Helen continued, as though she were the Sphinx, pronouncing doom.

"You've left out the only one that counted" Ridley grumbled.

"He was offered a degree" she finished. "Then he complains. Then he finds fault with people. Really, Ridley— I sometimes think you're the vainest man I know—which," she continued, "is saying a good deal."

By these means Ridley was prevented from exclaiming aloud that he suffered the tortures of the damned, bored to extinction by the incessant chatter of two worthy jackasses.

Dinner over, Dalloway confided to Vinrace that he still felt off colour, and that he would go to bed without a cigar.

"I thought he wasn't quite him self" Willoughby said to Helen. "But it seemed best to take no notice. Making the effort often does people good I'm afraid. We bored Ridley?"

"You're much too good, Willoughby" said Helen, touched by his modesty. "It's William Pepper, I think. Ridley's seen too much of him."

"A thorough good chap—Dalloway" said Vinrace. "I wish Ridley and he could have had a good talk. But they're landing. He tells me he must see Morocco. These risings mean more, he thinks, than the people at home realise. It's interesting to talk to some one behind the scenes. I suppose he'll be at the top one of these days." He swung off to annotate papers, and left Helen wondering. There were no facts for her to wonder about, but there were symptoms.

"It was just his eyes and his hands" she concluded, "at dinner."

Rachel too had seen those eyes. They were eyes that no longer saw clearly. The unreasonable heart which seemed to have a separate life of its own, began beating; but when Richard did not come, dragged again. Her pallor struck Helen.

"Aren't you tired?" she asked.

"Sleepy" said Rachel. She went to bed.

She slept, but she dreamt. Alone she walked a long tunnel; it grew dark and narrow; at length she saw a dim light, and found that the tunnel led nowhere, but ended in a vault, where a crouching little man waited for her, gibbering, with long nails. The wall behind him dripped with wet. Still as death and cold she lay, until she broke the agony by tossing herself across the bed, and woke crying "Oh!"

Light showed her the familiar things—her own clothes and the water jug. But the horror did not go at once. She was certain that some one was after her. She actually locked the door. She would see Richard's eyes; and hear his voice. To comfort herself she repeated "But it's only the body they destroy." The soul? When she sought for it, it appeared an abject thing. "Well then—sleep." She fell asleep, with her hands clasping her forehead. All night long barbarian men harassed the ship; they came scuffling down the passages; and snuffed at her door.

CHAPTER EIGHT

"You've never had that lesson" said Ridley. Once more Mrs Dalloway was dressed in her long fur cloak; once more rich boxes stood on top of each other.

"That's the tragedy of life" she returned. "One's always beginning and having to end. Still, I'm not going to let this end, if you're willing!"

"D'you suppose we shall ever meet in London?" said Ridley ironically. "You'll have forgotten all about me by the time you step out there."

He pointed to the shore, where they could now see the separate trees with moving branches.

"How horrid you are!" she laughed. "Rachel's coming to see me anyhow. Ah, I remember" Rachel was leaning over the rail, looking at the shore. She turned.

"You've promised to come, the instant you get back" said Clarissa. "Now you've no excuse!" She wrote her name and address on the fly leaf of Persuasion, and gave the book to Rachel.

Sailors were shouldering the luggage. People were beginning to congregate. There were Captain Cobbild, Willoughby, Helen and Richard Dalloway.

"Oh, it's time" said Clarissa.

"Well, goodbye" she said; she kissed Rachel. "I do like you" she murmured. Richard raised his hat. People in the way made it unnecessary for him to shake hands with Rachel; but he managed to look at her very stiffly for a second. The boat separated from the ship, and made off towards the land. For some minutes Helen Ridley and Rachel stood watching. Once Mrs Dalloway turned and waved. But the boat steadily grew smaller; and nothing could be seen save two backs.

"Well—that's over" said Ridley, turning to go to his books. They felt melancholy. Ridley had spoke the truth. They were never to meet again.

CHAPTER NINE

Directly people have left either a house or a ship the traces of them begin to be swept up. No one is quite easy until the rose petals have been brushed off the dressing table and the basins emptied. Mrs Chailey was doing her part to obliterate the Dalloways; Helen and Rachel did theirs. They wanted at least to get things straight again.

"Well," said Helen turning from the rail when the boat was very small. "That's a relief."

"Were you bored?" said Rachel.

"I should have been" said Helen. "You liked them didn't you?"

It became clear to Rachel that she would now tell Helen about the kiss; although she had not meant to.

"How difficult—" she began.

"To know people?"

"Yes. He kissed me."

Helen drew in her breath. "Tell me" she said. "When was it?"

"It was after the storm. The day before yesterday. He came in to see me, and he kissed me."

"I suspected something" said Helen. "Let's sit down."

The day was fair and blue, and they sat in two long chairs looking towards the shore, where even now the Dalloways mingled in the swarm of active little bodies by the pier. Rachel told the story as well as she could remember it. She related how they had talked about politics and Burke, and

Richard's youth. Suddenly she had felt something queer. Then he kissed her.

"I thought he was that kind of man" said Helen.

In telling the story Rachel had grown flushed once more; but Helen in hearing it grew calm.

"It's odd how one can always tell" she added.

"Why did it happen?" said Rachel.

"Men are like that—a great many of them" said Helen.

"That's why life's so difficult—that's why one can't walk alone" flung out Rachel.

"I don't see why there should be any difficulty whatever" said Helen. "After all, it doesn't matter."

But to Rachel it did seem to matter, partly because she took it for a compliment.

"It destroys talk" she said.

"Honestly, Rachel did you mind?"

Rachel thought of the excitement, the exaltation, then of the exhaustion and of the horrors at night.

"Not at the moment" she said. "But afterwards—think of the women in Piccadilly. I'm furious to think that that's at the bottom of everything. That's why we can't go about alone."

"If you once get that into your head, you'll lose all sense of proportion" said Helen. "It's like noticing the noises people make when they eat, or men spitting."

"How do you look at it then?" asked Rachel.

"Well—it's beautiful" said Helen considering. "It's really very pleasant. I've never minded being kissed!"

Beside the rich store of Helen's amorous experiences, Rachel's one kiss lost something of its importance.

"But beautiful" she said "—why beautiful?"

"Of course it's nothing in itself" said Helen. "But if one cares, there's nothing like it."

"That's what Mrs Dalloway said" Rachel reflected. "Yet her husband kissed me."

"And why not?" asked Helen. "You're nice to kiss I've no doubt."

"If that's just that," said Rachel, "like washing one's hands, why was I afraid?"

"Partly because you've heard a lot of nonsense we all have. Partly no doubt because Mr Dalloway was a stupid sentimental man."

Rachel described her dream of the little man with the long nails crouched in the dripping vault.

"No" said Helen considering, "I can't remember ever feeling that."

"I felt weak you see" said Rachel. "I felt he could do what he chose with me. I remember looking at his hand. It takes one back to pre-historic times I suppose. It makes one feel queer."

"I suppose we're very different people" Helen concluded. "But aren't you feeling what you think you ought to feel?"

"A theory wouldn't have made me wake up would it?"

"Excitement would. Then you begin inventing reasons. I grant that sentimental nuzzling is disgusting."

"But you don't understand! To me it wasn't sentimental nuzzling—oh it's all so mixed!"

"Look Rachel. You were flattered by his talking to you; then he kissed you; and you can't make out how to combine the two things. You don't want to admit that he was attracted by you as he is I've no doubt by heaps of other women."

"If you were me you'd dismiss him?"

"I'm vain too! It's the great compliment after all."

"But you do dismiss them both. You say 'That's a relief' when they go. If he'd kissed you you'd say the same."

"It was amusing to see them" said Helen, "I daresay I should have liked him to kiss me. I daresay, if I'm honest, that I'm a little jealous that he kissed you instead. Still, I'm quite convinced of this—two kisses would have been enough. So it's a relief that they're gone. There's the boat coming back!"

"In spite of my adventure" (she was now shy about it) "I do want to see them again" said Rachel. "I like hearing them talk."

Helen paused and then said,

"It becomes more and more clear to me that you will always be the dupe of the second rate."

"Shall we have time to finish this conversation?" said Rachel, "Because I want to understand."

"We've got at least two hours. But I really don't think love is a thing to be explained to people who've never felt it. One splits hairs—that's all."

"But what are you there for if it's not to talk about love?" Rachel hazarded.

"Well, there's some sense in that" Helen owned.

"Besides I don't want to talk about love. I want to talk about the Dalloways. Did you ever read a little red book that's lying about—'The House of Commons' I think it's called? It gives biographies of Members. It gives facts like these—Born in Sheffield. Son of. Educated at Rugby; Became an Engineer and so on. There are hundreds and hundreds like that."

"Well?"

"Only I find it very impressive. Mr Dalloway was one of them. Wouldn't you be impressed if you read it. Wouldn't all those men doing things make you feel small?"

"Ten thousand Mr Dalloways would make me feel if any thing rather larger."

Rachel tried hard to recall the image of the world as a live thing that Mr Dalloway had given her; with drains like nerves, and bad roads like patches of diseased skin. She recalled his watch words. Unity. The Organism. She recalled that first evening and how painfully but wonderfully Mr and Mrs Dalloway had added a big world to her little one, like bubbles meeting in a tea cup.

"I admit" said Helen who had drawn a large piece of embroidery to her and was choosing a thread from many bright skeins, that our position is damnable. There are ten of us and ten million Dalloways. It comes to this. The only philanthropy is to hate people. That sounds rather foolish, but I believe it's true. People like that," she continued, "poison the air. Wherever they go they do harm. They encourage bad books and bad pictures; they loathe good ones. Still, that wouldn't matter; but it does matter that they should have children, and increase the general muddle. Either they force one to withdraw, as we have done, or they spoil one; or they make reformers. Shelley for instance."

"But what was there to hate in the Dalloways?" Rachel asked.

"Their feelings" said Helen. "Think what lies Mrs Dalloway told to make herself agreeable! Fish and the Greek Alphabet! Think of his attitude to her—to all women. She has daughters to bring up. He rules us. A fine mess they'll make of it! Still, hating's no good. In many ways they're very nice people. If I were you, Rachel, I wouldn't attempt to compromise. Don't let them try to convert you. She did, didn't she?"

With some awkwardness, Rachel remembered how she had talked to Mrs Dalloway about her mother; how much charmed she had been by a nature which, if Helen was right, was pitted as by the small pox.

"That's one of their vilest habits" Helen continued. "They want to make people like themselves. They're always talking at one. They try to impose their own views. No one's any business to do that."

"Did she try?" said Rachel. "Didn't she only show me something new? He did that too. He told me about girls in Manchester. If they exist how can we ignore them? His life too—the way he was brought up—the canaries and the lemur—how he argued—if I'd seen more of him, I should have heard how he fell in love."

"All that you can get from books with much less trouble."

Rachel thought of the pair now driving over cobbled streets and washing their faces in a shabby little hotel on shore. Did Richard think of her? Did Clarissa guess?

"It's the human soul!" she ejaculated. "Things go on and on." She followed them travelling through Morocco, observing, chattering, meeting at night, and telling each other what they had felt.

"I wonder if Mr Dalloway has told his wife about me" she said.

"I should think not, but perhaps she guesses."

"And it doesn't matter?"

"You see, they've got children" said Helen. "That means so much more than—just kisses."

The affair looked small enough now. Rachel was ashamed of her exaggeration.

"It may be all true" she said, "but—the human soul? One gets so close to something—one things it's going to blaze, and then—one gets kissed."

"The dupe of the second rate!" Helen laughed. "You're doomed Rachel. There's no escape!"

"It mightn't always be like that. Perhaps with a Liberal—"

"Liberals? They're no different from Conservatives!"

"I don't mind being kissed—"

"I thought not."

"You see I thought people were images. Somehow they're becoming real."

"Oh yes, they're real enough" said Helen; "Only, you'll have to discriminate."

"How?" asked Rachel. "Tell me how one knows?"

Helen was sweeping a piece of charcoal in circles over her canvas. She was drawing trees hanging fruit over a river.

"One knows everything for oneself" she said. "What one really wishes even for one's own children is that they should find things out for themselves."

"We're very different people!" Rachel sighed, reviewing the points which Helen had not understood.

"I suppose you think I don't understand?" said Helen.

"Not altogether."

"Now's your chance then. Your chance of being a person, I mean."

"I can be myself in spite of you, in spite of the Dalloways, in spite of William Pepper, and my father, and Darwin?"

"You can; but I don't say you will. But I like you Rachel."

"That," cried Rachel, her eyes lighting up, and gazing wide awake for the first time into Helen's, "that is what matters!"

An exquisite happiness filled them both.

Now Willoughby Vinrace had a great objection to women talking in private with women, and had never left his wife alone with Helen without indicating the hour at which they ought to part. His reason was that nothing was ever done as the result of such talks, and that things were said that had better remain unsaid. Action alone justifying talk, it followed that women should be silent, for they seldom do anything. They may talk with cooks, nurses and plumbers, but not with friends.

The talk just recorded, was however an exception to this rule, for it bore a little fruit, of a kind which Willoughby himself could handle, a few days later. Helen sought him in his work room, where he was applying a stout blue pencil to bundles of filmy paper.

"If you are willing to leave Rachel with us, when we land," she said, "we shall be very glad to have her. We will take good care of her."

There were obvious advantages in the plan, for to take a girl on a long voyage up the Amazons, to a port where business would claim her father, and the social conditions as Willoughby put it, were primitive, did not recommend itself to reason. Willoughby had agreed, because Rachel had wished it; because they did without any doubt love each other.

"You would take care of her?" he asked.

"Yes" said Helen. "I am very fond of her. But it depends of course what she wants herself."

"She's the only thing that's left to me" said Willoughby glancing at his wife's photograph.

"There is a likeness" said Helen.

["We go on year after year without talking about these things—" He broke off. "Life's very hard. But it's better so. Only, life's hard."

Helen pitied him, and patted him on the shoulder, but she felt uncomfortable. She praised Rachel, and explained how the visit might be arranged.

"True" said Willoughby when she had done. "The social conditions...are certainly primitive. I should be out a good deal. I agreed because she wished it. But of course I have complete confidence in you. You see, Helen, I want to bring her up as her mother would have wished. I don't hold with these modern views—nor do you eh? She's a nice quiet girl, devoted to her music—a little less of that would do no harm. Still, it's kept her happy, and we lead a very quiet life at Richmond. I should like her to begin to see more people. I want to take her about with me when I get home. I've half a mind to rent a house in London, leaving my sisters at Richmond, and take her to see one or two people who'd be kind to her for my sake....

Rachel when consulted showed less enthusiasm than Helen could have wished. One moment she was eager, the next doubtful.... She occupied herself with] miscellaneous reading about the soul riding safe among tumultuous circumstances, a moon among racing clouds, kept her calm until the very moment of parting. Then it seemed to her that pain was more real than happiness. If Helen could have read her mind she would have felt more sure than ever that destiny marked her for a dupe.

CHAPTER TEN

The extreme insignificance of the Euphrosyne, and, it seemed to follow, of her freight, was perfectly apparent to young officers and the daughters of South African millionaires as they strolled upon the upper deck acquiring a right to dine, and swept the sea for something to talk about. She was called alternately a Tramp, a cattle boat, a Cargo boat and "one of those wretched little passenger steamers." Of the love and the reason on board, no one recked. The insect like figures of Dalloways Ambroses and Vinraces were also derided both from the extreme smallness of their persons, and the doubt which only strong glasses could dispel, as to whether they were really live creatures or lumps on the rigging. Mr Pepper had been mistaken for a cormorant, and then transformed into a cow.

After dinner indeed when the waltzes were booming, a more sentimental view would be induced by the sight of ships shrunk to a few beads of light and one high in air upon the mast head. "Ships that pass in the night"—many knew that line, without being able to say what happened to them. But it was easy enough to supply "Awfully like life," the young man being a Captain in the army, the young woman going out to keep house for a brother in the mines.

The sea being covered with ships, the ships swarming with human beings, who each found that isolation on board spread strange ideas about life, the historian will not attempt to say which view was the right one, or which ship really mattered most. Since religion has gone out of fashion, and the soul is called the brain, these enormous spaces of silence in which our deeds and words are but as points of rock in an ocean, are discreetly ignored; the novelist respects but does not attempt to render them. Miss Löbstein writing home to her mother summed up the situation thus. "Nothing has happened to tell you about, but if I were to be shut up much longer on this stuffy old ship, I should be fit to join the loonies I know." This disaster was prevented by a woman having a baby in the steerage, and as the baby had no clothes and the mother had no milk, Miss Löbstein's fingers kept her brain from thinking.

All ocean liners were accounted for in Mrs Ambrose's mind. The incident of Miss Löbstein and the baby would not have surprised her. "How people love the chance of a scene!" would have been her comment. She was content that half the population of England should be lifted to the African shore, and the void filled by negroes as she was content to mix her coffee with milk. This economy of emotion left her with strong passions for the objects she selected.

She was pale with suspense while the boat with mail bags was making towards them. Absorbed in her letters she did not notice that she had left the Euphrosyne; she felt no sadness when the ship lifted up her voice and bellowed thrice like a cow separated from its calf.

"The children are well!" she exclaimed. Mr Pepper who sat opposite with a great mound of bag and rug upon his knee, said "Gratifying." Rachel to whom the end of the voyage meant a complete change of perspective, was too much bewildered by the approach of the shore to realise what children were well or why it was gratifying. Helen went on reading.

What Rachel saw was this. At dawn they had entered the bay, and the boat was now nearing a white crescent of sand. She saw a deep green valley, and distinct hills on either side. On the slope of the right hand hill white houses with brown roofs were settled, like nesting sea birds. Cypresses striped the hill with black bars. Mountains whose sides were flushed with red, but whose crowns were bald, rose behind. As the hour was still early, the whole view was exquisitely light and airy. The blues and greens were intense but not sultry. An air seemed to be moving among the trees. On her the effect was exhilarating; after the sea, the hot earth was exciting.

"Three hundred years old" said Mr Pepper, meditatively.

As nobody said "What?" he merely extracted a bottle and swallowed a pill. The piece of information that died within him was this. Three hundred years ago five Elizabethan barques had anchored where the Euphrosyne now floated. Half drawn up upon the beach lay an equal number of Spanish galleons, unmanned, for the country lay still behind a veil. Slipping across the water, the English sailors bore away bars of silver, bales of linen, timbers of cedar wood, golden crucifixes knobbed with emeralds. When the Spaniards came down from their drinking, a fight ensured, the parties churning up the sand, and driving each other into the surf. The Spaniards bloated with fine living upon the fruit of the miraculous land, fell in heaps. The hardy English men, tawny with sea voyaging, hairy for lack of razors, with muscles like wire, fangs greedy for flesh and fingers itching for gold, despatched the wounded, drove the dying into the sea, and soon reduced the natives to a state of superstitious wonderment. Here a settlement was made; women were imported; children grew. All seemed to favour the expansion of the British Empire; had there been men like Richard Dalloway in the time of Charles the First the map would undoubtedly be red where it is now an odious green. But the political mind of that age lacked imagination, and, merely for want of a few thousand pounds and a few thousand men, the spark died that should have been a conflagration. From the interior came Indians with subtle poisons, naked bodies and painted idols; from the sea came vengeful Spaniards and rapacious Portugese; exposed to all these enemies (though the climate proved wonderfully kind and the earth abundant) the English dwindled and all but disappeared. Somewhere about the middle of the seventeenth century a single sloop watched its season and slipped out by night, bearing within it all that was left of the great British colony, a few men, a few women, and perhaps a dozen dusky children. English history then denies all knowledge of the place. Owing to one cause and another civilization shifted its centre to a spot some four or five hundred miles to the south and to day Santa Rosa is not much larger than it was three hundred years ago. Its population is a happy compromise. Portugese fathers wed Indian mothers, and their children intermarry with the Spanish. In arts and industries the place is still where it was in Elizabethan days. Although they get their ploughs from Manchester, they make their coats from their own sheep, their silk from their own worms, their furniture from their own cedar trees.

Knowing historians, pale men, with endearing eccentricities, which render them incapable of crossing roads, or joining talk, for the mere look of them inspires respect, we no longer hope to find in their works what has really happened. The history of Santa Rosa is a case in point. There is a chapter which will never be written.

When the capital was founded elsewhere, this little town became popular as a place to go to when one wished for mountain air and scenery. Rich men built themselves villas on the slopes of the hills. But the Latin races lack enterprise, and except for a dozen white houses and a few shops, there was nothing until yesterday to show that Santa Rosa was a town where one enjoyed oneself. Love and friendship and happiness with all the sorrows they bring, flourished here unrecorded.

To explain what brought the English across the sea it would be necessary to write much about modern life which has not yet been written; as the cause was neither love of conquest, love of rule or love of money we may expect that this chapter will escape the learned too. The English were dissatisfied with their own civilisation. Chapters might be written explaining and describing the disease. On the surface, it had the appearance of severing one limb from another. With money one could live the life of a bird or a fish, a hermit or an epicure, the machinery having grown so perfect that what one wished would be granted if one could pay for it. This being so, it is manifestly absurd to talk of 'The English' or to impute to them one desire. A single little group then, an infinitely small conspiracy, tired of their isolation blamed wealth, machines, all skill and knowledge acquired by the help of money in solitude, and began to seek out what they felt. Some, it was obvious, felt nothing at all. The majority discovered that there was a happy twinship between the nature of man and the nature of the earth. The poets and painters had done nothing all these ages but spin veils between man and his comrade. Without special talent, one possessed at least a body, which if exposed at night grew cold, if exercised rejoiced, if plunged into running water, thrilled. But although one could strip one's body, it was hard to find a stretch of water in England not overlooked by farms, or subject to the gaze of maidens coming home from church. One cried for Pan, and startled women fled shrieking at the sight of a man without trousers. In Italy one could live more simply, but it is impossible to find a view without churches and pictures, the landscape even striking one as a background. Greece was hopeless; a land full of malaria and bits of old stone. In short it was a case for the tropics; the South Seas being very distant, South America did instead.

The movement began very humbly by a few school-masters going out as Pursers, the nature of their occupation requiring them to drink a more drastic dose than other people. They came back windswept and vigorous with stories of sea captains and nights at sea, some of them bringing a yard of bright silk, or a primitive beast, carved out of cedar wood and painted blue and gold. People began to enquire whether one could not enjoy these delights more comfortably, and, as in the whole of the modern world there is no ear so sensitive to the public pulse as the business man's, before three seasons had passed, there was not only a special passenger service to the spot, but a hotel (which had been a monastery) to receive the pilgrims.

Oddly enough, Helen Ambrose had a brother who at this very moment came to an entirely opposite conclusion. He had been sent out to make his living from the land, which he had done with moderate success. But the one merit of the place in his eyes was that it enabled one to leave it. Again and again the sultry evening found him in his verandah with eyes fixed upon the blue rim of the sea, and the magic ship now steaming across the bay which had come from England with an English schoolmaster for Purser. With a pessimism akin to his sister's, he would brush aside all the qualities of the country, its fruits climate beauty health and the virgin splendour so rightly prized by his countrymen, because there was no race course, no Derby Day. What children and philosophy were to Helen, a race horse was to him. When they met, each politely made room in their scheme of the universe for the other's hobby, although in private they spoke of 'poor Harry' and "Poor Helen." Harry's villa was now at Helen's disposal. Having been bothered for some time by scholastic friends of her husband's who said "Oh Mrs Ambrose, why go to Italy when you can go to South America!" or "I assure you the virgin forest did my husband more good in a week than Greece in three months!" Mrs Ambrose determined to see for herself. The day increased in heat as they drove up the hill. The road passed through the town, where men seemed to be beating brass and crying "Water," where the passage was blocked by mules and cleared by whips and curses, where the women walked barefoot their heads balancing baskets, and cripples hastily displayed mutilated members; it issued among steep green fields, not so green but that the earth showed through. Great trees now shaded all but the crest of the road, and a mountain stream, so shallow and so swift that it plaited itself into strands, as it ran, raced along the edge. Higher they went, until Ridley and Rachel walked behind; next they turned along a lane scattered with stones. Mr Pepper raised his stick and silently indicated a shrub, bearing among sparse leaves a voluminous purple blossom. At a rickety canter the last stage of the way was accomplished.

The villa was a roomy white house, which, as is the case with most continental houses, looked to an English eye frail ramshackle and absurdly frivolous, more like a Pagoda in a tea garden than where one slept. The garden called urgently for the services of a gardener. Bushes waved their branches across the paths; the blades of grass could be counted. In the circular piece of ground in front of the verandah were two cracked vases, from which red flowers drooped, with a stone fountain between them, now parched in the sun. The circular garden led to a long garden, where the gardener's shears had scarcely been, unless now and then, when he cut a bough of blossom for his beloved. Trees shaded it; round bushes with wax like flowers mobbed their heads together. A garden smoothly laid with turf, divided by thick hedges, with raised beds of bright flowers, such as we keep within walls in England, would have been out of place upon the side of this hot hill. There was no ugliness to shut out; the villa looked straight across the shoulder of a slope, ribbed with olive trees to the sea.

The indecency of the whole place struck Mrs Chailey forcibly. There were no blinds to shut out the sun; there was no furniture for the sun to spoil. She further ventured the opinion that there were rats, as large as terriers at home, and that if one put one's foot down, one would come through the floor. Water—at this point her investigations left her speechless.

"Poor creature!" she murmured when introduced to the sallow Spanish servant girl, "no wonder you hardly look like a human being!" Maria accepted the compliment with an exquisite Spanish grace. In Chailey's opinion they would have done better to stay on board an English ship. Yet her duty commanded her to stay. No one knew why Mr Pepper had chosen to stay. Efforts had been made for some days before landing to point out the beauties of the Amazon.

"That great stream!" Helen would begin. "I've a good mind to go with you myself, Willoughby,—only I can't. Think of the sunsets and the moon rises—I believe the colours are unimaginable!"

"There are wild peacocks" Rachel would hazard.

"And marvellous creatures in the water" Helen asserted.

"One might discover a new reptile" added Rachel.

"There's certain to be a revolution I'm told."

But the effect of these ingenious subterfuges was spoilt by Ridley, who after regarding Pepper for some moments, sighed aloud "Poor fellow!"

Any one else as Helen and Rachel agreed, would have taken this as a hint to go; Mr Pepper took it as an invitation to stay.

"One wouldn't mind his staying if he'd talk about love" said Rachel.

Helen laughed at her. "How your bees do buzz!" she said, implying that there were other things to talk about.

But there was some truth in what she said; Mr Pepper perpetually snubbed the natural human wish to feel things. Women at any rate felt him unadventurous; one who hugged the coast, and offered no help to those in distress among the waves.

But they were too hasty.

The dinner table was set between two long windows, which were left uncurtained by Helen's order. Darkness fell as sharply as a knife in this climate, and the town then sprang out in circles and lines of bright dots beneath them. Buildings which did not show by day showed by night. Moreover, the sea flowed over the land, judging by the moving lights of the steamers. The sight fulfilled the same purpose as an orchestra in a London restaurant. Silence had its setting.

On the sixth night of their stay William Pepper raised his spectacles to contemplate the scene.

"I've identified the big block to the left" he observed, and pointed with a fork.

"One should infer that they can cook vegetables."

"An hotel?" said Helen.

"Once a monastery" said Mr Pepper.

Nothing more was said then, but the day after, Mr Pepper returned from a midday walk, stood silently before Helen who was reading in the verandah.

"I've taken a room over there" he said.

"You're not going?" she exclaimed.

"On the whole—yes" he remarked. "No private cook *can* cook vegetables."

Knowing his dislike of questions, which she to some extent shared, Helen asked no more. Still, an uneasy suspicion lurked in her mind that William was hiding a wound. She flushed to think that her words or her husband's or Rachel's had penetrated and stung. A tear actually came to her eye. She was half moved to cry, "Stop William; explain!" and would have returned to the subject if William had not shown himself inscrutable and chill, lifting fragments of salad on the point of his fork, with the gesture of a man pronging sea weed, detecting gravel, suspecting germs.

"If you all die of typhoid I won't be responsible!" he snapped.

"If you die of dullness, neither will I" Helen echoed in her heart. "That's the penalty of putting one's trust in vegetables" she added.

She meant that if one had not the courage to use live words instead of dead ones one must expect to be treated as a log; to be smothered in refuse. What did the log feel? No one knew. If Rachel had listened instead of looking out of the window, she could have made some profoundly gloomy reflections upon the state of human relationships. "We live to hurt each other!" she might have exclaimed. Happily, she dreamt.

CHAPTER ELEVEN

Three months passed. Mrs Ambrose had a friend, an elderly mathematician, famous even in Pekin, to whom she wrote when ever, after drinking three cups of hot tea, or scaling a steep chapter, she seemed to see life by the light of the setting sun.

"Three months!" she wrote, then she dipped her pen deep and drew a figure which might have been a diagram of the flaming edge of the sun. There was a circle, and rays shot from it, and were drawn back into it. She contrived to make them look as though they were shot out and sucked in forcibly. This was a diagram of three months' life at the Villa San Gervasio; the circle represented the villa, and the vigorous strokes the excursions of the people in it, which, so her allegory might be interpreted, really centred in the villa itself. They had seen few strangers, but they had come to know each other. Then she gave him a list of the things now happening round her. "For I am not what one would call a writer. It is now ten minutes to six. One hears a great deal more than one would expect directly one listens. The clock for example. Ridley is writing an article about Greek Mysticism over my head. There! he chokes, having swallowed some nicotine. He swears. Rachel is going over and over a difficult passage. It is not Bach. Am I boring you with all these noises? There is Mrs Chailey singing 'Far down the Swanee river' as she washes up the tea things. Various tropical birds are singing. Dogs bark in the town below. They should be killed, not that I am afraid of rabies, but the hot weather will make them infested. There are now some great red flowers out. London must be detestable; Cambridge worse; the place I should like to be in is Cornwall. How difficult girls are! Suppose you saw some one bound to make a fool of herself, what would you do? Let her alone, I suppose. They'll come home. It may be tailless though." The figure of a manx cat was drawn upon the blotting paper.

"A steamer is trumpeting in the bay. It shall take back this letter. Perhaps it brings one from you. Are we really doomed to loneliness, or can we board the souls of others? That is the kind of thing we talk about. You asked. Also, what is meant by real? Love too. Oh, and religion."

Excited by the mere mention of these topics, Mrs Ambrose was here led to embark upon a definition of reality, which filled six pages though it proved nothing, and occupied her until dinner was ready.

Three months had made but little change in Ridley or Rachel. Their skins were browner; the careless comfort of their manners reminded one of a well worn coat. The vagueness of their behaviour, resulting in long easy silences and a blankness of the eyes, proved that Rachel was on that decline which Mrs Dalloway had so sadly foretold for her. Six months of the London season would have been her instant prescription, preceded by a course of sitting up right, with a sharp quill pen under the chin, and a dozen lessons in the management of arms and legs.

"A lovely night" said Ridley, indicating the dusky view beneath them.

"D'you realise the season's begun?" said Mrs Ambrose.

"Damn the season!" said Ridley.

"Rows and rows of lights" said Rachel, pointing to the big white house, where lights were opening like evening primroses.

"That reminds me—I have a letter to post" said Helen.

"All my friends are dead" said Ridley.

"Nonsense" said Helen.

"Shall I take your letter?" said Rachel.

"We'll both take it" said Helen.

"We'll go and see life. Coming Ridley?"

"Lord no," said Ridley. "Rachel I expect to be a fool; you might know better." He was examining his whiskers in the looking glass as he spoke.

Helen laid hold of his beard.

"Am I a fool?" she said.

"Let me go, Helen."

"Am I a fool?" she repeated.

"Vile woman!" he exclaimed, and kissed her.

"We'll leave you to your vanities" Helen called as they shut the door.

"It isn't vain to look in looking glasses" said Rachel.

"Not if you're as beautiful as I am" said Helen.

"Perhaps one looks for moral virtues" Rachel pondered. "The light of genius, or the sadness of a self sacrificing mother."

"You're quite vain enough to look for all three" said Helen.

Having dropped her letter in the pillar box, which was let into a wall where the lane joined the road, Helen was for turning back.

"We're going to see life—you promised" Rachel urged.

Seeing life was their phrase for walking in the streets after dark. The social life of Santa Rose was carried on almost [entirely by lamp light. The young women with their hair magnificently dressed, a red flower behind the ear, sat on the door steps, or issued onto balconies, while the young men ranged up and down beneath shouting out a challenge from time to time, and stopping here and there to make love.

At the open windows merchants could be seen making up the day's accounts, and older women lifting jars from shelf to shelf. The streets were full of people, men for the most part, who interchanged their views of the world as they walked, or gathered round the wine tables at the street corner where some old cripple was twanging his guitar strings, while a poor girl cried her passionate song in the gutter. The two Englishwomen excited some friendly curiosity but no one molested them.

Helen sauntered on, observing the different people in their shabby clothes who seemed so careless and so natural with satisfaction.

"Just think of the Mall tonight!" she exclaimed, at length. "It's the fifteenth of March. Perhaps there's a Court." She thought of the crowd waiting in the cold spring air to see the grand carriages go by. "It's very cold even if it's not raining" she said. "First there are men selling picture postcards; then there are wretched little shop girls with band boxes; then there are bank clerks; in tail coats; and—dressmakers. People from South Kensington drive up in a hired fly; officials have a pair of bays; earls on the other hand are allowed one footman to stand up behind; Dukes have two, Royal Dukes—so I was told—have three; the King I suppose can have as many as he likes. And the people believe in it!"

Out here it seemed as though the people of England must be shaped in the body like the Kings and Queens, Knights and Pawns of the Chessboard. Their differences were so distinct.

Here they had to part in order to circumvent a crowd.

"They believe in God" said Rachel as they regained each other. She meant that the people here believed in Him; for she remembered the crosses with awful plaster figures that stood where foot paths joined, and the inscrutable mystery of a service in a Roman Catholic church.

"We shall never understand!" she sighed.]

"Do you mean to go right up to the hotel?" said Helen.

A private road—but nothing was private in Santa Rosa—led to the platform of ground upon which the hotel was built. Talking idly, they had gone some distance. It was now night.

The monks had chosen what was called a "lovely situation" for their monastery. On one side there was only a strip of land set with twisted little trees between them and the sea; on the other there was a garden with shady walks for meditation, and fruit trees to make liqueur of. But tennis lawns had been flattened out upon the slope; and the only part of the building that survived was the chapel, which had been given over to the charge of an English chaplin. Solemn allusion was made to this in the steamship prospectuses. "Embellished as the hotel is with the latest conveniences carried out in a highly artistic manner by a well known firm of English upholsterers, we would respectfully draw the attention of British tourists to a unique figure, consisting of a chapel, where worship is conducted on Sundays (in the season) after the rites of the Anglican church, by the Rev. Alex Maclean, feeling confident etc. &c &."

Ignorant of this convenience, Helen and Rachel were fascinated by the display of modern luxury exhibited before them. A broad gravel terrace ran round the building. The large windows were all of them uncurtained, and each revealed a section of the hotel. The dining room was being swept; a waiter was eating a bunch of grapes with his leg across a corner of the table. In the kitchen next door the white cooks were dipping their hairy arms in to cauldrons, while the waiters made their meal voraciously off broken meats, sopping up the gravy with bits of crumb. Creeping on, they came next to the drawing room, where the ladies and gentlemen having dined well lay back in deep arm chairs occasionally speaking or turning over the pages of magazines.

"What is a dahabeeyah, Charles," a widow seated near the window asked her son. As a thin lady had just finished a daring run upon the piano the answer was lost in the general clearing of throats and tapping of knees.

"They're all old in this room" Rachel whispered.

The next window revealed men in shirtsleeves playing billiards with two young ladies.

"He pinched my arm!" the plump young woman cried as she missed her stroke.

"Now you two—no ragging" said the young man with a red face who was marking.

"D'you think they're engaged?" asked Rachel.

"Take care or we shall be seen" Helen whispered.

Turning the corner they came to the largest room in the hotel, which boasted of four windows and was called the Lounge. Hung with armour, and the embroideries of the natives, furnished with divans and screens supplied with mysterious corners, the room was the haunt of youth. Signor Rodriguez, manager, would often take a moment from his ledgers at about this hour of the evening, and standing at the doorway survey the scene with righteous satisfaction.

"Without our lounge," he proclaimed to the furtive woman peeping round his side, "where should we be? Smoking rooms, billiard rooms, drawing rooms—all very well, but without a lounge—swhit!" It had been a conservatory, a warm stone room with pots on trestles, until he came and made a lounge of it; just as the chapel had been used for storing deck chairs and jars of oil until he came and made a place of worship of it.

People were scattered about in couples or parties of four. Either they were actually better acquainted, or the informal room made their manners easier. Through the open window came an uneven sound like that which rises from a flock of sheep pent within hurdles at dusk. A card party occupied the centre of the foreground.

Helen and Rachel watched them play for some minutes without being able to distinguish a word.

"I'm sure I know that man's face" said Helen at length. She was observing a clean shaven lean man of about her own age, who was the partner of a straight forward looking English girl. By watching his lips they could hear him say,

"All you want is practise, Miss Warrington; courage and practise—one's no good without the other."

"Hughling Elliot of course!" Helen exclaimed. She ducked, because he looked round.

The game was broken up at this instant by the approach of a wheeled chair, containing a voluminous old lady who paused by the table and said,

"Better luck tonight Susan?"

"All the luck's on our side" said a young man who until now had kept his back to the window. He was inclined to be stout, but his face was lively.

"Luck, Mr Hewet?" said his partner, a lady with spectacles and grey hair. "I assure you Mrs Paley, our success is due solely to my brilliant play."

"Unless I go to bed early I get practically no sleep at all" Mrs Paley was heard to explain, to justify the seizure of Susan, who proceeded to wheel the chair to the door.

"Oh they'll find someone else to take my place" said Susan cheerfully.

But she was wrong. No attempt was made to find another player, and after the young man had built two storeys of a card house, they strolled off in different directions.

Mr Hewet whose full face showed that he had large eyes obscured by glasses, a rosy complexion, and clean shaven lips, advanced towards the window; but his eyes were fixed not upon the eavesdroppers, but upon a spot where the curtain hung in folds.

"Asleep?" he said.

Helen and Rachel started to think that some one had been sitting near to them unobserved all the time. There were legs in the shadow. A melancholy voice issued from above them.

"Two women" it said.

A scuffling was heard on the gravel. The women had fled.

CHAPTER TWELVE

Not as much pains as one could wish, so Miss Allen said, had been taken to secure privacy in the hotel. She alluded to the thickness of the partitions between the bedrooms. "Match board" she announced, tapping the wall with a thick knuckle. "For married couples I should imagine, it must be particularly awkward" she continued.

Her grey petticoat slipped to the ground. The great rooms downstairs were all deserted, and the little box like squares above them were all irradiated. Some forty or fifty people were going to bed. The thump of jugs set down on the floor could be heard, and the chink on china. Miss Allen having folded her clothes with neat but not loving fingers and screwed her hair into a plait, wound her father's watch, and opened Wordsworth. There are fourteen books in the Prelude; if you read one every night therefore it will last a fortnight. Miss Allen had to keep in touch with the classics because she made her living and supported an invalid sister by teaching girls in the north modern languages and English literature. She was now engaged upon a primer. Wordsworth's philosophy had six hundred words allotted to it. But though she had a pencil with which she pinned down fragments of philosophy, she made slow way with her book tonight.

Boots fell heavily above her.

"I should like to know" she said, shutting the book upon the pencil, "exactly what is going on over my head!" and as a swishing sound came through the wall, "what's that next door?"

Ye Presences of Nature in the sky
And on the Earth! Ye visions of the hills!
And Souls of lonely places!
she resumed—

"All that's very noble of course but—" A great impatience
with those match board partitions over came her.

"Considering we're made for each other" she said.

Rapidly casting her mind over her entire life, and fore-
casting the future she sighed, and to a spectator would have
looked gaunt enough. But the hour being rather late, she took
her pencil and resumed her Wordsworth, a worthy disciple.
For some time longer the swishing and tapping went on next
door, so that Miss Allen dropped off to sleep murmuring

And certain hopes are with me that to thee
This labour will be welcome, honoured Friend!
and thinking, "She's a nice kind girl, I wonder why she hasn't
married."

Very different was the room through the wall, though as
like in shape as one egg box is like another. By the time that
Miss Allen had read her book, Miss Warrington had just
reached that solemn stage in the ceremony of undressing
known as "brushing the hair." Ages have consecrated this
hour—for an hour it can be, or two, or three—to talk of love
between women. Miss Warrington being alone could not
talk, but she could look in the glass. Seated before the looking glass in a long white dressing gown she looked
meditatively at her reflection, as she turned her head from
side to side, tossing heavy locks now this way now that.

She liked to see that her cheeks were red and her eyes
were blue. "I'm nice looking decidedly" she thought; "Not
pretty; possibly"—she shut her mouth—"possibly handsome." Withdrawing slightly, she composed her self into a
stately picture. "It seems plain enough" she thought, meaning by this that she was a suitable person to be wife and

mother. Her eyes now became blank, as though fixed on someone else.

"It's true he didn't ask me to play, but he did follow me into the hall."

The figure of Mr Arthur Venning became so clear at this point that she might have been looking at a picture. Truthful, robust and clean, simple but wise in man's knowledge, she could love him if she let herself; nothing could prevent her from honouring him.

"There's no harm in that" she said aloud almost, when after a few minutes pause, she again took brush in hand.

Miss Warrington could not get undressed in much less than an hour because she did it so well. Merely to see her capable handling of brushes and bottles was a pleasure, or the deftness with which shining hair coiled where it should. Possibly there was more assurance in her processes to night than usual, since there was promise of an object. At the age of thirty, having no proposals to manipulate, the hour of undressing was often a sad one. She had no confidences to give. She had been known to go to bed in tears, treating her hair unkindly. She was just about to pull back the bedclothes, when she cried "Oh but I'm forgetting!" and went to her writing table. A brown volume lay there, stamped with the year; she never missed a day; for ten years she had kept a diary. She wrote a square child's hand; "A. M. Talked to Mrs H. Elliot. About country neighbours. How small the world is! She knows the Hunts, also the Careys. Like her. Hope to know her better. Read a chapter of Kenilworth to Aunt Bessie. P. M. Played tennis with Mr Perrott and Evelyn M. Beat them. Dont like Mr P. have a feeling about his being not 'quite.' though clever certainly. Day very fine view magnificent; one gets used to no trees though much too bare at first. Cards after dinner. Ab. B. Cheerful. Tho' twingy, I fear. *Am enjoying myself.*"

The line drawn beneath the last words was really a private signal to show that her hopes flourished. That diaries would prove useful, and were somehow an incentive to frugality and order she believed; to write them generally meant that one got one's toes cold, and thus one's soul benefited. At any rate having accomplished this paragraph which was too private for any one but herself to read, and yet left all she thought unsaid, she knelt in prayer, and leapt into bed. Soon her breathing with its adorable little sighs and hesitations reminding one of a cow met by night asleep in a meadow, showed that she was well on her way to another pleasant morning.

A glance into the next room revealed little more than a nose. Growing accustomed to the darkness, but the windows were open and showed grey squares with splinters of starlight, one could distinguish a lean form, terribly like the body of a dead person. Even in sleep, Mr Pepper was more silent than other people. Thirty six, thirty seven, thirty eight, here were three Portugese men of business, asleep presumably, since a snore came with the regularity of a great ticking clock. Thirty nine was a corner room at the end of the passage; late though it was—'one' struck gently downstairs—, a line of light under the door showed that some one was still awake.

"How late you are Hugh!" a woman, lying in bed, said in a peevish but solicitous voice. Her husband was tying a cord round his pyjamas before getting into bed.

"You should have gone to sleep" he answered. "I was talking to Thornbury."

"But I never can sleep when I'm waiting for you" she said.

To that he made no answer, but only remarked, "Well then we'll turn out the light." They were silent.

The faint but penetrating pulse of an electric bell could be heard in the corridor. Old Mrs Paley, having woken hungry but without her spectacles, was summoning her maid to find the biscuit box. The maid having answered the bell, drearily respectful even at this hour though muffled in a mackintosh, the passage was left in silence. Downstairs all was empty and dark; but on the upper floor a light still burnt in the room where the boots had dropped so heavily above Miss Allen's head. Here was the gentleman who a few hours previously, had seemed to consist of legs in the shade of the curtain. Deep in an arm chair he was now reading the 3rd volume of Gibbon by candlelight. Automatically he knocked the ash now and again from his cigarette and turned the page, while a whole procession of splendid sentences entered his capacious brow and went marching through his brain in order. It seemed likely that this process might continue for an hour or more, until the entire regiment had shifted their quarters. But the door opened, and the young man who inclined to be stout came in with fat naked feet.

"Oh Hirst, what I forgot to say was—"

"Two minutes" said Hirst, raising his finger.

He safely stowed away the last word of the paragraph, "What was it you forgot to say?" he asked.

"D'you think we make enough allowance for feelings?" asked Hewet.

After intense contemplation of the immaculate Gibbon Mr Hirst smiled at the question of his friend.

"I should call yours a singularly untidy mind" he observed. "Feelings? aren't they just what we do allow for? We put love up there, and all the rest somewhere down below." With his left hand he indicated the top of a pyramid; with his right the base. "But you didn't get out of bed to tell me that" he added severely.

"I got out of bed" said Hewet vaguely, "to talk I suppose."

"Meanwhile I shall undress," said Hirst. When naked of all but his shirt, and bent over the basin, Mr Hirst no longer impressed one with the majesty of his intellect, but with the pathos of his young yet ugly body.

"Women interest me" said Hewet, who, sitting on the bed with his chin resting on his knees, paid no attention to the undressing of Mr Hirst.

"They're so stupid" said Hirst. "You're sitting on my pyjamas."

"I suppose they *are* stupid?" Hewet wondered.

"There can't be two opinions about that, I imagine," said Hirst, hopping briskly across the room, "unless you're in love. That fat woman Warrington?" he enquired.

"Not one fat woman—all fat women," said Hewet.

"The women I saw tonight were not fat" said Hirst, who was taking advantage of Hewet's company to cut his toe nails.

"Describe them" said Hewet.

"You know I can't describe things!" said Hirst. "They were much like other women, I should think. They always are."

"That's where we differ," said Hewet. "I say everything's different."

"So I used to think once" said Hirst. "But now they're all types. Take this hotel. You could draw circles round the whole lot of them, and they'd never stray outside."

"You can kill a hen by doing that" Hewet murmured.

"Mr Hughling Elliot, Mrs Hughling Elliot, Miss Allen, Mr and Mrs Thornbury—one circle—" said Hirst. "Miss Warrington, Mr Arthur Venning, Mr Perrott, Evelyn M. another circle; then there are a whole lot of natives; finally ourselves."

"Are we all alone in our circle?" asked Hewet.

"Quite alone" said Hirst. "You try to get out but you can't."

"I'm not a hen in a circle," said Hewet, "I'm a dove on a tree top."

"I wonder if this is what they call an ingrowing toe nail?" said Hirst examining the big toe on his left foot.

"I flit from branch to branch" continued Hewet. "The world is profoundly pleasant." He lay back on the bed, upon his arms.

"I wonder if it's really pleasant to be as vague as you are?" asked Hirst. "It's the lack of continuity—that's what's so odd about you" he went on. "At the age of twenty seven, which is nearly thirty, you seem to have drawn no conclusions. A party of old women excites you still as though you were three."

Hewet contemplated the angular young man who was neatly brushing the rims of toe nail into the fire place in silence for a moment.

"I respect you Hirst" he remarked.

"I envy you—some things" said Hirst. "One; your capacity for not thinking; two; people like you, better than they like me. Women like you, I suppose."

"I wonder whether that isn't what matters most" said Hewet. Lying now flat on the bed he waved his hand in vague circles above him.

"Of course it is" said Hirst. "But that's not the difficulty. The difficulty is, isn't it, to find an appropriate object."

"There are no female hens in your circle" said Hewet.

"Not the ghost of one" said Hirst.

Although they had known each other for three years Hirst had never yet heard the true story of Hewet's loves. In general conversation it was taken for granted that they were many; but in private the subject lapsed. The fact that he had money enough to do no work, and that he had left Cambridge after two terms owing to a difference with the authorities, made his life strange at many points where his friends' lives were all of a piece.

"I don't see your circles—I don't see them" said Hewet. "I see a thing like a teetotum spinning in and out—knocking into things—dashing from side to side—collecting numbers—

more and more and more, till the whole place is thick with them. Round and round they go—out there, over the rim out of sight."

His fingers showed that the waltzing teetotums had spun over the edge of the counterpane and fallen off the bed into infinity.

"Could you contemplate three weeks alone in this hotel?" asked Hirst.

Hewet proceeded to think.

"The truth of it is that one never is alone, and one never is in company" he concluded.

"Meaning?" said Hirst.

"Meaning? oh, something about bubbles—auras—what d'you call 'em? You can't see my bubble; I can't see yours; all we see of each other is a speck, like the wick in the middle of that flame. The flame goes about with us everywhere; it's not our selves exactly, but what we feel; the world in short. People mainly; all people. No one gets inside; but they colour stain the bubble. So, it follows, we're never alone and we never get out."

"A nice streaky bubble yours must be!" said Hirst.

"And suppose my bubble could run into someone else's bubble."

"And they both burst?" put in Hirst.

"Then—then—then" pondered Hewet, "It would be an e—nor—mous world" he said stretching his arms to their full width, as though even so they could hardly clasp the billowy universe.

"I don't think you're altogether as foolish as I used to be Hewet" said Hirst. "You don't know what you mean but you try to say it."

"But aren't you enjoying yourself here?" said Hewet.

"On the whole—yes" said Hirst. "I like looking at things. This country is amazingly beautiful. Did you notice how the top of the mountain turned yellow tonight? Really we must take our lunch and spend the day out. You're getting disgustingly fat." He pointed at the calf of Hewet's bare leg.

"We'll get up an expedition" said Hewet. "We'll ask the entire hotel. We'll hire donkeys and—"

"O Lord" said Hirst, "do shut it! I can see Miss Warrington and Miss Allen and Mrs Elliot and all the rest squatting on the stones and saying 'How jolly!'"

"We'll ask Venning and Perrott and Miss Murgatroyd—every one we can lay hands on" went on Hewet. "What's the name of the little old grasshopper with the eyeglasses? Pepper? Pepper shall lead us."

"Thank God, you'll never get the donkeys" said Hirst.

"I must make a note of that" said Hewet, slowly dropping his feet to the floor. "Hirst escorts Miss Warrington; Pepper advances alone on white ass; provisions equally distributed—or shall we hire a mule? The matrons—there's Mrs Paley, by Jove!—share a carriage."

"That's where you'll go wrong" said Hirst, "Putting virgins among matrons."

"How long should you think that a procession like that would take Hirst?" asked Hewet.

"From twelve to sixteen hours I should say" said Hirst. "The time usually occupied by a first confinement." It will need considerable organisation" said Hewet. He was now padding softly round the room, and stopped to stir the books on the table.

"We shall want some poets too" he remarked. "Not Gibbon; no; d'you happen to have Modern Love or John Donne? You see, I contemplate pauses when people get tired of looking at the view, and then it would be nice to read something rather difficult aloud."

"Mrs Paley will enjoy herself" said Hirst.

"Mrs Paley will enjoy it certainly" said Hewet. "It's one of the saddest things I know—the way elderly ladies cease to read poetry. And yet how appropriate this is—

"I speak as one who plumbs
Life's dim profound,
One who at length can sound
Clear views and certain.
But—after love what comes?
A scene that lours,
A few sad vacant hours,
And then, the Curtain"

I daresay Mrs Paley is the only one of us who can really understand that."

"We'll ask her" said Hirst. "Please Hewet, if you must go to bed, draw my curtain. Few things distress me more than moonlight."

Hewet retreated, pressing the poems of Thomas Hardy beneath his arm.

Between the extinction of Hewet's candle and the rising of a dusky Spanish boy who was the first to survey the desolation of the hotel in the early morning, a few hours of silence intervened. One could almost hear a hundred people breathing deeply. It would have been hard to escape sleep in the middle of so much sleep. All over the shadowed half of the world people lay prone, and only flickering lights in empty streets marked their cities. Red and yellow omnibuses were crowding each other in Piccadilly; sumptuous women were rocking at a standstill; but here in the darkness the owl fluted from tree to tree. When the breeze lifted the branches the moon flashed as if it were a torch. Until all people should awake again the houseless animals were abroad. There were tigers; there were stags; there were bisons drinking at pools. On one side of the world there were the carts and the men; on the other the animals. If we had done nothing to wound the earth, if the wind blew straight over hills and forests and sea, the day would be as the night. For six hours this profound beauty existed; then it became clearer and clearer, as the ground swam to the surface, that there are roads all over the earth, houses and details; we walk with short steps, and use short words. At nine o'clock precisely, the breakfast bell rang.

CHAPTER THIRTEEN

Breakfast being over, the ladies generally circled vaguely, picking up papers and putting them down again, about the hall.

"And what are you going to do today?" asked Mrs Elliot drifting up against Miss Warrington.

"I'm going to try to get Aunt Bessie out into the town" said Susan. "She's not seen a thing yet."

"I call it so spirited of her at her age" said Mrs Elliot, "coming all this way from her own fireside."

"We always tell her she'll die on board ship" said Susan. "She was born on one."

"In the old days" said Mrs Elliot, "a great many people were. I always pity the poor women so! We've got a lot to complain of!" She shook her head. "The poor little Queen of Holland! Newspaper reporters practically, one may say, at her bed room door!"

"Were you talking of the Queen of Holland?" said the pleasant voice of Miss Allen, who was searching for the thick pages of the Times among a litter of thin foreign sheets.

"I always envy any one who lives in such an excessively flat country."

"How very strange!" said Mrs Elliot. "I find a flat country so depressing."

"I'm afraid you can't be very happy here then Miss Allen," said Miss Warrington.

"On the contrary" said Miss Allen. "I am exceedingly fond of mountains." Perceiving the Times at some distance, she moved off to secure it.

"Well, I must find my husband" said Mrs Elliot.

"And I must go to My Aunt" said Miss Warrington.

Whether the flimsiness of foreign sheets and the coarseness of their type is any proof of frivolity and ignorance, there is no doubt that English people scarcely consider news read there as news, any more than programmes brought from men in the street inspire complete confidence. A very respectable elderly pair having inspected the long tables of newspapers, did not think it worth their while to read more than the headlines.

"The debate on the fifteenth should have reached us by now" said Mrs Thornbury. Mr Thornbury who was beautifully clean and had red rubbed into his handsome worn face like traces of paint on a weather beaten wooden figure, looked over his glasses and saw that Miss Allen had the Times.

The couple therefore sat themselves down in arm chairs and waited.

"Ah, there's Mr Hewet" said Mrs Thornbury. "Mr Hewet," she continued, "do come and sit by us. I was telling my husband how much you reminded me of a dear old friend of mine—Mary Appleby. She was a most delightful woman I assure you. She grew roses. We used to stay with her in the old days."

"No young man likes to resemble an elderly spinster" said Mr Thornbury.

"On the contrary" said Mr Hewet; "I take it as a compliment. Why did Miss Appleby grow roses?"

"Ah, poor thing," said Mrs Thornbury, "—that's a long story. She had gone through dreadful sorrows. At one time I think she would have lost her senses if it hadn't been for her garden. The soil was very much against her—a blessing in disguise; she had to be up at dawn—out in all weathers. And then there are creatures that eat roses. But she triumphed. She always did. She was a brave soul." She sighed profoundly.

"I did not realise that I was absorbing the paper" said Miss Allen.

"We were so anxious to read about the debate" said Mrs Thornbury accepting it on behalf of her husband. "One doesn't realise how interesting a debate can be until one has sons in the navy. My interests are equally balanced though; I have sons in the army too; one son who makes speeches at the Union—my baby!"

"Hirst would know him I expect" said Hewet.

"Mr Hirst has such an interesting face" said Mrs Thornbury. "But I feel one ought to be very clever to talk to him. Well William?" she enquired, for Mr Thornbury grunted.

"They're making a mess of it" said Mr Thornbury. He had reached the second column of the report; the Irish members had been brawling three weeks ago at Westminster. It was a question of naval efficiency. After a disturbed paragraph or two, the column of print once more ran smoothly.

"You have read it?" Mrs Thornbury asked Miss Allen.

"I am ashamed to say I have only read about the discoveries in Crete" said Miss Allen.

"Oh but I would give so much to realise the ancient world!" cried Mrs Thornbury. "Now that we old people are alone I am really going to put myself to school again. After all we are founded on the past, aren't we Mr Hewet? My soldier son says that there is still a great deal to be learnt from Hannibal. One ought to know so much more than one does. Somehow when I read the paper, I begin with the debates first, and before I've done the door always opens—But *you* begin at the beginning. I envy you Miss Allen."

"When I think of the Greeks I think of them as naked black men" said Miss Allen, "which is quite incorrect I'm sure."

"I'm afraid I don't think of them very much" Hewet confessed. "Except as people lying under trees talking perpetually. I read wherever I happen to open."

"And you, Mr Hirst? I'm sure you read everything," said Mrs Thornbury, perceiving that the gaunt young man was near.

"I confine myself to cricket and crime" said Hirst. It was not true.

Mr Thornbury threw down the paper, and emphatically dropped his eyeglasses. The sheets fell in the middle of the group, and were eyed by them all.

"It's not gone well?" asked his wife, solicitously.

Hewet picked up one sheet and read, "An aged lady was walking yesterday in the streets of Westminster when she perceived a cat in the window of a deserted house. The famished animal—"

"I shall be out of it anyway" Mr Thornbury interrupted.

"Cats are often forgotten" said Miss Allen.

"Remember John, the Prime Minister has reserved his answer" said Mrs Thornbury.

"At the age of eighty, Mr William Harris of Eeles Park, Brondesbury, has had a son" said Hirst.

"—the famished animal, which had been noticed by workmen for some days, was rescued, but—by Jove! It bit the man's hand to pieces!"

"Wild with hunger I suppose" commented Miss Allen.

"You're all neglecting the chief advantage of being abroad" said Mr Hughling Elliot, who had joined the group. "You might read your news in French, which is equivalent to reading no news at all."

Mr Elliot disguised his profound knowledge of mathematics by always talking about the French, and quoting phrases, upon which such exquisite care was spent that it seemed improbable that he could talk French which was useful.

"Coming?" he asked the two young men. "We ought to start before it's really hot."

"I beg of you not to walk in the heat, Hugh" his wife pleaded, giving him an angular parcel enclosing half a chicken and some raisins.

"Hewet will be our barometer" said Mr Elliot. "He will melt before I shall."

Indeed, if so much as a drop had melted off his spare ribs, the bones would have lain bare.

The ladies were left alone, surrounding the Times. Miss Allen looked at her father's watch.

"Ten minutes to eleven" she said.

"Work?" asked Mr Thornbury.

"Work" replied Miss Allen.

"What a fine creature she is!" murmured Mrs Thornbury, as the square figure in its manly coat, withdrew.

"And I'm sure she has a hard life" sighed Mrs Elliot.

"Oh it *is* a hard life" said Mrs Thornbury. "Unmarried women—earning their livings—it's the hardest life of all."

"Yet she seems pretty cheerful" said Mrs Elliot.

"It must be very interesting" said Mrs Thornbury. "I envy her her knowledge."

"But that isn't what women want" said Mrs Elliot.

"I'm afraid it's all a great man can hope to have" said Mrs Thornbury. "I believe that there are more of us than ever now. Sir Harley Lethbridge was telling me only the other day how difficult it is to find boys for the navy—partly because of their teeth, it is true. And I have heard young women talk quite openly of—"

"Dreadful dreadful" said Mrs Elliot. "The crown, as one may call it, of a woman's life. I, who know what it is to be childless—" she sighed and ceased.

"But we must not be hard" said Mrs Thornbury. "The conditions are so much changed since I was a young woman."

"Surely maternity does not change" said Mrs Elliot.

"In some ways we can learn a great deal from the young" said Mrs Thornbury. "I learn so much from my own daughters."

"I believe that Hughling really doesn't mind" said Mrs Elliot. "But then he has his work."

"Women without children can do so much for the children of others" said Mrs Thornbury.

"I sketch a great deal" said Mrs Elliot, "but that isn't really an occupation. It's so disconcerting to find girls just beginning doing better than one does oneself!"

"Are there not institutions—clubs—that you could help?" asked Mrs Thornbury.

"They are so exhausting" said Mrs Elliot. "I look strong, because of my colour; but I'm not; the youngest of eleven never is."

"If the mother is careful before" said Mrs Thornbury, "there is no reason why the size of the family should make any difference. I believe the statistics prove that the younger children are more interesting than the elder. In our family, the baby, Edward, is certainly the cleverest; though the eldest Ralph, is very clever in his own way, and he is always so nice about his brother's successes. You can't imagine two boys more devoted, though they're so different."

"My mother had two miscarriages I know" said Mrs Elliot, meditatively, touching two fingers. "One because she met a bear unexpectedly; the other—oh it was a dreadful story—The cook had a child, and there was a dinner party. So I put my dyspepsia down to that."

"And a miscarriage is so much worse than a confinement" said Mrs Thornbury, adjusting her eyeglasses, and taking up the Times.

Having heard what that one voice of the million voices speaking in the paper had to say, and noticing that a second cousin had married a clergyman at Minehead, ignoring the drunken women, the Cretan golden animals, the movements of battalions, the dinners, the reforms, the fires, the indignant, the learned and the benevolent, Mrs Thornbury went to write a letter for the mail. The paper lay directly beneath the clock; the two seemed to represent stability in a changing world. Mr Perrott, passed through; Mr Venning poised for a second on the edge of the table. Mrs Paley was wheeled past. Susan followed. Mr Venning strolled after her. Portuguese military families, their clothes suggesting late rising in untidy bedrooms, trailed across, attended by confidential nurses, carrying noisy children.

As midday drew on, and the sun beat straight upon the roof, an eddy of great flies droned in a circle; iced drinks were served under the palms; the long blinds were pulled down with a shriek, turning all the light yellow. The clock now had a silent hall to tick in, and an audience of four or five somnolent merchants. By degrees white figures with shady hats came in at the door, admitting a wedge of the hot summer day, and shutting it out again. After resting in the dimness for a minute, they went up stairs. Simultaneously, the clock wheezed One, and the gong sounded, beginning softly, working itself into a frenzy, and ceasing. There was a pause. Then all those who had gone up stairs came down; cripples came, planting both feet on the same step, lest they should slip; prim little girls came, holding the nurse's finger; fat old men came still buttoning waistcoats. The gong had been sounded in the garden, and by degrees recumbent figures rose and strolled in to eat, since the time had come. There were pools and bars of shade in the garden even at midday.

Partly owing to the heat, partly to the fact that lunch was the prelude to rest, conversation was never luxurious at lunch. Distributed at many small tables, people eat, for the most part, in silence, grateful if there was some one new to look at, for then fresh guesses could be made.

"The diplomatist has got a friend" said Mrs Paley to Susan.

"I shouldn't like to say what *she* is" the old lady chuckled, surveying a tall woman from whose festive appearance and painted hollows the worst conclusions were always drawn in whispers. Susan, although she was thirty, still blushed, admitted to the talk of matrons.

Lunch went on methodically, until each of the seven courses was left in fragments and the fruit was merely a toy, to be peeled and sliced as a child destroys a daisy petal by petal. The food served as an extinguisher upon any faint flame of the human spirit that might survive the midday heat. To the old it was pleasant to yield; the young were disturbed to find themselves no longer able to carve patterns on the world, and were therefore surly until they gave way. But Susan who was no egoist lay on her bed in a state of secure happiness, for Mr Venning had certainly moved a step further that morning.

From two to four it might be said without exaggeration that the hotel was inhabited by bodies without souls. Disastrous would have been the result if a fire or a death had suddenly demanded something heroic of human nature. But tragedies come in the hungry hours. Towards four o'clock the human spirit again began to lick the body, as a flame licks a black promontory of coal. Mrs Paley felt it unseemly to open her toothless jaw so widely, though there was no one near. Mrs Elliot surveyed her round flushed face anxiously in the looking glass. Great as the heat still was, the tide had turned; the blue was not going to burst into roaring fire, but to subside slowly into darkness. Indeed, the hours between tea and dinner were the pleasantest of the twenty four, for the hot spell filled the place of industry, so that both men and woman felt that they deserved the cool.

"You like your cup of tea too, don't you?" Mrs Paley said to Mrs Elliot, as she rolled through the hall. "Come and join us in the garden. Angelo had laid a table for us under the tree. A little silver goes a long way in this country" she chuckled. Susan was sent for a cup.

"They have such excellent biscuits in this hotel" said Mrs Paley. "Not sweet biscuits, which I don't like—dry biscuits…. Have you been sketching?"

"Oh I've done two or three little daubs" said Mrs Elliot, speaking rather louder than usual, "But it's so difficult after Oxfordshire, where there are so many trees. The light's so strong here. Some people admire it I know; but I find it very fatiguing."

"I really don't need cooking, Susan" said Mrs Paley, when her niece returned. "I must trouble you to move me."

Everything had to be moved. Finally the old lady was placed so that the light wavered over her, as though she were a fish in a net. Susan poured out tea, and was just remarking that they were having hot weather in Wiltshire too, when Mr Venning asked whether he might join them.

"It's so nice to find a young man who doesn't despise tea" said Mrs Paley, good humoured again. "One of my nephews the other day asked for a glass of sherry—at five o'clock! I told him he could get it at the public house round the corner but not in my drawing room."

"I'd rather go without lunch than tea" said Mr Venning, "That's not strictly true. I want both."

Mr Venning was a lean energetic young man, aged about thirty two. His friend Mr Perrott was a solicitor, of unprepossessing manners, and as Mr Perrott never went any where without Mr Venning, it was necessary when Mr Perrott came to Santa Rosa, about a company, for Mr

Venning to come too. He was a barrister by profession, but his passion was for aeroplanes. So long as his widowed mother lived, he had promised not to lose touch with the ground; but directly she was in her grave—"But she's a dear old lady—" he added, explaining the case to Susan—"Phit!" Mr Venning would mount high in air. Susan could only hope devoutly that another tie would then pin him to the earth.

"Don't you think it dreadfully cruel the way they treat dogs in this country?" asked Mrs Paley.

"I'd have 'em all shot" said Mr Venning.

"Oh, but the darling puppies" said Susan.

"Jolly little chaps" said Mr Venning. "Look here, you've got nothing to eat." A great wedge of cake was handed Susan on the point of a trembling knife. Her hand trembled too.

"I have such a dear dog at home" said Mrs Elliot.

"My parrot can't bear dogs" said Mrs Paley, with the air of one making a confidence. "I always suspect that he or she was teased by a dog when I was abroad."

"You didn't get far this morning, Miss Warrington" said Mr Venning.

"It was hot" she answered. Their conversation became private, owing to Mrs Paley's deafness, and the long sad history which Mrs Elliot had embarked upon of a wire haired terrier belonging to a deceased uncle which had committed suicide. "Animals do, I fear" she sighed.

"Couldn't we explore the town this evening?" Mr Venning suggested.

"My Aunt—" Susan began.

"You deserve a holiday" he said. "You're always doing things for other people."

"But that's my life" she said, under cover of refilling the tea pot.

"That's no one's life" he returned, "no young person's. You'll come?"

"I should like to come" she murmured.

At this moment Mrs Elliot jumped up and cried "Oh Hugh!"

"He's bringing someone" she added.

"He would like some tea" said Mrs Paley. "Susan, run and get some cups—there are the two young men."

"We're thirsting for tea" said Mr Elliot. "You know Mr Ambrose, Hilda? We met on the hill."

"He dragged me in" said Ridley, "or I should have been ashamed. I'm dusty, and dirty and disagreeable." He pointed to his boots which were white with dust; a dejected flower drooping in his button hole, like an exhausted animal over a gate, added to the odd effect of length and untidiness. He was introduced to the others. Mr Hewet and Mr Hirst brought chairs, and tea began again, Susan pouring cascades of water from pot to pot.

"I should explain that my wife's brother has a house, over there; and we are staying here; and I was sitting on a rock, filling my pipe, when your husband started up like a fairy in the pantomime," Ridley explained to Mrs Elliot.

["Our chicken got into the salt," Hewet said dolefully to Susan. "Nor is it true that bananas include moisture as well as sustenance."]

Mr Hirst was already drinking.

"And your wife?" asked Mrs Elliot.

"Helen's here, and so is Rachel, my niece."

"It's so delightful to meet friends in a foreign country."

"We've been cursing you" said Ambrose. "You tourists eat all the eggs, Helen tells me. That's a dreadful eyesore too" he pointed at the hotel. "We live with hens in the draw-ing room."

"The food is not what it ought to be considering the price" said Mrs Paley, "but unless one goes to a hotel where is one to go?"

"Stay at home, I should" said Ridley, "But nobody will."

"I believe in foreign travel myself" said Mrs Paley who had conceived a certain grudge against Mr Ambrose, "if one knows one's native land. I should certainly not allow any one to travel until they had visited Kent and Dorsetshire."

"Kent" said Mrs Elliot, "the hops—of course. But Surrey is my favourite."

"Some people like the flat and some people like the downs" Susan observed; but in her defence it must be observed that she was still pouring.

"Oh but we are all agreed by this time," Mr Hirst suddenly broke in, "that nature's a mistake. She's either hideous or she's terrifying. I don't know which alarms me most—a cow or a tree. I once met a cow in a field by night; it turned my hair grey. The creature looked at me."

"What did the cow think of him?" Mr Venning mumbled to Susan.

The crackle of cultivated paradox was as incense in the nostrils of Mr Elliot.

"Nature's too intractable, I suppose?" he remarked. "In my day the adjective was uncomfortable. Some one discovered the fact that we have hip bones."

Mr Hirst shut his mouth as though it were a spinster's purse. He saw through Mr Elliot and pronounced him shallow, a distinction quite beyond the grasp of Mrs Elliot who merely knew that her husband was being clever, and Mr Hirst was being clever, and she only wished she could be clever herself, but she wasn't as stupid as the others. For example, she could glide on quite naturally, turning to Mr Ambrose, "Wordsworth was a little over done perhaps."

"Poor old Wordsworth" said Ridley, who by reason of that simple remark, struck Mr Hirst as a fellow possibly worth talking to. Ridley was not the man to waste his time in uncomfortable quarters. The sun being less hot, and the mountains now purple with great angles of shadow across them, he was eager to be on his feet again, striding home. Politeness required him to thank Mrs Elliot for his tea, and to add, "You must come and see us." He glanced at every one. "We shall like it very much" said Mr Hewet. Ridley then left them.

CHAPTER FOURTEEN.

S tupendous though it seemed to hire donkeys and assemble people to ride them at the same spot at the same hour, in roughly equal numbers of the opposite sexes, some fifty minutes of less arduous thought than is needed to read a philosophic article, achieved the task. When next day Helen's note came, saying "My niece and I shall be glad to accept your invitation" it seemed to Hewet that to be a great general would not need much genius; rather the power of focusing the mind on facts instead of ideas, which was painful, as it is painful to count pebbles on a path, but not difficult.

Hirst was quick to point out that all the difficulties remained. "You've got your pebbles together; now what are you going to do with them?" "Oh they'll settle that" said Hewet.

"Remember, there are two women you've never seen" said Hirst. "Suppose one of them has a tendency to mountain sickness or only talks German, and the other—"

"has a hump on her back and a long black tail—I shall introduce her to you" said Hewet.

Nevertheless, as he walked in advance of the carriages to the meeting place, one fine hot Friday, he felt nervous. The least philosophic, when they have committed themselves to action, ponder for a moment on the brink. What do we expect to get from all this stirring about of bodies? Mr Hewet reflected. Cows draw together in the damp; ships in a calm; so, too, men and women when they are unoccupied.

Is it to prevent ourselves from seeing to the bottom, as a child disturbs a shallow pool to create phantom caves and submerged ranges, is it that we love each other, or is it that we have learnt nothing, know nothing, but leap from moment to moment as from world to world? A little stream crossed the road, which Hirst took almost in his stride; Hewet paused.

"Now I've boarded the new world!" he cried within himself, leaping high into the air and landing on both feet.

Half a mile further, they came to a group of plane trees and the salmon pink farm house standing by the stream which had been chosen as meeting place. It was a shady spot, lying conveniently just where the hill sprung out from the flat. Between the thin stems of the plane trees the young men could see little knots of donkeys pasturing; a tall woman was rubbing the nose of one of them; another woman was kneeling by the stream lapping water out of her palms.

As they entered the shady place, Helen looked up and then held out her hand.

"I must introduce myself" she said, "I am Mrs Ambrose."

Having shaken hands, she said "That's my niece."

Rachel approached sadly and awkwardly. She held out her hand, but withdrew it. "It's all wet" she said.

Scarcely had they spoken, when the first carriage drew up. The donkeys were quickly jerked into attention; then the second carriage arrived. The grove filled with people—the Elliots, the Thornburys, Mr Venning and Susan, Miss Allen, Evelyn Murgatroyd, and Mr Perrott. Mr Hirst acted the part of a hoarse energetic sheep dog. By means of a few words of caustic Latin he had the animals marshalled; by inclining a sharp shoulder he lifted the ladies. "What Hewet fails to understand" he remarked, "is that we must break the back of the ascent before midday." He was assisting Evelyn Murgatroyd as he spoke. She rose light as a bubble to her seat. With a feather dropping from a broad brimmed hat, in white from top to toe, she looked like a gallant lady of the time of Charles the First leading royalist troops into action.

"Ride with me" she commanded; and, as soon as Hirst had swung himself across a mule, the tow started, heading the cavalcade. "You're not going to call me Miss Murgatroyd. I hate it" she said. "My name's Evelyn. What's yours?"

"St John" he said.

"I like that" said Evelyn. "And what's your friend's name?"

"His initials being R. S. T., we call him Monk" said Hirst.

"Oh you're all too clever" she said, "Which way? Pick me a branch. Let's canter."

Evelyn's career which being full and romantic must be summarised, is best hit off by her own words. "Call me Evelyn; and I'll call you St John;…. I hate Miss Murgatroyd." She was always saying that; great numbers of young men had made the spirited answer; but she went on saying it, as though determined not to suffer the romantic spirit of her age to die discouraged.

But, sitting on an ass instead of a horse, she could not give wings to romance at present; she jogged on solitary, for the path when it began to ascend one of the spines of the hill became narrow and scattered with stones. The cavalcade wound on like a jointed caterpillar, tufted with the white parasols of the ladies, and the panama hats of the gentlemen. At one point where the ground rose sharply, Evelyn M. jumped off, threw her reins to the native boy, and adjured St John Hirst to dismount too. Their example was followed by those who felt the need of stretching.

"I don't see any need to get off" said Miss Allen to Mrs Elliot just behind her, "considering the difficulty I had in getting on."

"These little donkeys stand anything, n'est ce pas?" Mrs Elliot addressed the guide; who obligingly bowed his head.

"Flowers" said Helen stooping to pick the lovely little bright flowers which grew separately here and there.

"You pinch their leaves and then they smell" she said laying one on Miss Allen's knee.

"I think we must have met before" said Miss Allen.

"I was taking it for granted" Helen laughed.

"How sensible!" chirped Mrs Elliot. "That's just what one would always like—only unfortunately it's not possible."

"Not possible?" said Mr Hewet, "Everything's possible, Mrs Elliot, "Who knows what mayn't happen before nightfall?" Helen continued mocking the poor lady's timidity. She depended so implicitly upon one thing following another that the mere glimpse of a world where dinner could be disregarded, or the table moved one inch from its accustomed place, filled her with fears for her own stability.

Higher and higher they went, becoming separated from the world. The world when they turned to look back, flattened itself out, and was marked with squares of thin green and grey.

"The world's so big—the towns are so small" Rachel breathed, obscuring Santa Rosa with one hand. The sea filled in all the angles smoothly, breaking in a white frill, and out upon the flat blue, ships were set like toys. The sea was stained with purple and green blots and there was a glittering line upon the rim. All these things were observed by the party when they halted and sat for a time in a quarry on the hill side. Those who spoke—speech was a duty to some of them—said that the sight was beautiful—so clear—so unlike anything in England. The sense of expanded eyes, which overcomes certain people on a height, and makes speech impossible and sleep desirable, kept Helen and one or two others silent. Evelyn M. her chin upon her hand, surveyed the land with the eye of a conqueror.

"D'you think Garibaldi was ever up here?" she asked Mr Hirst. Oh, if she had been his bride. If, instead of a picnic party, this was a party of patriots, and she, red shirted like the rest, had lain among grim men, flat on the turf, aiming her gun at the white turrets beneath them, screening her eyes to pierce through the smoke! She stirred restlessly, and exclaimed "I don't call this life, do you?"

"What do you call life?" said St John angular upon his elbow.

"Fighting—revolution" she said, still gazing at the doomed city. "You only care for books I know."

"You're quite wrong," said St John.

"Explain" she urged, for as there were no guns to be aimed at bodies she turned to another kind of warfare.

"What do I care for? People" he said.

"Well I *am* surprised!" she exclaimed. "You look so awfully serious. Do let's be friends and tell each other what we're like. I hate being cautious, don't you?"

But she shut the spinster's purse, if that is not too wild an image to apply to St John's neat pale lips. He was decidedly cautious; he believed neither in the honesty of women; nor in making himself ridiculous.

"The ass is eating my hat" he said, and reached out for it. Miss Murgatroyd looked at him sharply. She knew that she was beaten; she flinched, but turned her guns with the decision of a great commander upon Mr Perrott. He should lead her donkey. St John had lost his chance, for ever.

A French proverb about eating one's omelette when one had laid one's eggs, exquisitely pronounced by Mr Elliot was taken even by those who knew no French to mean that they must push on. The midday which Mr Hirst had foretold was upon them. The higher they got the more of the sky appeared, until the mountain was only a small tent of earth against an enormous blue back ground. The English fell silent, but the natives sang. It was obvious to everyone that a greater strain was being put upon their bodies than is quite legitimate in a party of pleasure. It was necessary for the ladies to exercise some self control, and they had forgotten their hats in the desire for comfort, which if Hewet observed it, was an ominous sign. Mrs Elliot said something peevish about expeditions in the heat being a mistake; but Miss Allen merely answered "I always like to get to the top." The vivacious white figure, now crowned with leaves, rode well in front, two gentlemen at her side, and with such a spirit urging on, the older riders might well despair.

"The view will be wonderful" Hewet remarked, turning his in saddle. He raised no comment, but Rachel meeting his eyes, smiled. Then they saw that Evelyn was off her ass, and that Mr Perrott was standing like a statesman in Parliament Square, stretching an arm of stone towards the view. A mound loaded with blocks of stone lent shade.

"That must be the old watch tower" said Hirst, and looked back to see whether the sumpter mules carrying wine and food were at hand. "Thank Goodness" Mrs Elliot murmured, "I really couldn't have stood the heat much longer" she confided to Mrs Thornbury, who conscious that her own heart was legitimately weakened by the bearing of eleven healthy children only said "The view no doubt will be magnificent."

Coming out upon the other side of a familiar object has often a chilling effect. A sense of smallness overcomes the gazer; and this is more true in a foreign land where the far off hills and scattered villages have no names than in England. Even Susan who had as she called it 'many ties' or reasons for believing in the reality of a great many people, suddenly felt herself free. Class rooms, store rooms, had no power over her, beholding the grey sands, the dark forests, and the infinite distances of South America. As for Rachel she was spell bound, imagining herself a Victory who could fly. A cold breeze played upon them refreshing as the spray of a douche. Despondency or fatigue gave way to a triumphant feeling.

"I am glad we came" said Mrs Elliot, turning her back on the view and feeling a strange superiority to friends of hers who were now bicycling along the streets of Oxford.

"Oh isn't it splendid!" cried Evelyn M. grasping the first hand she felt—it was Miss Allen's.

"North South East West" said Miss Allen; the first line of a lyric poem. Their skirts flapped like flags on a high staff, and Mr Hewet crouched binding his knees with his arms, observed how strangely the row of figures bending slightly forward and plastered with cloth, suggested naked pieces of sculpture.

Set thus on a pedestal of earth human beings looked strange and noble. But they must eat.

"Chicken—no that's cheese—Eggs or raisins first? There must be green food somewhere" Hirst explored the baskets. They were to dine beneath the ruined wall.

"Our ancestors came up here three hundred years ago" said Mr Elliot to Helen. "Have you such a thing as a historical imagination?" he asked Rachel. "I haven't."

Rachel liked thinking about the past; but there seemed little welcome for her theory about a river with little islands in it, at present; she considered Hughling, to Helen's amusement, judged him a dry old Devil, and said "No."

But Hewet brought her a stone which had been chisselled.

"They shot a man and buried him up here" he said.

"I'd like to dig him up, wouldn't you?" Rachel remarked, handling it.

"I'd like to see people who've been dead hundreds of years" she continued.

"There are such numbers of them" said Hewet, ruefully turning the stone in his hands.

"Folded in bed with pink cheeks and silver embroideries" said Rachel.

"Yes they never are a mass of worms, as one expects" said Helen. "They're almost always dry."

When St John Hirst handed her a parcel of food she looked up at him and said, "Do you remember—two women?"

"I do" he returned.

"I knew you by your legs" she said.

"They came and spied and ran away" St John explained. "They were laughing at us."

"We were seeing life" Helen told Mr Elliot who had fixed his eyeglasses with a view to understanding the situation. "Your lights looked so tempting. We crept round and watched you playing cards. We thought no one saw us—but he did."

"Oh you're the two women!" Hewet burst in, "And we were thinking you might have mountain sickness and tails! Hirst couldn't describe you."

"I could describe every one of you" said Helen.

"It was like a thing in a play to us" said Rachel. "One expected it all to drop into Hell the next moment."

"I don't know whether you agree, but there is something dreadful in being seen when one isn't conscious of it" said Mr Elliot.

"Looking at one's tongue in a hansom?" said Hewet.

"I like looking glasses in hansoms" said Rachel, "because—" then she turned shy, for Miss Allen and the others had come to sit in a circle round the hampers.

"Because?" said Miss Allen.

"One has a nose or a mouth alone, you see" Rachel stumbled, "Most people get ugly somewhere."

"But too true" Mr Elliot laughed.

"There will soon be very few hansoms left" said Mrs Elliot. "I wonder what becomes of the poor dear horses. Every change means pain to some creature" she sighed.

"When they see us falling out of aeroplanes they must laugh" said Mr Venning. Susan shuddered.

"You fly?" said Mr Thornbury, and every one gazed at him.

"I hope to fly some day" said Mr Venning modestly, unable to explain that to leave the earth was only possible when his mother lay beneath it.

"It will be quite necessary in time of war" said Mrs Thornbury in her sweet judicial voice. "My boy tells me that there is already a great demand for instruction."

The opinion of the party was that to fly was terrible.

"No" she said, "I think it's fine. If I were a young fellow I should certainly learn. We are a great people and cannot flinch from knowledge. We must go on, or we shall be left behind."

"One would never think it, of a modest little old lady eating a sandwich on a hill top" Mr Hewet reflected. "But she's put us back in Whitehall in an instant."

The ants however removed the burden. They had a home in the loose brown earth piled between the gaps in the wall; and Miss Allen was in the line of their march.

"I'm covered with little creatures" she suddenly announced, gently brushing her skirts. "Although they are not little—they are remarkably large." She held out one on the back of her hand for Helen to look at.

"Suppose they sting?" said Helen.

"They will not sting" said Miss Allen. "But they may infest the victuals."

The ants were irresistible. Susan and Mr Venning loved ants. They called them Great Aunts. They laughed whenever they say an Ant. They laughed when Miss Allen said she always called them Emmets. They built barricades of crust and dug trenches of salt. The unprepossessing Mr Perrott said "Permit me" and removed an Ant from Evelyn's neck. "Miss Vinrace is all over Ants" they cried, and Rachel blushed and stammered until it struck her that the way to feel at ease was to offer to undress and search for Ants.

"It would be no laughing matter really" Mrs Elliot murmured to Miss Allen "if an Ant did get between the skin and the vest."

"I don't wear a vest" said Miss Allen, and Helen asked her to name her underclothes.

Suddenly as a pallor crosses the surface of water, Hewet felt despair. If you do not laugh when others are laughing you are liable to feel despair.

"They are not satisfactory; they are ignoble" he thought. "I brought them up here, and I've nothing to do with them. After all these centuries" he meditated, "these are men and women! I've been stooping to walk with you; if one stands erect—how contemptible!" He glanced round the circle; saw many sweet amiable modest eyes, lovable in their contentment, respectable in their discipline, but how mediocre in their soul, and capable of what insipid cruelty! Mrs Thornbury so sweet but so trivial in her maternal egoism; Mrs Elliot a woman to sting greatness whenever she found it; her husband a dry pea in a pod; Miss Warrington a woman who had sacrificed herself and could never be used in a great adventure; Venning as honest and as brutal as a schoolboy; Mr Thornbury a worn mill horse plodding out his round; Evelyn M.—! and these were the pick of the race who had money and managed the world! One had only to put someone who was in sorrow among them, to imagine anyone who cared much for life or beauty, and what a long toil, what a waste would be inflicted on him, if he tried to share with them and not to scourge!

"There's Hirst" he pondered, coming to the figure of his friend, who with his usual concentration was peeling the skin off his chicken. "And he's as ugly as sin." For the ugliness of that honest man the rest were responsible, condemning him to live alone. Then he came to Helen who was laughing over Miss Allen's underclothes. The sound of it relaxed his tension, and he passed on to Rachel in a gentler mood. The look of vague speculation with which she regarded Mrs Elliott, now more than suspicious of an Ant in the middle of her back, aroused his curiosity.

"Bread?" he asked, "I want to know" he said, giving it her, "—what are you looking at?"

"Human beings" she answered, taking the slice. "At least—I would have told a lie, if you'd given me time."

"Perhaps you wouldn't mind?" said Mrs Elliot offering her back. "There—there—just where I can't reach." Rachel's unskilful fumbling with hook and eye stopped the talk.

"Why is it," Hewet speculated, "that all one's theories vanish, directly people move?"

When they all stood up, Susan and Mr Venning were seen to stand near each other, looking at the Ants.

"They are wonderful little creatures" said Susan and stooped to peer into one of the tunnels through which they poured. She had the look of a person seeing through a veil which intensifies and yet makes things dance a little.

The odd mood passed from one to the other. They might have been waiting for a great gun to go off. Presently the figures separated, some to lie in the shade, others to move the lunch things. Everyone was conscious that Susan and Mr Venning had gone off together, but no one looked, for to look would have been indecent. Susan knew that she had been left alone with a man, as though all the world had stared at her and with drawn.

"Shall we go there—over there to that rock?" Mr Venning said. Getting beneath its shade, he sat down first and then held out his hand. When she took it and looked at him there was no need to speak. This was the tremendous moment, when she gave herself, and felt her soul slip over the waterfall before she knew that he lay below to catch it. Inarticulately murmuring he drew her down to his breast, and after lying in his arms she murmured, "Was there ever such happiness as this?"

After a time they began to say irrelevant things—what they had first liked—"A buckle you wore one night at sea" said Arthur, and what Mr Perrott had been called at school, and how Susan liked peas, and Arthur—it was one of the first things she had noticed—didn't.

"And we've found each other" Arthur went on. She gave herself up to his embracing.

"They guessed at lunch" said Susan. "Perhaps they did" said Arthur. "Those Ants" Susan laughed. She trembled when she laughed, and then cried on his shoulder. At last they lay still hand in hand.

[One after another they rose and stretched themselves, and in a few minutes divided more or less into two separate parties. One of these parties was dominated by Hughling Elliot and Mrs. Thornbury, who, having both read the same books and considered the same questions, were now anxious to name the places beneath them and to hang upon them stores of information about navies and armies, political parties, natives and mineral products—all of which combined, they said, to prove that South America was the country of the future.

Evelyn M. listened with her bright blue eyes fixed upon the oracles.

"How it makes one long to be a man!" she exclaimed.

Mr. Perrott answered, surveying the plain, that a country with a future was a very fine thing.

"If I were you," said Evelyn, turning to him and drawing her glove vehemently through her fingers, "I'd raise a troop and conquer some great territory and make it splendid. You'd want women for that. I'd love to start life from the very beginning as it ought to be—nothing squalid—but great halls and gardens and splendid men and women. But you— you only like Law Courts!"

"And would you really be content without pretty frocks and sweets and all the things young ladies like?" asked Mr. Perrott, concealing a certain amount of pain beneath his ironical manner.

"I'm not a young lady," Evelyn flashed; she bit her underlip. "Just because I like splendid things you laugh at me. Why are there no men like Garibaldi now?" she demanded.]

[[Mr. Perrott, during]] years of toil had educated himself, and now supported himself and a sister and was worn and seasoned like a ruddy herring by hundreds and hundreds of hours over law books in a back room, "you don't give me a chance. You think we ought to begin things fresh. Good. But I don't see precisely—conquer a territory? But they're all conquered already aren't they?"

"It isn't any territory in particular" Evelyn explained. "It's the idea, don't you see? We lead such tame lives. And I feel you have splendid things in you."

The way matters would now go was sufficiently clear to Hewet who had been dreamily listening. He saw the scars and hollows in Perrott's sagacious face relax pathetically. He could even imagine the little calculation that was going on in his mind. Marriage was still beyond his means; and he was over forty.

Hewet strolled off to the ruin, where Mr Thornbury was instructing the ladies. The cultivated but somewhat cantankerous old gentleman was of opinion that the tower was not a tower, but a place for keeping cattle. "The pound or barton as we call it in England" he said. Helen, by suggesting that it really looked more like a tower, had to listen to a great many reasons to follow Mr Thornbury's argument, deduced from irregularities in the soil, and to sympathise

while he confuted the antiquaries of England who call everything a camp when it ought to be called a place for keeping
cattle.

"On my own ground in Sussex"—he began; an ominous
beginning.

Helen looked at Rachel and drooped an eyelid, which
meant, "Do what you like; I'm doomed."

"D'you think it matters?" Hewet asked Rachel, turning
away with her. "D'you mind whether that's a cattle shed or a
tower?"

"Not in the least" said Rachel.

"I do," said Hewet. "And what did you mean by saying
that if I'd given you time you would have told a lie?"

"I meant that I was afraid of you—not of you but of the
world" she answered.

"What has the world done to you?" he asked.

"It would probably laugh if I said what I thought" she
answered. "And men—" she hesitated.

"Yes?" he enquired.

"They're not easy to talk to because they suspect one.
Besides," she added, "women are kissed."

"Honestly," said Hewet, "I did not suspect you."

"You've a load of virtue on your back" said Rachel, "like
one of those ants, stealing the tongue."

Hewet who was filling his pipe, regarded Rachel, and
thought her more interesting than beautiful to look at,
because too pale and irregular in feature for beauty, she had
grey, long-shaped eyes, and a broad forehead.

"It's a pity that you should tell lies" he said, "and it's a
pity" here he began to puff "that when people meet they
should discuss dreary things. I want to read poetry. Do you
like poetry?"

"Yes, I like poetry" said Rachel, "I like Keats better than
Shelley."

"Now as I live," exclaimed Hewet, slapping himself, "I've lost that book: Wordsworth. I picked it up and put it in my pocket just as I was starting, along with my tobacco. Well it can't be helped. Hirst shall have another copy. But what are we to do. I can only remember bits.

"Duty Stern daughter of the Voice of God" he began.

"No hungry generations tread thee down" Rachel continued.

"No no no," he cried. "We shall have to talk instead of reading. Tell me, who is that beautiful lady?"

"Helen Ambrose" Rachel answered.

"What are you doing here?" he asked.

"Just living" said Rachel. "I play the piano, she's embroidering a great picture of a river, and Uncle Ridley edits Pindar. And now we're all on the top of a hill together. Who are they all?"

"Human beings" he answered. "Nothing in the world would make it possible for me to tell a lie."

"Then you shall explain" she said. "What d'you think of them?"

"Well," he answered, "when they sit still I hate them; and when they move I love—like them, that is to say."

"Is it that they join instead of being separate?" she asked.

"You can dislike any live thing" he said emphatically. "The things we hate are stays and horsehair. If I hadn't lost that book of poetry,—God knows how I did it—I could explain. I overslept this morning, so I just ran into Hirst's room, and took the first book I saw—but the question is, did I put it in my pocket or did I leave it in—the smoking room?"

"Go on talking" Rachel said within her, "I like your voice." It was a soft voice with a tendency to blur the edges of words and hesitate.

"D'ya have a feeling," she said aloud, that something is happening?"

He smiled at her.

"It may only be this odd prickly kind of air" he said. "How clear it all is! The mountains might have been shaved by razors. And the colour—" He drew in his breath, and stopped to gaze at the sharp range the body of which seemed made of intense blue mist.

They walked on a pace or two looking right away to the horizon, and then both dropped their eyes to earth simultaneously. They beheld a man and woman beneath them, pressed in each other's arms. They rolled slightly this way and that, as the embrace tightened and slackened. Then Susan pushed Arthur away, and they saw her head laid back upon the turf, the eyes shut, and a queer look of pallor upon it, as though she had suffered and must soon suffer again. She did not seem altogether conscious, which affected both Hewet and Rachel unpleasantly. When Arthur began butting her as a lamb butts a ewe, they turned away. Hewet looked, half shyly at Rachel, and saw that her cheeks were white.

"Oh how I hate it—how I hate it!" she cried to him.

"Yes" he said. "It's odd how terrible that seems, until one gets used to it. But you know, you must get used to it, because if you don't you will exaggerate its importance."

Already, under the influence of his kind tone which she had not expected, Rachel's terror passed.

"It's absurd of course" she said.

"We may take it for granted that they are engaged" said Hewet. "He'll never fly—or d'you think he'll have the strength of mind to persist?"

She understood that he was calming her, but did not resent it. "What a strange thing love is," she said, "making one's heart beat!"

"It's the only thing that has much effect" he answered. "You see, their lives are now altered for ever."

"One feels a queer kind of sympathy for them" said Rachel.

"D'you know, I could cry? and yet I don't know them."

"Just because they're in love" said Hewet. "I understand that. There is something horribly pathetic about it."

At this moment it struck them both that they did not know each other.

"I never heard your name" she said.

"Hewet" he answered. "Roger, Sydney, Terence Hewet.... A great encampment of tents" he said looking at the mountains. "I've been wondering what they looked like. Or a water colour drying in ridges."

They had walked to the edge of the mountain top, and Hewet proposed that they should sit down. He lay with his back to the rock apparently matching the view with other objects. His eyes were dreamy, reminding Rachel in their colour of the green flesh of a snail. She did not like to tell him so. She was much occupied with the idea that something was happening. She curled up beside him, and they both surrendered themselves to the content which great beauty inspires. After looking at the view, until her eyes felt enlarged, Rachel began considering the insect population in the grass. Here she made a red beetle into a Bishop kneeling in a vast cathedral, roofed with green; here she sent ants flying from blade to blade, in order that they might have adventures.

"Did you tell me your name?" Hewet said suddenly.

"Vinrace—Rachel."

"I had an Aunt called Rachel" said Hewet, "who put the life of Father Damien into verse."

"I have two Aunts. What are they doing at this moment I wonder. Buying wool! They are small rosy little women" she continued, "very clean." He signified interest and she went on. "They live in Richmond. They have a dog who will only eat the marrow out of bones. They—" Then the difficulty of describing people overcame her.

"It seems very insignificant here!" she concluded.

The sun was behind them, and two long shadows suddenly lay in front of them, one waving, because it was made by a skirt, the other stationary because thrown by a man in trousers.

"You look very comfortable!" said Helen.

"Those legs are the legs of Hirst" said Hewet, pointing to the scissor like shadow, and then rolled round to look up at them. "Won't you come and look at the view too?"

"Did you congratulate the young couple?" asked Hirst, when they had all settled down in a row upon the ground.

"They were not exactly in a condition to be congratulated" said Hewet.

"Embracing?" said Hirst "or what?"

"They seemed very happy" Hewet answered.

"Well," said Helen, "so long as I needn't marry either of them—"

"We were profoundly moved" said Hewet.

"I thought you would be" said Hirst. "Which was it? the thought of the immortal passions, or the thought of new born males, to keep the Roman Catholics out?" "He's capable of being moved by either" he said to Helen. Rachel was stung by his banter, and burst out "You can't deny that something has happened."

"It's the quality of the thing, isn't it?" said Hirst, who was now extended, with his head upon his hands, and his knee cocked up in the air.

"Or does everything move you equally?"

"Most things move her a good deal" Helen explained.

"Nothing moves Hirst" Hewet laughed, "unless it were a trans-finite number falling in love with a finite one."

"On the contrary" said Hirst, "I am a person of very strong passions. Don't you agree?" he said turning to Helen.

She saw that he was serious.

"I've known you four hours" she answered.

"Five and a half to be precise" he returned. "Well?"

"Ask me again when I've known you five and a half days" she said.

"A bargain" he concluded.

"By the way, Hirst" said Hewet, after they had sat silent for a minute or two, "I have a confession to make. Your book—"

"I know. Lost," said Hirst.

"There is still a chance," Hewet urged, "that I left it behind."

"There is not" said Hirst. "It is here" he slapped his breast.

"Thank God!" said Hewet. "I need no longer feel as though I had murdered a child!"

"Are you a person who always loses things?" Helen asked.

"Hirst wouldn't share a cabin with me because of my habits" he said.

"You came out together?"

"We are travelling together" he answered.

"I propose that each member of this party now gives a short biographical sketch of himself or herself" said Hirst sitting upright. "Miss Vinrace—you come first. Begin."

"I am the daughter of a man who owns ships" Rachel began. "Aged twenty four—That is my age, I mean. I live with Aunts at Richmond." ("Who keep a dog who eats marrow" Hewet murmured.) "Sometimes I travel with my father."

"Education?" Hirst asked.

"None."

"Tastes?" Hewet asked.

"Music."

"Brothers and sisters?"

"None."

"Mother alive?"

"No."

"Next" said Hirst having taken in these facts. "Hewet."

"I am the son of an English gentleman, aged twenty seven," said Hewet. "He died when I was ten, in the hunting field. I can remember his body coming home on a shutter (I suppose), just as I was—"

"Facts" Hirst interrupted.

"Yes. He left me an independence. I was educated at Winchester. I had to leave Cambridge after a time. I have done a good many things—"

"Profession?" "None—at least—"

"Tastes?" "Literary—decidedly literary and what I may call general."

"Brothers and sisters?"

"Three sisters and a mother."

"Is that all we're to hear about you?" said Helen. "I'm next? Well, I'm immensely old—forty last October. My father was a solicitor in the city. I have two sisters and three brothers."

"Education?" said Hirst. "A very mixed education" said Helen. "If I were to tell you everything—" she smiled and stopped.

"Do tell us everything" Hirst urged.

"It mightn't interest you" she said. "I had practically no education. An elder brother used to lend me books. Then I married when I was twenty eight, and I have two children. Now you" she pointed at Hirst.

"(You've left out a great deal" he reproved her.)

"My name is St John Alaric Hirst. I am twenty five years of age, the son of the reverend Mr Hirst, vicar of Great Wappyng in Norfolk. Oh I got scholarships everywhere—Westminster—Cambridge—I am now a Fellow of Kings. Doesn't it sound dreary? Parents both alive (alas). One sister living; no brothers."

"I suppose," said Rachel "you are what they call a distinguished man?"

"I am one of the three most distinguished men in England" said Hirst.

"Of course we've left out the only questions that matter" said Helen.

"Just what I was going to say" said Hewet.

"For instance—are we Christians?" said Helen. "I am not."

"I am not" said Hewet. "I am not" said Hirst.

"I suppose I am aren't I?" asked Rachel.

"You believe in a personal God?" Hirst demanded.

"I believe—I believe—I believe that there are things we don't know about which we feel and the world might change in a minute and any thing appear."

"No" said Helen. "She's not a Christian. She hasn't thought what she is really. Then there are other questions, which we can't ask yet."

"The most important of all—" said Hewet. "The really interesting ones."

"Whether we've ever been in love you mean" said Rachel. "That kind of question."

Helen burst out laughing.

"Having Rachel is like having a puppy in the house" she said. "She's always bringing underclothes down into the hall. Oh look!"

Again fantastic shapes moved across their feet—the shadows of men and women.

"There they are!" exclaimed Mrs Elliot. "Lying on the grass. And we've had such a hunt to find you. Do you know what the time is?" She playfully tapped the face of her watch.

"Time for tea" said Hewet rising.

"Time for putting on one's wraps" said Mrs Elliot. "It's quite chilly isn't it?" she asked Mrs Thornbury.

As Hewet had made himself responsible for all chills and discomforts felt that afternoon he led the way to the ruined watch tower, which Evelyn M. and Mr Perrott were decorating with a crimson scarf. The heat had changed just so far that instead of sitting in the shadow they sat in the sun; which was still hot enough to paint their faces red and yellow, and to colour great sections of the earth. The flasks of hot tea were passed round and round, and a delicious feeling of cheerful comfort ran through their veins.

"There's nothing so nice as tea!" said Mrs Thornbury.

"Nothing half so nice" said Helen speaking more quickly than usual. "Can't you remember as a child chopping up hay and pretending it was tea and getting scolded by nurses—why I can't imagine except that nurses are such brutes, won't allow pepper instead of salt though there's no earthly harm in it—weren't your nurses just the same?"

She began the sentence seeing Susan advancing; she went on with it while Susan made her way into the group and sat down by Helen's side. A minute later Mr Venning strolled up from the other direction,

"Oh how nice!" said Susan drinking.

"What have you been doing to that old chap's grave?" said Arthur in the tone of one who will laugh whatever answer is made.

"We have tried to make him forget his misfortune in having died three hundred years ago," said Mr Perrott.

"It would be awful—to be dead!" said Evelyn M.

"I wonder if any of us realises what it would be like to be dead?"

"It's quite easy to imagine" said Hewet. "When you go to bed to night, fold your hands so—breathe slower and slower" he lay back and shut his eyes. "Now I shall never move again."

"This is a horrible exhibition!" cried Mrs Thornbury.

"More cake for us!" cried Arthur.

"I assure you, it's quite easy to imagine," said Hewet, sitting up, and securing the cake.

"I was asking myself just now" said Mr Thornbury, "whether you would consider this a suitable spot to make an aeroplane ascent from? What are your exact requirements now?"

Arthur explained with unnecessary hilarity.

"You think there's going to be a great future for aeroplanes in England?" Susan asked Mrs Thornbury.

"We are sadly behindhand now" sighed Mrs Thornbury.

"Yet I scarcely see how one could be glad for one's son or anyone one cares about to adopt that profession" said Mrs Elliot.

"But one does want what is best for one's children— one does want that" said Mrs Thornbury. "With all the most profound feelings of one's life" she went on, speaking to the matrons, "one is conscious I think of a great division in one self and yet.... Well, one would cheerfully go to the stake rather than let a hair of their head be injured! She smiled seraphically. "You have children?" she asked Helen seeing that Helen's eyes were contemplative and mournful.

"Two" said Helen. She hastily emptied the cups on to the earth, conscious of sudden tears,

"I too!" thought Susan. "I am a woman with children too—one of the great company." She felt admitted to it, rather than framed the words. She marched one of the regiment which toils all through middle life in the heat.

"Come come—no time for lamentation or farewell, ladies and gentlemen," cried Hughling Elliot leading a fine grey donkey into their midst. "What do you think of this for a bargain? fine bright colour isn't it?"

He held out a silk hand kerchief, so bright that it made his hand look pale.

"I bought it from that fine fellow over there" he said. "It won't suit you Hilda; it's just the thing for Mrs Raymond Parry."

"Mrs Raymond Parry!" cried Helen and Mrs Thornbury simultaneously. They looked at each other as though a mist hitherto obscuring their faces had been blown away.

"You know Mrs Raymond Parry?" they said with one voice.

"Those wonderful parties!" Mrs Elliot exclaimed.

Mrs Parry's drawing room, though hidden behind a vast curve of water on a tiny piece of earth seemed to be the place where they were all anchored. Perhaps they had been in it at the same moment. There was no time to follow up the discovery, for the donkeys were gathering together. The older ladies began buttoning up their cloaks and making clothes fast in a way which reminded Rachel of servants bolting and barring the front door—a mediaeval custom, now superstitious. They filed off, down the hill side. Scraps of talk kept floating back from one to the other. Susan laughed tremulously; Mr Venning joked. Mr Elliot called back "Now who writes the best Latin verse in your college?"

But this was before the dusk came on; in the dusk the riders were almost silent, their minds spilling out as it were into the great blue space.

Suddenly, some one cried "Ah—!"

In a moment a slow yellow drop rose again from the town beneath them; it rose, paused, opened like a flower, and fell in a shower of drops.

"Fire works!" they cried.

Another went up more quickly; they could almost hear it twist and roar.

"That's just it" Rachel mused. "When people fall in love they seem to rush up like that; and we stare; our faces are white."

"Friday" said Mr Thornbury. "Some Saint or patriot I suppose."

Then the fireworks became erratic. Soon they stopped altogether, and the rest of the journey was made almost in darkness. Among the plane trees they separated, bundling into carriages and driving off.

It was so late that no interval of normal conversation intervened between their arrival at the hotel and bed.

"Well Hewet" said Hirst with his collar in his hand on the crest of a yawn. "It was a great success I consider." He yawned. "But take care you don't find yourself landed with that young woman" he added. "I don't really like young women."

Hewet was too much drugged by hours of fresh air to answer. In fact, every one of the party was sound asleep save Susan. She was lying in bed, a lighted candle beside her, with her two hands clasped above her heart. All articulate thought had deserted her. Her heart seemed to irradiate her entire being, and to have grown to the size of a sun, shedding, like the sun, a steady flood of warmth.

"This is happiness," she said. "I love every one. How easy to be good!"

Loving everyone she fell asleep.

CHAPTER FIFTEEN

By Wednesday the wires had flashed Arthur's name and Susan's name twice beneath the ocean. When the shock reached the breakfast table at Beryton parsonage in Wiltshire, it struck Mr Warrington speechless. Mary, behind her tea pot, flew round and read over his shoulder. Then she sang out, "Susan engaged!" and spun round the table. Arthur was described (leaving out the indefinite articles) as a barrister, aged thirty two; a blessing was asked; his mother's address in London followed. Mr. Warrington in his best clothes caught the afternoon train, supplied by Mary's forethought with a photograph of Susan holding a racquet, saw Mrs Venning, found her re-reading Arthur's wire, in which the adjective 'beautiful' had been inserted; and the interview between the two parents passed in each congratulating the other. They composed a joint message ("This is now my privilege" remarked Mr Warrington giving the maid a sovereign to send it with) in which their blessing rang with a double voice.

It was handed to Susan late on Tuesday evening; and before nightfall the splendid news was abroad. At first handshake Susan's eyes filled with tears; and Mrs Elliot got a kiss which made her suddenly feel very tenderly towards Hughling. Mr Perrott had long foreseen that his friend would marry; he knew what it meant; but he showed his usual sad dignity, only remarking with some point that he considered "Miss Warrington" "Susan" she interrupted,

"Miss Susan—the most fortunate of women." His business was only half through, and this determined the couple to miss the next boat and keep him company. Although Susan would have preferred to sail at once, and appear before the world engaged, she saw that Arthur disliked the thought, the feelings of engaged men being different on this point from the feelings of engaged women.

After all this handshaking had taken place, people were still unsatisfied. There are times when desires are general, as public inscriptions testify; this was one. The desire of the public was to do something to please the engaged couple; the desire of the engaged couple was to show their gratitude to the public.

"We must contrive some festivity" said Miss Allen.

"Something in which everybody can join" said Hewet.

"The worst of mountain expeditions is the insufficiency of asses."

"How would a dance do?" said Miss Allen.

"O do let's dance!" cried Evelyn M. who had joined the group under the leopard which held a lamp in his paws. "Nothing's such fun as a dance!" She whirled round on her toe. Hirst was seen to purse his lips.

The result of the talk was that a committee was formed, who promised to organise an entertainment satisfactory to everybody on Friday night. On Friday night there were always ices for dinner; Friday was the first anniversary—"Or what would be the proper term?" asked Miss Allen,—of the event. After all, the preparations were simple. Public feeling ran strongly in favour of a dance. The lounge had a floor which would do; and if there were any so sick or so surly as to prefer arm chairs or needlework or Bridge to spinning and watching others spin the drawing room and the billiard room were theirs. Music again could be supplied. There was an old Spaniard who could play the fiddle so as to make a tortoise waltz, and his daughter in spite of her melancholy black eyes had the same power over the piano. Hewet's part was to beseech dowagers and those ringed round according to Hirst with indelible circles of chalk, to spin across them into the ball room. At dinner he professed himself satisfied.

"They're all coming!" he announced to Hirst. "Pepper!" he cried, seeing William Pepper slip past in the wake of the soup, with a pamphlet beneath his arm, "We're counting on you to open the ball."

"You will certainly make sleep impossible," said William.

"You are to take the floor with Miss Allen" said Hewet consulting a sheet of pencil notes.

William Pepper smiled; then he propped his pamphlet—a work upon sedges, with illustrations which represented sections of plants as though they were slices of battleships—upon the decanter and began his dinner.

The dining room had a certain resemblance at this moment to a farm yard scattered with grain upon which bright pigeons kept descending. All the ladies wore dresses not yet shown; some were so wonderfully crowned with hair as to be new women.

The dinner was shorter and less formal than usual.

Ten minutes before the clock struck half past nine, the committee made a tour through the ball room.

"I think it looks nice and festive" said Miss Allen, who had arranged it with Evelyn M.

The lounge when emptied of its furniture brilliantly lit, and scented with flowers, presented a wonderful appearance of aetherial gaiety. "It's like a starlit sky" said Hewet.

"And a heavenly floor" said Evelyn, sliding daintily.

"It's a fine night too" said Hirst. "Must we have the curtains drawn?"

"On the whole—yes" said Hewet. "Curtains inspire confidence—don't you think so, Miss Murgatroyd?"

"O I love the night!" cried Evelyn.

"Elderly people will imagine there are draughts" said Miss Allen, and her word always settled arguments.

The father, the daughter, and the son in law who played the horn here flourished with one accord. Like the rats who followed the piper heads instantly appeared in the doorway. There was another flourish, and then the trio dashed spontaneously into the triumphant swing of the waltz. It was as though the room were instantly flooded with water. After a moment's hesitation first one couple, then another, leapt into midstream, and went round and round in the eddies. The rhythmic swish of the dancers sounded like a swirling pool. By degrees the room got perceptibly hotter. The smell of kid gloves mingled with the strong flower scent. The eddies seemed to circle faster and faster, until the music wrought itself into a crash; stopped; and the circles were smashed into little separate bits. The couples struck off in different directions, leaving a thin row of elderly people stuck fast to the walls. Here and there a piece of trimming or a handkerchief or a flower lay upon the floor.

When this had happened about five times, Hirst who leant against a window frame, like some singular gargoyle, perceived Helen Ambrose and Rachel in the doorway. The crowd was such that they could not move. What he could see of them, a piece of Helen's shoulder, Rachel's long blue skirt, seemed to him very interesting. As for Hirst's attire, rosy buttons grew in a cream coloured waistcoat. He made his way to them; they greeted him with relief.

"We are suffering the tortures of the damned" said Helen.

"This is my idea of Hell" said Rachel.

Her eyes were bright and she looked bewildered.

Hewet and Miss Allen who had been waltzing somewhat laboriously paused and greeted the new comers.

"This is nice" said Hewet. "But where is Mr Ambrose?"

"Pindar" said Helen. "May a married woman who was forty in October dance? I can't stand still." She seemed to fade into Hewet and they both dissolved in the crowd.

"We must follow suit" said Hirst to Rachel, and with a glance of despair mingled with determination they started. A single circuit of the room proved to them that their anatomies were unsuited; instead of fitting in to each other, the bones seemed to collide, making smooth turning an impossibility. The angles they made cut into the circular progress of the other dancers.

"Shall we stop?" said Hirst. Rachel agreed, profoundly conscious of her guilt. They found seats from which the dancing could be viewed.

"An amazing scene" said Hirst. "Do you dance much in London?"

"Not much. Do you?"

"My family gives one dance every Christmas. You see, I'm at Cambridge most of the year."

"The most distinguished man in England" Rachel quoted.

"One of the three" he corrected. "Was that all nonsense what you said the other day about being a Christian and having no education?"

"Practically true" said Rachel. "The thing is—what was I going to say—oh, I play the piano better than almost any body else."

Helen tossed a fan into Rachel's lap, whirling past.

"She is very beautiful" Hirst remarked.

"I wonder if you think me nice looking" Rachel reflected.

"About books now," said Hirst. "What have you read. Just Shakespeare and the Bible?"

"Why can't he talk simply." Rachel again reflected.

"I don't read much" she said aloud.

"D'you mean you've reached the age of twenty four without reading Gibbon?"

"Yes" she answered.

"Then you must begin tomorrow. What I want to know is—can one talk to you? I should have thought you might be intelligent."

"It's the Decline and Fall isn't it?" said Rachel.

"But what's the use of your reading it if you can't understand it?" said Hirst fixing her with his severe honest eyes. "I should think it quite possible that you have a mind, but it is doubtful if you can think honestly because of your sex you see."

"Well after all," sighed Rachel, "we can only wait and see."

"I was going to say that I could lend you books if you liked" Hirst continued. "Oh, they're beginning again. I am going to leave you."

He got up and went. Rachel was left like a child at a party, surrounded, so she fancied, by great hostile faces, hooked noses, and sneering indifferent eyes. But she was near a window, and she pushed it open with a jerk and stepped into the garden. The swinging and trampling had excited her; Hirst's words had roused a feeling of fury; the garden with its pale green squares where the light fell, swam for a moment behind tears.

"Considering that there are trees" she said, speaking half aloud to impress herself.

"There are trees" said Hewet, coming through the window.

"How wonderful they are! Even dance music can do it— can make them come out real." Smoothed of their detail the forms of the trees, and the mass of the earth, had a monumental look, as of stationary things, waiting. Now that the music had stopped it was possible to hear the leaves rustle and cease.

"You were dancing with Hirst?" said Hewet.

"He has made me furious" she cried vehemently, facing Hewet. "No one has any right to be insolent."

"Insolent.... Hirst?"

"It is insolent to say that women can't be honest, to condescend to me because I am a woman."

"Let us walk and explain" said Hewet, stepping on to the grass.

"I can't explain" she flashed. "But if I had a gun I would shoot him!"

"I feel sure he did not mean to hurt you" said Hewet.

"No: Helen would laugh" said Rachel more calmly. Hewet saw that soon the whole incident would be stored away in her mind to take its place in the view she had of life.

"Now you'll hate him" he said, "which is wrong. Poor old Hirst—he can't help his method. And really Miss Vinrace he was trying to pay you a compliment. He was trying—he was trying—" he could not finish for laughter. The thought of the interview tickled him immensely. Rachel veered round suddenly to the comic standpoint and laughed out too.

"He was trying to kiss me I suppose!" she cried.

"Of that I am not so sure" said Hewet, "But he was preparing the way."

"Then I shall do my part too" said Rachel. "'Mr Hirst'" I shall say, 'ugly in body and repulsive in mind as you are—'"

"Hear hear" cried Hewet. "That's the way to treat him. I see you'll get on splendidly. And now we must dance. Oh there's Pepper writing to his Aunt. You didn't know he had one? He takes her for walking tours in the New Forest. "Pepper" he cried, "come along and do your duty! Miss Allen is waiting. Now Miss Vinrace—" They swept off into the great swirling pool.

It was midnight and the dance was now at its height. Servants were peeping in at the windows; the garden was sprinkled with couples sitting out. Mrs Thornbury and Mrs Elliot sat side by side, holding fans, handkerchiefs, and brooches deposited by flushed maidens. Occasionally they exchanged comments.

"Miss Warrington does look happy" said Mrs Elliot; they both smiled and sighed.

"He has a great deal of character" said Mrs Thornbury, alluding to Arthur.

"And character is what one wants" said Mrs Elliot. "Now that young man is clever enough" she added, nodding at Hirst, who came past with Helen on his arm.

"He does not look strong" said Mrs Thornbury, "His complexion is not good.—Shall I tear it off?" she asked, for Rachel had stopped, conscious of a long strip trailing behind.

"Are you enjoying yourselves?" Hewet asked the ladies.

"This is a very familiar position for me!" said Mrs Thornbury. I have brought out five daughters—and they all loved dancing!" You love it too Miss Vinrace?" she asked looking at Rachel with maternal eyes. "I know I did when I was your age. How I used to beg my mother to let me stay— and now I sympathise with the poor mothers—but I sympathise with the daughters too."

"She is what you call a sympathetic woman" said Rachel as they turned.

"Yes; but I don't think she bullies her daughters" said Hewet. "Or is she a terrific tyrant at home?"

"I think she might be" said Rachel, "supposing one didn't love dancing."

"They seem to find a great deal to say to each other" said Mrs Elliot, smiling significantly at the backs of Hewet and Rachel. "Did you notice at the picnic? He was the only person who could make her utter."

"Her father is a very interesting man" said Mrs Thornbury. "He has one of the largest businesses in Hull.

He made a very able reply you remember, to Mr Balfour at the last election. It is so interesting that a man of his experience should be a strong Protectionist."

But Mrs Elliot would only talk about the Empire in a less abstract form.

"There are dreadful accounts from England" she said, "about the rats. A sister in law, who lives in Norwich, tells me it is quite unsafe to order game. The plague—you see. It attacks the rats and through them other creatures."

"And the local authorities are not taking proper steps?" asked Mrs Thornbury.

"That she does not say. But she describes the attitude of the educated people—who should know better—as callous in the extreme. Of course my sister in law is one of those active modern women, who always takes things up you know—the kind of woman one admires though one does not feel, at least I do not feel—But then she has a constitution of iron."

Mrs Elliot brought back to the consideration of her own delicacy here sighed.

"A very animated face" said Mrs Thornbury, looking at Evelyn M. who had stopped near them to pin tight a scarlet flower at her breast. It would not stay, and with a spirited gesture of impatience she thrust it into her partner's button hole. He was a tall melancholy youth who received the gift as a knight his lady's token.

"Very trying to the eyes" was Mrs Elliot's next remark, after watching the yellow whirl in which so few of the whirlers had either name or character for her, for a few minutes.

"May I sit by you?" said Helen, breathing fast, "I suppose I ought to be ashamed of myself," she said sitting down. "At my age."

Her beauty now that she was flushed and animated was more expansive than usual. Both the ladies felt the same desire to touch her.

"I am enjoying myself" she panted. "Movement—isn't it amazing."

"I have always heard that nothing comes up to dancing if one is a good dancer" said Mrs Thornbury.

Helen swayed slightly as if still on wires.

"I could dance for ever" she said. "They ought to let themselves go more" she exclaimed. "They ought to leap and swing. Look! How they mince!"

"Have you seen those wonderful Russian dancers?" began Mrs Elliot. But Helen saw her partner coming and rose as the moon rises. She was half round the room before they took their eyes off her.

Directly she was left alone, the gentleman having gone to find an ice, St John Hirst stood beside her.

"Are you disengaged?" he said. "Should you hate sitting out? I am quite incapable of dancing." The ice was brought; the anonymous gentleman whose blood ran darker than is nice, bowed, hoped for another opportunity, and disappeared.

"How like a toad!" said St John. He piloted Helen to a corner on the verge of the dancing area, where two arm chairs stood empty.

"Do you really enjoy this kind of thing?" he asked.

"Love it," said Helen. "You don't?"

"Perhaps I might" he answered. "But I always connect it with large family parties at Christmas—snow holly, cousins, all that's most detestable."

"Don't you get on with your family?" Helen asked.

"Does any one?" he replied.

"You see, I think one does want the society of one's intellectual equals. There's no one here—excepting ourselves—that one can talk to—though poor old Hewet does try."

"You can talk to us?" said Helen smiling.

"Of course" he said. "I'm not quite sure though about Miss Vinrace. Somehow, I don't think we got on."

"O you should laugh at her" said Helen.

"But I knew the moment I saw you that I should be able to talk to you" said Hirst. "I think you have an honest mind."

"That's a great compliment" said Helen, she looked greatly pleased.

"There are fearfully few people one can talk to" he said. "Or perhaps I've been unfortunate. I haven't got many friends. Should you say I was a difficult kind of person to get on with?"

"All clever people are difficult when they are young" said Helen. "I'm rather like it myself."

"Yes; I am immensely clever" said Hirst. "I'm infinitely cleverer than Hewet. Besides being clever I'm really rather important. D'you understand the distinction? There are lots of people who are clever (Hughling Elliot for example) but only two or three who really matter. That's what one's family doesn't see."

"They want you to be something I suppose?"

"They would like me to be a Peer and a Privy Councillor. My father wants me to go to the Bar."

"What do you want?"

"That's just the difficulty" said Hirst sighing. "I've come to the turning point. Either I must go to the Bar, or I must stay at Cambridge. There are drawbacks to both. I am conscious too of great powers of affection. On the other hand I am not really passionate, as Hewet is for instance. I am very fond of a few people. I think for example that there's something to be said for my mother, though she is in many ways so deplorable. Well, if I stay on at Cambridge I shall inevitably become the most eminent person there. London on the other hand—do you live in London?"

"Yes" said Helen, "we live in Richmond Square."

"Should you mind if I came to see you?"

"I should like it" said Helen.

"You can't think," he said almost with emotion, "what a difference it makes finding someone to talk to. I feel as if you understood me. I'm very fond of Hewet, but he hasn't the remotest idea what I'm like. D'you think there's any truth in what people say about women's intuition?"

"I expect it's age in my case" said Helen.

"The odd thing is I feel as though we were exactly the same age" said Hirst. "What's more, I feel as if one could talk quite plainly to you—about the relations between the sexes, about...., and...."(Mr Hirst's words must be represented by stars; public opinion being what it is.)

"But of course you can" said Helen.

"Could one to Miss Vinrace?"

"She's not my daughter," said Helen, "but if she were, I should let you say whatever you liked to her. In fact, I should ask you to."

"Then there's no real reason for all this mystery between the sexes?"

"Except that most men and most women are very stupid people" said Helen—"worse than stupid, sentimental. It stands to reason: if you see a person naked every day, you never think of one part more than another; whereas if some parts are hidden, you think only of them. I felt that just now dancing with my toad. One's always feeling it."

"Life would become incredibly simpler" said Hirst.

"The real difficulties will always remain" said Helen. "What I mean is facts are so much more beautiful than anything else. How, all these years, people have gone on muffling them up, why they've done it, passes my comprehension. Christianity I suppose. Consider the state of mind of a woman like Mrs Elliot or Mrs Thornbury."

"Will you tell me what you wouldn't tell me the other day," said Hirst, "about yourself?"

Helen laughed, but told him the facts of her life. There was nothing specially strange about them, but the narrative was one of the most exciting events Hirst had ever known. After what they had just said their simplest statements had an extraordinary significance, because they could say anything. When, at last, Helen exclaimed, "I'm hungry with so much talking!" and they went in search of food, they had begun an intimacy to last a lifetime.

It was now half past one; a critical moment in the life of a dance. Some talked of bed, others scoured the idea. The little tables in the dining room were almost all engaged. As Helen and St John made their way to seats, they passed Rachel on Mr Venning's arm.

"Enjoying yourself?" asked Helen.

"Miss Vinrace," Arthur answered for her, "has just made a confession. She'd no idea that dances could be so delightful."

"Yes" said Rachel, "I've changed my view of life completely."

"You don't say so," Helen mocked. "You see," she said to Hirst, as they went on, "I've got my work cut out—looking after Rachel."

"I do not understand Miss Vinrace" said Hirst.

Meanwhile Rachel danced the lancers with Arthur. Their set was made up of Miss Allen, Hughling Elliot, Susan and Hewet. South America with its great red flowers, with velvet petals, its blue mountains, and ink dark shadows, had already affected Mr Elliot in a remarkable way. It was too late for him to forget the seven languages, the entire history of Europe from the year 1216, all the squabbles of Oxford, the university cricket scores for the past fifteen years, which he had by heart; but he could still use slang, dance the lancers, and regret with real sincerity the fate which had bound him to a suburban ninny instead of a woman with a mind, and the doleful life in lecture rooms and studies which had crooked his back, paled his flesh, and set him apart from his kind, before he was fifty.

At half past one in the morning he was protesting against the thought of bed.

"I have to despatch Alexander Pope tomorrow" said Miss Allen consulting her watch.

"Pope!" snorted Mr Elliot, "Who reads Pope I should like to know—and as for reading about him—! No Miss Allen, be persuaded; you will benefit the world much more by dancing than by writing."

"It's a question of bread and butter" said Miss Allen calmly. "However: they seem to expect me."

She took her place, and pointed her square black toe. "Mr Hewet, you bow to me." It was soon obvious that Miss Allen was the only one of the set who knew precisely how the lancers should be danced.

After the lancers there was a waltz; after the waltz a polka. Then a dreadful thing happened. The lady with the dark eyes was seen to swathe her violin in silk, and lay it in its case. She was at once surrounded by imploring couples. In French, in English, in German, she was begged to go on. Perhaps she would have yielded; but the old man at the piano merely exhibited his watch and shook his head. Strange as it seemed, the players were all pale and heavy eyed. The glory had left them. Rachel who was turning over the music on the piano, said to Venning, "Why do we only dance waltzes and polkas? No wonder these people get sick of playing them. I dare say you and Miss Warrington feel all kinds of other things. Isn't there some music that's really happy?"

With her right hand she tried to recall a melody by Gluck.

"What sort of dance could one dance to that?" Arthur asked.

Susan answered. "We're not meant to dance; we're meant to listen. It's lovely."

"But you are meant to dance" said Rachel. "Invent the steps." Sure of her melody now, she struck off boldly, marking rhythm, so as to simplify the way. Helen caught the idea, seized Miss Allen by the arm, and whirled round the room, now making the steps of the minuet, now curtseying, now spinning round, now darting, like a child in a meadow.

"This is the dance for people who don't know how to dance!" she cried.

The tune quickened; and St John hopped with incredible swiftness first on his left leg, then on his right. The tune swerved; Hewet sawing his arms, and holding out the skirts of his coat imitated the voluptuous dreamy dance of an Indian maiden dancing before her Rajah. The tune marched; and Miss Allen sailed down the room, skirts extended, and bowed profoundly to the engaged pair. By degrees every person there was leaping or tripping, in pairs or alone. Once their feet got into the rhythm they showed a complete lack of self consciousness. In a far corner, Mr Pepper even executed an ingenious pointed step of his own, derived from figure skating at which he was an expert. Mrs Thornbury danced a quadrille. As for Mr and Mrs Elliot they gallopaded round and round the room with such impetuosity that the other dancers shivered at their approach.

"Now for the great round dance!" cried Rachel, and struck into the Mulberry tree. Instantly a gigantic circle was formed, the dancers holding hands and swinging round faster and faster, shouting out the tune as they swung. The last chord crashed; the chain burst, people went staggering about in every direction, leaving Arthur and Susan sprawling back to back upon the floor.

It struck them that the electric lights pricked the air very vainly, and instinctively a great many eyes turned to the windows. Yes—there was the dawn. Outside the mountains rose pure and remote; there was dew on the grass and the sky was washed almost clean white, save for the pale yellows and pinks in the east. The dancers came crowding to the windows pushed them open and here and there ventured a foot upon the grass.

"How silly the poor old lights look!" said Evelyn M. who was one of the bold. "And ourselves; it isn't becoming!" It was true; the untidy hair, and the green and yellow gems which had seemed so festive half an hour ago, now suggested all the horrors of dirty bedrooms. In particular it affected the elder ladies unpleasantly. Their tufts and necklaces looked absurd. As if conscious that a cold eye had been turned upon them, they began to say good night.

"You're a witch" said Mrs Thornbury kissing Rachel upon the forehead. "I've not danced for forty years!"

The younger people could not make up their mind to part. Susan wanted to say how happy she was. But she had the greatest difficulty in saying anything she meant. She merely appeared garrulous and uneasy.

"We musn't go to bed yet" said Hewet. That was clear. But what were they to do?

"Suppose Miss Vinrace were to play something classical?" said Hirst.

"Now that would be nice" said Susan. "That would just make the evening perfect. I do adore music don't you? It seems to say just what one can't say oneself." She laughed nervously, to show perhaps that she did not mean to be taken seriously.

In obedience to the general desire, Rachel began to play. Whether or not it was due to the fact that the music was classical, it had certainly a strange effect. With the first notes, nerves relaxed; the tightness round lips that had laughed and talked much, loosened; in the quiet thus produced the beautiful tune with spaces like the spaces between columns reared itself. That there are no people, only music, seemed for a few minutes to be true and desirable. Then of course, the different people began to see different things. They saw themselves and their aims; they saw the trees; they saw the whole world in a fixed rhythmic career as though dancing forward. But one or two kept steadfastly to the idea of the lovely building with its columns. What Hewet had imagined that the music might do, it had done, when Rachel stopped. Quiet had stolen over them; they wanted no more; they were desirous only of sleep.

"I think this has been the happiest night of my life" said Susan. "Every one has been so good. I hope we shall meet many many times." They were all shaking hands. But she kissed Rachel she kissed Helen.

"How shall you go home?" said Hirst, as Helen and Rachel began to look for cloaks.

"We shall walk" said Helen. "There'll be no carriages, and after all it's broad daylight."

"I was just going to suggest a bathe" said Hewet. "Put before yourselves the two pictures—a little dark bedroom, just light enough to see the wash stand, and soft stuffing all round one; and the cold waves, with the sun bobbing up on the horizon. Can there be any question which you prefer?"

"None" said Helen. "Sleep is far more romantic than swimming, if you consider that there are dreams."

"Dreams versus sharks" said Hirst.

"Well—may we walk with you?" said Hewet.

"Look! That's where you live—It's all sound asleep." He pointed to the little white and black house on the hill side, which seemed to have its eyes shut.

"Can you see a light?" Helen asked. One was just perceptible, burning through the daylight.

"That's my husband" she said. "He's reading Greek. All this time he has been reading Greek. And he promised to go to bed." They set out up the steep pathway, scattered with stones, which led to the villa. While the road was perfectly clear, the sun was not strong enough to cast shadows. Partly because they were tired, partly because the early light subdued them, they did not talk much. After walking some way, Helen exclaimed "Now let's sit in the ditch and look at the sea!" Still as the sea was, rippling beneath the sky, lines of green and blue were beginning to stripe it. There were as yet no sailing boats, only one steamer, ghostly in the mist.

"And so you've changed your view of life" said Hewet dreamily.

"Perhaps when it's midday I shall remember" said Rachel, yawning, "Just now—" She took one of the grey stones in her hand, and put it carefully on Helen's knee. "There seem to be nothing but stones."

"On the contrary," said Hirst, "my brain's in an abnormally active condition. I feel as though I could see through everything. Life has no more mysteries for me. And you?" he asked Helen.

"Life?" said Helen, who had not been attending. Instead of answering, she merely smiled. Then she recollected herself and remarked, "What a lot of nonsense you all talk, to be sure."

"D'you know Helen I almost expected to see angels then" said Rachel.

"Well—you were disappointed" said Helen.

"One in each eye" said Rachel.

"And all those people down there going to sleep; thinking such different things; Miss Warrington so happy, on her knees I expect; the Elliots a little startled (it's not often they get out of breath) the poor lean young man putting his flower in water, and asking himself, is this love? Some so dreadfully disappointed, because somebody's slighted them, others all of a quiver, still. No Hirst—" Hewet wound up—"I don't think it's altogether simple."

"I have a key" said Hirst cryptically.

A long silence followed. It was broken by Helen, who said she felt cold. As she rose she remarked, "I suppose you've all been thinking. I haven't had a single thought."

"Are you sure?" Hewet asked her. "You have been conscious, you know."

"I have been conscious of that hill, the colour of the sea, the road and—There is something else, yes," she said. They walked on, reached the villa, and Helen invited the young men to come in and drink. She took them up stairs, and opened Ridley's door. Suddenly they were back in the night again. His lamp burnt, though the room was almost sunny.

"Oh Ridley" she cried, "what an hour to be up!"

Ridley sat like an idol in a temple; with a great volume spread upon his knees; beneath him were scattered other volumes so that one could not come near.

"What a fantastic apparition!" he exclaimed, regarding the white shirts and the brightly coloured cloaks of his visitors. "As you didn't come, I finished my job. Done!" he groaned, and pointed to the floor. "That's Pindar finished. And now, what's to come next?"

"Bed" said Helen.

But the daylight had gone too far to be ousted by either of the young men. They decided to walk off into the country.

All the blinds being pulled down something like night was restored to the villa.

CHAPTER SIXTEEN

That vague dissatisfaction with the ordinary events of the day which is the result of a night spent dancing attacked both Helen and Rachel next morning. Fragments of talk kept running in their heads, like barrel organ tunes. The answers they might have made but had not made tormented them. Helen thrust her needle listlessly in and out, and made no attempt to balance a philosophical volume upon a music stand, which was her usual practise, the difficulty of the point being judged by the swiftness of her needle, which, in crises, speared the cheek of an apple, and stuck there. This morning she seemed in doubt about the trees in the background, and fretted by Rachel's desire for a troupe of naked knights in the distance. As always happens the most interesting events of the night before did not bear repetition. Each wished to think in private.

"What I shall do," said Rachel stretching herself, "is to go and walk."

"I advise you to be careful in this heat" said Helen.

"I shall take a book" said Rachel. She knocked at her uncle's door. He sat reading.

"Have you such a thing as a Gibbon Uncle Ridley?" she demanded. She had to say it again. "What on earth d'you want with a Gibbon" he asked. "It might be very interesting" she said.

"Books can be very interesting" he remarked. "Homer, Shakespeare, Boswell." He stroked the backs of the books as he passed.

"Lovely too" said Rachel, stroking some Greek books, in yellow parchment with gold lines.

"You ought to talk to me more, Rachel" he said. "I could tell you a great many things, I daresay worth your knowing. Who tells you to read Gibbon?"

"Mr Hirst" said Rachel.

"I could have told you that, if you'd ever asked me."

"Mr Dalloway told me to read Burke" said Rachel.

"They come in here, take things off the table, and pop 'em in wherever there's room!" cried Ridley uprooting an interloper. "There's an enormous amount for you to read Rachel!" he exclaimed. "You might begin at the beginning. I think I shall draw up a scheme for you."

"I wonder why people read," said Rachel, vaguely thinking that so learned a man must be deaf.

"If you're going to ask me silly questions you'd better go" said her uncle. "All sensible people love reading."

He had discovered a fresh crime. "And as I say, I'd better teach you. When you're old, you can creep off out of people's way. There's the first volume." He dropped it into her hands. "Just look at all I've done!" He took up a whole volume of exquisitely written manuscript and began turning the pages. "It's a miracle of method—look! Every page is numbered twice; I can put my finger on any passage I want at once. Admire the writing, Every letter perfectly formed, you see—no spiders sprawling in the ink. Now kiss me." She kissed her uncle with real affection. A few minutes in this work room, with the books scattered on the bare planks of the floor, and the few volumes disposed about on the shelves, and the papers lying in piles all hazy with tobacco smoke, impressed her profoundly. She paused at the door to look back. Her uncle was lost again, returned to the Greeks.

With the first volume of the Decline and Fall beneath her arm, Rachel started on her walk. It was too hot for climbing hills, but along the valley there were trees, and a thread of water running in the river bed. In this land, where the population was centred in the towns, it was easily possible to lose sight of civilisation, and to feel oneself an explorer even in the course of one afternoon. About half an hour after she had started, Rachel was by a path, scarcely trodden, which led along the bank of the river. She chose it and left the road. The trees spread leaves like fans above her; on her left the water ran at the bottom of a steep bank of dry stones. She passed bushes with crimson blossoms; tall single stems with white flowers above which the butterflies floated. To her right, lay the flat space of the valley marked with dark green lines of trees, which ran to the base of the mountains. She likened the ridge of the mountains to the long lash of a whip, flying out energetically. Each flower, each tree, she observed distinctly; those who walk much alone come to feel that trees and flowers are friends. Seeing them alone, they strike the mind with a shock, scarcely to be felt when others are there. Rubbing her hand upon a tree, kneeling to pick a little flower, Rachel went through the rite which shame would have prevented in company. "I've loved you—I've loved you" she repeated. The exertion of talking to people had made it more than usually exciting to be alone. Splendid and tumultuous the world appeared there were live people and solitude. She went on naturally, to make the two into a kind of pattern as she walked; unconsciously, she walked fast and spoke aloud.

"It is love that matters" she murmured, "love and flying. Up up up you go. But Mr Hirst would say no. What does matter then I wonder? Trees, perhaps, more than any thing. Why take upon ourselves the burden of faults? But place the two together. Let me think what other people are doing. Mr Venning and Susan. Are they playing tennis? Ah! That's the world one is asked to enter!" (for the suggestion of tennis had made appear in her mind's eye a number of human beings vaguely centring in the hotel running hither and thither upon unknown errands).

"Mr Hirst—Mr Hewet," she continued. "Mr Hirst" she pondered, "sees through everything. He always speaks the truth." The thought of Mr Hirst caused her to keep silence and to walk slower. "There is room for extreme diversity of opinion in this world" she concluded, as if she quoted, and having switched her mind on to another track sped on again. Hewet was the companion of her thoughts, a more pleasing companion because she knew that he liked her. She recalled all the views he had expressed since they had known each other; and from these tried to make up a character. She opposed the character of Hirst to the character of Hewet. The two characters were alike in this—each was of the noblest stature; and overwhelmed all the other little puppets which Rachel brought up from her memory to stand beside them. The figure of poor Richard Dalloway was a mere ghost and vanished.

Conscious that if they knew everything about her they would disapprove, Rachel dismissed them, ran, and filled her eyes with sights. Tired at length, she lay beneath a tree, throwing aside her hat and clasping her forehead in her hands. She looked into deep green shade; a gaudy bird startled perhaps by the vehemence with which she threw the first volume of Gibbon on the ground went creaking in and out. Gibbon! he was a message from Mr Hirst. "In the second century of the Christian era," she read, "the Empire of Rome comprehended the fairest part of the earth, and the most civilised portion of mankind." The work had a miraculous value in her eyes, because it must be the book that really clever people liked. She tried hard to give each word its volume: "decent reverence" "ancient renown and disciplined valour" "active emulation of the consuls." In common with all who read little, she took every sentence very seriously handling it more as a drawer or a table than as a row of words. She was soon driven to conclude that her imagination was not strong enough to read out of doors. The majestic style, the incomparable wit, had on her the effect of a roll of oil cloth spinning smoothly round. The pages were now and then lifted by a breeze; darting dragon flies caught the tail of her eye. A mood of drowsy happiness over came her; into which suddenly there shot a pang, making her jump up, and stride off with Gibbon beneath her arm. It was the idea of love. What was it that made this day different from other days? It was the fullness of the life in everything. What words those were on the opposite page—Aethiopia—Arabia Felix! Even the leaves, and the hills seemed to have a tremendous motion in them. Gigantic melodies seemed to float between the hills and come across the valleys. Nevertheless she dreaded to find that her suspicion was right, much as a person coming from a sick room dreads to find the signs of infection. As she swung along between the trees she fled from the idea, welcoming a rise in the ground, a fall over a grass tuft, because thus the mind was silenced. However, the summit attained, she stood erect, and asked out loud of the sky and mountains, "Am I in love?"

Only the truth was ever spoken by things of such beauty; speaking to them lies were vain. She paused that all unreal foolish excitement might subside; and then answered, aloud but very low, "I am in love."

There had been two people in her, one who asked, and one who answered. But now there was one only. For a long time she sat, clasping her knees upon the top of the little hill. Strings of long necked birds, whom the sun made golden, passed her; the tall grasses in the plain waved apart, bowed their heads, and stood erect again; a vast yellow butterfly slowly opened his wings and closed them upon a stone in front of her. Only now had she ever seen how the earth lived, now that she herself was alive. When at length she rose, stretched herself, picked up her book, and turned to see how the sun had crossed to the opposite range of mountains she once more cried aloud, "I love you I love you!" This was addressed to the mountains. Something in the speed with which they rushed up into the sky falling here rising there, rejoiced her, because she was for rushing too, up and up.

CHAPTER SEVENTEEN

The sun had crossed over to the other range of mountains, and after illuminating the forlorn English camp for perhaps the three hundred and eighty seventh time, had dropped to the other side of the world. The pools and forests there flashed blue and green; whereas in the hotel at Santa Rosa dinner had just been cleared from the tables, and the lights in the sitting rooms were all ablaze. Lethargy marked most of the figures who were now sipping coffee, or glancing at the newspapers. The silence was notable; as though all the heads had been emptied of talk the night before. The post had come in, not long ago and several of the ladies were now settling down to the perusal of many scored sheets from home. Mrs Thornbury was completely engrossed; when she had finished a page she gave it to her husband. Sometimes she gave him the sense of what she was reading in a series of short quotations linked together by a sound at the back of her throat. "'Evie writes that George has gone to Glasgow. He finds Mr Chadbourne so nice to work with, and we hope to spend Christmas together, but I should not like to move Betty and Alfred any great distance' (no quite right) 'though it is difficult to imagine cold weather in this heat.... Eleanor and Roger drove over in the new trap.... Eleanor certainly looked more like herself than I've seen her since the winter. She has put Baby on three bottles now, which I'm sure is wise (I'm sure it is too) and so gets better nights.... My hair still falls out. I find it on the pillow! but I am cheered by hearing from Tottie Hall Green.... Muriel is in Torquay enjoying herself greatly at dances. She is going to show her black pug after all.... A line from Herbert—so busy poor fellow! Ah Margaret says 'poor Mrs Fairbank died on the eighth, quite suddenly in the conservatory, only a maid in the house, who hadn't the presence of mind to lift her up, which they think might have saved her, but the doctor says it might have come at any moment, and one can only feel thankful that it was in her house and not in the street—' (I should think so!) 'The pigeons have increased terribly, just as the rabbits did five years ago....'"

Miss Allen was engaged in the same occupation, but her letters caused her to assume an air of concentration. The wheat crop had failed in New Zealand. What then would become of Hubert? The Allens had always had a struggle to make both ends meet, chiefly owing to old Mr Allen's inordinate taste for China. Hubert the only boy, lacked his sister's grit, and chiefly by their help had been enabled to start life fresh (having started it once wrong) on a farm. It was not certain how far Hubert would suffer. All that Emily the younger sister said was that they ought to be prepared. The Allen family was noted for the way in which it understated things; and this explained no doubt the smoothness of Miss Allen's forehead. She had the expression of a heavily burdened but not over burdened cart horse.

Having given the news about Hubert, Emily went on to describe the pleasant holiday she was spending on the Lakes. "They looked exceedingly pretty just now. I have seldom seen the trees so forward at this time of year. We have taken our lunch out several days. Old Alice is as young as ever and asks after everyone affectionately. The days pass very quickly, and term will soon be here. Political prospects not good, I think, privately, but do not like to damp Ellen's enthusiasm. Lloyd George has taken the Bill up, but so have many before now, and we are where we are, but trust to find myself mistaken. Anyhow we have our work cut out for us. Surely Meredith lacks the human note one likes in W.W.?"

Emily was one of the first authorities in Europe upon the works of Rabelais. She was one of those middle aged spinsters who keep the classics alive, somewhat one may suppose to their surprise, if they know it.

Underneath the palm which afforded some shelter, Susan and Arthur were reading each other's letters. The big bold manuscripts of the hockey players of Wiltshire lay on Arthur's knee; while Susan deciphered neat little legal hands, curt and jocular in style.

"I do hope Mr Hutchinson will like me, Arthur" she said. "He writes such a nice letter. He's evidently so fond of you."

"I must say we've got a jolly set of friends between us" he replied.

"Oh Kitty's a perfect dear" she said. "You will like each other." Already Susan's mind was busy with schemes for the benefit of her friends; with a house in London she could do much. She hoped, before the year was out to have married Kitty and Hester; and Blanche even might be made to forget the detestable Mr Vincent. "Is Mr Hutchinson married?" she asked. Her mind ran on marriage. If one of these young women could have seen Susan now they would have noticed a change. She was far more confident than of old, and, if you spoke to her, you spoke not only to her but to Arthur. The bolder spirits might even regret the change, which had replaced a friend by a matron, but the general opinion would be that Susan was much improved, and had obviously done the right thing. The mellowness and firmness of her manner were partly due to the fact that she would foretell the general opinion, and had a profound respect for it. To be thirty years of age, to have had no one in love with you, and to recur on tennis lawns and ball rooms like some old plant whose white petals begin to yellow, was not a pleasant experience and who can wonder if Susan was glad to end it, to hood those malicious eyes, irrespective of her love? Even Mrs Paley, who owing to her failing eyesight, did not like to travel without a niece, considered that Susan had been wise. Instinctively, she treated her with more respect, and positively protested when Susan knelt down to lace her shoes. For twenty years Mrs Paley had not been able to lace her own shoes, or even to see them, the disappearance of her feet having coincided more or less with the death of her husband a fox hunter, soon after which Mrs Paley began to grow stout. Susan's engagement had relieved her of the one great anxiety of her life—that her son Christopher should "entangle himself" with his cousin. Now that this interest was removed, she felt a little low, and inclined to see more in Susan than she used to. Her wedding present, a cheque, should be very handsome, she determined. With a newspaper on her knee, and a ball of wool in her hand, she looked vaguely in to a thicket of native spears and considered many things. "If I were to die," she thought, "nobody would miss me but Dakyns, and she'll be consoled by the will! The young are very selfish, but then so are the old. How selfish Gervase was, and Thomas is." With a queer thrill of feeling she began to think of the only people she had known in her seventy five years who had not seemed to her selfish. She had had a brother who died suddenly when he was young; and she had also had a niece who had died young too, when her first baby was born. "They ought not to have died" she thought, "However, they did—and we selfish old creatures go on." This was the utmost intensity of emotion that she ever felt; but such as it was, it was genuine. A tear sparkled in her eye, but dried before it fell.

Her real life was lived in the adventures of imaginary people, as represented by modern English novelists, and in order to give her evenings a zest she ran nightly all the hazard of a difficult kind of patience.

Just behind the spears, Mr Elliot was suffering defeat at the hands of Mr Pepper. The game was chess; Mr Pepper wore an air of grim taciturnity which the inevitable triumph would not disturb, or the entry which he would then make in his pocket book to the effect that on such and such a day he had won his one thousand six hundred and twenty third game out of a total of two thousand and eighty four. Mr Elliot's game was not improved by the conversation which he flung out over his shoulder between the moves of Mr Wilfrid Flushing, a new comer.

"Old Truefit had a son at Oxford. I've often stayed with them at the paternal mansion. Some lovely Greuzes, and one or two Dutch pictures which the old boy kept in the cellars. Then there were stacks upon stacks of prints. Oh the dirt in that house! The queer thing was that the son adored his father. He married a daughter of Lord Pinwell's. I've stayed there too. The collecting mania I observe is hereditary. This man collects buckles. Now that would be reasonable enough, but the sign of your true collector is that he hedges himself with all kinds of limitations. They must be shoe buckles, worn by gentlemen, after the year 1580, and before the year 1660. (I may not be right in my dates but the fact's as I say.) On other points he's as levelheaded as a cattle breeder, which is what happens to be. Then the Pinwells, as you probably know, have their share of eccentricity too. Lady Maud for instance—" he was interrupted here by the need of considering his move—"Lady Maud" he began again, "inherits the temper of her Aunt, the famous Lady Egborough. You've heard the story of Lady Egborough and the footman? Lady Maud has a hatred of cats and clergymen. To me she's always been civility itself. She dabbles in literature—likes to collect a few of us round her tea table but mention a clergyman, a bishop even—nay the Archbishop himself—and she gobbles like a Turkey cock. Yes," he continued, observing that the end of his game was drawing near, "I always like to know something about the grandmothers of fashionable young men. In my opinion, these great ladies preserve all that we admire in the eighteenth century with the advantage (in the majority of cases) of personal cleanliness. Not that one would insult old lady Barborough by calling her clean. How often, d'you think Hilda," he called across to his wife, "that her Ladyship takes a bath?"

"I should hardly like to say Hugh," Mrs Elliot tittered, "but wearing puce velvet as she does, (even on the hottest August day) it somehow doesn't show."

"Pepper, you have me" said Elliot, "My chess is even worse than I remembered." He pushed out his chair, and, fixing his glass, turned to examine the case of native manufactures which were set out to tempt visitors.

"Are these at all in your line Flushing?" he asked.

"Pretty little bits of colour, eh?"

"Shams all of them" said Flushing, a tall man with a distinguished head. "Just look at that gold work beside a piece of the real stuff. Alice, lend me your brooch." Mrs Flushing who was reading, unfastened her brooch and gave it her husband scarcely raising her eyes as she did so. She had not listened to a word that Mr Elliot spoke, or she might have been amused by his reference to the uncleanliness of old Lady Barborough who was her great Aunt. She continued to read, with intense concentration, the memoirs of a great traveller who had left his trail in faint red ink across the map, like the trail of a slug.

"Whatever you may say, Hewet," said Hirst, who had been for some time looking straight in front of him with a frown upon his brow, "the human race, as exemplified before us, is divisable into species; hogs, horses, cows and parrots.

It seems to me doubtful whether you can fairly say that they are alive. Do they think? no. Do they feel? Can one feel without thinking? The Vennings distress me. Children ought not to be born of a feeling like that. D'you suppose that Venning feels any thing more than I do when I have a hot bath? The woman in particular is repulsive. I detest the female breast. What are they all doing I ask you? scattered about under lamps in that grotesque way? Look! The creatures begin to stir."

The clock after wheezing for some moments like an old man about to cough struck nine; the eyes of certain merchants who were lying somnolent were raised for an instant; and then closed. They had the appearance of crocodiles so fully gorged with their last meal that the prospect of their next gives them no anxiety whatever.

Hewet though he was not reading, had scarcely noticed any of the people round him. On the contrary his eyes were fixed upon the opposite wall; but he was thinking, not seeing. He had only gathered a part of Hirst's speech.

"Rather dull, I own" he remarked absent mindedly. "How do you know what you feel, Hirst?" he enquired.

"You are in love I conclude" Hirst answered.

"No," said Hewet "I wish I were."

"I feel practically nothing," said Hirst, "except certain attractions and repulsions which have most of them an intellectual origin. For example I am conscious of a great deal of intellectual disapproval at this moment. What hope can there be for a world which is peopled almost entirely by Vennings? I shan't speak to you any more; you're not attending" he broke off.

"I know it all by heart" sighed Hewet. He leant his head on his hand and gazed at the floor. Each continued to meditate, in silence. Their thoughts ran near together. St John thought how the evening would change if Mrs

Ambrose came into the room. The melancholy wreckage would disappear, and he would have a live person to speak to. Hewet was conscious of a curious discontent as though something he held had been snatched from him; he wanted to talk to Rachel.

"But what is talk?" he pondered. "Talk—talk—talk." He said this aloud.

"If we talk we shall only quarrel" said St John; You had much better go to bed."

"I shall go out" said Hewet. He wanted to exchange this hot yellow room with its burble of talk for a great silent space. Out he went into the garden then along the road which was striped with moon shadows. The hills were dark now, and the houses only points of light anchored in darkness. The soft booming of the sea was again audible. His eye sought the light which marked the villa where the Ambroses lived. Without any plan in his head he took the road which led up there, and soon stood by the gate. Still scarcely thinking what he did he pushed the gate open, and, treading on the grass border crept silently round to the front, and stood in the shadow so that he could see half the drawing room. He saw Helen sitting with her embroidery on her knee. She was stitching quietly. A voice went on in the background. After a time it stopped. Then Rachel came behind the chair, and watched the picture grow. Now and then she looked out into the garden. She took the needle from Helen's hand and pointed to the window. He moved back, lest they should come out. But they only stood on the terrace.

"It's not the wet, it's the toads I dislike" said Helen softly.

"I saw millions of snakes this afternoon" said Rachel, in the same soft distinct tones. "The lights of the hotel" she murmured. They paused looking at them. Then Helen remarked, "How odd to be dead!" "Not odder than this" said Rachel.

Helen yawned. She stretched her arms above her head. Rachel took advantage of the raised arms to clasp her round the waist and kiss her. Then they went in, and two minutes later Ridley stooped and fastened the windows, after which the room suddenly became dark.

Now there was nothing to be heard but the whispering of bushes round the house, and Hewet, after crushing a leaf for a minute or two in his fingers found his way to the gate again. His irritation was soothed; the voices which had gone on speaking in ignorance of his presence composed him. Now sleep would come; and then a sane day, and then more certainty. But he was not to get to bed directly, although he wished it. When he reached the hotel the hall was empty, but he paused for a moment to look for a book he had left among the coffee cups and ash trays. He heard the swishing of a skirt, and Evelyn M. stood beside him.

"I wanted to talk to you" she said, "so I came down. D'you mind? I must talk to some one. I like you. You seem more sympathetic than most men."

"You will not find me very intelligent" he said. "I skipped last night. I explain this so that if I yawn you may not think it due to boredom." He yawned. He sat down in the chair he had sat in before, and lit a cigarette.

"What did you want to tell me?" he asked.

"Are you really sympathetic, or is it just a pose?" Evelyn demanded.

"I'm interested" he replied. "But it's for you to say."

"Interested!" she cried. "Any one can be interested. Your friend Mr Hirst's interested I daresay. However, I do believe in you. I don't know why. You look as if you'd got a nice sister. Anyhow here's my story. D'you ever make a fool of yourself, d'you ever get into a state when you don't know your own mind? Well, that's what I've done. You see last night at the dance Raymond Oliver—he's the tall dark boy who looks half Indian but he says he's not really—well, we were sitting out together, and he told me all about himself, and how unhappy he is at home, and how he hates being out here, and how he felt I could help him, and so I felt awfully sorry for him; and you see when he asked me to let him kiss me I did; and then this morning he said he thought I'd meant something more; and I wasn't the sort to let anyone kiss me. And we talked and talked, and I felt fearfully sorry for him; any how you see," she broke off, "I've given him half a promise; and then, well then—there's Mr Perrott."

"Let me see," said Hewet, "Mr Perrott is the melancholy lawyer, who doesn't approve of women smoking."

"We got to know each other on that picnic" said Evelyn. "I couldn't help being sorry for him. He was so unhappy about his friend's engagement. Of course it wasn't known then; but I knew that was in his mind, and we had quite a long talk, when you were looking at the ruins, and he told me all about his life and his struggles, and how fearfully hard it had been. He began as a telegraph boy. That interested me awfully, because I always say it doesn't matter how you're born if you've got the right stuff in you. And then he told me about his sister, who's paralyzed, poor thing; and he's done everything for her. Well, I did like him awfully, and last night we walked about the garden together and I couldn't help seeing what he wanted to say—only then there's Raymond Oliver. One can't be in love with two people at once—or can one? That's what I want you to explain.

"It probably depends what sort of person you are" said Hewet. "What sort of person are you?"

That she was pretty, lively, and about twenty eight or nine was obvious.

"Who are you, what are you, I know nothing about you" Hewet continued, regarding her.

"Well, I'm the daughter of a mother and no father, if that interests you," said Evelyn. "It's not exactly a nice thing to be. Poor mother! She's had a very sad life; father behaved awfully badly to her. I know all that, but I can't help liking him—the things I hear about him. I never saw him. He left her before they were properly married you see. She was the clergyman's daughter, and he was the handsome young son at the big house. I believe much more of that kind of thing goes on in the country than one's any idea of. He made her an allowance and all that; then he married some one else, and was very unhappy and left her; and he was killed in the war. I can't help feeling that if I'd only known him I might have kept him straight. You see, mother's had all the life crushed out of her. The world—oh people can be horrid to a woman like that!"

"And you," said Hewet, "Who looked after you?"

"I've looked after myself mostly" she laughed. "I've had splendid friends. I do like people. That's the trouble. Now what would you do if you liked two people both of them tremendously and you couldn't tell which most? Oh the world! How exciting it all is! Don't you feel sometimes as though you couldn't sleep in case you might be missing something? Well, but you haven't answered?" "I should go on liking them both" said Hewet, "Why not?"

"But you see one has to make up one's mind" said Evelyn. "Or don't you believe in marriage? Look here; this isn't fair. I do all the telling, and you tell nothing. Perhaps you're the same as your friend; perhaps you don't like me?"

"I think I like you" said Hewet.

"How cautious you all are! I know when I like a person, at once. I knew I liked you directly I saw you. Oh dear," she ran on, "what a lot of bother would be saved if only people could say the thing they think straight out. I'm made like that. I can't help it."

"But don't you find it lands you in difficulties like this" Hewet asked.

"Mmm yes I suppose it does" said Evelyn. "But that's men's fault. They always drag it in—love, I mean."

"And so you've gone on, having one proposal after another" Hewet meditated.

"Well," said Evelyn, "I don't suppose I've had more than most people."

"Five? Six? Eight—ten?" Hewet enquired.

Ten seemed to be about the right number.

"I believe you're thinking me a heartless flirt" she protested. "But I don't care if you are. Just because one's interested, and likes to be friends, and talk about real things, and behave to men as though they were women, one's called a flirt."

"But Miss Murgatroyd—"

"I wish you'd call me Evelyn" she interrupted.

"Do you honestly think that men are the same as women?"

"Honestly—honestly—how I hate that word!" said Evelyn. "It's always used by prigs. Honestly, I think they ought to be."

"That's what I cannot understand" said Hewet. "After ten proposals to think that."

"That's what's so disappointing" said Evelyn. "Every time one thinks it's not going to happen; every time it does."

Hewet laughed out loud. "The Pursuit of Friendship"; that might be the title of a comedy."

"You're horrid" she cried. "You don't care a bit really; you're only interested."

"No" said Hewet. "I should like to understand. Let us think now; what are you going to do? You've promised to marry both Oliver and Perrott?"

"Not exactly promised," said Evelyn. "Oh how I detest modern life! I think it must have been so much easier for the

Elizabethans, don't you? I thought the other day up on that hill how I should have liked to be one of those colonists—to cut down trees and make laws and all that." "I'm afraid," she went on after a slight pause," right down in my heart, that Alfred Perrott won't do. He's not strong is he?"

"Perhaps he couldn't cut down a tree" said Hewet. "But have you never cared for anybody?"

"Not to marry them" said Evelyn. "I wanted somebody splendid somebody one could look up to, somebody great and big and splendid."

"Splendid? What d'you mean by splendid? People are; nothing more."

"I don't see what you mean" she said.

"Nor do I" said Hewet. "But I think there's something in it, after all; we don't care for people because of their qualities. Or do we? Isn't it just them that we love—" He struck a match. "Just that" he said, pointing to the flame.

"No" said Evelyn. "I think I'm very good about people. I know at once what kind of things they've got in them. I think you may be rather splendid; but I'm quite certain Mr Hirst isn't."

"I don't think I agree" said Hewet. "In many ways he's finer than I am. But I don't know why."

"He's not nearly so unselfish, or so sympathetic, or so big, or so understanding," said Evelyn.

Hewet sat silently smoking his cigarette.

"I should hate cutting down trees" he remarked.

"I suppose you think I'm trying to flirt with you!" she cried.

"But I don't blame you" said Hewet.

"Well, I'm not; and you can believe me or not as you choose" she answered. "I wouldn't have told you all this if I hadn't thought you could understand without thinking odious things of me all the time." Tears came to her eyes.

"Do you never flirt?" he asked.

"Of course I don't" she protested. "Haven't I told you? All my life I've longed for a true friendship with some one greater and nobler than I am; and if they fall in love, it isn't my fault; I don't want it; I hate it."

"Well," said Hewet, "if you want my advise, you had better tell Perrott and Oliver tomorrow that you've made up your mind, and you don't mean to marry them. They're sensible people; they'll understand, I'm sure, and then all this bother will be over."

He got up although Evelyn did not move, but sat looking at him, with bright cheeks and eyes. He found his book and said "Good night." "They're heaps of things I want to say to you still" said Evelyn. "And I'm going to some time. But I suppose you must go to bed now?"

"Yes" said Hewet. "I'm half asleep."

He went leaving her alone in the empty hall. As he walked along the dim corridors to his room, he said to himself, "Why is it that they won't be honest?"

CHAPTER EIGHTEEN

Ridley's dressing room opened out of Helen's bed room. By leaving the door between them open, conversation could be carried on while she did her hair and he washed his face. It being about four in the afternoon, they were dressing after their sleep.

"Dearest," said Ridley, through a cascade of water, "have you noticed anything about Rachel?"

"What sort of thing?" said Helen after a pause.

Ridley appeared in the doorway in his shirt sleeves.

"I think she is becoming intimate with one of those young men" he said significantly.

"It's amazing what you notice" said Helen. "After all it's not safe to treat you like a mat."

"I have my reasons" said Ridley. "Young gentlemen do not interest themselves in young women's education without a motive. The worst of it is"—he sighed profoundly— "young men tend to be spotty."

"Oh, you're not as clever as I thought" said Helen. "It isn't Hirst?"

"I don't know that it's anyone" said Helen. "How can one know with Rachel? She's as undependable as a child of four. You never know who she's going to like, or what she's going to think, or why she does anything. She'd marry that dreadful flying man I believe if he'd ask her. Are girls always like that, d'you suppose? There's nothing one can take hold of in them." Her brush handle seemed satisfactory in that respect, judging by the strength with which she wielded it.

"I thought you liked her" said Ridley.

"Yes, I do like her" said Helen looking steadily at her self in the glass. "That's the odd thing; I see that women can be quite interesting in their own way. But one feels so much in the dark. Now, with either of those two young men one knows where one is directly. D'you think I'm hard on women, Ridley?"

"You don't admire beautiful women such as I do" he teased her. "That I've always observed. No nice woman does."

"Rachel is beautiful in some lights," said Helen. "I'm not unfair to her Ridley; I think she has great possibilities."

"Unfair! Don't talk nonsense!" said Ridley. "Fasten my collar and my dear, would it possible, or am I making too great demands, if I asked you to implore Chailey to leave my links in my cuffs in future?"

He was now ready to go down.

"If it's not Hirst it's Hewet" he said, looking keenly at her. "What she can see in either of them passes me. Seriously, Helen, we must be circumspect. There's Willoughby remember." He groaned.

Willoughby lay on Helen's dressing table in the shape of a fat letter. He write from a port far down the Amazons, and the terse sentences which seemed to say all that was to be said and to rob that part of the world of mystery, brought the burly figure of the merchant clearly before her. His solicitude for his daughter might be read in the humorous hope expressed towards the end that his girl was not giving trouble. "If so, you have only to put her on the next ship and forward her to me. I am more than grateful for your care. She is a good child."

Then came the narrative of a strike among native work-men, which Willoughby had subdued by leaning out of his bedroom window in his shirt sleeves and roaring loudly in English. He was up to his eyes in work, triumphant over Germany.

"If Theresa married you, I don't see why Rachel shouldn't marry—anyone" Helen speculated, as she turned the page with a hair pin. But the thought of Theresa softened her mind towards Willoughby. She remembered the sight of them together, and reflected once more that one can scarcely judge any relationship fairly the essential thing being hidden.

She went down stairs thoughtfully. Rachel was apparently reading Gibbon; but the page she read was written not printed and ran thus. "You said you had not read Gibbon. I can scarcely believe it; but should blame myself if I did not take all steps to repair the mistake. I shall send my copy. Ibsen? Butler? Personally I find little to be said for the moderns, but should like to draw your attention to Mr Shaw. Life here is incredibly dismal. And you?" The letter had neither beginning nor end, save the flourish of an initial. When Helen came into the room Rachel had just said to herself, "Perhaps I am in love with him." But the question could not be answered, for Ridley appeared in the doorway in some agitation.

"Carriages are coming in at the gates with females in feathers!"

"Oh it's all Mrs Raymond Parry!" Helen exclaimed.

Sure enough, the first words that Mrs Thornbury spoke as she came into the room were, "I brought Mrs Flushing. She is a great friend of our common friend, Mrs Raymond Parry."

Now that Mrs Flushing was not reading the memoirs of a great traveller, it was possible to see that she had remarkable blue eyes. Her figure though short was full of energy and character. She looked straight in Helen's face and said "You have a charmin' house."

In the confusion of setting chairs round the tea table, it was only obvious that Mrs Flushing was nervous, and sat very upright, jerking her head from side to side. Mrs Thornbury smoothed the way.

"You know the country very well, Mr Ambrose? We are going to ask your advise. Mr Flushing is a collector. Can you tell us anything about native manufactures?"

"Not old things, new things" said Mrs Flushing. "That is if he takes my advise."

It appeared that Mr Flushing kept a little shop in Red Lion Square. It all came back to Helen. She remembered hearing of him—the man who could not marry because most women have red cheeks, the man who could not take a house because most houses have narrow staircases, the man who could not eat beef because oxen bleed when they are killed. He was also the man who had done all these things.

She looked with interest at the woman who had converted him. Mrs Flushing, although she had helped herself to jam, was using her knife to threaten Ridley with.

"Nothin' that's more than twenty years old interests me" she said. "Mouldy old pictures, dirty old books, they stick 'em in Museums when they're only fit for burnin'."

The groan with which Ridley answered her caused her to slice her bread like an executioner.

"I quite agree," said Helen, "But my husband spends his life in digging up manuscripts, which nobody reads. But where do you find your new things?"

"Galleries" said Mrs Flushing. "There's a clever man in London called Steer who paints ever so much better than the old masters. I like things that excite me—nothin' old excites me."

"Even his pictures will become old" said Mrs Thornbury.

"Yes I know and then I'll have 'em burnt—or I'll put it in my will."

"And Mrs Flushing lives in one of the most beautiful old houses in England" said Mrs Thornbury. "Chillingly."

"If I'd my way I'd burn that tomorrow" Mrs Flushing laughed, with a laugh like the cry of a jay startling and joyless. "What does any sane person want with these great big houses? If you go down stairs after dark you're covered with black beetles, and the electric lights always goin' out. Tell me," she said, fixing Mrs Ambrose with her eye, "what would you do if spiders came out of the tap when you turned on the hot water?"

Mrs Ambrose only laughed.

"This is what I like" Mrs Flushing went on, jerking her head so as to get a view of all sides of the room. "A little house in a garden. I had one once in Ireland. I lay in bed in the mornin' and picked the roses outside the window with my toes."

"I quite understand the feeling of wishing to pick things with one's toes" Mrs Thornbury remarked to Ridley. "But I should be afraid of the effect upon the gardener. A single foot...."

"There were no gardeners" Mrs Flushing chuckled. "Nobody but myself and an old woman without any teeth. You know the poor in Ireland lose their teeth after they're twenty. But you couldn't expect a politician to understand that." Again she chuckled.

"I don't expect anybody to understand anything," said Ridley.

"Rachel believes in politicians" said Mrs Ambrose.

"Yes yes?" said Mrs Flushing. "Which? Balfour, Lloyd George, Haldane?"

"It's an argument" said Rachel. "My Aunt thinks that some things are better than others. I say every thing's the same."

"This is the perfectly futile kind of argument that attacks people in foreign countries" said Ridley. "To look at them, you would think that my wife and my niece were nice domestic Englishwomen. But they talk more nonsense than I have ever heard out of an undergraduates' debating club. Last night they were arguing whether tea cups were round—"

"Blue" put in Helen.

"And now they'll begin about whether politicians have souls. The advantage of extreme old age I may tell you is that nothing interests one except one's food and one's digestion. It becomes obvious after fifty that the world's going rapidly to—the nethermost pit, and all one can do is sit still and consume as much of one's own smoke as possible."

"I always contradict my husband when he says that" said Mrs Thornbury. "You men? Where would you be if it weren't for the women?"

"Read the Symposium" said Ridley.

"Symposium?" asked Mrs Flushing. "That's Latin or Greek? Tell me, is there a good translation?"

"No" said Ridley, "you will have to learn Greek."

Mrs Flushing laughed like a jay. "Catch me!" she cried, "I'd rather break stones in the road, in fact I always envy men who break stones and sit on those nice little piles all day wearing spectacles."

At this Rachel laughed so loud that Mrs Flushing demanded, "Are you learned too?"

"Rachel?" snorted Ridley, "You might as well ask an old cab horse. A more ignorant creature doesn't walk the earth. By the way, how do you get on with Gibbon?"

The question had the effect of making Ridley blush; for at that moment the names of Hirst and Hewet were oddly mispronounced by the sallow Spanish maid.

Hewet's voice was heard,

"Please don't stop; we will find places."

"Suppose we sit in the garden in the shade" said Helen.

Carrying their tea cups they moved the chairs under the hedge, which was now set here and there with gigantic white flowers, whose petals were thick as blotting paper.

"Gibbon?" enquired Mrs Flushing. I connect him with the happiest hours of my life. We used to lie in bed and read him when we were supposed to be asleep. That's why we liked him I suppose. It's so difficult to read by a night light. And then the moths were always gettin' in. Tiger moths, yellow moths, and horrid cockchafers, because Louisa would have the window open. Have you ever seen a moth dyin' in a night light? Ah, the fight we've had over that window!"

As Mrs Flushing spoke, Rachel looked first at Hewet then at Hirst, and said to herself, drawing her breath easily, "Thank God, I'm not in love with you or with you."

When Hirst asked her how she liked the book she answered, "Not much."

"Then I despair of you" he remarked.

"And I despair of you" she returned, and catching Hewet's eye, laughed remembering her phrase "Ugly in body repulsive in mind as you are"...

"Because?" he enquired.

"Because to judge a person by the books they like seems to me the action of a penny in the slot machine," she hazarded.

"You agree with my spinster Aunt then" said Hirst. "Be good &c. I thought my Aunt and Mr Kingsley were now obsolete."

"No" said Mrs Thornbury, "I have lived all my life with people like your Aunt, Mr Hirst. They had never heard of Gibbon. They only cared for their pheasants and their peasants. They were great red faced men who looked so fine on horse back, as people did I always supposed in the days of the great wars. Say what you like 'gainst them, they are animal, they are unintellectual; they don't read and they don't want others to read; but they are some of the finest and kindest human beings on the face of the earth. You would be surprised at some of the stories I could tell. You would never guess perhaps, at all the romances and the queer unlikely things that go on in the heart of the country. In those old houses, up among the downs—"

"My Aunt" said Hirst "spends her life in East Lambeth. I only introduced my Aunt, because she persecutes those whom she calls intellectual which is what I suspect Miss Vinrace of doing. I am quite ready though I have no proof, to allow your country gentlemen great merits. For one thing they are probably quite frank about their passions, which we are not. My father who is a clergyman in Norfolk, says that there is hardly a Squire in the country who does not". . . .

"But why don't you like Gibbon?" Hewet interrupted, thus relaxing the nervous tension which was observed on every face.

"I haven't read him" said Rachel. "Only three sentences about the Consuls."

"The Satrap of Etruria" said Mrs Flushing so abruptly that the orange plumes almost touched her nose.

"Have you heard from Mrs Raymond Parry lately?" she asked Helen.

The three ladies now became united in sharing what they knew about Mrs Raymond Parry. This lady was celebrated for her character. She was a despotic woman, a socialist and an aristocrat. Owing to the violence of her temper, many stories were current about her, but no one knew whether they liked her or what to think of her relations with her husband, a wax like figure of a man, who spent all the golden hours when his wife was trouncing celebrated people up stairs in arranging gems in a vault like chamber underground. Towards the end of the discussion, Mrs Flushing cried out that Mrs Parry was her first cousin, and once more giving her singular laugh, rose to her feet.

"You must come—you must all come" she said. "I shall write and ask you." She swept majestically to the carriage, Mrs Thornbury following with laughter in her eyes. Hewet saw that the eleven healthy children had not dimmed her spirit, however loosely one was inclined to confound her with other matrons at first sight.

CHAPTER NINETEEN.

Ridley having announced that he should go back to his labours now that that unattractive but remarkable woman was gone, Hewet still remained standing tilting his chair on its hind legs.

"Suppose suppose" he began looking vaguely at Helen, "that we were all to go and climb a mountain."

"Your suggestion is not received with enthusiasm" said Hirst after a momentary silence.

"Surely looking at mountains is enough" said Helen, looking across at the purple mass speckled with white villages.

Rachel found Hewet looking at her.

"I shall go" she said jumping up. "I want to look at the sea." She fetched her hat, and they turned away together just hearing Hirst begin, "Ten days have now passed"—

"—since he asked Mrs Ambrose whether she thought him a man of strong passions." Hewet finished the sentence as he opened the gate.

"And how she is to answer him, I don't know. How anyone knows anything about anyone I don't know."

They did not take the road which led up to the mountain but turned round behind the villa, so as to climb the vineyard which overlooked the sea. The path between the vines was narrow; Hewet's back blocked it completely. Rachel followed behind, thinking, "Undoubtedly I am in love with him."

When the vineyard ended, and they stood beneath a little cluster of thin-stemmed trees, which wore a garland of leaves on their heads, Hewet repeated,

"How we know anything I don't know."

Rachel dropped down on her elbow. It was at this moment that Helen's old taunt—"Oh Rachel, you'll always be the dupe of the second rate!" recurred to her; and she determined to strip a long blade of every tassel before she answered. Hewet sat down deliberately beside her. "I want to know you" he remarked. Rachel was much relieved. "I want to know you" she said, and threw away her stem of grass. "There are so many things to talk about.... All that—" she waved her hand to indicate the sea and the town and the mountain beyond.

"And ourselves" said Hewet. He spoke with some tremor in his voice.

"I like you" said Rachel. "And I like you" he answered. "But I shall not lend you books. I should like—" he hesitated "I should like to talk to you as I talk to men. I have never done that to any woman. And perhaps after all it is not possible."

So miserable was she, fearing that he despised her, that she could only answer, "Try and see."

"When I first saw you," said Hewet, looking through the great jungle of corn which cut the sea into strips, "I thought you were like a creature who had lived among pearls and old bones. Your hands were wet. Tell me what you think about."

"About images and spirits and the sea" said Rachel.

"There is a great war you understand; or there was a great war. But now the images are becoming real; Mrs Flushing seemed to me quite real."

"Am I real?" asked Hewet.

"I see you as I saw you in the vineyard just now," said Rachel, "a great bulk like a cathedral."

"It is true my grandfather was carried out the drawing room window" said Hewet. "But tell me more. The sea? Why the sea?"

"O if one lives with Aunts at Richmond one thinks of nothing else!" Rachel burst out. "We have quite a nice house; it is red brick; but oh the horror of the dusting and the meals and the cook and the butter boxes! If I had a daughter I should give her a square of cardboard painted blue and make her think of infinity every day. No adventures. We sit and hear the dining room clock tick. And all the time there are hair dressers' shops round the corner, and one need only go in and ask a question and something would happen."

"It is a great thing" said Hewet, contemplating his hands, "to cultivate a passion for facts. You see anything that is—like my hand for example—is infinitely wonderful. Now I often prowl about London when the lamps are being lit and look in at all the windows and I'd give my eyes to know what people are really doing. You might know. I consider myself worse off than you are. I live so much among ideas. In my family we talk; we talk about everything."

"I've never talked," said Rachel.

"You have spent your life in thinking about the sea?" asked Hewet.

"Yes, and in violent emotions."

"And I was thinking you'd never felt a thing" said Hewet. "Am I being insolent?" he asked, seeing her suddenly flush.

"After all" said Rachel, "what's the use of men talking to women? We're so different. We hate and fear each other. If you could strip off my skin now you would see all my nerves gone white with fear of you."

"Has that been one of your emotions?" asked Hewet.

"The first I think" said Rachel.

"Will you tell me?" Hewet asked, the back of his head rested against the trunk of a tree; and his eyes watched the sea as though he were matching things.

"It would mean beginning at the beginning" said Rachel. "The way my father treated my mother. I once heard him abuse her when she asked him for money. Feelings come in flashes like that and last all one's life. That was one flash. Then dishonesty. He never treated me fairly. Then when I was eighteen he forbade me to walk down Bond Street alone. Suppose anyone had forbidden you to walk down Bond Street alone when you were eighteen! because of the women! It made me feel robbed of my life. When you think that you have only one life—just for a second and all that waste of sea behind you and before you—and that other human beings should interfere with the smallest moment of it—then you hate them more than anything in the world. I shall never never never have all feelings I might have because of you."

She stopped; as he said nothing she went on.

"And then if you had lain awake chased by men because of the women you saw under lamps in Piccadilly driving home—Besides women see the worst of men. How cruel they are at home, how they believe in ranks and ceremonies, how they want praise and management. Even Uncle Ridley who is far better than most wants praise all day long and things made easy by Helen. As for men talking to women as though they were men, no; it's the worst relationship there is; we bring out all that's bad in each other; we should live separate."

Hewet forebore to pick holes in the argument because clearly she felt what she said. He restrained his irritation, knowing that in a moment they would quarrel.

"Try this plan" he said after a moment. "Forget yourself. Think of people in myriads, like a great sea. How does it work out then, this question of men? The general opinion surely is that they are"—he paused for his word—"more satisfactory."

"But then we have no poet" said Rachel, when she had reduced the population of the world to tiny waves. "The world I know is made of good people, but not one who sees things new."

"We must go to Shakespeare you mean" said Hewet. "And Shakespeare's really no good because he's dead" he added. "We must be our own Shakespeares. We must see things new. If I try, will you?"

"I come burdened with all this," Rachel sighed, "I fear you, I want to coax you, I carry a wound in my heart; and you come despising, suspecting—'honestly' as Mr Hirst would say, you come despising, suspecting?"

"If I am to be quite honest," said Hewet, "I think I did. And for me the whole question is complicated by the fact—well, that you're a woman. Save for that I feel to you as I feel to another man. Do you believe me?"

"It's quite clear I do," said Rachel, "because of the way I talk."

"That is what I should have said," said Hewet. He lit a cigarette. "Now I shall call you Rachel, and you shall call me Terence, I think; though my friends call me Monk."

"Monk? why Monk?"

"Oh that story belongs to another day" said Hewet. "What are the things you feel besides the fear of men?"

"My mother died" said Rachel. "I hated death."

"No one I cared for has ever died" said Hewet. "What is death like?"

"The queerest thing," said Rachel. "Only one's not supposed to talk about it. Here we all sit, never talking; and then a great hand reaches out and takes one; and still we never talk about it. Then it is painful to know that you will never see a person again."

Unable to finish her sentence for tears she stretched out her hand for a yellow poppy and as she picked it controlled herself. "So I love the sea and music because they don't die" she said. "And because after all—aren't they after all the things that matter most—so much more than the wrigglers." She pointed her poppy to the hotel, which stood out on its mound as though guarding the waters.

"There I disagree with you entirely" said Hewet. "I like a little music after dinner, and what is the sea? only water. But people believe me are far more interesting than all the music and all the seas and all the mountains and all the dreams and Death and Birth and Personifications and Elements and all the rest of the abstractions put together. They feel poor devils, and then they're so odd. You agree really; I know you agree."

"Yes I do" said Rachel with sudden excitement, "I love people. If we were to walk down there" she said, "d'you think we could throw a stone into the sea?"

As Hewet strolled behind her he reflected upon the instability of her mind. No feeling no conviction occupied her for long. It was not only her lack of training for that she shared with most of the women he knew. But his sisters at the age of twenty four had character; and could love. Whether Rachel could ever feel a passion for one man rather than another seemed to him profoundly doubtful; at the same time there might be something in her—something one could love.

He looked at her throwing stones and a chill came over him the result of his doubts.

There was no beach, the earth having broken off here with extreme abruptness. Rachel's stones fell plump into the sea, which was so full and calm this evening that it washed against the cliff without a wave. It still hoarded the deepest blue of the midday sky. They crawled on their knees to the edge and lay upon their arms looking into the depths.

"For all this beauty I shan't be sorry to get back," said Hewet. "I want England. All this seems to me unreal—too good to be [[true."]]

["What novels do you write?" she asked.]

[["My novel]] [is about a young man who is obsessed by an idea—the idea of being a gentleman. He manages to exist at Cambridge on a hundred pounds a year. He has a coat; it was once a very good coat. But the trousers—they're not so good.] The story then deals with his adventures in London. He has one splendid coat, and a pair of trousers which is not quite so splendid. You can imagine the wretched man who has had only a herring for his breakfast, arranging the garments over the end of his bed, now in full light now just in shade, and wondering whether they will survive him or he will survive them; and undecided which will be the worst fate. Then the landlady has a daughter, with whom he falls passionately in love; but at the critical moment, just in fact as she is giving him her heart, she drops an aitch,—but I had forgotten about his meeting with Lady Theodoar on the banks of the Serpentine in the early morning. My hero has by this time been reduced to one coat—which we may call the coat; he is taking his morning bathe, (he is scrupulously clean—he observes all the habits of a gentleman) when Lady Theo's bay mare flashes past. In an instant he has thrown on his clothes, is after the beast, seizes the bridle, and brings it to a standstill. Now the poor fellow is in a desperate fix. Lord Gorbottle, the lady's father, insists upon knowing his name. His name—it is one of his chief curses—is plain Bott, Albert Bott—. He yields to the temptation and describes himself as Herbert Warrington; his mother he says is Lady Warrington of Warrington Place. He gets deeper and deeper into mendacity—and the more lies he tells the older his coat is getting. Here I shall describe fashionable life. I shall have to do this at length because it is very important for the course of my story that the significance of the coat in fashionable life should be clearly understood. But do you perceive the fatal drawback? It has just occurred to me. It is a comedy, not a tragedy; inevitably it will become a mere burlesque."

He drew his hand over his eyes to consider the question. Rachel stared out across the sea. After a minute or two Hewet sat up and said, "The same thing happened with my Stuart tragedy. The cow was fatal. I wished to prove that there is absolutely no difference between people in those days and people now. I said nothing about 'Regent of the Skies' and 'clapping spurs to their horses.' But the milk maid of St James Park had a cow; and the cow became symbolical—a type of Destiny, like a figure in Greek tragedy, which was fatal in a psychological novel. In writing" he continued, "the great thing is to find your mood and stick to it. My difficulty is that things shift so. The Gods are always stirring the cauldron—dropping gold and silver and mud into it. I am not like Hirst, who sees neat little circles between people's feet. I tend, as far as I can see, to make fewer and fewer judgements. Perhaps that was how Socrates died, staring into the air, his mind a blank."

"How then do you account for warmth, cold, blues and red things happiness rage, music and so on?" Rachel asked, counting up at hazard the events of the day. "Why aren't you content to feel without explaining?"

"No one is who knows how to read" said Hewet. "Behind every sensation there is a shape. Have you ever seen great flowers made of fireworks? They are made of dots of light. Sensations are dots; combine them and you have a flower or a cow or a tea pot. To combine them, to find out their shape, that is my trade. I've never done it so far, because the sensations themselves are so overwhelming. Have you ever walked about London at night, or been to a music hall, or talked to old men in the street—I forgot," he said, "you've never done any of these things, because of me. I'm very sorry. It seems monstrous when one comes to think of it."

"Yes" said Rachel, "think of me at midnight, say in the middle of June; the doors locked and barred; lights all out; a kind of throb in the house when one listens. Whether it is the creaking of the boards, or the hot water pipes, I have never been able to make out."

It appeared that Hewet had rooms in the Temple; with carved mantlepieces; the walls for the most part covered with books; and an old woman who did for him who also did for the Marchants who lived over head. The main advantages of the place were the neighbourhood of the river and the Strand, and the quiet essential for one who writes.

As he finished this statement, the air became noticeably cold. They turned from autumnal London to the intensely coloured southern evening. The beauty of the town, the valley with the dark trees and the violet mountains kept them from talking; they looked at these things and at floating crimson feathers in the sky; Hewet left her at the gate of the villa.

At the precise moment when Rachel and Hewet were seeing the jelly fish, Hirst lit his sixth cigarette and staring intensely at the dead match exclaimed,

"I suffer tortures!"

Helen drew her thread through her canvas and asked "Why?"

"I envy everybody" said Hirst, "And everybody hates me. I'm essentially mean. I'm so mean that I can hide it from everyone—except perhaps from you. I envy Hewet—everything. I envy Venning because Susan's in love with him; I envy Pepper his learning; I envy waiters because they can balance half a dozen plates without breaking them. I envy old women their comfort; and I envy natives."

"Nonsense" said Helen.

"It's partly my appearance" said Hirst. "I'm infernally ugly, though I've not got a drop of Jewish blood in me. Partly of course that I've not yet had a chance of showing people what I can do. The question is—can I do anything? Aren't I a fraud? Five people admire me; true. What are those five people worth? Before I knew you," he continued, "I should have said that they were worth all the rest put together— Even now—Yes" he exclaimed, after a pause, "they are worth all the rest put together. You'll have to be sixth—that's all."

Helen already knew the five by name. There was Bingham the philosopher, Hughes the mathematician; Bennett the scholar; and Morley and Carpeneter, who "merely existed." Indeed when she asked for particulars, Hirst had snubbed her.

"It isn't what people do but what they are" he remarked; nor was it easy to describe how they were.

"When I think what I was when I left Westminster— what a muddled sentimental little ass—and what happened to me afterwards I can see how amazing they must have been. You see, they taught me to speak the truth."

He meant much more than the simple virtue learnt at his nurse's knee.

"That is why I like you" said Helen. "Practically no woman speaks the truth."

"And very few men" said Hirst. "Fundamentally," he continued, "I'm convinced that I'm sound; these miseries are only on the surface."

"I don't understand your miseries" said Helen.

"Envies jealousies hatreds horrors—you'd think them too despicable. I've practically had to shut myself away from my kind. The awful thing is—I wobble. I should like to be like Swift; really I'm only a male edition of an old lady in a cathedral close—except for my mind. When I'm working I'm really rather sublime. Why can't one always be working? Perhaps when I'm immensely celebrated I shall be happy. Only then there's love" he added, and dropped his cigarette.

"Considering how many people in my family have either come to bad ends or gone wrong," said Helen, "I suppose I am amazingly happy."

"Marriage?" said Hirst.

"Yes" said Helen. Her relationship with Ridley was a thing she never discussed, because people with insight could judge directly, and she did not trouble to enlighten gulls. In her day she had been much criticized—a beautiful girl and a pedant of forty!

"But not only marriage" she continued.

"Children?" asked St. John.

"But besides children I don't know why I'm happy" she gave it up and took to her needle again.

"I see an abyss between us" said St John in a voice which seemed to issue from a hollow rock. "Do you really think? The difficulty of any relationship between the sexes is that one never knows how a woman gets there, therefore whether to trust her or not. My instinct is to trust you, but supposing you don't really understand? vice versa; supposing all the time you're saying 'O what a morbid young man!'"

"Difficulties abound" said Helen. "All the same, if you let yourself go and take the risks things may be all right; on the other hand I admit you may come a cropper."

"I suppose you've never paid any one a compliment in the course of your life?" said St. John.

"Most people say I spoil Ridley" said Helen.

"I must ask you point blank—do you like me?"

"Yes I do" said Helen.

"That's one mercy" said St John.

"Now will you tell me whether you think I am as I said, fundamentally sound?"

He did not look at her while she considered his question. After a perceptible pause, she said, "I think you are—certainly."

"You don't know how tremendously that pleases me" he said speaking with emotion.

"Because you see—or perhaps you don't see—I would rather you approve of me than any one else in the world. I've never met any one in the least like you."

Helen flushed with pleasure. "You're absurd" she said. "You know quite well, when you get back to Cambridge, and meet the five philosophers you'll forget all about me."

"I wonder what you'd think of them" Hirst pondered.

"You'd like Bennett and Morley; I think it might take you some time to appreciate Hughes; of course Bingham's the test. Bingham's superb! If God had made Bingham only one could forgive him the rest! I've never heard Bingham say a thing that wasn't absolutely true. You can't conceive his mind harbouring a lie for the fraction of a second. I suppose he's done more for the world than anyone since Socrates. And yet if you put him out here among the Elliots and the Thornburys what sort of figure d'you think he'd cut? Did you notice at tea? How they were all ready to swoop upon me because I made some stand against their inane prudery? Poor old Hewet had to change the conversation. Now, if Bingham had been here, he'd have stuck to it. He'd have said exactly what he'd meant to, or he'd have got up and gone. He wouldn't have cared a hang what any one thought of him. But I can't help thinking it's bad for the character to have perpetually to get up and go—only Bingham's so stupendous nothing does seem to hurt him. It tends to make one bitter. I'm inclined to be bitter, because though I've only half Bingham's mind, I'm always finding myself the only sensible man among a crowd of gabies. Couldn't you make Rachel understand or is it too late?"

Helen tossed her embroidery into a chair and sprang up, for the splendours of the sunset made her restless.

"Have you any notion what a girl of twenty four is like?" she said. "I never had. She's not a bit like a man.... I'm very fond of her" she concluded, as though in the interval she had run over her qualities.

"But what is she like?" Hirst pursued; as they walked side by side down the grass path which led between the great bushes in the long garden.

"I mean does she reason—does she feel. She seems to me so hopelessly vague. I offered to lend her books, but I doubt whether it's any use. Of course she's obviously attractive, but I don't think I feel any more.... You're not attending" he broke off.

The same sunset that silenced Hewet and Rachel silenced Helen too. She looked from the purple land to the blue mountains, upon which the clouds curled, yellow and crimson.

"Amazing" said Hirst.

"About Rachel" said Helen after a considerable pause. "I some times think I don't know her at all; and sometimes that she's about the same as my right hand. The truth of it is Mr Hirst," she added with a laugh, "I'm not analytic by nature, and when you insist, I talk nonsense."

"You have now made me exceedingly angry" he returned.

"For the tenth time, my name is St John."

"For the twentieth time," said Helen, "it's the name of a character in Thackery whom I particularly detest."

CHAPTER TWENTY

Now Sunday came a mood rather than a day. Those hens, which did figuratively at least, over run the drawing room of the villa, rendered the mood of no avail there. On the other hand every person in the hotel awoke to find it in possession. Where linen was worn it was uncomfortably starched, and dresses of cloth had an unreasonable allowance of jet. But the mood went deeper than dress. Surely, breakfast was eaten with greater sobriety than usual, and after breakfast even the most energetic visitors sat about, instead of preparing parcels of food, and checking their watches by the great clock in the hall. One little group in particular seemed to be united by the same influences. There was Susan, her skirt as white as a wedding cake, and so stiff that it seemed to resist the chair when she sat down, with a string of bright beads round her neck, there was Mrs Thornbury and her husband; Mrs Elliot, Arthur Venning and Miss Allen. Come and go they did; but as the hands of the clock neared eleven, they tended to draw together, clasping little red leaved books in their hands. The clock marked a few minutes to the hour when a small black figure, acknowledging the presence of the others by a slight formal bow, passed through the hall and disappeared down the corridor which led from it.

"Mr Bax" said Mrs Thornbury under her breath.

They were preparing to follow, when Mrs Flushing swept across, and, making for Mrs Thornbury demanded in an agitated voice, "Where? Where?"

"We are all going" Mrs Thornbury stated quietly, and therewith led the way. Loungers by the door looked after them; one or two appeared from other parts and joined them; Hewet and Hirst came in at the rear, provided it seemed with only one thin light blue volume between them. The elegant but melancholy Raymond Oliver deliberately lit a cigarette, and pushed through the door into the garden as they passed. It was a soft bright morning.

Perhaps there were twenty people assembled in the chapel, a profound cool place, where it was said, the monks had once eaten. By the disposition of several yellow benches and claret coloured foot stools, and the erection of an altar near the end, and the laying of mats upon the floor, and the writing of words upon an arch, and the embroidery of a long piece of stuff with gilt tassels, the illusion of a place of Protestant worship was created. Miss Willett was striking solemn chords upon the harmonium as they entered, and several immediately fell upon their knees.

Mr Bax had replaced Mr McClean. He was a very young man, anxious to mix with ordinary people in an ordinary way though a clergy man. To Hewet he had confided his aim—which was to prove that there is nothing unmanly in the Christian religion, and thus to bring back young men who from lack of sympathy were now indifferent. "Play bridge with them—tennis with them—mix with them—show them that you're made of flesh and blood just as they are—" that, he exclaimed was the way for a man to set to work nowadays. The learning of the older men, much though we owe them, had in some ways been a mistake.

He wished Hewet to realise that there was new blood in the church as there was in science and medicine and art. Here he laughed at the latest art movement, which was good though because it proved life, and we should, he wound up, all be alive and all share as much of our good things as possible.

When the chords had ceased to vibrate Mr Bax began, "Dearly beloved Brethren...."

At once the room filled with the ghosts of innumerable services on innumerable Sundays, in thousands of churches, London churches, country churches and great Cathedrals. The words that followed rose almost automatically as smoke from a lit fire; "Almighty and most merciful Father. We have erred and strayed from thy ways like lost sheep." The twenty odd people who had met for the most part on the stair case or in the dining room now felt themselves pathetically united and well disposed towards each other. Susan's mind in particular was flooded with the sweetest emotions of calm sisterhood. Her sisters knelt, her brothers knelt, in Wiltshire; and she, who had gone away, found the world here full of brothers and sisters too.

The Lord's Prayer continued the pure and exalted mood which filled her; there was no stress in the demands, for they were too familiar to seem like desires. She knelt and felt herself like a child, and could not help her joy at feeling that God had kept her so right up to the greatest event of her life. She was a virgin, in soul as well as body. This beatific mood had spread and completely overwhelmed them all, bringing charity and calm and the associations of country Sundays in England among them, when suddenly Mr Bax turned the pages of his Bible and read a Psalm. Although his voice remained in much the same key, it was impossible for the most pious not to feel that the words were different, and the mood broken. "Be merciful unto me O God, for man goeth about to devour me; he is daily fighting and troubling me."

There was nothing in Susan's experience at all like that.

"They daily mistake my words; all that they imagine is to do me evil. They hold all together and keep themselves close."

"They?" who were "they?" She followed the words with respectful courtesy, as she followed the somewhat distraught exclamations of characters in Shakespeare, and where she could, joined honestly in praise of the might of God.

"Break their teeth, O God, in their mouths; smite the jaw-bones of the lions, O Lord; let them fall away like water that runneth apace; and when they shoot their arrows let them be rooted out." Her lips moved smoothly in an apologetic murmur over such passages.

Every one felt the inconvenience of the sudden intrusion of the old savage. He had completely dissipated the peace of Sunday. Instead of visualising themselves, toilworn but peaceful after the week's work, and their rewards and virtues and suffering, they were called upon to listen to the ravings of an old black man with a cloth round his loins cursing with vehement gesture by a camp fire in the desert. A critical literary look replaced the devout look. After that they dipped into the Old Testament, reading a little bit of history about making a well much as schoolboys after their French lesson translate an easy passage from the Anabasis. Next came the chapter from the New Testament, which though it had the same disadvantage of being as it were an exercise, moved them back to England, and the mood with which they started. The character of Christ was very familiar to them. The sad, mystical words might have been spoken by an Englishman whom Susan had seen. He did absolutely sympathise with her life, and gave her sufficient directions and reasons, so that she floated over the next passages though dictated by the fear of a night attack upon her camp, serenely, and spoke with conviction when it came to saying what she believed. Custom had smoothed these passages to such an extent that she settled herself to listen to the sermon without feeling jolted or breathless. Her vision of Christ, a sad beautiful man, and her conception of the world and life and right and wrong and her duty, which all depended upon her version of this man's teaching, were too long established to suffer from the sudden apparition of an old savage. But there were others who did not share Susan's mood. Mrs Flushing having been late for church, had taken up a Bible instead of a prayer book, and finding herself next to Hirst, began to read over his shoulder. He politely laid the book before her. As Mr Bax intoned "I believe in God the Father Almighty" Hirst pointed to the Ode to Aphrodite.

Mrs Flushing rapidly read the verse, then enquired, "What's this?"

"The works of Sappho" whispered Hirst. "Sappho? That's Greek ain't it?" said Mrs Flushing, and studied the title page. She glanced through the Ode to Aphrodite and was just about to make some brisk enquiry, when Mr Bax's voice became threatening, and she hastily repeated, "The forgiveness of sins; the Resurrection of the body, and the life everlastin'. Amen."

"This is by far the most beautiful thing ever written" Hirst continued. "It's the one Swinburne did, you know."

Mrs Flushing could not resist looking, though she murmured 'Hush.'" She tried to kneel devoutly, but the corner of one vivid blue eye glanced unhidden. Hirst read openly, letting the patter of praying voices fall round him like leaves.

Hewet with his legs extended gazed profoundly at the ceiling. The mixture of modern symbolism and splendid heathen poetry roused his curiosity and love of language; and then—the worshippers? What were they worshipping? What on earth did it all mean? The question pressed so hard, as he ran his eyes over the merchants, women, and young people, that he was relieved when Mr Bax twitched his robe and began to preach. The sermon was about the duties which visitors owe to natives. You cannot go anywhere without leaving some trace behind you. "We," said Mr Bax, "leaving our offices, our desks, our domestic duties at home, come out here saying in our hearts 'Now we'll have a jolly good time. We have earned our holiday, we need it; it is right that we should take it.' But do we ever think what effect our taking it will have upon those who are not holiday makers, not strangers, but the people of the land, who are intent upon their daily lives? The mistake we are perhaps inclined to make," Mr Bax went on, qualifying his advice kindly for the mild eyes of women old enough to be his grandparents were upon him, "is to think that because one man speaks English and another Spanish, they're different—radically different—beneath their skins. I don't know whether any of you have stopped to look at the little chaps who mind donkeys outside the hotel gates. If you did, you'd find them after precisely the same games as little chaps in London streets. There is a saying which you may have heard—The child is father of the man. This teaches us that we must not pass them by saying 'Nay, he is not my brother—what can such as I say to such as him?' Believe me you can say a great deal; you can teach him you can help him you can—no less surely—harm him. Now some people are inclined to think that if you are what they call a religious person there is only one way in which you can help others by bringing them back to the church, by convincing them of the truth of the Christian dogma. Well; that is one way, a very splendid way; the lives of our great missionaries make up noble reading; but it is not the only way. Life," said Mr Bax, expanding his chest, "has many manifestations. Now, more than ever, we are aware of the possibilities which life holds. You have only to pick up a modern book, or to go into a modern picture gallery, to realise how the human mind is as it were breaking into fresh leaf and bud and promise. Then there are the great scientific discoveries—the aeroplane—the wireless telegraph. New manifestations, I said; and you can only enter into sympathy with the eternal human brain and human heart behind them by sympathising with the form which that spirit takes. So many of us nowadays are inclined to say, 'O he's very clever—he's such a modern chap' and so to pass on taking it for granted that such a one is beyond our pale, will have none of the simple old doctrine of Christianity. But we are wrong—we are very wrong. It is precisely that man who needs our help—whom we can help. And in all humility let me say it, do we not need his help too? Do we not need the strongest and the most brilliant minds among us?—not to make excuses, not to plead, not to reform our faith, we have no need of that—but to prove how splendidly the old beliefs fulfil the needs of the modern man. But if he is to be one of us we must show him that we can sympathise. Very likely he will say, 'O that fellow—he's a parson.' What we want him to say is, 'Oh, I know so and so—he's a good fellow'—in other words 'That man is my brother.' Yes my brethren, that is the work of the true Christian. To reveal brotherhood. Again and again you will meet with rebuffs, do not be despondent; perhaps you have failed in sympathy; perhaps you have been over sure of yourself, thinking of yourself and not of the master. But believe me the man who truly and sincerely reveals himself to another man, in his strength and weakness, above all in his beliefs, that man is sure of sympathy in the long run; he is the true Evangelist; he is the missionary, who goes not from white man to black man, but from one man to another man.

"Therefore," he continued, seeming conscious that he might have said enough, "let us remember that whether we are together in this spot, English people with English people, or whether we are with those who speak another tongue the same need is laid upon us. We have not shifted our burden by changing our climate and for the time being our habits. Indeed this is the season when we can give freely of the best we have, unfettered by business, unhampered by all those ties which custom lays upon us in our native land. We are in a sense released, uncloaked. And who knows, who would take upon himself to foretell, what results may not spring from our seemingly accidental meeting here—the words we may let fall unthinkingly, the things we may do when apparently there is none or only an ignorant native to witness. As a drop of water, seemingly detached alone separate from others, falling from the cloud and entering the great ocean, alters so scientists tell us, not only the immediate spot where it falls, but all the myriad drops which together compose the great universe of waters, and by this means alters the configuration of the globe and the lives of millions of sea creatures, and finally the lives of the men and women who seek their living upon the shores—as all this is within the compass of a single drop of water, so is a marvel comparable to this within the reach of each one of us, who dropping a little word or a little deed into the great universe alters it—yea alters it—for good or for evil, not for one instant or for one hour, but for all eternity." Whipping round, as though to avoid applause, he began with the same breath, "And now to God the Father...."

He blessed them, and then Miss Willett burst into a triumphant march tune, under cover of which the scraping and rustling of worshippers going out was scarcely heard, or sounded only as the bustle of life beginning again under the divine banner. Before the last had left the chapel, the march had dwindled to a few intense but widely spaced chords, which became further and further apart until they ceased altogether dying rather than coming to an end.

CHAPTER TWENTY-ONE

Halfway up the stairs which led back to the upper world, Rachel felt a hand violently grasping her shoulder.

"Miss Vinrace!" said Mrs Flushing. "We met the other day. Are you goin' back? Won't you stay to luncheon? Sunday's such a dismal day, and they don't even give one beef for luncheon here, which at any rate makes one go to sleep afterwards. That's what I miss—roast beef. It would be awfully kind of you to stay."

"I should like to stay" said Rachel, "except," she looked from one to another. They were now in the hall, and the congregation stood about as though the service still had power over them. "Everyone looks so respectable" she ventured.

"Ain't they awful?" returned Mrs Flushing, with a vivid flash of malice. "English people abroad.... We won't stay here," she continued, plucking at Rachel's skirt. "Come up to my room. I've some things to show you." She bore Rachel past Hewet and Hirst and the Thornburys and Elliots. Hewet stepped forward.

"Luncheon" he began.

"Miss Vinrace lunches with me" said Mrs Flushing, and began to pound energetically up the staircase, as though the middle classes of England were in pursuit.

"What did you think of it?" she demanded, planting slightly. "The sermon I mean? Did you like it, or did you think it awful rot?"

"Some I thought nonsense, some rather good" said Rachel. "On the whole I pitied him, having to make a fool of himself."

"Yes yes poor man" said Mrs Flushing, pausing with her hand on the handle of her door, "Did you see that Mr Hirst was reading Greek? I looked over his shoulder. I meant to ask him what it was, and now I can't remember. Poetry. I always take the wrong book. That's what comes of havin' 'em bound alike."

She opened the door and made Rachel go in first. She had one of the best bedrooms in the hotel. From the bow window you could see both the town scrambling up to the mountains, the mountains, and on the right hand a considerable space of sea. Rachel went at once to the window to look, for an old view seen from a new standpoint is always interesting.

"That's where we live" she said, pointing to the villa. "It's odd how different things look. I'd no idea we lived where we do. Do the windows always blaze in the sun like that? That's my uncle's window."

"Which? Show me," said Mrs Flushing. "Tell me. What does your Uncle do? Greek? Is he a professor? And your Aunt? Is that lady your Aunt?"

"No; he's my Uncle" said Rachel. She looked about the room, and observed that a great many oil sketches were pinned to the walls or stood upon chairs and chests of drawers.

"O I'd forgotten!" Mrs Flushing cried, and quickly turned as many as she could with their faces to the wall. "You're not to look at them," she commanded, nervously watching to see whether Rachel looked. "I've somethin' much better worth your lookin' at."

"But I want to see" said Rachel. "I know nothing about painting." She took up a large piece of yellow cardboard, upon which there was a great glow of colour; the sun, it seemed to be, violently attacked by the earth in motion. A gigantic tree was tearing its hands at the firmament.

"That's nothin'" said Mrs Flushing, who while making as though to snatch the picture yet seemed to await criticism. For some reason or other either because of the gaudy colours, or because of the abrupt shapes, the picture seemed to Rachel oddly like the painter. Unable to give this as a reason for liking it she merely said with a flourish of her hand, accurately copied from someone else, "It moves."

"Now you've said exactly what I wanted you to say!" exclaimed Mrs Flushing, highly pleased. "I'd give both my ears to make things move—I don't mind which way. I don't care a fig for shape or likeness and all that—so long as things move." She screwed her eyes up and looked out of the window. "That's how I see everything whirling round and round. Now you've looked long enough at that. Look here!"

So saying she flung open the wings of her wardrobe. Inside all in a row, so that they looked like victims of a gamekeeper's gun, hung a variety of long, tasselled shawls, some white some fawn coloured, and some intense black. Mrs Flushing took an armfull and laid them on the bed. "These are what the women wore hundreds of years ago" she said. But the flowers and trees embroidered upon them were so bright that it was difficult to believe how much they had seen.

"My husband rides about all day and finds 'em" she said. "The women don't know what they're worth so we get 'em cheap. I call it cheatin' but my husband doesn't; and it ain't any of my business. He says they'd cheat us. This is what they do now; they like it much better than the old; so do I."

She pulled out a handfull of scarves from a drawer embroidered with realistic butterflies and convolvuli. "More life in 'em, don't you think? They're done for people in Birmingham. You buy 'em in the shops down there." She unlocked a leather case, and from it took strings of beads, gold brooches, earrings made of grotesque pearls, golden bracelets, tassels knobbed with red and green stones, and beautiful tortoiseshell combs. She tumbled them out among the shawls. Rachel and Mrs Flushing sat on either side of the bed, and played with them, now holding some semi transparent stone to the light, now draping the necklaces upon a shawl draped upon a bed post.

"And you sell these in a shop?" asked Rachel.

"We shall sell every single one for double what we paid," said Mrs Flushing. "You've no idea what fools women in London are—smart women, you know. They'll buy anythin' if it's out of the way. Some old frump with a neck like a pea hens will deck herself out with this. Won't she look a guy?" Mrs Flushing chuckled, holding up a splendid tuft, which was meant to sway upon the brow of some springing young Spanish woman with naked feet.

"I tell you what I want to do" Mrs Flushing went on, nervously picking up one jewel after another. "I want to go out there and see things for myself. It's silly, stayin' here with a pack of old maids just as though one was at the sea side in England. I want to go up the river and see the women in their camps. It's only a matter of ten days under canvas. And no one to bother you with chatter. That's what I detest; chatter, chatter, chatter." She flung the necklaces down and paced about the room. "One would lie out under the trees at night, and be towed down the river by day; and if we saw any thin' nice we'd just shout out and tell 'em to stop. Don't it sound to you jolly?"

"What d'you think it looks like?" said Rachel. "Are there trees all the way, and then clearings with huts, and painted women sitting making baskets, and men on little horses with long tails?"

Mrs Flushing cried. "Yes! Yes! You'll come! One must have a party you see, and a man to make bargains or one gets horribly cheated. We'll settle it between us, and then we'll tell my husband. If we tell him now he'll make difficulties; men always do. Now will Mr Hirst and the other gentleman come? Will Mrs—the lady you call Helen—come? What about your Uncle?"

The party had spring up with such suddenness that Rachel scarcely knew how to deal with it. Was it all as fantastic as her description of it, or could it really be that eight people all wonderful new and happy should spend ten days together out upon the river?

"You should ask Mr Pepper" she said, "an old old gentleman, who knows everything. He knows everything," she laughed, "but his heart's a piece of old shoe leather."

Mrs Flushing stopped her pacing and fixed Rachel with her suspicious blue eye.

"Which d'you like best?" she said. "Mr Hirst or t'other gentleman? (I call 'em both Mr Hirst" she said, "only one of 'em isn't.) To tell you a secret," she continued, not waiting for an answer, "I'm horribly frightened of both of them, only there's one who's not so frightening as the other."

From this description Rachel supplied the names.

"Hewet" she said "is tall, rather large, with ruffled hair and spectacles. Hirst is tall, thin, with a moustache, very dark with eyeglasses. I expect he is the one you find frightening. So do I. He has a gigantic brain."

"And Mr Hewet?" asked Mrs Flushing.

Rachel found that she could not talk of Hewet without losing some control over her voice.

"He is a writer, travelling for his amusement. I think he writes novels" she said.

"I know a man who writes novels" said Mrs Flushing. "At least I did; he's dead now poor man. They have to drink more than's good for them always, and that's why their wives are so unhappy. But it's nothin' to the painters. If it ain't beatin' it's some thin' worse!" and she gave her sinister chuckle.

"I go to see Maddock sometimes. He's as polite as he can be to me; but it don't take me in; I know there's some poor wretch of a woman cookin' his dinner downstairs, and My! won't she catch it if Maddock don't like it! I've often stayed to dinner on purpose, though he didn't mean me to, just for the run of watchin' him behave to her. But the party" she broke off. "Did you really mean you'd come?" "Yes, of course" said Rachel, standing as well as she could the searchlight which Mrs Flushing turned upon her.

"That's right" said Mrs Flushing, and began to count upon her fingers. "Ten days—let's see. Where are we now? Eight people. Two days for gettin' ready. That brings us— where's my diary?" She began to open and shut the drawers of her writing table, and suddenly cried, "Yarmouth! Yarmouth! Drat the woman! She's always downstairs."

At this point the gong went into its daily frenzy. Mrs Flushing gave up the search, and rang the bell violently. The door was opened by a handsome maid, whose bearing was almost as upright as her mistress's.

"Look here Yarmouth," said Mrs Flushing pointing to the bed, "Put those things away will you; and put 'em in their right places there's a good girl, or it fusses Mr Flushin'. Now." She pointed to the door with a superb forefinger, so that Rachel had to lead the way.

"O and Yarmouth!" Mrs Flushing called back over her shoulder, "just take my diary and find out where ten days from now would bring us to, and ask the hall porter how many men'd be wanted to row eight people up the river for a week, and what it 'ud cost, and put it on a slip of paper and leave it on my dressin' table."

"Yes, Mam" said Yarmouth.

As they entered the long dining room it was quite obvious that the day was still Sunday. The mood was still victorious. Mrs Flushing's table was set by the side in the window, so that without seeming rude she could scrutinise each figure as it entered. "Old Mrs Paley" she whispered, as the wheeled chair slowly made its way through the door, Susan pushing behind. "Thornburys" came next. "That nice woman" she nudged Rachel, to look at Miss Allen, "What's her name?"

The painted lady who always came in late, tripping into the room with a prepared smile, as though she came out upon a stage, might well have quailed before Mrs Flushing's glance; it expressed a steely hostility. Next, there were the two young men whom Mrs Flushing called collectively, "The Hirsts" then all alone, with a black book beneath his arm, William Pepper.

"That's my old gentleman" said Rachel. He saw her, considered for a moment, and then approached.

"An unexpected sight" he said. "All well?"

"What is your book, Mr Pepper?" Rachel asked, instead of answering.

"Metaphilostratos Hippopotidorum" Mr Pepper answered, and made off to his little round table at the end of the room, where the cruet served for reading desk.

"I tell you," Mrs Flushing began, "that's the most interestin' man in the place. I'm always tryin' to hear what he says. What did he say?"

"He always says the same thing" said Rachel. "Metaphilostratos Hippopotidorum; only sometimes he says it the other way round."

"I want to know" said Mrs Flushing abruptly; she seized the fork and gave the table a smart rap, as though she were an auctioneer.

"Yes?" asked Rachel.

"No; I shan't tell you" said Mrs Flushing.

"Please" said Rachel.

"I want to know" Mrs Flushing began again. She paused so long that Rachel was afraid she had repented.

"Do you like me?" Mrs Flushing suddenly brought out, now seizing a knife also for support.

"Yes, of course I do," said Rachel shaken with laughter.

"I sometimes think that I have seen you laughin'" said Mrs Flushing.

"That's because I like you" said Rachel. "If I admired you I should be as glum as the grave. I want to know" she imitated Mrs Flushing's voice and seized the vase in the middle of the table, "Do you like me?"

"I shan't answer that" said Mrs Flushing grimly, "until we have slept at least one night under the same roof."

Hirst and Hewet whose table was opposite across the gangway, observed the laughter and gestures of the two ladies rather sourly. Ever since they had left the chapel they had been arguing about the sermon and Christianity. Both agreed that the sermon was a repulsive exhibition, but both did not agree upon the merits of the service. Hewet had secretly been annoyed with Hirst for his display of ostentatious paganism.

"Even if you want literature merely," he said, "the Psalms are every bit as good as Sappho."

Hirst hooted. "You can't read Greek; so how d'you know?"

"All I say," Hewet then remarked, growing surly, "is that it's silly not to see that there's something in it.

"You can't dismiss what half the human race feels. It's so easy. If you're merely going to read Sappho why go to church at all?"

"If you'd been less absorbed in your devotions," said Hirst, who, having already earlier in the day confuted all Hewet's arguments and forced him to own that a man's emotion for an unknown God is a bad emotion, now felt disposed to tease him, "you'd have seen that I was doing a great many other things besides reading Sappho. I attended to every word of the sermon, as I'd prove if you like to introduce me to your friend Mr Bax. Moreover, while you were obviously engrossed in the beauties of the female form, I wrote on the back of the envelope of my aunt's last letter, three of the most superb lines in English poetry. They are the beginning of my address to the Creator. I assure you, Mr Bax brought him very vividly before me."

"Well, let's hear them" said Hewet, slightly mollified by the prospect of a literary discussion.

"My dear Hewet, do you wish us both to be flung out of the hotel by an enraged mob of Thornburys and Elliots?" Hirst enquired.

"The merest whisper would be sufficient to incriminate me for ever. God," he broke out, "what's the use of attempting to write when the world's peopled by such damned fools? Seriously Hewet, I advise you to give up literature. What on earth's the use of it? There's your audience!" He nodded his head at the tables, where the portly men of business, lean women and fat women, bronzed young athletes and surly old fogies were eating their stringy foreign fowls. Hewet was not exhilarated by the sight, but remarked,

"You can write well without being indecent."

"Names" demanded Hirst. "Jane Austen's the only great writer who'd be allowed to write now."

"That depends" said Hewet, "whom you call great."

Whether it was that unlucky sermon, or the fact that a fly died without any legs in the mustard, or whether there was some less obvious cause, the literary discussion was by no means calm.

"If you refuse to call Meredith a great writer," said Hewet, "you merely prove, what I've always suspected, that you've no feeling for literature. Style, I grant you; you know a good style when you see one, because you can measure a sentence by a foot rule. But when it comes to the really important qualities, you're all of you simply hidebound with humbug."

"All of me?" Hirst enquired. In argument with Hewet he always kept his temper, used his brains, and won the day.

"All Cambridge I mean" said Hewet.

Here they touched upon another old grievance. Hewet's acquaintance with the university had been short, and it was due to this he maintained that he preserved any force, any originality, any joy in life. Naturally it was a proposition that often had to be disproved.

"You're very silly about Cambridge" Hirst continued calmly, choosing an orange with great perspicacity. "One; you've practically never been there. Two; you have to admit that the only people worth knowing are Cambridge men. Bingham; Bennett; Carpenter; with all his faults you can't beat old Mozley either."

"Bingham I admit" said Hewet. "The others I totally refuse to accept. If you consider that they've done nothing but sharpen their noses since they had noses to sharpen, well, it's nothing wonderful if they are sharp. They can all write prose that might be mistaken for somebody else's. I grant you that."

"My dear Hewet, don't get cross" said Hirst, who felt for Hewet on these occasions as for a truculent small boy, and treated him as such.

"If you were capable of calm judgment, which you are not, you would be forced to own up. You call yourself a man of the world; I defy you to produce a single human being, white black, or striped, who's fit to compare for any of the qualities you've named with any of the people I've named. I give you till I've peeled this orange. Now; go."

"I'm not going to play absurd games" said Hewet; he grumbled himself into silence. He would not admit that it was not the truth of Christianity, or the genius of George Meredith, or the defects of the University system that lay at the base of his ill humor. No; it was an altogether far more trivial cause than any of these—that Rachel Vinrace was sitting at the table opposite, very much enjoying her talk with Wilfrid Flushing, an elderly married man.

Coffee was served in the lounge, but even after luncheon, though two hours had passed since the religious service, the effects seemed still to linger.

"Do you know anything about Mr Bax?" said Mrs Thornbury drawing a chair near Miss Allen.

"His father was a Professor of Geology" said Miss Allen.

"There was so much that one liked in what he said" said Mrs Thornbury.

"And so much that one did not like" said Miss Allen.

"Yes, yes" said Mrs Thornbury, "and I'm afraid that applies to the whole service, magnificent as it is."

"One just has to think of something else" said Miss Allen, "as I always say God Save the Queen instead of King. I rather like the savage bits, taken as poetry."

"But for anyone who does not understand," said Mrs Thornbury, "I always fear it may seem strange. I make a point of explaining to my girls at home as much as I can explain. I have a little club in our village, and I talk to them on Sundays and we read together. Of course they are easier than the boys. The young men are the great problem—how to reconcile modern ideas with the old teaching. Even where we are they get hold of pamphlets. And that is what one wishes to do, as Mr Bax very rightly said this morning. When

I think what our faith has been to us—to William and me, I mean—it seems terrible that young people should grow up without it. It makes a background doesn't it?"

She looked about the room as though she meant that the figures she saw were passing in front of something permanent. Miss Allen said nothing.

"I was glad to see Mr Hirst and Mr Hewet there" Mrs Thornbury continued. "Yes" said Miss Allen dryly. The silence was felt by them both to be awkward, it was probably the result of some difference in what they believed, and also of the fact that Miss Allen resented attacks upon her reserve.

"I make a point of going to church when I'm abroad" she said at length deliberately stirring her coffee, "just as I should make a point of going to a sailor's funeral."

"Yes?" asked Mrs Thornbury.

"I cannot explain more than that" said Miss Allen.

As a matter of fact Miss Allen had never been baptised, old Dr Allen having been one of the first men to call himself Agnostic in England, and the eighth person to be cremated.

"I do not think there is a need to explain" said Mrs Thornbury gently. "What a lovely bird!" A blue bird, about the shape and size of a magpie, opportunely perched on the gravel outside, flitting its tail up and down, and glittering in a metallic way in the bright sunshine. "And yet, I believe that if all our sparrows were blue, we should soon get tired of it—what do you think William?" She touched her husband on the knee; he was engaged as usual, in raising his eyeglasses, dusting them, and putting them on again—an occupation which seemed to make it unnecessary for him ever to take part in a conversation. "When I can see to my satisfaction" his argument seemed to be, "I will give my opinion; until then, I prefer to abstain." "If all our sparrows were blue" he said; and took his glasses off. "They would not live long in Wiltshire." He put them on again.

"Blue sparrows" said Miss Allen meditatively. "Would one like them or not?" Miss Allen Mr and Mrs Thornbury now gazed in silence at the bird, which obligingly stayed in the middle of the view for a considerable time and thus made it unnecessary for them to speak.

Hirst had done what Hewet either had not the courage or the temper to do. He had approached the Flushing party, where they sat in the corner, with a cigarette in his hand.

"What did you think of the sermon?" he demanded, with a little constriction of the lips to show that he quoted.

"Now you've done it!" cried Mrs Flushing. "I'd quite forgotten it was Sunday!" She hastily knocked her cigarette into ashes. "It's a little late in the day for that Alice" said Mr Flushing producing his cigarette case.

"They'll be shocked" said Mrs Flushing, glancing surreptitiously round the room, while she fingered a fresh cigarette. "Besides it's no use." She met Mrs Thornbury's eye and instead of taking a cigarette grasped her handkerchief, and blew her nose, as though to protest her innocence.

"Ain't they depressin'?"

Rachel looked at the three elderly people who were inspecting the bird.

"Middle age! How awful!" she ejaculated. "Just follow them until you get to their eyes."

"But you are a Christian too?" said Hirst looking from the Thornburys to Rachel. "I suppose you enjoyed the service."

Rachel pondered. The desire to contradict Mr Hirst mingled with fear of his strong ruthless mind; but, when they talked of honesty did they mean, these god like young men, that private ideas would be respected?

"There are two things I like about the service" she began, and then knowing that her two might become five or one corrected herself, "the things I like about the service are, that it continues things, and that the preacher generally makes a fool of himself; in fact we all make fools of ourselves."

"Continues?" said Hirst as though the first stumbling block must be removed.

"I see what Miss Vinrace means. I feel it myself" said Mr Flushing.

"Imagine" said Rachel much encouraged, "a summer day; the sky is blue without a cloud; enormous like the top of a hall."

"Yes?" said Hirst.

"A blue dome" said Mr Flushing.

"Well, that's the service you see; even if one doesn't attend, and I don't, because it's so old."

"Why should it please you to imagine a blue dome?" said Hirst.

"What Miss Vinrace means, I think," said Mr Flushing, "is that she enjoys the sense of community which worship gives."

"Yes, and making a fool of oneself. It's what I felt," she continued "when the Vennings became engaged."

Hirst could imagine the vague sentimental indolent emotions which filled Rachel's mind. Freshmen were often like that. He did not approve but liked her for her confession; and credited her with the power of owning her mistakes, if some one took the trouble to reason with her. As for Mr Flushing, he judged him to be a weak but very amiable man.

"Churches" said Rachel. "I once spent six weeks near York Minster. It was the first thing I saw in the morning. But I never understood—the churches."

"I don't think we shall ever understand again" said Mr Flushing. "It doesn't worry me now, as it used to."

"It worries me when I think of them, standing about all over England" said Rachel "such vast things."

Hirst had just remembered that Mr Flushing was an authority upon architecture, and was about to ask for information, for the subject interested him, when Mrs Flushing broke in,

"You don't ever make a fool of yourself, Mr Hirst!" and thus recalled him to the fact that he was hated by every body. Accordingly he pursed his lips and said,

"I certainly don't think it's a virtue to make a fool of myself" which Rachel took to be a hit at her.

Hewet sitting out in the garden in a remote part, where a gigantic bush cast shade, did not know that for a moment at least one person ardently desired him. On the contrary, he had come to the conclusion since luncheon that Rachel was completely and eternally indifferent to him. Two or three books as usual solaced him, but after reading for a page or so, he gazed up into the sky. His ordinary expression of dreamy content, was now clouded with gloom. Not for the first time he ran over the unsympathetic qualities of his friend, St John Hirst, and of the country where he was.

"How tired one gets of blue skies, white roads, olive trees, sea, the picturesque" he reflected, "and of hotel life. Rachel—do I love her, or don't I?" He sighed and stretched himself, so that Sir Thomas Browne fell upon the gravel. At this moment Evelyn M. approached, with young Oliver to hold her parasol for her. She was slapping her bare arm energetically with her gloves and from the obsequious droop of his back Hewet could guess that Oliver's career was being shaped for him.

"What, you here—all alone?" she said, stopping for an instant; "Well, good luck to you!" she cried, and passed on, the white parasol leading, still leading her procession it seemed to the top of a high mountain.

"Too public" Hewet commented. He picked up his books, put his hat firm upon his head, and laced a loose boot lace. Then, trim and equipped, he walked out of the hotel grounds, in spite of the fact that this was the hot hour when every one slept. There were two roads from the hotel, one of which, becoming steep and scraggy, led to the Ambroses' villa, the other struck into the heart of the country, and foot paths led off it, across the great dry fields, to scattered farm houses, washed light pinks and yellows. Hewet chose one of these, so as to avoid the carts which raised the white dust as they carried parties of festive peasants, or turkeys, swelling like entrapped air balloons, beneath netting, or the bed room furniture of some newly wedded pair. He found himself after walking quickly for an hour, on the banks of what had once been a river for the sides were steep, and down the bottom ran a rivulet of hot dry stones. Drops of perspiration were sliding from his forehead down his cheeks. He came to a tree which spread its shade and murmured over the dry river bed. He leant against it, so that his hat fell back, and his forehead was pressed to the bark. "I love her." He murmured aloud, in a voice that was half a sob, "I love her, I love her I love her" and then sobbed, so that he could stand no longer, but sat in the shade of the tree still, except for the movement which his sobs made, irregularly. When he unclasped his knees, and raised his face, an enormous happiness was to be seen there. He saw nothing, not the leaves, or the great blue dragon fly, or the lizard slipping between the stones in the sun; he saw nothing but the tender and magnificent world; he felt nothing but the sublime relief of allowing himself to love.

CHAPTER TWENTY-TWO

When a few minutes after three o'clock, the different parties began to disperse, the blue bird having flown away and St John having quitted the Flushings to add some particularly caustic lines to his sacrilegious poem, Rachel was left standing in the hall, beneath the clock. Mrs Flushing as she swept off to smoke cigarettes in her bed room, and perhaps cover another square, had commanded her to stay to tea. Seeing no one she knew to speak to, Rachel picked up an old copy of an American magazine, and lay back in a deep arm chair. There was only Miss Willett in the middle distance nervously playing scales with her fingers upon a sheet of sacred music, and half a dozen white or sausage coloured faces scattered round the sides. Unknown to herself, Rachel was the object at once of passionate admiration and of intense dislike. The admiration was bestowed by a girl of fifteen, a long legged American with her hair tied in a bow so large that from the front she appeared winged like a bat. When the unknown lady was there the commonest objects were wonderful, because her eye fell on them; and she crossed the hall again and again, and stood talking in the middle of the room, so that Rachel might see her. But Rachel knew nothing except that she wore a bow. The dislike on the other hand was felt in common by a young married couple, he was a soldier and she had once been on the stage. From the first they had disliked Rachel instinctively. It was not dislike so much as contempt, which in the woman's case fed on clothes, hair, shoes, everything. Again, Rachel was unconscious, except once, as she went into luncheon, and Mrs Carter slid her eye from top to toe, with a peculiar glance which Rachel did not on that occasion interpret. Once disliked, she became a type; they called her "The Spring Chicken." But, for the rest the white or sausage coloured faces were as unwitting of her as she was of them.

Suddenly, the swing door swung, a wedge of light fell upon the floor, and a small white figure, on whom the sunshine seemed concentrated, made straight across for Rachel.

"How cool you look!" she exclaimed, flinging herself into the next chair, "I'm baking!" But the spirit seemed to burn as well as the flesh.

"Not the weather for raking out one's emotions is it?" she said, panting as much with excitement as with the heat, "But I daresay you're like your friends and never do that in any weather. I wish I could keep cool—but I can't—never could. And so you see I'm always in scrapes—but I don't care a hang what they say—why should one if one knows one's right?—and let 'em all go to blazes—them's my opinions!" Saying this, she went on slapping her bare brown arms energetically, "I suppose you think I'm quite mad?" she continued, looking at Rachel.

"What has happened is this," Rachel exclaimed; "somebody's been proposing to you!"

"It isn't only that" said Evelyn. She prepared to unbosom herself. "Look here, we don't want an audience. Come up to my room." [She took Rachel by the wrist, and forced her out of the hall, up the stairs. As they ran up the stairs, Evelyn who still kept hold of Rachel's arm ejaculated some broken sentences about not caring a hang what anyone said—"Why should one if one knows one's right?"

…"What's happened to me isn't a proposal—exactly. It's—O it's a muddle—a detestable, horrible, disgusting muddle!" She went to the washstand and began sponging her cheeks with cold water; they were flaming red. "Alfred Perrott says I've promised to marry him, and I say I never did. Raymond says he'll shoot himself if I don't marry him and I say "Well. Shoot yourself!" but of course he doesn't—they never do—And Raymond got hold of me this afternoon, and began bothering me to give an answer…; in another instant Evelyn was off upon quite a different train of thought; that the finest men were like women, and that women were nobler than men, for example one couldn't imagine a woman like Lillah Harris thinking a base thing, or having any thing mean about her.

"How I wish you knew her!" she exclaimed.

…"Lillah runs a home for inebriate women in the Deptford Road. She started it, managed it, did everything off her own bat, and now it's the biggest of its kind in England. You can't think what some of those women are like,—and their homes. But she goes among them at all hours of the day and night. I've often been with her.]

[[There was a plan for]] some other man or woman who would dedicate a life to it, and needed money too, it was still admittedly vague. There was to be a band of young men and women, who wore white badges, went about the streets at night, met every other Thursday, behaved as though sex did not exist, and made the fallen women feel at their ease.

Rachel was interested, but exclaimed,

"People don't think. You've only to look at them here. They feel."

"That's awfully interesting" said Evelyn. "And I quite agree. Look here you must join. Name and address please."

Down they went into a note book already well supplied with the names of those ready one of these days to speak the truth, and wear white badges in Piccadilly.

"What's wrong with Lillah—if there is any thing wrong," said Evelyn, writing 12 Bury Road, Richmond, "is that she seems to think of temperance, not of women. Now I'm going to start the other way round, and think of the women first and let the abstract ideas take care of themselves. There's one thing I'll say to my credit," she continued, "I'm not intellectual, or artistic, or anything of that sort, but I'm jolly human." She slipped off the bed, and sat on the floor looking up at Rachel.

"And I think you are too" she said, smiled, searching into Rachel's face, "though I didn't think so at first. Now I'm Evelyn; you're Rachel."

The friendship was further ratified by the clasp of their hands, "It is being human that counts," said Evelyn "whatever Mr Hirst may say. That's why I want a revolution. If only some thing would happen! We all sit jawing away, and we're all so clever and I feel that we get further and further from the things that really matter."

"If you were binding up a wound, and I were sitting on a camel—" Rachel suggested.

"If we believed in freedom or God" said Evelyn.

"I suppose you don't believe in anything?"

"In everything!" cried Rachel. "In you, in the bed, in the photographs, in the pot, in the balcony, in the sun, in Mrs Flushing, in Miss Allen, in Susan Warrington—"

"In Mr Hirst?" asked Evelyn.

"Only parts of him, and Mr Pepper not at all."

"What I mean is" said Evelyn, "you've no cause that you'd die for."

"If I thought that by dying I could give birth to twenty—no thirty—children, all beautiful and very charming, I'd die for that" said Rachel, "Perhaps." Candour forced her to consider the extreme horror of feeling the water give under her, of losing her head, splashing wildly, sinking again with every vein smarting and bursting, an enormous weight sealing her mouth, and pressing salt water down her lungs when she breathed. A recent sip wreck suggested drowning as the form her death would take.

"That's just why one must marry" said Evelyn. "That's what makes us so much finer than men are. Who shall you marry? Is it Mr Hewet? You needn't answer if you don't want to."

Rachel did not want to; she said "It isn't any one."

"I think I could die for the Russians" said Evelyn. "Liberty is what I'm keen on."

A single sentence dropped right at the beginning of their talk, had been pricking Rachel now this way now that. Were Hewet and Evelyn intimate friends as Evelyn seemed to suggest? If he had tried to kiss her—She had recourse to movement. "Could we explore the hotel before tea?" she asked. She went out upon the balcony and looked into a wilderness. "When Helen and I came that night we only saw two sides."

"That's where they kill chickens" said Evelyn. "They chase 'em for ever so long before they catch 'em. Why is it that foreigners can't do that kind of thing? Then they cut their heads off."

Indeed, they looked down upon triangular figures, doing some thing vigorous to bodies on their knees.

"Let us explore" said Rachel again. As a matter of fact, Evelyn had no wish to explore; she wished to talk; she wished as usual to become intimate. She wished to talk of parents and experiences.

"Doesn't it seem to you strange," she exclaimed, "how one suddenly meets a new person, and knows nothing about them,—I wish you'd tell me about yourself."

"I can't" said Rachel. "I don't know."

"What don't you know?" said Evelyn her eyes brightening as she observed Rachel's excitement.

"Nothing" said Rachel. ""Who I am, what I feel, or what this strange adventure is." She checked herself, and her eyes lost their light. "You know how one takes hold of a chair, to be sure, to be certain that the world exists?"

"Yes?" Evelyn enquired.

"So I take hold of a chair now" said Rachel, leaning on the back of one, "I do not know who I am." It seemed as though she had lost her consciousness.

"Wake up" said Evelyn brightly.

But it was some moments before Rachel's soft grey eyes lit up again.

"I don't like it" she said with a little shudder, "going under like that. But does it never strike you," she continued, making an effort to explain, "that the great procession, these people we see going about, scattered everywhere without any connection, and you and me—we are not real, we cannot touch each other. And the present is only an instant."

Instead of answering Evelyn said

"What has suddenly made you gloomy?"

"I want to be assured. I want courage" said Rachel. "In fact what I want" she said with a complete change of mood, "is to explore the hotel."

"Right you are" cried Evelyn, jumping off the bed, "And you shall tell me about yourself another time."

But they had not gone half way down the corridor before Rachel flagged and stopped; it happened that there was a window, and that Guiseppe the manager had seen fit to nail a plaster image of Christ upon the Cross to the frame. It was one of the relics that the monks had left behind them.

"You have been in love" she said. "I wish you'd tell me what it feels like, because people talk as much about it as about religion."

She knelt on the floor, crossed her arms upon the window sill and looked out into the garden.

"How can one explain?" said Evelyn rather tartly. "Anyhow, not here, where the servants are always fetching cans."

Rachel with her head outside continued to speak.

"Years ago," she said, "I read two books—Thomas a Kempis, and the Love letters of a Portuguese Nun. I did not understand either of them. But I said—I wrote it in a pocket book—'in ten years time I shall understand both.' When I get home the first thing I shall do is see. Do you feel that?" she said, now drawing her head in, so as to look up at Evelyn, "Do you feel that the past has hung sealed packets upon the branches which we break open one by one?"

"Sort of" said Evelyn, "Only it's not quite so pretty if one happens to be an illegitimate child."

This communication had the effect of taking away whatever wish Rachel may have had to continue her voyage of discovery. She sank upon the floor saying,

"You? Illegitimate?"

"Well, it isn't a kind of skin disease" said Evelyn for Rachel continued to gaze at her. "And I wasn't born in a ditch either. But it's the sort of thing that makes a difference. There was a man who wouldn't marry me because of it— spoilt his quarterings I suppose. That's why I'm going to help other women." Seeing that Rachel was once more sinking into meditation or mere blankness of mind, Evelyn gave her wrist a tug exclaiming, "Now come along! D'you always take ten minutes to think of something to say?"

Much though she resented the interruption, Rachel had to get up, ejaculating, "They were in love!"

Evelyn's object now was to get her past other windows tempting her to other soliloquies. Ready though she was to tell the unhappy story of her mother's life, she had no wish to begin now, feeling certain that Rachel would merely keep her standing about indefinitely, while she speculated in the vaguest possible fashion upon love and death. But a balcony on the floor beneath proved a trap—a terrible opportunity for abstract reflection, since it was but a few feet above the scrubby back garden where the women sat killing fowls. Rachel showed her determination. "I want to look" she said. There was practically nothing to see, only two large women in cotton dresses, sitting on a bench with tin trays in front of them, and chickens on their knees.

"Now what are they talking about?" Rachel asked, but Evelyn was saved from answering by Miss Allen who came out of her room at this moment and holding up a half written page of manuscript, said, "Sacrilegious—an i or an e?"

She came and looked over the balcony railing. For all that Evelyn might say, it was a strange sight. It was the wrong side so to speak of hotel life; the place where the old tins were thrown away and bushes wore towels and handkerchiefs upon their heads to dry. Every now and then a waiter in his shirtsleeves ran out and threw rubbish on to a heap. The two large women spoke of interesting things as they plucked the fowls, for every now and then the one on the left hand side shook her fist in the air instead of pulling feathers. Then her companion would shrug her shoulders. Suddenly a fowl came floundering half flying half running into the space; pursued by a third woman whose age could hardly be under eighty. Although wizened and lame she kept up the chase, egged on by the cheers of the others, her face was twisted with rage and as she hobbled she swore in Spanish. Frightened by hand clapping here, a napkin there, the bird dodged round and round, and finally fluttered straight at its enemy. The old woman promptly enclosed it in her skirts, and then—at this point Evelyn turned away— drew her knife and cut its head off with an intensity of vindictive energy which might have accompanied the death of a traitor.

The blood and the ugly wriggling were sufficient excuse for leaving the balcony had Evelyn wanted one. But Miss Allen and Rachel stood fascinated. Miss Allen turned to Rachel, more intimately than if they had seen nothing ugly together.

"You have never seen my room" she said.

It was another of those small hotel rooms which though identical when empty become so different directly a box has been unpacked there. The small writing table was neatly piled with manuscripts, divided into sections. The scrupulous tidiness was almost masculine and rather ugly.

"Age of Chaucer. Age of Elizabeth. Age of Dryden" said Miss Allen, lifting the sections. "I'm glad there aren't many more ages. The difficulty in work of this kind is to be at once instructive and entertaining. I do not find it difficult to instruct, but I should like to be able to jest as some of my colleagues can. (Won't you sit down Miss Vinrace? The chair, though small is firm.) Do you jest, or are you serious, or perhaps you are both. (If you put your finger into this jar you may be able to extract a small piece of preserved ginger.) The best thing about a college education is that it teaches the young people to laugh. But that was after my time. I belong to the age of ball room misses."

"That explains," said Rachel, "how you knew the Lancers."

"I did not enjoy dances" said Miss Allen. "But we were very thoroughly taught. If we had been of your generation it would have been Greek or Science, not dancing."

"Or nothing at all" said Rachel.

"With my parents it would certainly have been something" said Miss Allen. "And I expect it was something with yours too" she added kindly. She had an affectionate feeling for all young women, and it was this that encouraged Rachel to continue those spasmodic utterances which represented her attempts to grapple with the world. Accustomed to think in music, unused to being one of a great number, for with her aunts at home she was solitary she was of a type well known to Miss Allen; they came up in October from remote country homes; who gazed benignly at her, as she fished ineffectually for ginger, and gazed about her now with fire and now with blank eyes.

"Nothing!" she exclaimed. "Nothing! I was taught nothing, nothing but lies. And then I was dropped here, where you are all so different."

"We are not very alarming, when you come to know us" said Miss Allen. "I think we are rather shy, and that makes us seem awkward."

"Were you shy when you looked at the blue bird?" Rachel asked.

"Well, slightly," said Miss Allen. "I am not a person who makes friends easily. Now I have a colleague who knows whether she likes you or not—let me see how does she do it?—by the way you say good morning at breakfast. I am not at all that kind of person."

By this time Rachel had fished out her lump of ginger and incautiously bitten it.

"I must spit it out!" she cried. "I did not know that ginger was disgusting."

"Experiences everywhere" said Miss Allen calmly. "Let me see—I have nothing else to offer you, unless you would like to taste this. To avoid temptation it is locked." She unlocked a cup board, above the washstand, and took out a bottle containing a vivid green liquid.

"Crème de Menthe" she said. "When I went to Dresden six and twenty years ago a certain friend of mine announced her intention of making me a present. She thought that in the event of a ship wreck or accident strong drink might be useful. However I had no occasion for it, having met with no adventures. Therefore when I came back I returned it. On the eve of any foreign journey the same bottle appears with the same note; on my return it is always handed back. Yes" she continued, addressing the bottle, we have seen many climes and cupboards together, have we not? I intend one of these days to have a label printed with an inscription. It is a gentleman, as you may observe, and his name is Oliver."

Rachel was holding the bottle to the light.

"Can one have a friend for twenty six years?" she asked.

"Indeed one can" said Miss Allen. She paused. "May I ask who you live with?"

"With my father and two Aunts" said Rachel still turning the bottle. As to look intently at a brightly coloured globe takes away self consciousness, she added something unintelligible to Miss Allen "and spirits and the sea."

"A sister is a good sort of relationship" said Miss Allen.

"My three sisters" she observed, giving Rachel a case containing three photographs. "Emily, Hilda, and Edith, so called after the three Northumbrian saints."

"I suppose you say everything to them?" said Rachel looking at the three ladies who looked at the photographer so brightly and at the world so doggedly.

"We are not great people for talking" said Miss Allen. "Of the three I consider Hilda the most communicative, and Emily the least. Some people get so devoted to their dogs. And have you nobody you can say everything to?" she added as she replaced the case?

"To tell you the truth," said Rachel, instantly desiring to explain her entire life to the kind woman whom she had seen perhaps three times, "I don't know how to speak. I want—"

"When we are young we want a great deal" said Miss Allen.

"And do we get it?" Rachel asked.

"I have a great deal of reason to be satisfied with my life" said Miss Allen, "But I always thought I should marry. You are very young however. You have time to get everything you want, and I hope you will. But I believe it is wise to make the most of our opportunities. I do not think I could forgive you if you broke my Oliver, Miss Vinrace" she said, firmly taking the bottle out of Rachel's hand. Absorbed in Miss Allen, the sisters, and her own sensations, Rachel had been swinging Oliver idly by the neck.

"If I seriously thought I was not going to have what I want" she said, taking up her favourite position by the window, so that she could look alternately out of doors and indoors, "I should kill myself."

"I have often heard young people say that" said Miss Allen, locking the cupboard. "And then they get interested in something else. Our Miss Murray used to say just that kind of thing. I think it was the Suffrage that upset her. And then she took to breeding guinea pigs for their spots and forgot all about killing herself, I suppose. I must ask her."

Miss Allen then looked at her watch and said that it was tea time. "Not that I am in a fit state to encounter my fellow beings" she said, glancing at herself in the glass; and patting her back hair. Instead of leaving her to dress, Rachel still leant against the window.

"But Miss Allen," she said, "is there any reason why one should not have everything? So far, my life has been quite wonderful."

"Let us hope that it will go on being wonderful" said Miss Allen abstractedly.

"Wonderful" said Rachel, now addressing the outer world. "The trees, and the mountains and the people; and when the statue gets off his horse...."

Miss Allen said rather loudly, "I fear you are wasting your eloquence—and I should be grateful for a pin behind."

"What was it I kissed?" she enquired.

"O nothing" said Rachel, confused and irritated.

"Then shall we descend?" said Miss Allen, who now that the pin had been administered, looked again as though her dress of brown cloth with its green trimming were the skin God had clothed her in at her birth.

"But we will only consider this as a beginning, Miss Vinrace" she said, putting her arm around Rachel's shoulder, and causing her to blush with pleasure.

They walked slowly along the corridor, and Miss Allen observed the different pairs of boots.

"People are so like their boots" she said. But Mrs Elliot came abruptly out of her room, and the Mrs Paley rolled out in her chair, and a thin foreign lady came scudding past, all obedient to the hour of tea, and Miss Allen repeated her remark rather loudly for the benefit of the old widow.—"I was saying that people are so like their boots." But as the statement was of a metaphorical nature, it had to be said a third time, and even then Mrs Paley regarded it with suspicion. Rachel as they slowly got round the corner, misunderstanding each other, stopped dead, and slipped back the opposite way. She was weighed down by the burden of a question which no one would answer.

"If all these doors were to open," she said, passing numbers 21, 23, 25, 27, 29, and 31, "and I stopped every one as he came out, and said, 'Answer this' they would say what Evelyn said, and Miss Allen said. 'In this world we are completely alone.'" In her erratic pursuit of the odd numbers, which remained obstinately shut, Rachel found herself at the end of a cul de sac, where there was a round table and on the round table lay an illustrated news paper and an ash tray. She began to turn the pages, but soon ceased, and fell into the attitude which was characteristic of her when not playing the piano. She leant both her elbows on the table, and supported her head as though it were something separate and precious set on the top of her body. She contemplated number thirty three as if the answer to her question dwelt behind the door, and a head, with moving lips might suddenly appear in the panel where the number was painted. An old fairy tale was running in her head. It was about a traveller who walked all a summer's day along a high road, and first he met a rich man in a coach with golden wheels, and asked him a question; but the rich man whipped up his horses and disappeared; next he met a merchant carrying a sack of rice; next there came a goose girl with her geese, and next a convict from the salt mines of Siberia. To all of them he put the same question but they were all too busy with their own affairs to answer him; "and that," said Rachel, "is exactly what has happened to me." She was the traveller, and she went not only from person to person, but from country to country and from age to age, asked her question: in the streets of Baghdad she asked it of men sitting by the roadside, and now in the city of London; she asked it of the Greeks and of the Italians, of poems and of music. But whereas the traveller in the fairy tale fell asleep and had a vision, she travelled on and on, still asking. Beginning with that rainy evening on board the Euphrosyne in the Thames when she had looked at the lights of London lying behind her, and Helen's face so strange in the lamplight and the wind, she passed on to the Dalloways, and then to Richard's kiss, and their backs as thy rowed away getting smaller and smaller; and then she came to Santa Rosa, and all the faces crowded round her, like Chinese lanterns, for so she had seen them that first night, as they sat playing cards; and gradually they became distinct, Evelyn's face, Hirst's face, Susan's face lying white upon the turf, with Arthur's face above it; she saw them all dancing now, and crowding to the window to look at the dawn; her uncle she saw, reading Greek with the sunlight joining with lamplight upon his page; and Helen sitting with her book before her, stitching at the picture of a river; and she saw herself sitting on the ground, saying "Am I in love? I am in love."

In her fancy she saw herself going up to each of these in turn and asking her question; but not one of them answered. "And how foolish," she said, "to sit on the ground and say 'I am in love' for I had no notion of what I meant."

One person only had not been asked the question, and that was Hewet. "If I could ask him—if I could tell him everything" she murmured, and was reminded of the difficulty of speaking to him, and of the immense distance between them, by the sensation which even here, at the end of the corridor, over came her, as of little waves raising her heart. Again she found it necessary to stir, and flung up the window and thrust her head out. To her surprise she found herself that a sunny green lawn lay beneath, alive with bright white figures. They were moving tables under the tree; then suddenly she saw Helen Ambrose who was standing still, looking straight up at her, laughing. But she did not see Rachel; she was laughing at something, Hirst said in answer to something said by Mrs Wilfrid Flushing.

CHAPTER TWENTY-THREE

In an obedience to an impulse which comes as suddenly as water boils over, the big tea table attracted the little tea tables. It was begun by a few rapid glances; and then St John and Mr Flushing began moving chairs, and Arthur Venning said stoutly "Marching orders, Aunt Emily" and moved the old lady so that she commanded the centre. Mrs Flushing was undoubtedly the central fire, and Helen Ambrose was her guest; but the Elliots the Thornburys, Hirst and Miss Allen had all the right to join in, and if a single figure wavered on the outskirts any one could beckon or call, and a cup would be forth coming somewhere.

Dismissing the heat, tea, the blueness of the sky, and the character of Signor Rodriguez as topics that demanded only a frown, a stare, or a sudden caw of laughter, Mrs Flushing concentrated herself upon the following speech addressed to Helen, and accompanied by the most systematic buttering of a horn of dry roll.

"Your niece and I have made a plan, Mrs Ambrose. We're goin' up the river on a boat. You'll come? We're goin' to hire a boat, and we're goin' to hire men; and we're goin' to see the most wonderful things that have ever been seen. Wilfrid's been. Everyone ought to go. I invite you and your husband. Ten days under canvas; no comforts; if you want comforts, don't come. I tell you, if you don't come you'll regret it all your life. Now, you say yes?"

Helen naturally turned to Wilfrid who put his wife's speech into prose.

"It is not a matter of ten days but of five" he said. "And the arrangements are not difficult."

All the others who had suspended their eating and opened their mouths now began to talk.

"I should think it would be hot. But very cold at night. I should think it would be rather uncomfortable. What a splendid idea! But are there any boats? Won't you have to talk the language?"

Mr Flushing merely told Helen that he had made the trip twice himself, and found it well worth doing for the sight of the native villages and the river scenery which was different from anything here.

"And we go back so soon" said Helen.

"Quinine and sleeping bags" said Mr Pepper.

Again the voices rose, but this time they were more deliberate, and several pieces of information were gravely imparted. Mrs Thornbury asked whether they had read the travels of Charles Bruce, whose book she believed was still the great authority; of course they knew the memoirs of Dom Miguel, who really might have been another Garibaldi, given the opportunity; Mr Thornbury interrupted her; "If a pair of binoculars would be of use they are at your service" he remarked, putting on his spectacles and looking straight in front of him. Mrs Paley having had Susan at one ear and Arthur at the other informing her in distinct simple sentences of the proposed plan, pronounced her opinion that they should take nice canned vegetables, insect powder and fur cloaks. She leant across to Mrs Flushing, and her old eyes which were becoming ringed with white, twinkled over the word "Bugs."

Helen paid no attention to these voices; she was considering. "So Rachel has agreed to go?" she said at length, smiling a little.

"Where is she?" asked Mrs Flushing, darting glances hither and thither. She was annoyed at missing her ally.

"Some one's been looking out of that window all this time" said Arthur. "A splendid shot from here. If it was Miss Vinrace she's just vanished."

"I left her looking at a chicken being killed" said Evelyn. "She was so absorbed that I couldn't get her on."

"A chicken? How disgusting!" breathed Susan.

"She left us in the passage I suppose," said Miss Allen, "I never noticed it until this moment." She looked about her as though Rachel might be there all the time.

"Are musical people always like that?" said Evelyn boldly, reaching her bare arm across the table, "flopping down and asking questions?"

"I shouldn't mind their asking questions if they'd listen to the answers" said St. John.

"I always tell you to laugh at Rachel" Helen remarked privately. "Laugh at her and enlighten her. That's your duty."

"I know. But I want to talk to you" said St. John.

Across the table Susan ventured her remark, prepared beforehand. "I always think that people who are very much interested in something else, like art or music, don't know people as well as quite ordinary people like myself, for instance know them."

"Do you know people?" St John demanded.

"Yes I think I do" said Susan candidly. "But then I'm interested in them, and I daresay you're not."

At this saying Arthur concealed his face behind a pocket hand kerchief.

Again the talk dropped to a few shots; again it crossed the tables and the shots knocked into each other.

"Everyone here, I'll be bound, thinks he knows everything about all the others."

"I wish you'd tell me. What am I?"

"O I never said I'd tell."

"Then I don't believe you."

A bird or two hopped near and were fed with crumbs. In the middle the flame of the tea urn made the air waver all round like a faulty sheet of glass. Little particles of dust or blossom fell on the plates now and then when the branches sighed above. Evelyn kept calling to a white dog belonging to a party of Portuguese children, and at last induced it to beg for a lump of sugar. Susan and Mrs Elliot kept up a gentle steady narrative, of a semi-confidential nature, inaudible to the rest.

Such was the group that Rachel saw directly she turned the corner of the building. But, owing to the sunshine after the shaded passages, and to the substance of live people after dreams, she saw with startling intensity as though the dusty surface had been peeled off everything, leaving only the reality and the instant. So she would be able to print the scene on the dark at night—-the white and grey and purple figures sitting round wicker tables, wavering air in the middle, and a tree like a moving force held stationary as a sentinel above them. Evelyn's voice, "here then—here—good doggie, come here" did not break the spell. She stopped dead for a moment. Then the dust began to settle. She saw that Hewet was not there. Then Mrs Thornbury saw her. Then two or three people leant back and beckoned; she became abashed by the necessity of going up to them and beginning to talk.

Laughter greeted her. "Was it you looking out of the window?" "The penalty is you tell us your thoughts." "The penalty is tea like ink." Helen however with a curious protective movement of her arm, shielded her. She began in a clear slow voice to recite "Toll for the Brave"; it was apparently the outcome of a bet between her and St John Hirst, and while her Aunt intoned the verses rather to the surprise of the company, Rachel found shelter.

"There" said Helen, rather flushed, but triumphant. "Mr Hirst must eat his words."

Evelyn came across and sat on the ground at Rachel's feet, clasping her arms round her knees. Secure from observation Rachel drank her tea and looked round; she looked at Mr Elliot who held the table with anecdotes of a noble patron; she looked at Mrs Paley who with head slightly dropped regarded the cake with speculative affection; she looked at Susan murmuring while Arthur stared at her with complete confidence in his own love.

"It's when you look like that" said Evelyn suddenly. "I wonder what on earth you're thinking about?"

"Miss Warrington" said Rachel. Miss Warrington of course heard her own name.

"Well you looked as though you were thinking about the end of the world" said Evelyn.

"You're not very complimentary" Susan laughed.

"I hope there's not much of the end of the world about Arthur or me!"

Then Mr Pepper who had an odd habit of suddenly lifting whatever lay before him and naming it, said "Yellow Cushion" and examined a yellow cushion, as though he were a connoisseur.

"Yes," said Rachel, becoming rash at the sight, "that's what I meant. So solid, so yellow, I can imagine jumping out of bed and holding on to you." She stopped; and blushed.

Susan laughed with immense benignity; content seemed to dance over her like hot air over tiles, making her impervious to doubt or criticism.

"It's all very flattering," she said, "but I don't know that I should like it, and I'm quite sure that Arthur wouldn't!"

"Don't mind me" said Arthur and they went on talking.

After a few minutes Susan was telling Mrs Thornbury how busy she was at home.

"There's the ordering and the dogs, and the garden, and the child coming to be taught," her voice proceeded, rhythmically, as if checking the list, " and my tennis, and the village and letters to write for father, and a thousand little things that don't sound much, but I never have a moment to myself, and when I go to bed I'm so sleepy that I'm off before my head touches the pillow—"

"My mother used to do that kind of thing" said Evelyn, in a low voice.

"Besides I like to be a great deal with my Aunts—I'm a great bore, aren't I Aunt Emma?—and father has to be very careful about chills in winter which means a great deal of running about, because he won't look after himself, any more than you will Arthur. So it all mounts up!"

Her voice mounted too, in a mild ecstasy of satisfaction with her life and herself. Rachel suddenly disliked her; she was insincere; she was cruel; and saw her stout and prolific, the kind blue eyes now shallow and watery, the bloom of the cheeks congealed into a network of little red canals.

("Did you go to church?" Helen asked Rachel.

"For the last time," said Rachel.)

As preparation for putting on her gloves, Helen dropped them.

"You're not going?" asked Evelyn, keeping one.

"It's quite time to go," said Helen. "Don't you see how silent everyone's—getting?"

They were silent and for that reason their eyes wandered to someone who was approaching.

Helen only saw Rachel draw her breath with difficulty.

"So" she said within her self and her heart beat very distinctly, "it has come." She slowly drew on her gloves.

"You're just the person I want, Mr Hewet!" cried Mrs Flushing. "While we've all been snorin' on our beds, you've been climbin' mountains. Tell me. Do you know how one hires a steamer?"

As Hewet sat down, Helen rose, for she knew that everything now would come over again, and Hewet, though he looked at Rachel, was entangled in chairs, and tea, and people.

As Helen and Rachel turned away, some one said, "O but it's six o'clock." Therefore they did not go on sitting under the tree; it was Sunday and again the hour of service.

Rachel could not resist one look back, when they reached the corner of the hotel, and there Helen stopped to raise her parasol. Again the group appeared with strange distinctness; but this time she was tormented by the longing to return. So great was it, that Helen had to take her by the arm.

They walked some way along the road in silence until they came to the spot where they had at the morning after the dance.

"Don't dream Rachel; talk" said Helen.

As if a spring had been touched, Rachel burst forth,

"What's the use of talking Helen? No one ever understands. What's the use of anything? It's pain pain always pain." She stopped. "I tell you," she began again, and Helen looked up at the break in her voice, "the agony is almost unendurable—the agony of living, of wanting"—Here she burst into tears and turned her face to the roadside, tore leaves from the bush and crushed them. Helen waited in the middle of the road.

"Now you think me a fool" said Rachel facing her, but she was too much in earnest to be ashamed. "If you had felt as I have the cruelty of people, how they feel none of the things they pretend to feel, how they only wish to hurt, and how lonely"—She was unable to speak.

"My dear Rachel," said Helen, "does one live to be forty without feeling all those things? Do you think you are the only person—do you never imagine that we are all feeling what you feel. Think more of other people" she ended.

"But you are married," said Rachel.

"There's no cure in that" said Helen. "I'm alone just as you're alone. But shall I tell you what I think?" she continued, once more taking Rachel's arm and leading her on. "You only feel so keenly now because you want so much, and therefore you are rather to be envied. One doesn't envy Mrs Paley." Rachel was calmed as Helen had intended, and walked silently for a minute or two. Then she asked,

"Do you think I shall ever get what I want Helen?"

"Yes. Everything" said Helen, with great confidence. "I see no reason why you shouldn't have everything in the world."

The road suddenly became very beautiful and a little picture of the road unforgettable in Rachel's eyes.

"Now I shall say the things one never does say" she said.

"Every day I love you better Helen. It is wonderful that you should now be living. It is not because of anything you do" she continued. "It may be at breakfast, or merely when we're in the room together; suddenly it comes over me: This is happiness!"

They went on to talk about the voyage up the river, and it was not until Helen was pushing open the gate of the villa that she made anything that could be considered as an answer.

"If you take everything into consideration, Rachel" she observed leaning her chin for a moment upon the topmost bar of the gate, "there's an enormous amount of good in the world."

CHAPTER TWENTY-FOUR

The river on which they were to sail for a few days ran into the sea some forty miles to the south of Santa Rosa. From the hill top where they picnicked they had seen the great root of it, where it flowed into the sea, lying like the root of some enormous forest tree, massive in the middle, with the lesser roots lying blue across the sand. But before it reached the sea it passed through flat swamps, and then narrowed itself and ran beneath the shade of the trees. Where from the top of the mountain they could see a dark cloud of green, there the river ran, further and further away, leaving civilisation behind it, passing through unlit reaches, broadening sometimes to an enormous girth, here lashed into rapids, and here large and calm as a lake. To find the source of the river you must first pass through the towns, then the villages, then the solitary huts of Indians; you must become the only person in your world; you must be the first to cut through the thongs of creepers; the first who has ever trodden upon the mosses by the river side, or seen trees which have stood since the beginning of the world. No longer are the sounds of men and women heard; no cart wheels sound upon distant roads; there are no lights upon the sky when the moon rises; never does any whistle sound, calling men to work and cease from work; only birds cry, and trees come down, and the fruit can be heard slipping and dropping on the ground; and now and then some beast howls in agony or rage. Wild creatures seeing you glitter their eyes at you from the branch, and the butterflies circle in your path. After traversing the forest for weeks and weeks and months and months, you come at last to a great grey screen of mountains. You are now encircled by the earth, in the very heart of stone and dust.

As leopard and birds have been born of the forest, so have human beings. But after stepping a few hundred miles into this world, they have ceased as though on the verge of a precipice, or on the edge of the sea. The proposed voyage was from a riverside station to one of these camps, and already, a sign that human beings were creeping further and further inland, using up more and more of the great raft afloat upon the sea, a small steam boat panted up the river regularly once a month. The steam boat was like a wedge driving wild life in front of it. Those that would not eat the food it brought or wear the clothes, took to their canoes and pushed again into solitude. But wherever the steamer halted, there streets and squares would be built, in time, and eventually the statue of some lawgiver, clasping his roll of paper, would command the market place. In talking of the future of the country, three great facts had to be considered, which did not suffer themselves to be tampered with and had for millions of years done what they chose with beast and mad, till both were properly shaped and coloured. These three were the sun, the trees and the water.

On the evening of the twenty ninth of May, a steam launch lay in the middle of the stream, opposite a clearing in the forest, where a wooden inn had been built for the refreshment of river passengers. At seven o'clock in the evening, the elderly Spaniard who was sitting on deck spitting and smoking, smoking and spitting, observed a cavalcade of six horses canter into the open space and stop dead, for it was the last canter of horses tired by a long day's journey. Three English men dismounted and three English women. It became dark.

Later, an oval space of light lay upon the shore, containing a table, round which the strangers sat eating; at either end the table was framed so to speak by the thin columns of the verandah, twined with vivid green creepers.

As the dinner went on, two or three men began to rattle about on the steamer, and a greasy black head appeared on the level of the deck now and then gazed and disappeared. From the light cast by the lanterns it could be seen that the stern of the boat was covered with an awning, and hammocks were swung in the shelter. Soon the boat began the gentle throbbing which showed that she was alive, and from her bowels came at intervals the strange cries of men and work. Later still, the oval light on shore dwindled and vanished. All were now active on deck, and from beating softly the heart of the steamer beat with vigour. Cries from the deck were answered by cries from the shore, and presently a boat made out from the shadow by the bank and soon the dip and splash of the oars could be heard; then the faces of the passengers were seen; at last the boat lay alongside, and one after another the six travellers climbed onto the deck of the steamer.

Although they were tired with the long day's ride they did not go to bed, but sat under the awning watching the procession of tree tops moving across the stars and the wide ripples which wrinkled the black water as the boat pushed through. One lantern illuminated a cheek here, a hand there. Then Mrs Flushing was heard to breath portentously, half a sigh half a yawn, and deep as the breath of a quadruped.

"In the open air" she muttered, and crept off by herself to choose a corner for her mattress. One after another without speaking the rest stood up, great figures without features, and withdrew, so that by midnight only two Spaniards watched, and Hewet, swung high in his hammock. He watched the trees, arching, sinking, towering; he watched the sky between them whiten, and as the steamer drew his body he was conscious that mind and heart were drawn too, further and further on; he voyaged calmly, knowing himself committed now to travel to the journey's end.

Next morning found them a considerable way up the river, on the left was a high yellow bank of sand, tufted with trees on the top, on the right a swamp cut with streams. They were gathered in the fore part of the boat, Mrs Flushing and Helen seated while the others lay or squatted on rugs on the deck beneath them. Mrs Flushing was painting. She darted her head from side to side with the action of a bird nervously eating; and as she darted flicked the cardboard with the top of her brush. Helen was stitching at the embroidery for she had announced her intention of bringing it back finished. Hewet had tried to read aloud, but the number of moving things had entirely vanquished the words. There was now a covey of red birds feeding on one of the little islets to the left, or again a blue green parrot that flew shrieking from tree to tree. As they moved on the country grew wilder and wilder. It was as if the trees and the undergrowth left to themselves had been struggling and wrestling together for centuries. Down below they were often choked one growing upon another, an impenetrable hedge; but here and there a splendid tree towered high above the rest, shaking its thin green umbrellas lightly in the upper air. Moreover when Hewet tired to read aloud in his level, engaging voice, a bird gave a wild laugh, or a monkey yelled where there was no full stop. As the river narrowed and the high sandbanks fell to level ground thickly grown with trees the forest echoed like a hall. It reminded Mrs Flushing of a service in San Sofia. There were the same cries and silences. When questioned by Mr Flushing the sailors told him that there was a track through the forest but "we" they said, "would rather find ourselves upon the water." "They kill animals," they said, describing the lives of Indians who used the track.

After they had lunched the steamer, whether it was due to laziness or to some inexplicable mood on the part of the machinery, slowly came to a standstill. The river at this point was broad but so arched over by trees that the path way of blue water, reflecting the sky, was quite narrow, and the borders were wide of profound green shade. They towed two boats behind them, and with Hewet to row one and Mr Flushing the other the party took to the water and rowed along the bank seeking a landing place. At a certain point a little bay was scooped in the bank and drawing the boats up the shore and making them fast they disembarked and pushed into the forest. There was no pathway, but as the trees stood irregularly and a springy moss grew at their feet it was possible to make out a way zig zagging to the left and to the right, and sometimes leading straight like an English forest though perhaps the mosses here had never been pressed by human feet before. The undergrowth walled in the path, the dense creepers having knotted tree to tree swarmed up the trunk and burst out into crimson blossoms shaped like star fish. Although the sky above was a perfectly swept blue dome, the light within was green, save where a yellow round of pure yellow sunlight lay beneath a gap in the trees. They were now inside the hall and the voices were crying all round them. Owing to Mrs Flushing's sudden desire to depict the vigorous downfall of a great tree which had fallen roped up by creepers, like a mast entangled by rigging, Hewet and Rachel were left to explore by themselves, Hirst and Helen seating themselves upon the stump.

"It is worth going on a bit isn't it?" said Hewet.

"O yes" said Rachel. "I call this exciting."

They went on slowly marking the way; when a flower tempted her, Rachel pulled it.

"Are they laughing at us—these creatures?" said Hewet after a time, as the cries of monkeys rang near by. He picked up a cone and threw it as high as he could among the trees; they heard the flapping of great wings. They heard the cone patter through leaves and fall.

"If you were not here," said Rachel, "I should be frightened."

The silence was now profound.

"That's not my idea of you," said Hewet.

"Your idea of me" said Rachel. She stopped and looked at him. "You often know me better than I know myself. It's true. I'm not frightened."

"You're the least frightened person I've ever met" said Hewet. "You really want to know."

"Yes" she said. "Everything. Everything. Not only human beings—Besides people I love the world."

"And everything that comes to you" said Hewet. "You don't think I've known you without knowing that." He seemed to put some constraint upon himself.

"I wish you'd tell me all you can about yourself. Tell me everything—I want to know."

"What is there to tell? Richmond you know; I've told you about my Aunts, and my father. And the rest—how can one tell that?"

"That's just what I want to know," he pressed.

"I used to walk to talk; I never had any one to talk to. I used to think there must be a key to everything. I used to walk along those roads—I was very lonely I suppose, but happy," she broke off recollecting.

"Good God!" Hewet cried, "How lonely one was! What you say is true of me too. But then I fell in love and I suppose you never did?"

"Never."

"And when I say love I don't mean it," he said, "any more than Hirst does. But you care for people?" he asked abruptly.

"My mother was the person I cared for" she said. "And now Helen. When she speaks it's like the beginning of a song."

"I've always felt that" said Hewet. "Sometimes you've seemed so far away; but when I saw you with her I guessed that it was possible...."

In her intolerable nervousness Rachel interrupted him, "Had you no mother."

"O yes, I have a mother" he replied with less emotion. "She cares for dogs and horses more than she's ever cared for her children. She's a great hunter, an absolutely cold uninteresting woman who's never yet done a thing to make anyone care for her and who never will. She's ruined my sisters' lives for them. The elder one's crushed, but I'm determined to save the other. If it weren't for her I'd never go near the place, though it's the loveliest in the world. I cannot endure family quarrels!" he exclaimed.

"So now you live alone in the Temple?" Rachel asked.

"Yes" he said, "I live there alone. But don't think that I'm to be pitied. I sometimes think life's been too easy for me. I've had too much happiness. If I'm ever gloomy it's my own fault. It comes of wanting too much—of wanting something so tremendously that the whole of my life will be worthless without it." He stopped; the moments seemed to Rachel as messengers approaching.

"You know that I love you" he whispered. The messenger had arrived.

"Is it possible?" she exclaimed.

"And you?"

For answer she opened her arms.

More as people who grope, who push away a veil between them than as man and woman in midday they sought each other's arms. They embraced passionately.

"And now," Rachel murmured, releasing herself and looking with dazed eyes into the distance, "what have we done?"

"The most wonderful thing in the world" Hewet replied. He was trembling all over.

"Something terrible" she answered.

Sounds stood out from the background making as it were a bridge across their silence; there was the swish of the trees and far off the rush of the water.

"Tell me you are happy" Hewet begged her.

"Happy?" she said. "I am nothing."

He sat by her side not touching her.

"It will mean" she said after a time, "living with you all my life."

She paused and then looked at him for the first time with life in her eyes.

"What happiness!" she cried.

"Oh that you should say that!" he burst out, as if released from agony.

"We must not move" she said after a time. "We must let it all begin round us—life—this wonderful life." Again they heard the cries and the water.

"O Terence," she cried suddenly. "The dead! My mother is dead!"

He comforted her. "In everything we shall be together, Rachel. With you to help me.... Ever since I met you," he continued, "life's been different. It's over now, the waiting, playing about, observing. All that's been so unsatisfactory, all the things I've had to pretend, all I've had to put up with in default of better—I shan't waste time on them again. Half my life I've wasted—worse than wasted."

"And mine?" said Rachel. "Spirits and the sea!"

"You've nothing to regret" said Hewet. "I'd give anything now—When you talked about women the other day I should have told you. That's why I'm called Monk. I am not chaste. I've sinned as they call it."

"Sinned" said Rachel meditatively. "That's an odd word."

"A few weeks ago you'd have minded" said Hewet. "But now you don't." He searched her face as if they shared everything.

"You've taught me" said Rachel. "Terence you've taught me to have courage! to love feelings I mean; even when they're partly bad."

"It was the women's lives that made me give it up" he said, "the unspeakable filth of them…. I've kept the power to care for you so that I haven't wasted much" he continued. "But oh those years! Outwardly one seems so much like other people; inwardly one suffers such hell. And if I suffer how vilely others must suffer! You're to know the worst of me Rachel. I'm lustful; I'm lazy; I'm overcome by a sense of horror and of my own incompetence. It's the unreality, the pain the uselessness of it all. If one could do anything, instead of merely seeing and feeling—It's the feeling that one can do nothing. But with you Rachel"—He took her in his arms. "You my dearest, you, the one woman in the world—"

"What have we done?" she said dully disengaging herself. "Are we in love? Are we going to marry each other?"

She looked at him curiously. She noticed that he was dressed in grey flannel, and that a shabby purple tie was lying outside his waistcoat.

"Terence, you're untidy" she said.

"Ever since I was a boy" he answered.

"Now tell me a long story" she sighed, laying her head upon his knee. "I'll think no more."

~ 287 ~

"Ten years ago I was seventeen. Shall I tell you about that? We lived in Yorkshire and a cousin fell in love with me."

"You're attractive?" she asked.

"Very" he answered. "But I didn't fall in love with her. It's one of my faults that I'm horrible ambitious; only I'm also horribly modest. I wanted then to be the greatest man in the world; I even wanted, so repulsive am I, to make a great match. I began life a snob. So I treated her very badly. One night we met it the rose garden…. I made her marry a man who died on the Alps last June."

"I want you to talk about me" said Rachel moving her head.

"When we first met did you like me?"

"The first thing I remember about you," said Terence, "is your saying 'Human Beings' at the picnic. I almost proposed to you on the spot."

"Why?" she asked.

"You've a free soul!" he exclaimed. "That's what I love you for. To you time will make no difference, or marriage or anything else. We're both free. That's why our life together will be the most magnificent thing in the world!"

"Our life together!" she echoed. "Where shall we live, Terence."

"In London" he said. "In the middle of everything. Together Rachel, we can do anything. There'll be so many people—so many things. There'll be Hughes and Lapworth and old Mrs Nutt—"

Rachel dashed the picture of London away from her.

"It's too much" she said. "Don't add to it, Terence. Let's have the moment, and the rest afterwards."

They were silent for some time.

"Did I accept you?" she asked suddenly.

"You did."

"Without telling you that I loved you. I've let you tell me everything. I love you better—" but no comparisons came to her and the sentence ended in his arms.

"But I will tell you" she said, sitting apart from him. "You shall know that it is as a full grown woman that I love you, not as a girl, not as a child. I want it to be a battle between us, you with your faults, I with mine."

"Ah Rachel," he cried, "I love you for that! You fight; and I shall fight! We'll have something better than happiness!"

"But where I want to fight, you have compassion" she said, regarding him with tenderness. "Terence, you're so much finer than I am."

"Not finer" he said. "Older, lazier, a man not a woman."

"A man" she smiled looking up at him. "A queer creature, with eyebrows and bristles. You've not shaved today."

"And it's the happiest day of my life" he said, as he rubbed his chin. "Certainly the strangest. It still seems incredible. What had happened? Why did I propose then? I had not meant to. I'd meant to wait until you knew the worst of me. I've tried to tell you, but I haven't told you."

"We only know one thing about each other" she answered. "What is that thing Terence?"

"The thing behind it all" he said. "The thing we both have. You feel that too? Then all my tortures have been vain! I knew they were! Nothing matters having that."

"No nothing matters" she murmured. "It's as if we lay upon the ground."

"And your faults Terence" she began after a time—

"God Rachel!" he broke out, "What couldn't you do with me! Here I am a great strong animal and you can do what you like with me. I've never used an ounce of myself yet. I'm capable of anything. You've shown me. You've been so sure, so outside of things, going on in front—that's how I see you. You've made me wake up instead of muddling on, with loves and books and vague ideas of how to live. What nonsense I've talked! I've never been alive. I've never known what was in me. I've dreamt and wasted. I've been so lonely. No one understood till you came. With you I could always be myself, and speak straight out. I cared for everything you did and said. It always seemed to me unspeakably lovely."

"And I sat in the passage and wanted to ask you," she answered. "What is it that runs beneath Terence, why do we go on, and all those strange people so different passing each other—O Terence what is the meaning? I asked Evelyn; I asked Miss Allen; no one's ever told me except you. No one ever cares except you."

"We shall understand everything Rachel" he cried. "There'll be nothing too difficult for us in the whole world so long as we have each other!"

While they embraced they heard a faint cry; at first confusing it with the cry of an animal, they paid no attention. Rachel opened her lips to speak again; then the syllables became unmistakable; Hew—et Hew—et! It was a human voice calling them; it was Hirst's voice. Hewet had to answer him.

"And we've only just begun" said Rachel.

"We shall have all our lives" said Hewet, as he helped her up, and straightened her and kissed her.

Helen Ambrose paced to and fro by the river bank. This restlessness in one usually quiet was strange in itself. But there are times when places, people and one's own nature appear unnatural, and this was one of them. The feeling grew and became insupportable as she talked to Hirst. Perhaps he was conscious of it, for his habitual sprightliness was broken into by emotions which he could not express and yet tried to. Usually calm as she was, and tolerant of anything any one might say while they said it, Helen became nervously apprehensive as to what he might say next. She felt herself pursued.

"Come and see us in London" she begged.

"I don't expect to be remembered in London" he said bitterly.

She then looked at her watch and asked him to call Hewet and Rachel. After another difficult attempt, he went. His first shout sounded like the crack of a dry branch. Reproach for her own conduct now mingled with other sensations of discomfort and drove her in spite of the heat—the afternoon had turned yellow—to walk up and down looking from time to time into the trees. She was not a woman to feel anything disturbing without seeking for a reason. Hirst's attitude did not explain what she felt; nor was there anything to upset her in the fact that Hewet had gone with Rachel. She suddenly realised that she hated the place. She was frightened by something unseen, as a child is frightened.

"Why was I ever fool enough to agree to come?" she exclaimed looking at the trees and then at the river. Both of them seemed to her terrible and hostile. It was just such a moment as she remembered years ago when at a polite river party the boat had suddenly capsized. In a second they were struggling in the water. In the same way then they had been mocked at; now again they had ventured too far.

"At any moment the awful thing may happen" she breathed.

What did their pretence of competence and wisdom amount to? At her back was the awful waste of trees ringing with the cries of beasts; in front of her the enormous smooth-swirling water. All the disasters in her experience seemed to have come from civilised people forgetting how easily they may die.

As the time went on she fastened her mind upon the only possible anxiety—the absence of Hewet and Rachel.

"Come—come—come" she repeated as she paced up and down.

At every cry she started; when there was silence she could imagine the sunless hollows far away among the trees, and the rank swamps. She was just about to go to Mr Flushing and tell him that the others must be lost, when she saw them moving through the trees not three hundred yards away. They came out into the open.

"Where have you been?" she cried before she reached them. There was so much agitation in her manner that even Rachel noticed it.

"But you didn't think there'd been an accident?" Hewet asked, hastening towards her.

"I don't know what I thought" said Helen. "We must be careful here. It isn't like England. I don't think you realise that in the least—any of you, or how horrid it is to wait."

As she looked at them she guessed what had happened.

"I know Rachel's hopeless" she said trying to laugh, "so I shall put all the blame on you."

"That's just what I want" said Hewet.

As they walked toward the boat it was Helen who felt the most of the four. At her age she understood better than the pair themselves the immense seriousness of what had happened. She saw them as they could not see themselves a man and woman joined for life. She could hardly walk for tears.

CHAPTER TWENTY-FIVE

"This is what I like' said Mrs Flushing at about half past ten the next morning as she stood in the bow of the boat, which was moving steadily. Upright and defiant she might have been an heroic figure head to some Elizabethan barque though clad in coat and skirt. She spoke to Hewet. "But I'm the only one of us who does" she chuckled. "Truthfully you're longing to be home again—as my husband is. But what more can anyone want?" She swept her head round. "It's always fine, there's air, there's trees, there's no one to ask you what you think about anythin'. You need never speak to another human bein'!"

From the mist that still enwrapped him making contact with people outside very unreal, Hewet answered,

"Is that your ambition?"

Mrs Flushing paused. Then she returned, "I ask you, what d'you suppose would happen if this boat struck a rock and sank? Would you care for anythin' but savin' yourself—should I? Not one scrap! There's only two creatures the ordinary woman cares about—her husband and her dog. And I don't believe it's even two with men! Of course one reads a lot about love. That's why poetry's so dull. But what happens in real life. Eh? It ain't love!" she cried, grasping the rail and laughing.

"You must always remember Alice" said her husband, with his air of sympathetic detachment, "that your upbring-ing was very unusual. They had no mother," he explained to

Hewet, "and a father who cared only for racing and Greek statues. Tell him about the bath, Alice."

"It was in the stable yard" said Mrs Flushing. "Covered with ice in winter. We had to get in; if we didn't we were whipped. The strong ones lived; the others died. What you call the survival of the fittest. An excellent plan I daresay."

"And all this going on in the nineteenth century, in the heart of England!" exclaimed Mr Flushing.

"I'd treat my children just the same, if I had any" said Mrs Flushing.

"Don't believe her! Miss Vinrace!" said Wilfrid to Rachel who had joined them. Mrs Flushing appeared indifferent whether she was believed or not; she stared ahead at the river her eyes expressed nothing but her fierce love of the wild place they were passing through.

"It makes one awfully jumpy, don't you find?" Hirst said to Rachel. They were all now standing in the angle of the bow; they were passing an island in the middle of the river; two great white birds stood there on stilt like legs. It was a beautiful little island, with trees on it; but the beach was unmarked save by the prints of birds' feet.

"These trees get on one's nerves" he continued.

Strangely enough, he appeared no longer majestic a dictator; but young and to be pitied, standing as he did outside the illumination in cold daylight.

"We come to an open place soon" she answered gently. "Ah! Look!"

A lovely, bright crested bird flew across in front of them.

"There's something crazy about it all" Hirst complained, gazing ahead of him. "God is undoubtedly mad. What sane person could have conceived a wilderness like this and peopled it with apes and alligators? It gives me precisely the same sensation that a visit to Bedlam would give me."

Rachel's only answer would have seemed irrelevant. "Thirty or forty years of days like this!"

Hewet helped her.

"But you must admit Hirst that there is a certain grandeur—colour—" He waved his hand vaguely and ceased.

Then Helen spoke. "Grandeur and colour!" she mocked. "It's simply the most beautiful place I've ever seen. Look at the shapes of the trees, the amazing colours in the water, the way everything spaces out."

"Ahhhhh" breathed Mrs Flushing.

"And in my opinion," said Mr Flushing, "the absence of population which Hirst objects to, is precisely the significant touch. You must admit Hirst that a little Italian town even would vulgarise the whole scene, would detract from the space the sense of elemental grandeur—I own it makes us seem pretty small, us—but not them." He nodded his head at a sailor who leant over the side; he was bare footed, his face was very vivid and expressive, spitting into the river, a careless handsome man.

"That, if I do not mistake," he continued, turning to his wife, with something of the gesture of a plausible auctioneer, "is what my wife feels; it's the essential superiority of the peasant to the cultivated person, is it not, Alice?"

She swept round with her usual laugh.

"Go on talking, Wilfrid" she laughed, "You do amuse me!"

He was not daunted. "I quite agree; I should have been an awful windbag if you hadn't married me. While I talk," he explained to the others, "she goes straight for the real thing. It's an extraordinary fact; but Alice who's never had an hour's teaching in her life, hates books loathes shows, can't be got inside a concert room, knows more about art—what art really is I mean—than any learned man I've ever met."

Only a general sense of the comic relationship between husband and wife reached Rachel and Hewet. Terence whispered to her "A queer couple, aren't they?"

They had contrived so that their heads rested together on the rail, and their attitude was that of people scanning the horizon for a sail.

"Everything's odd today. Are you happy, or does it seem a dream, or have you repented?" Rachel had to run all her words into one senseless drone.

"Happy?" he said imitating her method, "I'm only just beginning to realise; yesterday I was stunned."

"I too" Rachel continued. "When I woke it was like being a child on Christmas day...... O that's an alligator!" she exclaimed for the benefit of the company.

"No one suspects" Hewet renewed "or does Helen? We won't tell till we get back. But we must contrive to get away alone."

"Yes for goodness sake, alone" Rachel breathed.

"And Hirst was writing poetry at dawn" Hewet added aloud.

"At five o'clock" said Hirst, "I gave up comparing the respective advantages of hammock and mattress; and took refuge in my God."

He produced some sheets of notepaper.

"Something awful's happened" he said pursing his lips, as he looked through them. "I can't produce a single argument against the existence of God. It is quite possible that by tomorrow I shall have definitely proved it. Then I shall have to wire to the Times—and to the Field, that he does exist."

Hewet and Rachel smiled at each other, queerly, and then Hewet murmured, "He's not very happy."

"What'll he say" she whispered, "when he knows?"

As Hewet would only laugh, she insisted, "He'll say I made you; he despises women; he hates me?"

"I think his own wife will be a very quiet woman" was the only answer Hewet could give. His respect for Hirst never altered. Here Mr Flushing who had been in talk with the handsome sailor, returned set up a number of folding chairs and bade every one sit down. "We're coming to the most magnificent part of all" he remarked. "Fernando was telling me the story of an Englishman who came out here to collect birds and lived in a little hut which we shall pass on our left. He appears to have died."

As it was Mr Flushing's wish they had to sit in a semi circle. The degree to which the country had been explored kept Hirst and Mr Flushing engaged in question and answer; the rest with legs stretched out, or chin poised upon hands, gazed silently.

Yellow and green shapes passed Rachel's eyes in a haze. She only knew that now one was big and now one was small she scarcely knew that they were trees; she felt she was marking time, since she could not talk to Terence, and her happiness seemed to her too great to be examined. Partly because no one knew of her engagement, she could not dwell upon the change in her future life. But her tension was such that she was unconscious of Helen's eye which looked at her steadily more than once. Helen had now had time to revise her opinion. She was not certain whether they were engaged or on the brink of it. But all kinds of sensations, partly physical, partly mental, assured her that something of great importance was in the air. When, driven from scrutiny of their faces she looked on shore, her old distrust returned. The beauty was as great as she had said, but mixed with something sultry and cruel. Oddly enough, the pain which she had felt as the Euphrosyne moved up the Thames, returned; as the steamer slipt steadily down the water she felt as if her children were drawn from her. They passed the hut where the Englishman had died. It stood in a small enclosure, where the ground had been stamped yellow; the roof was broken in; they could only see a few rusty tins scattered here and there.

"And then people go and marry!" she mused.

Human relationships seemed to her very transient, and as if they took place at an immense distance away. Nothing was said; they scarcely moved, except now to change a foot, or again to strike a match. Looking from one to the other it might be observed that all their lips were slightly pressed together, and all their eyes concentrated, as if the things they saw made them think.

"Your book Hewet?" said Hirst suddenly.

Hewet felt vaguely in his pocket and produced a book.

Without being asked he opened it and read aloud the first poem. It was obscure and for the most part unintelligible, for no one listened to more than a line or two at a time. By skipping and reading to himself he reached the end,

"Voyage to more than India!

O secret of the earth and sky!"

to which words Rachel suddenly attended.

"Sail forth—-steer for the deep waters only,

Reckless O soul, exploring, I with thee, and thou with me,

For we are bound where mariner has not yet dared to go,

And we will risk the ship ourselves and all.

O my brave soul!

O farther, farther sail!

O daring joy, but safe! are they not all the seas of God?

O farther farther farther sail"

She was the only person who listened, for they all looked roused when she exclaimed in a tone of awed rapture, "I never thought poems were like that!"

She took the book and began turning the pages as though they were made of something thicker than paper.

"Is there a great deal to read?" she suddenly asked Hewet.

"A great deal" he answered. He had been watching her.

"Well, that's a discovery" she sighed carefully shutting the volume.

"It's odd people should say what one thinks" she added, but so low that Hewet was the only one who heard her.

But Helen had seen enough to make her speculate about the future of Rachel and Hewet when married. Houses and income it was impossible to think of, out here; but she thought of their characters. She thought of Rachel's perpetual discoveries. "Is she a person ever to know the truth about anything?" she wondered. She seemed so young, by which Helen meant that she had only known kindly people, and would be shocked, disappointed, embittered, driven to despair, and altogether amazed if she knew how other men and women lived and behaved. How would she go through the experiences that were to draw wrinkles upon her forehead and cloud the fresh light in her eyes with contentment or patience? As to men, Helen as usual felt more certainty. But she thought of marriage; the solitary evenings, with the sense of growing up "I'm a man—you're a woman" of the sordid side of intimacy of the wrench and the nakedness; how would Terence stand them? As she turned her wedding ring unconsciously upon her finger she went over different scenes of marriage; trivial scenes; breakfast, catching trains; making plans; and, seeing them less and less distinctly passed to thoughts of her own children.

She had grown so accustomed to the darkness of trees on either side of her, that she looked up with a start when the space seemed suddenly to widen.

"It always reminds one of an English park" said Mr Flushing.

They had come to Rachel's open space. No change could have been greater. On either side of the river lay an open flat lawn, grass covered, and planted, for the look suggested human thought, with trees upon mounds; they swelled and sank gently; between them ran narrow rivulets.

"The camp's a mile or two away over there" said Mr Flushing. "No wonder our ancestors thought they'd discovered the garden of Eden. There may be rubies diamonds all kinds of precious stones beneath there; it's the country of the future.

As always happens the change of scene made them require change of position.

"But for the size" said Terence leaning over the rail, "this might be Arundel or Windsor; no; you'd have to cut down that bush with the yellow flowers; and by Jove! Look!"

A flock of deer paused for a moment and then leapt, with a motion as if they were springing over waves out of sight. No one could believe that they had seen them. The wild beasts careening in an open space woke a childish excitement in them.

"I've always longed to see wild beasts at home!" Hirst exclaimed. "I've never seen anything bigger than a hare."

A wild desire possessed them all to get out and walk at large, in spite of the heat. The captain agreed benevolently, to bring the steamer to a halt, as one whose duty it is to minister to the whims of the rich. A few strokes of the oar brought them to the bank. The sailors produced raisins and tobacco leant over the rail and watched the six English whose coats and dresses looked so strange wander off. Mrs Flushing pressed ahead; a joke that was by no means proper set all the sailors laughing; they turned round and lay at their ease upon the deck.

"The worst snakes are no bigger than twigs and they bite one's feet" said Hirst to Helen as they pushed through the rich thick grass. His concern was for her open stockings. But she was in a reckless mood.

At last she exclaimed, "I feel as if we did live in a beautiful world! I mean as if things were good of themselves."

The tremendous luxuriance of the place suggested benevolence and goodness arising from the heart; for who was there to enjoy the shade, the sun, and the cushion of grass, except the animals? In some ways the little flock of human beings resembled the herd of deer; for they pushed on eagerly, and the waving ground made them appear to rise and fall as though cantering.

Helen felt Rachel springing beside her.

She went ahead, and called back over her shoulder to Helen, "It's like wading out to sea!"

She left behind her a trail of whitened grass, like a track in water. Without thinking of her forty years, Helen cried "Spring on! I'm after you!" whereupon Rachel took longer leaps and at last ran. Helen pursued her. She plucked tufts of feathery blades and cast them at her. They outdistanced the others. Suddenly Rachel stopped and opened her arms so that Helen rushed into them and tumbled her over onto the ground. "Oh Helen Helen!" she could hear Rachel gasping as she rolled her, "Don't! For God's sake! Stop! I'll tell you a secret! I'm going to be married!"

Helen paused with one hand upon Rachel's throat holding her head down among the grasses.

"You think I didn't know that!" she cried.

For some seconds she did nothing but roll Rachel over and over, knocking her down when she tried to get up; stuffing grass into her mouth; finally laying her absolutely flat upon the ground, her arms out on either side of her, her hat off, her hair down.

"Own yourself beaten" she panted. "Beg my pardon, and say you worship me!"

Rachel saw Helen's head hanging over her, very large against the sky.

"I love Terence better!" she exclaimed.

"Terence" Helen exclaimed.

She sat clasping her knees and looking down upon Rachel who still lay with her head on the grass staring in to the sky.

"Are you happy?" she asked.

"Infinitely!" Rachel breathed, and turning round was clasped in Helen's arms.

"I had to tell you" she murmured.

"And if you hadn't, I knew" said Helen.

"He's unlike any one I've ever seen" said Rachel. "He understands." Lost in her knowledge of Terence, which she could not impart, she said no more.

The inevitable jealousy crossed Helen's mind as she saw Rachel pass almost visibly away into communion with someone else. "I've never told you, but you know I love you, my darling," she said, flushing as she spoke. Sometimes, the words were spoken with Rachel pressed to her—"you're so like Theresa, and I loved her."

"Why did she die?" said Rachel. "Or do people die?"

They sat opposite each other, with a sprinkling of long feathery blades between them.

"The great thing is love" said Helen. They were both pressed by the sense that the others were coming near.

"And your mother, the thing one remembers about her is that she enjoyed life tremendously."

Without really seeing them Helen was conscious of legs moving. "Tell Terence" she whispered. Rachel swiftly looked to the right. She pulled Helen to her feet.

"Hah!" cried Mr Flushing. "I thought I saw something moving in the grass. I almost suspected deer."

"If we don't walk pretty steadily we shan't get to the camp which is what I most want to see in the whole world" Mrs Flushing admonished them, pounding on still slightly in advance though her cheeks were the colour of strawberries in June.

She drew Hirst after her, for she had excited his pugnacity by denying that colleges were superior to trees. As usual Mr Flushing attended his wife, like a small cruiser circling round a battleship. In one moment Rachel had whispered her confession to Hewet, and with a sudden kindling of their eyes Helen and Hewet shook hands.

CHAPTER TWENTY-SIX

They stood in the native camp. The Indian women were squatting at the doors of their huts making baskets and did not stir from their triangular position when the strangers arrived though their long narrow eyes slid round and fixed upon them. As no on except Mr Flushing could speak to them the silent stare had to be continued. Recovering from their surprise they began to use their hands again, and the English moved carefully round. They looked into the shady little huts; they saw the ashes on the floor, the guns leaning in the corner, bowls and rushes; they saw the children clasped tight by some old grandmother. The eyes seemed to follow them without hostility but without great interest. A kind of shyness attacked both Hirst and Hewet; they stood together under a tree. A woman suckled her child close by them. Diamond shaped spots of sunshine slid over her, making her shawl now red now brown. The head man who was talking to Mr Flushing brought out a variety of very bright strips of embroidery, which the ladies were asked to handle.

"Aren't they magnificent?" Mr Flushing murmured as he stroked some of the glossy columbines which filled him with disgust. The woman was sent to fetch biscuits, drink and scented sweetmeats. She made a sign of reverence as she approached the strangers. Their hands felt strangely large and English as they took the food and their bodies well-nourished and formal, like soldiers in the midst of a crowd.

"But those are the things we want" Mr Flushing whispered pointing to the woman's shawl which was of thin blue stuff marked with great dark spots. She was summoned back. She brought out a number of handkerchiefs; her own, her best; and her dull black eyes expressed a certain sluggish wonder as she looked at the English women. Mr Flushing was left to do the bargaining. The ladies spoke together, keeping their voices low, although they could not have been understood.

"I see 'em moving about in the trees over there" said Alice Flushing.

"Then men are out I suppose" said Helen, looking at all the women.

Rachel tried to understand their faces, for she had thought that her own happiness would have made it easy for her. From one to the other she looked, as they plaited the straw, or shouted at the girls who were going in and out of the huts. Their faces were an oily brown, and this perhaps explained why they did not look like faces; they seemed neither old nor young, neither clever malicious women, or sweet sympathetic women; they seemed more like fruit hung high up in their own forest trees. She owned that she knew nothing about them.

Her happiness was dashed, as if it were a pool and a great stone had fallen which the waters could not embrace. Mr Flushing was long in bargaining, and rolled many cigarettes. The shawls ear rings and necklaces were spread out on a table before the hut; from a distance the process looked like a game of cards; the Indian looked at Mr Flushing and Mr Flushing looked at the goods; Mr Flushing looked at the goods and looked at the Indian; neither of them touched the goods; though their eyes kept returning to them. The eyes of the woman fell from one to the other silently. They were all motionless, save for an occasional gesture of Mr Flushing's arm. Meanwhile the life of the camp went on; the women plaiting their baskets and occasionally walking in and out of their huts. A great gabble of tongues suddenly rose; a child was beaten; it fell again. A woman fetched fresh grass, sat herself down and began to sing, rocking slightly from side to side. It was a chant rather than a song, sliding up a little way and down a little way and settling on the same note over and over again. She went on rocking and singing though her eyes wandered over the strangers when the bargains were over and the party walked past her.

"You're sad? Rachel?" said Terence lagging behind.

She lit up with joy that he had noticed it.

"Yes because it makes us seem small" she said.

"But what I have in my heart is as great as anything in the world" she added.

All the time that they walked to the river this feeling grew and grew. Something seemed urging her to tell him, as if her heart were thrusting its way out of her body. Inarticulately the sentences broke forth.

"Why do they ask so much of us Terence? It's a pain to love as I do."

He pressed her tight.

Again she was silent. "Loving you is like having iron thrust through one" she moaned.

Careless of risk they seized each other, and sobbed, embracing.

CHAPTER TWENTY-SEVEN

It was late that night and the steamer had turned and was retracing its way. It had gone as far up the river as it was accustomed to do, and the great stretch beyond was left unattempted. The day had been long and hot, and now the soft night air seemed to press fingers upon the eyelids. The sudden drop of Hirst's head upon his shoulder was the prelude to his withdrawal; and then the Flushings went. Helen Hewet and Rachel were left sitting in wicker chairs under the awning in the stern. The light which came from an oil lamp and from a sky whitened with stars left them with shapes and bodies, but without features at a little distance. Even in this dim atmosphere they felt each other very near when they were left alone. They sat thinking of the same thing and then Helen said, "So you're both very happy."

As if washed by the air her voice sounded more spiritual though lower than usual.

"If it's a dream it's a wonderful dream" said Terence.

"As for me, I've never been awake before" said Rachel.

"Are you prepared to take charge of her now that she's woken up?" said Helen.

A very low sound said that he was prepared to take charge of everything.

"I feel I ought to give you both good advice" she went on. Through the dimness she was trying to make out what Hewet looked like.

"I may call you Terence? Do you know what kind of person she is? When she's thinking of something else, will you be able to wake her up without making her angry?"

"But of course you know that better than I do." She had caught them glancing. "I shall superintend your mistakes" she said, apparently addressing herself to Rachel. "For the first twenty four years of her life I left her alone on principle. The experiment succeeded; she is nicer than most young women."

"Experiment! Laziness!" Rachel snorted.

"The question is now, what will you make of her? So far she's done practically nothing but come into the room and say 'O Human beings!'"

Terence suspected that Helen was really anxious to know about him.

"The magnificent thing is that she can make anything of me" he said. "I'm twenty seven, I've seven hundred a year, perfect health, good temper; I have been lazy, and not chaste; the worst of me is that I'm given to fits of gloom and that I don't do things. But I mean to. We mean to do everything."

Rachel echoed "Everything."

"Of course there are difficulties in marriage" Helen added, "particularly marriage with a person who's never had any experiences like Rachel. You must be prepared for revelations Terence."

"But on the whole you think we shall be the happiest people in the world?" Rachel broke out.

"And me the luckiest, don't you?" said Terence.

They shuffled their chairs nearer, and Helen gave her blessing by linking them together with her arms.

"But Good Lord!" she exclaimed throwing her head back and looking up at the sky, "how odd it all is!"

"Now we want to know about you" said Terence. "We've talked quite enough about ourselves."

"To have two children, to be half through one's life, to be married to a man who's fifteen years older than one is oneself, I'm in the thick of it all and you're just beginning .... I sometimes think it's a little disappointing," she hazarded. "I should say puzzling, very puzzling. After all what does it amount to? The great things never are as great as one expects. On the other hand I've been very happy when nobody knew. As you perceive Terence I'm not a good hand at talking," she broke off.

Both instinctively felt that their happiness had made her unhappy. They wished to comfort her but neither of them knew what to say.

She continued: "Anyhow it all goes on; and no one can deny that it's interesting." At this point both Rachel and Hewet became oddly conscious of the march of the dark trees on the banks, "or that there is a great deal of extraordinary pleasure mixed up with it.... It will be interesting to see what you make of it. I remember telling Rachel that she would always be the dupe of the second rate—and that reminds me, you will have to write to your father."

She rose as she spoke, though Rachel turned to stay her by clutching at her skirts and Terence implored her "Stay and tell us."

"I'm no good at explaining" she said detaching her skirt, "even if I had ideas, and I'm not particularly clever—just ordinary."

At this moment she appeared to them both vast and profoundly mysterious.

Rachel at length broke the silence in which they sat after she had disappeared.

"That's the oddest woman in the world!" she exclaimed. "She fills me with pleasure!"

Terence assented. "A woman who has nothing queer about her" he added. They moved to the side of the steamer, and looked down at the smooth surface slipping away beneath them.

"Does it never come over you that this is all quite unreal?" he said suddenly, "that we are now standing at midnight on the deck of a steamer on a river in South America, you and I—Rachel Vinrace and Terence Hewet? Or is it the most real thing that's ever been?" she asked.

"The forest and the Indians" he continued.

The great black world lay all about them. It seemed possessed of immense thickness and endurance. They could discern pointed tree tops and blunt rounded tree tops. Rachel looked slowly over them and up at the stars. They fixed her like a magnet. She looked so intently at the little points of frosty light infinitely far away that it seemed like falling a great distance when she determined to realise her own wrist again grasping the rail of the little steamer on the river in South America. Then she became conscious of Terence beside her; then of the boat going quickly down the river. "Terence" she urged, "it'll be nice to be in London won't it?"

"Men are very different from women" he returned. "You forget all about me; I never forget about you." They paced arm in arm. Terence pointed at figures lying like wounded soldiers upon mattresses. "All sound asleep" he said. For a moment they stood and listened to the concert of breathing.

"Good Lord! I'm happy" he exclaimed. For the last time they kissed each other and parted.

CHAPTER TWENTY-EIGHT

The villa seemed much the same as usual when they returned. Helen indeed noticed that the drawing room looked very shabby; more shabby than she remembered. When Oliver came back would he accuse her of carelessness? Always ramshackle and sun-faded the rooms seemed even more sparely furnished than usual, now that the great green blind was down outside, and the chairs in their proper places. Although they had been away but five days they went into all the rooms as people do after a long absence.

"You have the advantage of seeing Terence's window now" said Helen as they stood in Rachel's bed room.

The fact caused Rachel a sudden new pleasure. But they would soon be going and with that in her mind she looked about the large empty bed room where she had nursed the secret which was now a splendid fact. Much had happened since she slept in that bed, although the first volume of Decline and Fall of the Roman Empire still lay beside it. She recalled many wakings much music, very hot afternoons and a considerable amount of speculation. They went downstairs and out into the garden. The red flowers in the cracked basin were dead and Helen snapped them off. The little grass lawn looked perceptibly yellower and the blades of grass further apart. Instinctively they both looked out to the sea; Rachel's father was to come by that way soon, and soon they would take it themselves. For both of them England held much. Helen went in and disturbed the sitting room, which in her absence had taken on a rigid look; she tore up a quantity of envelopes. Rachel moved about restlessly, she scattered the books, and tried to straighten candles stooping with the heat. Through the open door they could hear Mrs Chailey singing as she washed up the tea things. Ridley stirred over head. A book dropped; he strode across the floor to take down another. It was strange to be back again in the shabby faded place.

When Hewet came up the next morning he had a confession to make. Overcome by his emotion and unable to withstand the lynx eye of Hirst he had allowed him to know all. But worse was to come. When Evelyn M. attacked him on the terrace after dinner asserting that he looked quite different and what had happened on the voyage, he had told her also, swearing her to secresy, "but I make no doubt the cat's out of the bag. Evelyn with all her merits is not a person to keep secrets."

Helen's advice was in keeping with the desires of each—to tell, because thus all barriers to their meeting would be removed. Accordingly Rachel received the cryptic congratulations of St John Hirst, and quite a number of ladies who had only seen Rachel once took occasion to smile brightly upon Terence when they passed him in the passage. She received also three letters from unexpected sources; a Greek line exquisitely written across a card from Mr Pepper; two pages upon happiness from Susan Warrington; and a curious statement from Miss Allen to the effect that marriage was good and wives were happy.

But it was Mrs Thornbury who came running after her and pulled her by the shoulder.

It was about a week after their return, and Rachel had gone down to the hotel in order to see Hewet's possessions, about which she was very curious. They were passing through the hall together when they caught Mrs Thornbury's eye.

"I must congratulate you" she said; her eyes were bright. "I must congratulate you both." Thereupon she drew Rachel's head down and kissed her. "You're going out together, so I will not stop you" she continued. All the time she kept hold of Rachel's hand and eyed her sympathetically. Terence saw Rachel's lip suddenly quiver.

"You're the first person who has made me believe it," she said, "that we shall be married I mean."

"And may I tell you this, Miss Vinrace," said Mrs Thornbury, looking at her with real tenderness, "there is happiness in girlhood, and happiness in being engaged, but no happiness can compare with the happiness of a married woman and of a mother." Her voice dropped very low as she spoke the last words. She was still holding Rachel's hand when Evelyn came flying down the stairs calling out, "O stop! you two! I want to speak to you!" As if her impetus was beyond her control, she fairly collided with them. "I call this splendid!" she exclaimed. "Quite splendid! I guessed it would happen! I saw you two were made for each other. I don't know either of you a bit, but I never make a mistake about people, and when I say a thing I mean it. Look here, you've got to sit down and spend five minutes in telling me all about it."

By sheer physical energy she propelled them into chairs. "You'll give up looking out of windows, won't you?" she said to Rachel. "And you'll make him take a rather kinder view of his fellow creatures I hope!"

This was directed towards St John who, considering that it was a challenge pursed up his lips and sat down opposite his tormentor. "I suppose you think them a horribly misguided couple?" she continued.

"Misguided?" said St John. "Not at all. Have you studied the German Navy estimates for the coming year Miss Murgatroyd?"

"What's that got to do with it?" she asked.

"I calculate" said St John, "that if every man in the British Isles has six male children by the year 1920 and sends them all into the navy we shall be able to keep our fleet in the Mediterranean; if less than six, the fleet disappears; if the fleet disappears, the Empire disappears; if the Empire disappears, I shall no longer be able to pursue my studies in the university of Cambridge."

Rachel laughed down Evelyn's vehement rejoinder.

"Then we may hope that you will be the next, Mr Hirst" said Mrs Thornbury with gentle malice.

A gloom descended on him which was not dispelled by the fact that Evelyn seemed to look at him with more interest than before. Possibly because she saw already to some extent through Terence's eyes, Rachel was no longer annoyed or daunted by St John's manner; she found him rather loveable and wished for his friendship.

"I think you'll marry" she said, "because you have an affectionate nature."

"Thank you" he returned, bowing ceremoniously, but that did not conceal the fact that he was pleased. Mrs Thornbury had been glancing from one to the other with bright but wistful eyes. They were all so young.

"I confess I envy you young people" she said. "So much seems possible now that was not possible when I was a girl. So many barriers seem to have been removed which were not necessary, though one thought them necessary. And the future!—what wouldn't I give to see what the next fifty years will bring! Great things I believe—very great things. In my life time—I'm almost seventy—I have seen great changes, but the best are still to come. Surely everything proves that. You cannot walk through London, or open a newspaper— even my dear old Times—without feeling it. I think you're going to be finer than we were. And I believe," she said, turning to Rachel, "that it's the women who are going to do it. All round me I see young women, women with children, with household cares of every sort, going out and doing things that we should not have thought it possible to do. And they remain women;" she concluded; "they give a great deal to their children."

Here Terence had to rise and shake hands first with Mrs Flushing and then with Miss Allen; in the background Mr Pepper hovered. He was stayed by a hand upon his shoulder. They all stood about talking. Many congratulated Rachel or began sentences meant to end that way. The news seemed to have produced a curiously genial feeling for the moment among so many different people. The reason which brought them all into the hall at this moment was that a tennis tournament was timed to begin in precisely five minutes. Unknown couples in flannels and white dresses kept passing through the swing doors, throwing back a glance or two over their shoulders. Mrs Elliot came down alone. Her wrinkles were rather deeper than usual, and her high colour slightly paler. In answer to enquiries she said that her husband was better but that his temperature would not stay normal, and she would very much like to get another doctor, "a proper doctor" she said dropping her voice. The only doctor was Giuseppe's brother and he was really no better than a chemist. "And Hughling is not an easy patient" she said. "He wants to know what his temperature is and if I tell him he gets anxious, and if I don't he suspects. Of course there are none of the proper appliances. But I think you'll find him more cheerful today, if you're so kind as to come and sit with him again," she said to Hewet. "O Miss Vinrace! I'm sure I congratulate you."

"I suppose you are not coming to the match?" said Miss Allen, when Mrs Thornbury had gone off to help Mrs Elliot in her struggle with the head waiter.

"I have made a small bet with Mr Venning."

"And is the book really finished?" Evelyn asked her.

"It is" Miss Allen answered. "From Chaucer to Tennyson. And all I can say is that if I had known beforehand how many great writers there are in English literature and how exceedingly verbose some of them have been I should never have undertaken the work. However I am glad to have done it. Best wishes for your happiness, Miss Vinrace" she said as she withdrew.

Now Mr Perrott whose face surely showed a deeper weariness than before, though his eyes were eager, claimed Evelyn M. "I don't want to watch that tiresome game!" she cried pettishly.

His lines increased. "Mighn't we just stroll round the grounds though?" he suggested. "We need not sit down."

His humility was such that she agreed to these conditions, though she looked boldly at the others so much as to say, "I'd definitely rather stay with you!"

"We'll meet again!" she called back

"It's like a cat playing with a mouse" said St John. "While we were away there was a crisis with Oliver; so now she's on with Perrott again. O and Venning's said to be tired of Susan; and I distinctly heard old Mrs Paley rapping out the most fearful oaths as I passed her bedroom door. I always thought she bullied her maid."

"Nonsense, nonsense, "said Hewet. "Venning and Susan are not an exciting pair of lovers, but they're as happy as turtle doves; and when you're eighty and the gout tweezes you you'll swear at the valet who helps you on with your trousers. Can't you imagine him Rachel? As bald as a coot, with a pair of sponge bag trousers, a little spotted tie, and a corporation!"

They were going back to the villa. St John asked whether he might come part of the way with them. He began by telling them the scandal of the painted lady, who lived with a very shabby female friend, was never seen to speak to any one, but was suspected to have nocturnal dealings with certain merchants. Hewet had met her on the stairs at midnight. One night while they were away something not precisely defined had happened in the hall. Next morning she was sent packing. Mr Thornbury and a man called Carter were said to have gone to the manager and insisted; in which case their behaviour had been monstrous, and Hirst proposed that Hewet should help him at once to investigate. Suddenly he broke off.

"Do you remember this spot?" he asked. They had come to that point on the road half way between the hotel and the villa from which there was a fine view of the sea, and of the town and of the mountains.

"It was here we sat the morning after the dance" he continued. "It was here that I had a revelation." He paused, and pursed his lips as he always did when excited. "Love. For the first time in my life I understood what love is. It seems to explain everything. What I want to say is that I am very glad you two are going to get married."

He shook Rachel's hand. They begged him to walk further with them. But he had said his say, and insisted upon turning back.

They breathed a sigh of relief as they always did when left alone.

"Do you know that he's in love with Helen?" said Hewet.

Rachel had never suspected it. She had enjoyed the theory that he was to be a bachelor in a government office. But these little accidents to her scheme of things no longer affected her seriously, for the world seemed to be a world where anything may happen. She drew a deep sigh and said "Well, it's odd!"

They had reached that stage in intimacy when silence was no longer the result of feelings too much crowded to issue. When silent they were like people walking hand in hand. At last Rachel exclaimed.

"It is odd! Extraordinarily odd!"

"The people at the hotel?" Hewet asked.

"Yes" she said. "What do they feel? And when St John says that love explains everything what does he mean? Loving you is the hardest thing I've ever done Terence!"

"People forget that love is also very interesting" said Terence. "But what Hirst meant I think, was that every one loves a little; and that gives a kind of reason to things. He's always looking for a reason. Up till now though he was a specialist in love, I don't believe he'd ever felt it."

But Hirst was too much unlike herself for Rachel ever to feel continuously interested in him.

"Nobody's ever been in love except our selves" she announced.

"I think there's some truth in that!" Terence laughed.

"We might find something about it in the poets" she went on. "Until I read that book it never struck me that poems are full of things we feel—things we really feel, that people never say."

"You'll love reading!" he exclaimed with triumph. "You'll go for the right things."

"That's because I love music" she said.

She then paused for a considerable time.

"There was a thing I put by to tell you" she began.

It was so solemn a thing that she stopped dead and looked him full in the face. "I love dew on a flower, I love the dawn beginning, I love things that go that no one sees,— things, you understand. I want to go on loving them; never to have eyes like Mrs Paley's. You're the only person I could say that to!"

"The more you say it, the more I love you!" he cried.

It was true. That was a gift of hers which he was without and loved her for.

"I suppose men always feel rather coarse beside women" he said. "I sometimes wonder how you ever said you'd marry me." He looked at her, and was struck again and this time almost painfully by the youthfulness of her face.

"And I too;" she answered; "what can you find in me?"

For a moment their union seemed impossible. There was nothing whatever to connect them.

"But you do love me?" he burst out.

"Everything about you" she answered.

They went on very slowly, up and up, for the road grew steeper and their content in each other's company was so great that they did not wish to end it. Every now and then they spoke saying whatever happened to strike them.

"It seems ages ago," said Terence, "that I first came here and walked up this road and looked at the view—ages ago since we sat on the cliff and argued—I was in love with you then."

"It's more wonderful for me!" she answered after a time.

"The people, Terence!"

Her mind was still busying itself with fragments of talk in the hall. "There'll be more people in London."

"One of my sisters you'll like, and one you won't get on with at all," said Terence. "Yes," he went on, "I think you've changed more than I have. Don't change too much. Stay as you are. Being a man," he went on lighting a cigarette, "I am far less sweeping than you are. Because I'm in love I don't want my friends less or my dinner less or my work less. I don't see everything differently as you do. The change is that everything seems to have a meaning, to be more profound." He waved his hand across the landscape. "I can't imagine death."

"You don't feel it painful as I do?" she asked. Then she burst out, "All that you've been talking of—work and people and London I can't take in that at all. I'm like a person exposed on a rock. To care as I do is too much."

As if she really suffered physical pain he put his arm round her and supported her.

"Don't tell me I give you pain" he said. "I want to give you nothing but happiness."

"Nobody knows what happiness is" she answered.

"No" he replied. He was silent for a minute or two.

"That's the kind of thing that makes me really gloomy" he said, "because they pretend. That's why these crises are so hideously difficult to manage. What does Mrs Elliot mean when she tells me that she has been the happiest of women—poor little soul, I should say she'd never known a moment's happiness in her life. But like all young people Rachel, you make the mistake of being too definite; you want to pin on labels here and there; and if you find more confusion than you expect you give it up as a bad job."

"Terence," she replied, "you narrowly escaped an evil fate—If I hadn't married you you'd have been an adviser of women. You'd have been a philosopher, an ant stealing the tongue a mountainous old prig."

"That's what I'm always telling you" he replied. "It's only thanks to you that I'm going to be a decent human being." "Tell me my faults" she cried. "Tell me that I'm utterly inferior, conceited, weak kneed, incapable creature; tell me those things or I shall hate you!"

"Those don't happen to be your faults" he replied quietly. "Your faults are that you are not always sympathetic, you're too theoretical, much too fastidious, and a trifle cold. You've never cared for anybody and you've lived in a dream world. You see Rachel, I know them all."

She pondered in silence for a minute or two, and then said, "I like things to be real."

"That is what one can't explain!" he continued. "I see it all. I see your faults more clearly than I've ever seen anyone's. But you might have any number of faults and it would make no difference. Nothing on earth would make any difference. I love you absolutely."

She said nothing in reply; a sound was her only answer, for words could not touch the great illumination.

Half an hour later they were seen by a peasant driving his cart into town, sitting together under a plane tree where the roads joined. There was a triangular patch of grass beneath it, and a prospect of great beauty all round, for the hill fell steeply, and showed the white roofs of the town and beyond them the blue of the sea.

CHAPTER TWENTY-NINE

Next morning a very strange thing had happened. Rachel woke up suddenly and felt as if she had been dried by fire. She was wide awake, but instead of being white and cheerful the wall opposite her stared, and the movement of the blind as it filled with air and dragged slowly out trailing the cord behind it seemed to her terrifying like the movement of a strange animal. She shut her eyes, and the pulses in her head beat so strongly that each thump seemed to tread upon a nerve. She turned from side to side opening her eyes now and then in the hope that this time the room would look as usual. But it never did and after the breakfast bell rang she resolved to settle the matter. She got out of bed and stood upright supporting herself by the brass ball at the end of the bedstead which cold at first soon became hot as her palm. The pains in her head and limbs proved that it would be far more intolerable to stand and walk than to lie in bed, so that she lay down again and accepted the idea that she was ill. The change was refreshing at first but soon the discomfort of the bed was as great as the discomfort of standing up.

When Helen came to find her and suddenly stopped her cheerful words looked startled and then unnaturally calm, and drew down the blinds the fact that she was ill became absolutely certain. It was confirmed when the whole household knew of it. Someone was singing; the song stopped in an instant. Maria when she brought water slipped in like a ghost averting her eyes from the bed.

There was all the morning to get through, and then all the afternoon. At one point the door opened and Helen came in with a little dark man dressed in a swallow tail coat with very hairy hands. Although he was a doctor, his tone was obsequious and furtive and Rachel scarcely troubled to answer him. At another point the door opened and Terence came in very gently, smiling too steadily to be natural. He sat down by the bed and stroked her hands, until it became irksome to her to lie in the same position and she turned round and when she next looked up Helen was there and Terence had gone. Helen was here and Helen was there all day long. When the room appeared to be very dim either because it was evening or because the blinds were drawn Helen said,

"Some one is going to sit with you tonight Rachel. Shall you mind?" Rachel opened her eyes and saw not only Helen but a middle aged woman in spectacles, who smiled steadily as they all did, and said that she did not find many people who were frightened of her.

Suddenly it appeared to be very very late; instead of ending at twelve Rachel thought, and beginning one two three, and so on, this night went on far into the double figures, twenty two twenty three twenty four. Of course she thought, there was never anything to stop nights from doing that if they chose. At a great distance the elderly woman sat with her head bent down; Rachel raised herself and saw with dismay that she was playing cards; a candle lighted her, which stood in the hollow of a newspaper. Rachel was terrified, and cried out, upon which the woman laid down her cards and came across the room shading the candle with her hand.

"Not asleep?" she said. "Let me make you comfortable." It struck Rachel that a woman who sat playing cards in a cavern all night long would have very cold hands and she shrank from the touch of them.

"Why, there's a toe all the way down there!" the woman said, proceeding to tuck in the bed clothes. Rachel never thought that the toe was hers. "You must try and lie still, because if you lie still will be less hot, and if you toss about you will make yourself more hot, and we don't want you to be any hotter than you are." The woman stood looking at Rachel for an enormous length of time.

"And the quieter you lie, the sooner you will be well" she repeated. The only thing that Rachel wished was that a peaked shadow upon the ceiling should be moved, for when it moved she supposed that the woman would disappear. She became desperately anxious for Helen, but as the night had all these hours in it she supposed that she never should. She cried out "Terence!" Again the woman who was playing cards crossed the room and stood by her and the peaked shadow also came and lay upon the ceiling.

"It's just as difficult to keep you in bed as it was to keep Mr Forrest in bed" she said, "and he was such a tall gentleman." After a time Rachel fell asleep and began to walk through tunnels with old women sitting in little archways playing cards, and the elderly nurse was able to finish her game of patience. She put out the candle when it became light enough to see, and shuffled the cards and continued her game by the pale light of day.

The day drew on much as in the same way as the day before had done. But Rachel was less conscious of what went on outside; she had forgotten the hours at which things happened; they happened so far away. She was surprised when Helen said "I must leave you for a moment to have my lunch." She thought it was some time in the evening after tea. When Terence came she did her best to bring her mind to remember certain facts about him.

"You have come up from the hotel" she said.

"No: I am always here" he answered, and then remembering that she was not supposed to know that, he added, "I have been lunching" he went on, "and reading the Times aloud to Uncle Ridley." But he saw with a pang that it was not possible to tell her of ordinary things.

"You see, there they go" she said, "rolling off the edge of the hill."

"No Rachel, nothing is rolling—you are in your own room" he said. But it gave her no comfort to be assured.

"I see them rolling" she answered. He took down a vase which stood on the shelf opposite her. "Now they can't roll any more" he said cheerfully.

But he saw that she was too much absorbed in watching to see whether the things rolled off the edge of the hill to pay any attention to him and it hurt him so profoundly that he left her. She was slightly relieved when he was gone, for his presence or Helen's interfered with her and she had to make an effort to remember them. Left alone she could give all her attention to the hot red quick sights that kept crossing her eyes. In the back of her mind she was convinced that it was of enormous importance that she should attend to these sights, but she was always being just too late to catch them, or unable to hear the last word they said. If she heard what was said something would happen, but the effort of seeing them and trying to hear and understand made her less and less able to remember what the important thing was; but she was goaded on by a sense that she must attend.

One afternoon she was unable to keep Helen's face distinct from the other faces. She tried to, had a sensation of slipping, and fell into a great crowd of red moving faces and loud voices. When Helen stood by her it was disturbing because she was generally out of proportion to the other heads. To the outer world it appeared that Rachel had lost consciousness. She herself was adventuring among strange sights with people whom she came to recognise; some she hated, some she thought ridiculous. The nature of what she was doing with them changed from hour to hour. It often happened that the real meaning of what she had done last only struck her as she was engaged in another adventure. The meaning of the whole was just about to come clear when invariably something happened which completely unsettled her mind again.

She began to be tormented by the sights, which now were always chasing her, and to try by swimming or jumping off high towers to escape from them. At last one afternoon she suffered sharp pain and found herself by a great dark pool into which she plunged. But it was not full of water but of a thick sticky substance which closed over her head. She saw nothing and heard nothing but a faint booming sound which was the sound of the sea rolling above her head. While all her tormentors thought that she was dead she knew that she was not dead, strangely enough, though right under the sea. The little man with the hairy hands had spurted opium into her arm.

But outside Rachel's bedroom the world was neither dark or quiet. Glasses and cups with saucers on top of them stood in the passage outside and downstairs Hewet sat in the drawing room with the door open, listening for any call from Helen. He always forgot to pull down the blinds so that he sat in the bright sunlight. He was conscious of discomfort but did not know what caused it. Sometimes he would sit for an hour, unable to read a line, and then just as he had fixed his mind on the page the soft call would come, which made him start and go running up the stairs in his stockings. Sometimes it was Mrs Chailey who came in, bringing a drink she had made, or ice just come from the town. They had the greatest difficulty in getting enough ice. Hewet and Hirst between them constructed a case to keep it in. Their distance from the town and the difficulty of getting out of the way things, made it necessary as the days went on to organise very carefully. Hewet's first task in the morning was to draw up a list of things to be done, which he pinned to the drawing room door and was for ever consulting. Hirst was the messenger because Hewet did like to leave the house, and the chief topic of conversation during the time of Rachel's illness was the behaviour of Hirst's horse, christened Sancho, which was or could be made to be an animal of character.

The illness had come on so suddenly and fiercely that Hewet could hardly grasp it. He kept thinking of the last day, when she had seemed perfectly well; he put off any attempt to explain it. He vaguely expected that it would go as suddenly as it came, and the stories which were told him in abundance of illnesses like hers conveyed little in him. He kept thinking "But of course Rachel's illness is quite different." It was more like a bad dream than anything else. His interviews with the doctor told him nothing. He had never been ill himself and had great faith in doctors. He understood the doctor's vague reports which were always very much the same to mean that the doctor completely understood the mystery. "A high temperature" the little man would say, looking furtively about the room, and rubbing his hands, "That is true. But you need not be alarmed at a high temperature. It is the pulse we go by (he tapped his own hairy wrist) and the pulse continues excellent." Thereupon he bowed and slipped out. It was strange that Hewet's respect for the medical profession should make him completely uncritical of the man.

But on the sixth day of the illness Helen came into the drawing room. It was about four in the afternoon and

Hewet was trying painfully to read a book. He was immediately struck by the change in Helen's face, for he had scarcely seen her in a bright light for a week. She was pale, thinner, and a strange look as of one harassed but determined was in her eyes.

"We can't go on like this" she said. She spoke as if she resented something. "Either we must get another doctor, or we must do something different. Rachel is getting iller every day and we are doing nothing to stop it."

Terence suffered a terrific shock of anxiety. He stilled it by reflecting that Helen was clearly overwrought.

"Do you think she's in danger?" he asked.

"Yes, I do," Helen answered. She had to go back at once. Nothing now could assuage Hewet's anxiety; it pricked through every attempt at reason, although when Hewet questioned him he would not admit that things were any worse than before. That being so, St John was naturally irritated when Hewet sat in complete silence all through dinner, and the story of Sancho and the geese carefully preserved for that hour failed entirely. It seemed like a breach of their contract. But part of his irritation came from the fact that he was for some reason more anxious himself.

The evening interview with the doctor made things even worse. "There is no reason for anxiety I tell you—none" he repeated in his execrable French, making little movements all the time as if to slip away. But Hewet would not let him go.

"Should you object to meeting another doctor?" he asked.

At this the little man became openly incensed.

"Ah!" he cried. "You have not confidence in me? You object to what I am doing? You wish me to give up the case to another." Hewet only said, "Not at all; all I want is the name of another doctor."

"There is no other doctor" he answered sullenly. "Everyone has confidence in me. Look! I will show you." He began talking papers from his pocket to prove what he said.

But Hewet stopped him. "I understand that you will not object to meeting another doctor tomorrow" he said; and went straight up to Rachel's room.

"Monsieur is over anxious" the little man said leering at Hirst. "The young lady is not seriously ill and I assure you there is no other doctor." He grimaced and left.

If this interview had not destroyed Hewet's belief in the doctor it would have gone when he saw Rachel. Her face had changed; she looked as though she were entirely concentrated upon keeping alive. Her lips were drawn, her cheeks sunken and flushed though without colour. Her eyes were not entirely shut, the lower half of the white part showed, but they seemed to remain open because she was too much exhausted to close them. She opened them completely when he kissed her. But she only saw an old woman slicing a man's head off with a great knife. "There it falls" she murmured. Terence was horrified to think of the furtive little man downstairs in connection with illness like this. He turned to Helen, almost in despair; but she had become too much used to it to realise how great the shock would be, and merely asked him in the same weary unnatural but determined voice to fetch her more ice and fresh candles. He waylaid the nurse on her way upstairs and asked her to tell him honestly in her opinion. But she would only repeat what the doctor had said, suspiciously as though she might be doing herself an injury if she spoke the truth.

Perhaps she knew that she did not satisfy Hewet for she added, "If you ask me I never like cases that begin with the new moon. Some say it's fancy, but I've had so many cases that began with the new moon and the patient never seemed to get over it. They do say that the moon has something to do with the brain Sir, don't they?" He could only let her pass, groaning at the fate which had put them in the hands of an illiterate chemist, and a superstitious, half cast, uneducated servant. The strangeness of the whole place terrified him. Though he went to bed he was unable to sleep. For a long time he leant out of the window surveying the dark world against the blue sky; he hated the slim black trees and all the unfamiliar noises of a southern night which show that the earth is still hot.

As they expected, Dr Allessandro had not spoken the truth; there was another doctor, a Frenchman, who was taking his holiday in the hills. Some hours were wasted in getting at the facts, before Hirst could start in pursuit of him.

It was midday when he came, and his curt speech and sulky masterful face impressed Hewet with confidence though it was also obvious that he was very much annoyed at the whole affair. He went straight up stairs; in a very short time he was down again; his directions were clear and emphatic, but it never occurred to him to give an opinion either because of the presence of Allessandro, who was now obsequious as well as malicious, or because he took it for granted that they knew already.

"Of course" he said with a little shrug of the shoulders when Hewet pressed him, "Do you think her very ill?"

But they were conscious of support when he was gone, and went back to their tasks now freshly made out on a new sheet of paper with greater spirit than before though the pallor and thinness of each struck the other. Ridley wandered in and out plaintive and dejected as an animal in the house of woe.

Meanwhile Rachel came slowly to the surface of the dark sticky sea. She had long ceased to have any will of her own in deciding what she did; she could not have escaped now if the faces had chased her. A wave seemed to bear her up and down with it; she lay on the top conscious only of pain—now thirst now headache now agony in a limb which was pinned to the bed. All these pains were so intense that the rest of her body was obliterated. But the adventures with the red faces and hairy bodies were over though she could remember some of them and tried to tell Helen.

Everything that went on in her roomed seemed to her now very pale and semi-transparent. Sometimes she could see through the wall in front of her. Sometimes when Helen went away she seemed to go so far that Rachel's eye could hardly follow her. The room also had an odd strange power of expanding and though she pushed her voice out as far as possible until sometimes it became a bird and flew away, she thought it doubtful whether it ever reached the person she was talking to. There were immense intervals or rather chasms, for things often became visible to her between one moment and the next; it sometimes took an hour for Helen to raise her arm, pausing long between each jerky movement, and pour our medicine. Helen's form stooping to raise her in bed was of gigantic size and came down upon her like the ceiling falling. But for long spaces of time she would merely lie on the top of the wave conscious of her body floating and of her mind flitting about the room like a moth.

As the pain went away her sense of weakness increased. Her body seemed to be sinking through the bed, like a drift of melting snow, while her knees stuck up bare bones, raised like peaked mountains above her. Shadows came round her. Every now and then after seeing nothing but black a face would become perfectly distinct, and when this happened she was tormented by a desire to know all about that person, and for a time after she had seen each face she remembered that she ought to fight for something.

This feeling came to her with great distinctness on the evening of the tenth day, when a large face appeared above her, with eyes that stared into hers and a dark moustache.

Ten minutes later Dr Paelletier for it was he, stood in the drawing room talking to Hewet and Hirst. As he had never grasped which of them was engaged to the young lady he addressed them both equally. Although his manner was still grave and formal he was no longer annoyed.

The first thing he said was, "I consider that her condition is very grave."

He then went on to tell them what he wished them to do. In silence but in such anxiety as he had never imagined, a pain in his side and his fingers ice cold, Terence went on all the evening ordering Mrs Chailey, fetching things, placing them quietly on the table outside Rachel's door. Once when they came down he found Mrs Flushing in the drawing room, talking emphatically. But she stopped when she saw him. They were all standing up.

Later in the evening Dr Paelletier who had been upstairs for some time again appeared in the drawing room. Hewet stepped forward; at last he was going to know. "If you wish to see her you should go up now" the doctor said. Hewet walked out of the room. All the way upstairs he kept saying to himself "This has not happened to me. It is not possible that this has happened to me." He looked very curiously at his own hand upon the bannisters.

Helen got up out of the chair in which she was sitting by Rachel's side. Her face was extraordinarily quiet. He took her place in silence. Rachel's face had again changed. It too was very quiet, as if a seal had been set upon lips and eyes, preventing them ever from opening or moving. The sound of the door shutting after Helen roused Terence to a sense that they were alone. He kissed her and said "Rachel." After a pause her eyes opened, first only the lower parts of the whites showed; then slowly the whole eye was revealed. She saw him for a moment distinctly; a large head above her; it became fringed with black and then became altogether black; she wished for a moment to fight for something, and then forgot, overwhelmed in the curves of blackness that were rising all round her. Sinking and sinking into them, she never heard him say "Rachel" a second time; she did not know that her hand lay in his.

After Rachel had shut her eyes Terence sat perfectly still. He knew that she was dying. But the dazed unreal feeling that such a thing as this could not happen to them which had haunted him ever since she fell ill disappeared completely. He was possessed by an extraordinary feeling of triumph and calm happiness.

"It is only us two in the world that this could have happened," was the thought that filled him. "Because we loved each other. Therefore we have this."

He believed that Rachel shared his feeling and that her face reflected back his triumph and calm. When he saw that she was dead he was only conscious of great triumph and calm. This death was such a little thing. It seemed that they were now absolutely free, more free more entirely united than they had ever been before. They had received the most wonderful thing in the world. He heard himself saying as he sat with her hand in his, "We have had what no people in the world have had. No one has ever loved as we love each other." He was conscious that there were people in the room at the back of him whispering. But he felt as though no one could disturb him. Someone put her arms round him and drew away the hand that was holding Rachel's hand and said "You must come away with me Terence. She is dead." He went because they wished it, but they could not disturb his happiness. As he saw the landing outside and the little tables with the cups and bottle on them he suddenly realised that in no other part of the world should he ever find Rachel again.

"Rachel Rachel!" he cried in agony, trying to rush back to her. Downstairs they could hear him as he stumbled to his room crying "Rachel! Rachel!"

CHAPTER THIRTY

Six hours after Rachel died, Mrs Thornbury and Miss Allen were standing after breakfast by the long table on which newspapers were displayed. After turning them over for some minutes in silence, Miss Allen said in an unnatural voice, "I suppose you have heard—"

Mrs Thornbury looked apprehensive.

"Miss Vinrace died this morning" said Miss Allen.

Mrs Thornbury dropped her Times. The tears instantly rose and slid down her cheeks.

"No," she said. "Poor things. Poor people. Poor child."

A tear stood in Miss Allen's eye though she controlled herself, so that she appeared more awkward than usual and the possessor of a large double chin, the result of squeezing her head back.

"It certainly does seem hard" she remarked.

"I can hardly believe it" said Mrs Thornbury. Her hands were still limp with shock. She looked through her tears at the sunny hall, at the nonchalant figures who were standing about, at the solid chairs and tables. Then it was they who seemed unreal, as people do who pass some startling sight without being conscious of it. Her mind became concentrated upon the dark room where Rachel lay dead, and upon the people sobbing downstairs.

"How did it happen?" she asked. "They did not expect this yesterday?"

But Miss Allen only knew what Yarmouth, Mrs Flushing's

maid had said when she happened to meet her. Mrs Thornbury still speaking in a dazed voice said that she should try and find Mrs Flushing. She wiped her eyes and went upstairs along the corridors which were busy with servants doing rooms. She met Evelyn M. She was sobbing openly.

"Isn't it hateful! Isn't it wicked!" she sobbed, seeing Mrs Thornbury. "I do think they might let happy people live. It's only yesterday that she was here." She leant against the window frame, and sobbed convulsively. Mrs Thornbury patted her gently on the shoulder.

"It is hard—very hard" she said. "And yet the older one grows the more certain one is that there is a reason. The world could not go on if there were no reason."

Her eyes which were no longer dim, but even brighter than usual, looked out of the window. She could see the villa.

Evelyn sobbed for some minutes and then grew quieter.

"That's what people say" she said; "That's what I believe really. I do honestly believe," she said, beginning to pull the blind up and down nervously, "that Rachel is in Heaven. But Terence—"

"Ah, poor fellow" Mrs Thornbury sighed. She pressed Evelyn's hand and went on down the passage to Mrs Flushing's bedroom. She found her sitting in an arm chair with her back to the light. Wilfrid was by her side. He took his arm from her shoulder as Mrs Thornbury came in.

"Ah, here is Mrs Thornbury" he said. "My wife feels this poor girl's death so terribly" he explained. "She feels that she was in some way responsible—that she urged her to come on that expedition. But we don't even know—In fact I think it most unlikely—that she caught her fever there. She was set on going—she would have gone whether you asked her or not. It is most unreasonable to feel responsible, is it not, Mrs Thornbury?"

"Don't Wilfrid," said Mrs Flushing, neither moving nor taking her eyes off the coal scuttle opposite where they rested. "By talking you only make things worse. After all, she's dead."

"I was coming to ask you how it happened?" said Mrs Thornbury, addressing Wilfrid for it was useless to speak to Alice. "Did they expect this sudden change? Did they know she was so ill?"

"She's been desperately ill for some days" he answered, but all the time he was watching his wife. She rose stiffly, turned her back to them and walked to the dressing room opposite. As she walked, they could see her great breasts slowly rise, and slowly fall. But her grief was silent. She shut the door behind her.

"That's the worst of these places" said Wilfrid. If he had not been much concerned he would have been irritable. "Unless people are fearfully careful they catch things. But it's absurd to say that they caught it with us. Pepper tells me— but this you won't repeat—that he left the house because he thought them so careless. He said they never washed their vegetables properly. Poor people! They must not know that."

There was nothing further he could tell her; there was nothing to be done. Mrs Thornbury went back to her room. The figures she passed were still strangely indifferent, but the incongruity of their life no longer shocked her. She sat down and thought about life. She thought of her own extraordinary happiness. She had brought eleven children into the world, they were all alive, all married, all the fathers and mothers of children. She did not attempt to explain why Rachel had been got ready for all this, and then taken away. But somehow, thinking of her own daughters, living here and there in England and in India, with babies at their breasts, with boys at school, with husbands at work, thinking of her sons, making bridges, making laws, carrying on the work of the world, thinking of all the various and vigorous life that had come from her own body her eyes lit with pride, and she repeated what she had said to Evelyn in the passage; there is a reason—there is a reason. So thinking, the tear she dropped for Rachel was without bitterness. She began to address Terence; "I must tell you how deeply shocked I am" when her husband came in, having missed her. It never occurred to Mrs Thornbury to tell him of Rachel's death; while she had gone on being interested in all kinds of things, he was more interested in public affairs. That was how she defined it. Therefore she gave her best attention to the letter, which was from William's partner in Canton, advising an extension of their business so as to include the carriage of cottons and silks.

At luncheon Evelyn, who was always outspoken, whose red eyelids spoke for her, broke out,

"I don't know how you feel, but I can simply think of nothing else!"

She was sitting at the round table in the window from which you could observe the people coming in without being seen. She was lunching with Arthur Venning, Susan Warrington, Mr Perrott and old Mrs Paley. Her soup stood untouched. She leant both elbows upon the table. Susan and Arthur had already heard the news.

"It's perfectly awful," said Susan. "When you think what a nice girl she was, only just engaged, and this need never have happened—it seems too tragic." She looked at Arthur.

"Hard lives" said Arthur. "But it was a fool thing to go up that river." He shook his head. "They should have known better." Old Mrs Paley hitherto contented with her soup, now intimated that she wished to know what they were talking about.

"Poor Miss Vinrace has died of the fever" said Susan. She could not speak of death in her usual voice; therefore Mrs Paley did not hear.

"Poor Miss Vinrace is dead" Arthur attempted; he was only successful the second time of saying it, and had to control a strong desire to laugh.

Facts that were outside her daily experience took some time to reach Mrs Paley's consciousness. She heard but sat vague-eyed for at least a minute before she realised.

"Mmmm" she muttered. "That's very sad. But I don't at the moment recollect which she was. We seem to have made so many new acquaintances in this hotel. A tall dark girl, who just missed being handsome with a high colour? She ought not to have died—she looked so strong. But people will drink the water—I can never make out why. It seems such a simple thing to order them to put a bottle of Seltzer water in your bed room. That's all the precaution I've ever taken and I've been in every country in Europe, Italy a dozen times over. But young people always think they know better and then they have to pay the penalty. Poor thing—I'm very sorry for her." But the difficulty of peering into a dish of potatoes and helping herself made her silent.

"I don't believe you care a bit!" said Evelyn turning savagely upon Mr Perrott who had not spoken.

"Indeed I do" he replied with obvious sincerity. He had a very deep sympathy for human suffering, which extended to people he did not know.

"It seems so inexplicable" said Evelyn "—death, I mean. Why should she be dead and not you or I? It was only ten days since she was here with the rest of us. What d'you believe? D'you believe that things go on—that she's still somewhere, or d'you think that it's simply a game; we crumple up to nothing. I'm perfectly positive that Rachel's not dead."

He would have said many things to please Evelyn; but to say that he believed in the immortality of the soul was beyond him. He sat silent, more deeply wrinkled than usual, crumbling his bread.

Lest Evelyn should begin to ask him what he believed, Arthur after making a pause equivalent to a full stop, started a completely different subject.

"Supposing a man were to write and tell you that he wanted five pounds because he had known your grandfather, what would you do? It was this way. My Grandfather—"

"Invented a stove" said Evelyn. "We had one in the conservatory to keep the plants warm. I know all about that."

"Didn't know I was so famous" said Arthur. "Well, the old chap being about the second best inventor of his age died without making a will. Now Fielding his clerk with how much justice I don't know, always claimed that he meant to do something for him. Poor old boy's come down in the world, lives at Penge over a tobacconists. Must I stump up or not? What does the abstract spirit of justice require, Perrott?"

"If you ask me" said Susan smiling complacently at Perrott, "I think he'll get the five pound whatever the abstract spirit of justice requires!"

Mr Perrott having to deliver an opinion, Evelyn being much of the opinion that he was much too stingy, and Mrs Paley requiring whenever a course came to an end an abstract of what had been said in the course of it, luncheon passed with out a silence. It happened that Mrs Paley's wheeled chair created a block in the doorway, for Mrs Flushing tried to pass. Brought thus to a standstill for a moment, Arthur and Susan congratulated Hughling Elliot upon his convalescence—he was down, cadaverous enough—for the first time—and Mr Perrott took the chance of saying something private to Evelyn.

"Would there be any chance of seeing you alone this afternoon between four and five. I shall be in the garden."

The block dissolved before Evelyn answered. But as she left them in the hall she looked at him brightly and said, "Half past four did you say? That'll suit me."

She ran upstairs with a feeling of excitement and exaltation which the prospect of an emotional scene always aroused in her. Although she thought a great deal about the proposal, she did not give a thought to what she meant to say. She always left that to be decided at the moment. One or two things she folded and put in her box, for in common with many English visitors she left in three days, and she made herself tidy, changing, and doing her hair.

"It's all too queer" she said, giving her hair little tugs and twists, "Here am I doing my hair as becomingly as possible because some one is going to propose to me in half and hour, and there's she lying dead. I wish there were an explanation, but all I can say is" she smiled with great intimacy at her face in the looking glass,—"it's no wonder men do fall in love with you!"

She whirled round on her toe, and went running along the passage to her interview conscious in every fibre that she was spinning round in a multitude of spinning things; and that it was all right. Honestly though she had wept, it was death that gave its peculiar zest and thrill to her emotion.

Mr Perrott was waiting for her; indeed he had been walking up and down the gravel path for over half an hour. She came along switching the bush with a twig which she had broken off on her way.

"Late as usual!" she exclaimed when in view of him.

"Well you must forgive me. I ran into an old friend unexpectedly. That's a new steamer isn't it? My word! It looks stormy." She looked at the bay in which a steamer was just dropping anchor the smoke still hanging about it.

But Mr Perrott paid no attention to the steamer or to the weather.

"Miss Murgatroyd" he began with his usual formality, "I asked you to come here from a very selfish motive I fear. I do not think you need to be assured once more of my feelings;

but as you are leaving so soon I felt that I could not let you go without asking you to tell me—have I any reason to hope that you will ever care for me?" He was very pale and unable to keep his lip from trembling. She felt impotent; when it came to the point how could she feel anything at all for this careworn elderly man? But she wised vehemently that she could care; and was dismayed to find neither words or feelings in her being.

"Let's sit down and talk it over" she said rather unsteadily. Mr Perrott followed her to the seat under the tree where Hewet had once sat.

"Of course I care for you," she said, "I should be a brute if I didn't. I think you're quite one of the nicest people I've ever met and one of the finest too. But I wish!—I wish you didn't care for me in that way. Are you sure you do?"

"Quite sure" said Mr Perrott.

"You see, I'm not so simple as most women" Evelyn continued. "I don't know exactly what I feel."

He sat by her watching her and refraining from speech.

"I sometimes think I haven't got a heart—Someone else would make you a better wife."

"If you think that there is any chance that you will come to care for me I am quite content to wait" said Mr Perrott.

"After all there's no desperate hurry is there" said Evelyn. "Suppose I thought it over and wrote and told you when I got back."

"You cannot give me any idea," said Mr Perrott, "I do not ask for a date—that would be most unreasonable." He paused, looking at the gravel. "You have no feeling when you consider it that it is quite out of the question?"

As she did not immediately answer he went on. "I know very well—that I am not—that I have not much to offer you either in my person or in my circumstances. And I forget; it cannot seem the miracle to you that it does to me. Until I met you I had gone on in my own quiet way—we are both very quiet people my sister and I—quite content with my lot. My friendship with Arthur was the most profound feeling in my life. Now that I know you all that has changed. You seem to put such spirit into everything. Life seems to hold so many more possibilities than I had ever dreamt of."

"That's splendid!" Evelyn exclaimed. "Now you'll go back and start all kinds of new things and make a great name in the world. And we'll go on being friends, whatever happens—whatever any one says."

"Oh Evelyn!" he moaned, and took her in his arms and kissed her. She did not resent it at all. "I never see any harm in kissing though some people do" she said, sitting upright again. "After all, these friendships do make a difference don't they? They are the kind of things that matter in one's life."

He looked at her with a strangely bewildered expression as if he did not really understand what she meant. With a considerable effort he collected himself and stood up. "Now I think I have told you what I feel" he said, "and I can wait as long as ever you wish."

With a kind of involuntary bow, he walked away; a little elderly figure, prim and decided in its walk, though the shoulders were prematurely hunched. As she watched him go, Evelyn could not help feeling as certain as she could be about anything that nothing on earth would ever make her his wife.

All that evening the clouds gathered. They came travelling slowly over the distant forest, and hung suspended over the mountain top. Shiver after shiver struck across the sea which lay still as if reined in. It was very hot, and the curve of a deep black cloud was an intense golden colour, the sun being visible behind it. The leaves hung close and the noises of birds and insects seemed shortened to a chirp.

So strange were the lights that far less chatter than usual rose from the numbers of tables in the dining room though between fifty and sixty people were eating there. The clatter of knives upon plates rose into prominence. The first roll of thunder and the first heavy drops striking the pane caused a little stir.

"It's coming" was said in three or four different languages. There was then an extraordinary silence, as if the thunder had withdrawn far away. Eating was again in full swing when a gust of cold air came through the open windows lifting skirts and table cloths, a light flashed, and was instantly followed by a clap of thunder right over the hotel; rain swished with it and immediately a dozen waiters ran about the room shutting windows. The room grew suddenly several degrees darker; the wind seemed to drive waves of darkness across the garden. Doors could be heard banging and windows shutting all over the house. All eating was suspended, people sitting with forks in air. Then another flash came, lighting up faces as if they were going to be photographed. The clap was close and violent upon it. Several women half rose from their chairs and then sat down again, but dinner was continued uneasily with eyes upon the garden. All the bushes there were showing the white undersides of their leaves; the wind pressed upon them so that they seemed to stoop to the ground. In a minute a large pool stood in the middle of the terrace, usually as dry and hard of surface as eggs in a basket. The waiter had to press dishes upon the diners' notice; and the diners had to draw the attention of waiters for they were all absorbed in looking at the storm. As the thunder showed no signs of withdrawing but seemed massed right overhead, while the lightning aimed straight at the garden every time a certain gloom replaced the first excitement. People congregated in the hall which felt more secure than any other place, because one could retreat far from the windows. A little Portuguese boy was carried away sobbing in the arms of his nurse.

For some reason no one seemed inclined to sit down, although two people less regardful of thunder than Mr Pepper and Mrs Thornbury could not well be imagined. They stood under the central skylight, as if they were standing at a religious service, and the look of them standing there under the queer yellow light gave undefined comfort to one or two like Susan, who felt vaguely uneasy. Unwittingly they became the centre of a little group of English people most of whom had come to know each other during the weeks of their stay.

Light sliced right across their faces and a terrific clap came, making the panes of the skylight lift at their joints.

"Ah" they breathed.

"Something's struck" said a man's voice.

The rain rushed down; the rain seemed now to extinguish the lightning and the thunder, and the hall became almost dark. After a minute or two when nothing was heard except the rattle of water upon the glass a voice said "The storm is over." It was Mr Pepper whose lean little form, the head raised looking upward was hardly to be distinguished.

Suddenly all the electric lights were turned on, and revealed a crowd of people all standing, all looking with somewhat strained faces up at the skylight. They dwindled away or sat down all talking about the storm except the English who sat down where they had stood. For some minutes the rain continued to rattle upon the skylight and the thunder gave another shake or two; but it was evident that the great disturbed ocean of air was travelling away from them passing high overhead with its yellow clouds and rods of fire. As it drew off out to sea the people in the hall of the hotel sat down and began to talk about storms and to produce their occupations for the evening.

The chess board was brought out, and Mr Elliot who wore a stock instead of a collar as a sign of weak health, but was otherwise as usual, challenged Mr Pepper to a final contest. Round them gathered a group of ladies with work, or in default of work with novels; to superintend the game, much as if the two elderly men were little boys playing marbles. Mrs Paley just round the corner had her cards already arranged in long ladders; with Susan near to sympathise but not to correct; and the moth which was now grey winged and grey of thorax, hit the lamps in turn with a thud. The conversation in these circumstances was very gentle fragmentary and intermittent.

Mrs Elliot was imparting a new stitch in knitting to Mrs Thornbury so that their heads came very near together upon the settee. Mrs Elliot disclaimed a compliment with evident pride. "I suppose we're all proud of something," she said, "and I'm proud of my knitting. I think things like that go in families. I had an uncle who knitted his own socks to the day of his death—he did it better than any of his daughters, dear old gentleman. Now I wonder that you Miss Allen, who use your eyes so much, don't take up knitting in the evenings. You'd find it such a relief I should say, and the bazaars are so glad of things."

Her voice assumed the smooth half conscious tone of the expert knitter, "as much as I can do I can always dispose of which is a comfort for then I feel I am not wasting my time."

Miss Allen shut her novel and observed the others placidly for a time.

"It is surely not natural to leave your wife because you discover that she is in love with you" she remarked at length.

"Very unnatural—very unnatural I should say" murmured the knitters in their absorbed voices.

"But that is what the gentleman in my book does" said Miss Allen.

"Marriage" by Michael Farren, I presume" said Mr Elliot who could not resist the temptation to talk while he played chess.

"I wish you could tell me of a good novel to read on the voyage back" said Mrs Thornbury.

"But d'you know I don't think people do write good novels now" said Mrs Elliot.

After a silence Miss Allen who had been watching the group while she evidently pursued a thought of her own, said aloud, "I wonder how many of us here have an imaginary uncle? I have an uncle" she continued, "who is always giving me presents. Sometimes it's a gold watch, sometimes it's a carriage and pair, sometimes it's a cottage in the New Forest with hot water lad on and a beautiful little conservatory. I don't know exactly what brought it into my head at this moment" she said, as they looked enquiringly at her; "unless it was Mrs Elliot's uncle who knitted and was certainly not imaginary; and our all sitting here not speaking."

She set them thinking of the things they wanted; Mrs Thornbury dismissed her own case—she had everything she wanted; but the Empire? "Ten, not twenty Dreadnoughts" she decided, and went on in her imagination to pass a law for the benefit of the whole world, on the strength of her twenty Dreadnoughts.

Mrs Elliot knew exactly what she wanted; a child; and the usual little pucker deepened on her brow.

"We're very lucky people—we really have no wants" she said aloud, looking at her husband. She was always anxious that people should think them an ideally devoted couple, and her husband did not hear what she said.

But she was prevented from wondering how far she carried conviction by the entrance of Mr and Mrs Flushing who came through the hall and stopped by the chess board. Mrs Flushing looked wilder than ever. A great strand of black hair looped down across her brow, her cheeks were whipped a dark blood red, and drops of rain made wet marks upon them. While she leant over the back of a chair and looked intently upon the chess board, Mr Flushing explained that they had been on the roof watching the storm.

"It was wonderful" he said, "The lightning went right out over the sea, and lit up the ships and the waves. You can't think how strange the mountains looked; with the lights on them, and the great masses of black; it's all over now."

He slid down into a chair becoming absorbed in the end of the game.

"And you go back tomorrow?" said Mrs Thornbury looking at Mrs Flushing.

"Yes" she replied.

"And indeed one is not sorry to go back" said Mrs Elliot assuming an air of mournful anxiety, "after all this illness."

"Are you afraid of dyin'?" Mrs Flushing demanded, scornfully.

"I think we're all afraid of that" said Mrs Elliot with dignity.

"We're all cowards when it comes to the point" said Mrs Flushing rubbing her cheek against the back of her chair. "I know I am."

"Not a bit of it" said Mr Flushing turning round for Mr Pepper contemplated long. "It's not cowardly to wish to live, Alice. Personally I should like to go on for a hundred years. Just think of all the things that are bound to happen!"

"That is what I feel" said Mrs Thornbury. "The changes, the improvements, the inventions—"

"And beauty" said Mr Flushing. "We lose all that by dying."

"It would certainly be dull to die before they have discovered whether there is life in Mars" said Miss Allen.

"D'you really believe there's life in Mars?" said Mrs Flushing turning vehemently upon her. "Who tells you that? someone who knows? D'you know a man called—"

Mrs Thornbury laid down her knitting, and a look of extreme solicitude came into her eyes.

"There is Mr Hirst" she said quietly.

St John had just come through the swing door. He was rather blown about by the wind, and his cheeks looked terribly pale and cavernous. After taking off his coat he was going to pass straight through the hall and upstairs, but he could not ignore the presence of so many people he knew, especially as Mrs Thornbury rose and went up to him, holding out her hand. But the shock of the warm lamp lit room, the shock of so many cheerful human beings sitting together and talking, after the dark and windy night, and the room where Rachel lay still with flowers scattered in the folds of her white sheets, and Hewet sat staring ahead of him, not speaking, his hand in Helen's, while upstairs Willoughby's tread was heard, up and down by his daughter's side,—the shock completely overcame him. He could not speak. Tears came to his eyes.

Every one was silent; even Mr Pepper's hand paused upon a Knight. Mrs Thornbury somehow moved him to a chair, sat her self beside him, and with tears in her own eyes said, gently "You have done everything for your friend."

Her action set them all talking again as if they had seen nothing.

"No one could do anything" said St John, speaking very slowly, spaces coming between his words. "I never imagined that such a thing was possible."

He drew his hand across his eyes as if some dream filled them and prevented him from seeing where he was.

"And that poor fellow—" said Mrs Thornbury, down whose cheeks the tears were sliding.

He could make no answer thinking of Terence.

"Impossible" he said at length.

"Did he have the consolation of knowing—" Mrs Thornbury began tentatively.

But St John was lying back in his chair looking at the others half seeing them, half hearing what they said. He was terribly tired, and the light and the warmth, the movements of hands, and the soft communicative voices brought him a strange sense of relief. He was too much tired even to think himself disloyal because he gave up thinking of Rachel and Terence and found it pleasant to think of other things.

The game was really a good one, and Mr Pepper and Mr Elliot were genuinely concentrated upon the struggle. Mrs Thornbury seeing that St John did not wish to talk, resumed her knitting.

"Lightning again!" Mrs Flushing suddenly exclaimed. A yellow light winked across the blue window. She strode to the door, pushed it open and stood half outside.

It was only the reflection of the storm. The rain had ceased, and the heavy clouds had gone, though vapourish mists were being driven at a great pace high up in the air. The sky was once more a deep solemn blue, and the earth was visible, enormous, dark and solid, rising over there into the tapering mass of the mountain, and pricked here and there with the tiny lights of villas. The driving air, the drone of the trees, and the flashing light, which now and again spread a broad illumination, filled Mrs Flushing with exaltation. Her breasts rose and fell. "Splendid! Splendid!" she muttered to herself. Then she turned to the hall inside, and exclaimed in a peremptory voice. "Come out and see. Wilfrid it's wonderful."

They half stirred; some rose; some dropped their balls of wool, and began to look for them.

"To bed—to bed" said Miss Allen.

"It was just that move with your Queen that gave it away, Pepper" exclaimed Mr Elliot triumphantly, sweeping his pieces together and standing up.

"What Pepper beaten? at last? I congratulate you?" said Arthur Venning, who was wheeling Mrs Paley to bed.

All these voices sounded gratefully in St John's ears as he lay half asleep, and yet vividly conscious of everything; across his eyes passed a procession of objects, black and indistinct, the figures of people picking up their books, their cards, their balls of wool, their work baskets, and passing him one after another on their way to bed.